The

Fash*ion K*itty

Collection

Book One

Fashion Kitty

Book Two

Fashion Kitty
versus the Fashion Queen

by Charise Mericle Harper

Disney Hyperion
Los Angeles   New York

First Paperback Edition of *Fashion Kitty*, September 2005

First Paperback Edition of *Fashion Kitty versus the Fashion Queen*, June 2007

First Bind-Up Edition, November 2019

10 9 8 7 6 5 4 3 2 1

FAC-029191-19221

Printed in Malaysia

This book is set in Belwe Mono/ITC; Julietrose, Kidprint/Monotype

Designed by Christine Kettner and David Hastings

Library of Congress Control Number for *Fashion Kitty*: 2005040435

Library of Congress Control Number for *Fashion Kitty versus the Fashion Queen* Hardcover: 2007299791

ISBN 978-1-368-04963-4

Visit www.DisneyBooks.com

Book One

Fashion

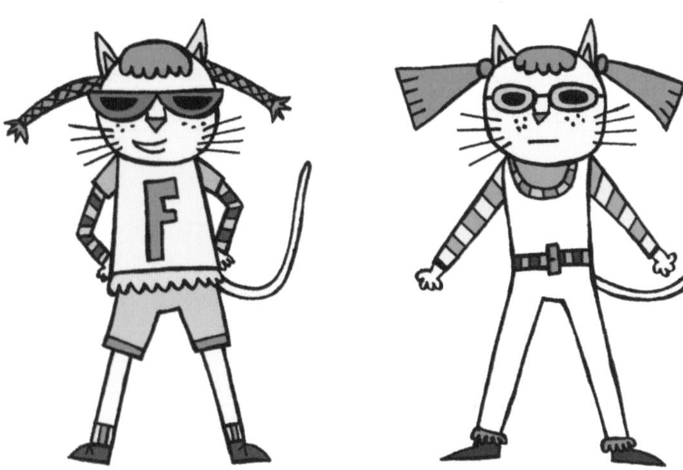
F

Kitty

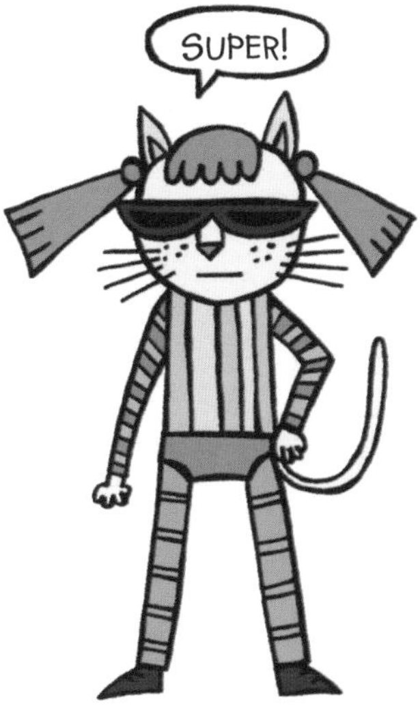
SUPER!

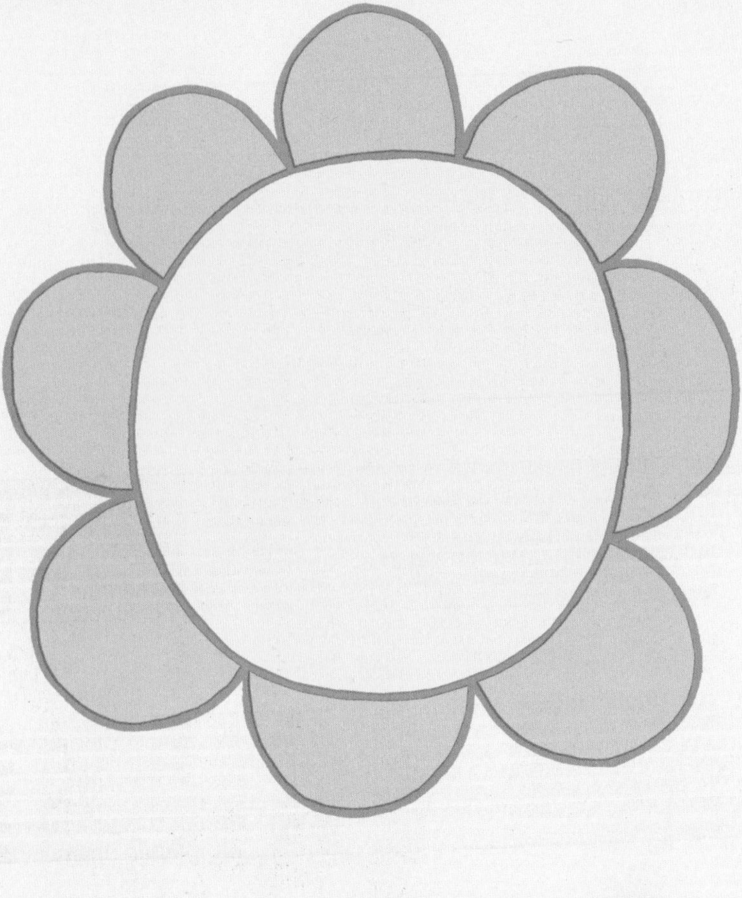

Christine, thanks for making this book

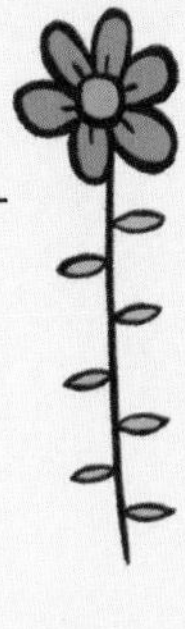

grow from this—

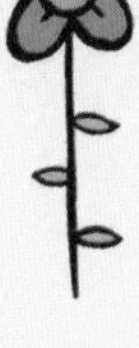

to this—

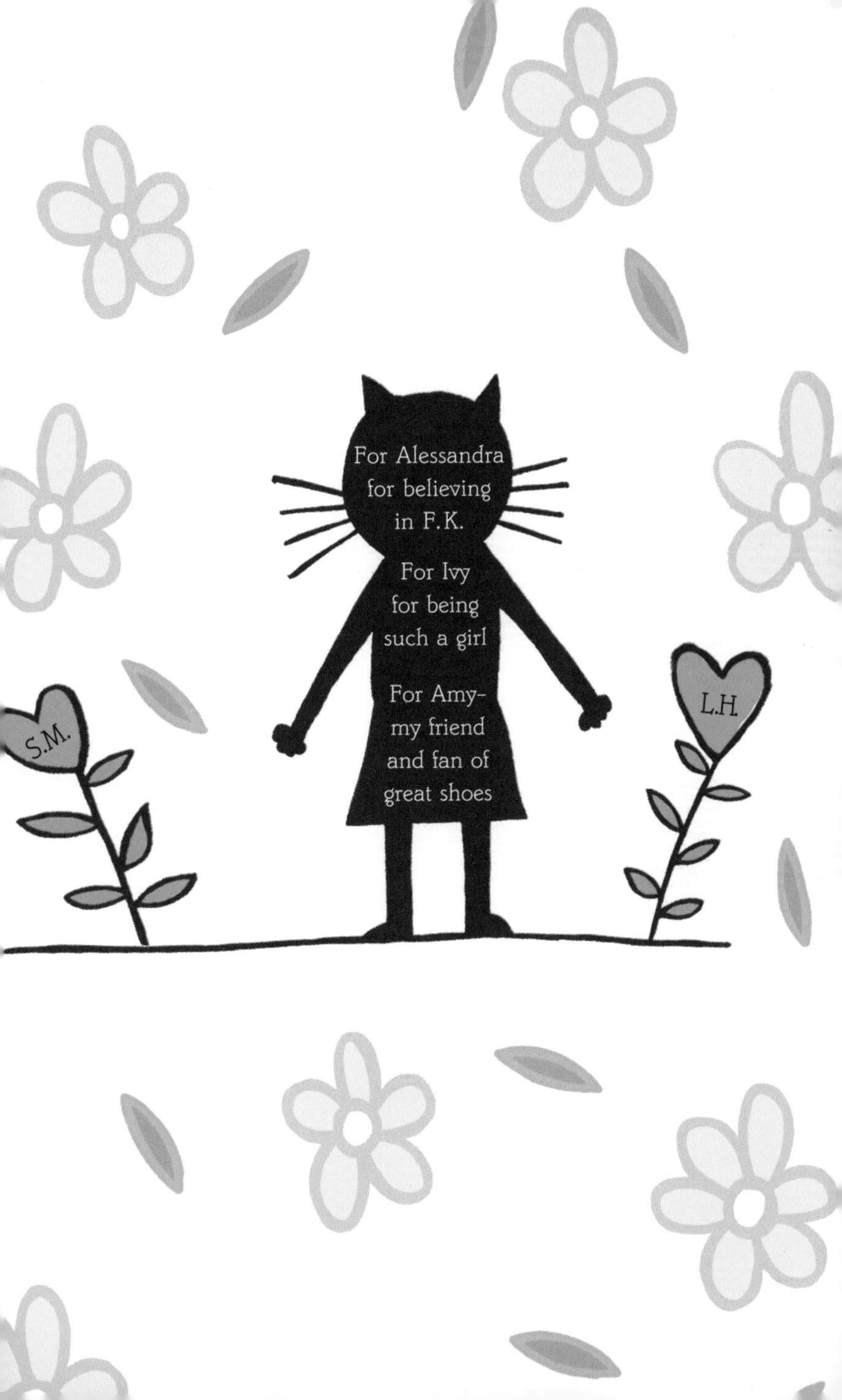
S.M.
L.H.

For Alessandra
for believing
in F.K.

For Ivy
for being
such a girl

For Amy-
my friend
and fan of
great shoes

This is Kiki Kittie.

She lives with her mother, father, little sister, Lana, and pet mouse named Mousie. The Kittie family is unusual for three reasons:

1 The Kittie family has a pet mouse.

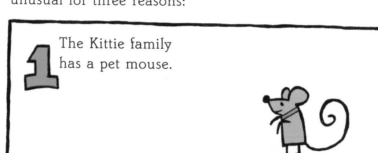

2 Kiki and Lana get to pick out all their own clothes.

3 The Kittie family knows the secret identity of Fashion Kitty.

The **FIRST** reason the Kittie family is unusual is that a cat having a mouse for a pet is similar to a human having a chocolate cake for a pet.

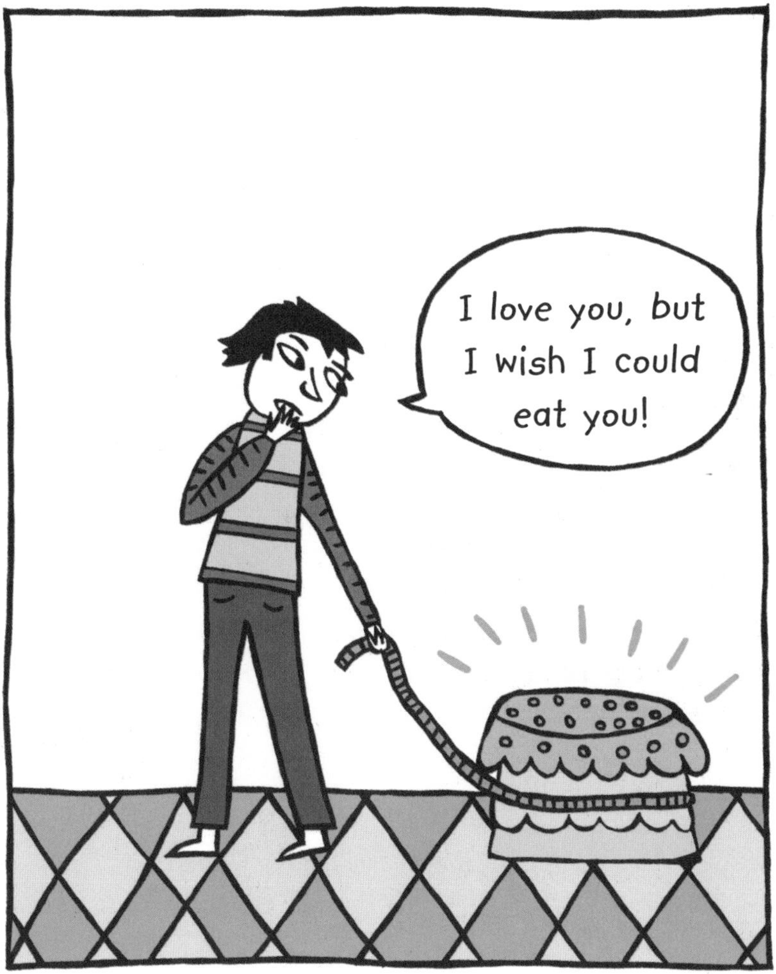
I love you, but I wish I could eat you!

Only, the Kittie family doesn't feel that way about Mousie, because they are vegetarians . . .

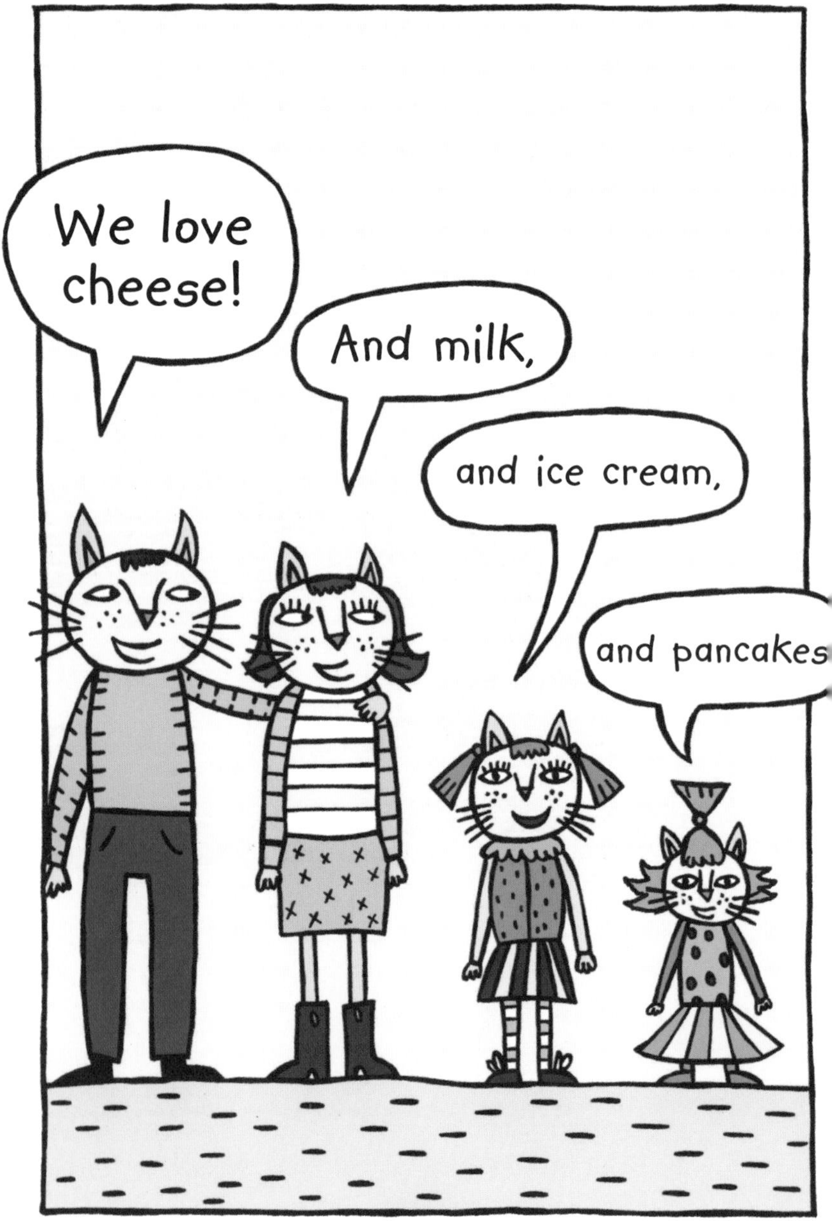
We love cheese!
And milk,
and ice cream,
and pancakes

. . . which means they don't eat meat.

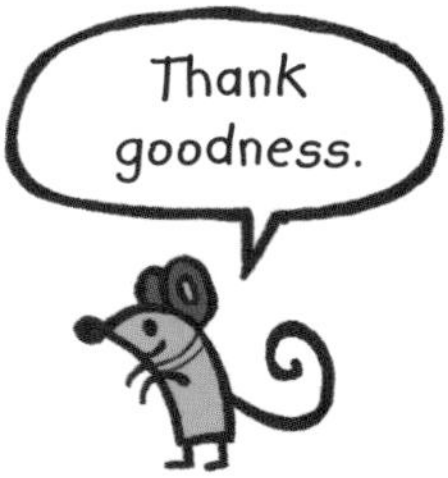
Thank goodness.

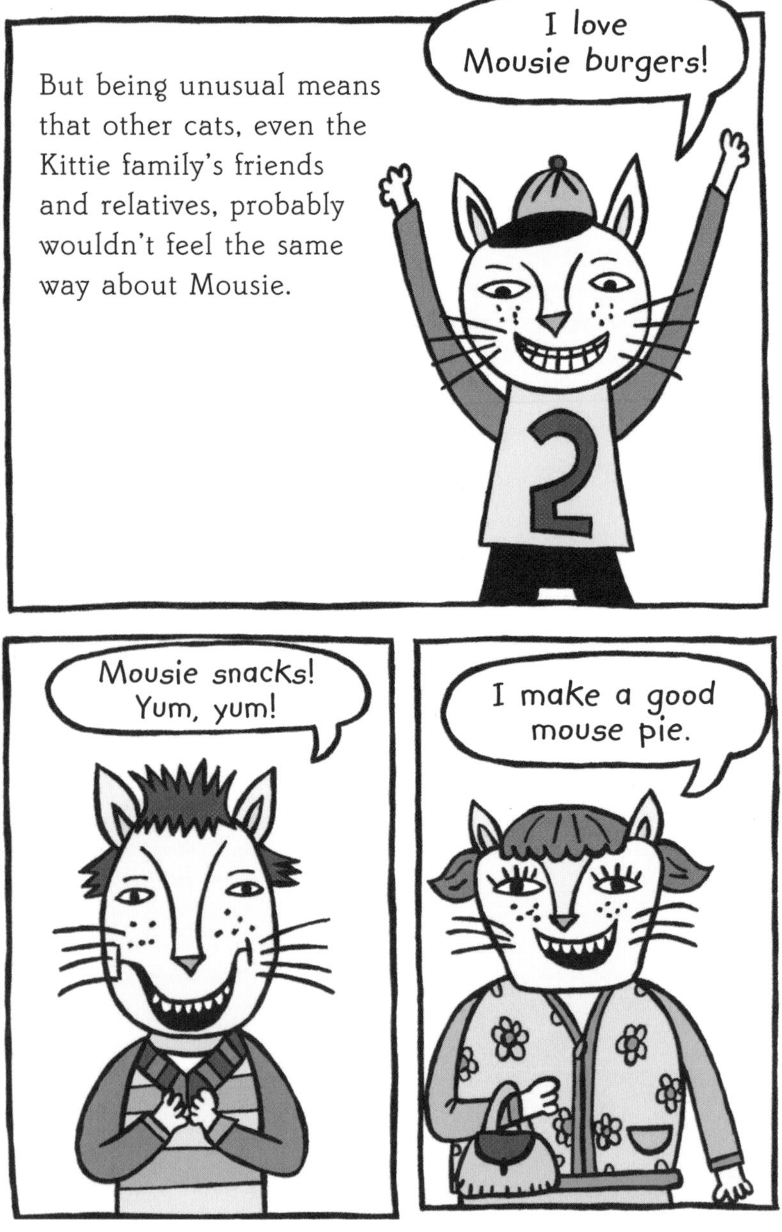
But being unusual means that other cats, even the Kittie family's friends and relatives, probably wouldn't feel the same way about Mousie.
I love Mousie burgers!
2
Mousie snacks! Yum, yum!
I make a good mouse pie.

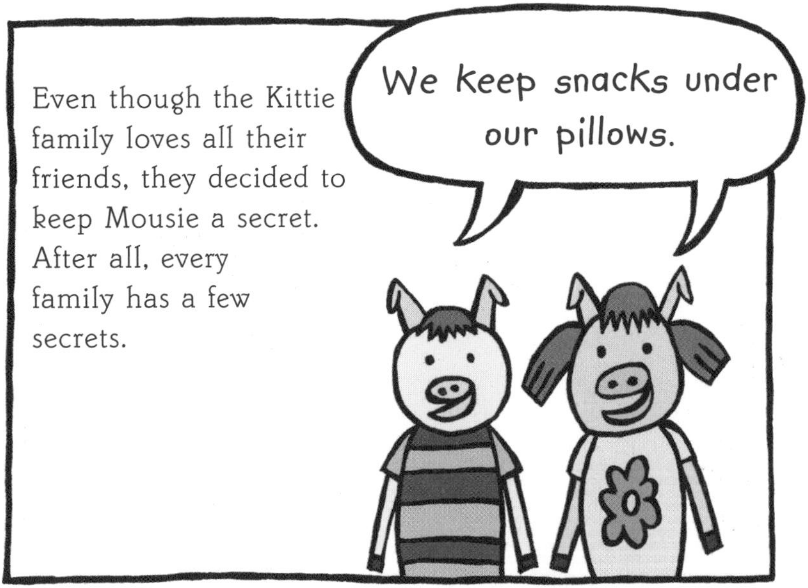
Even though the Kittie family loves all their friends, they decided to keep Mousie a secret. After all, every family has a few secrets.
We keep snacks under our pillows.

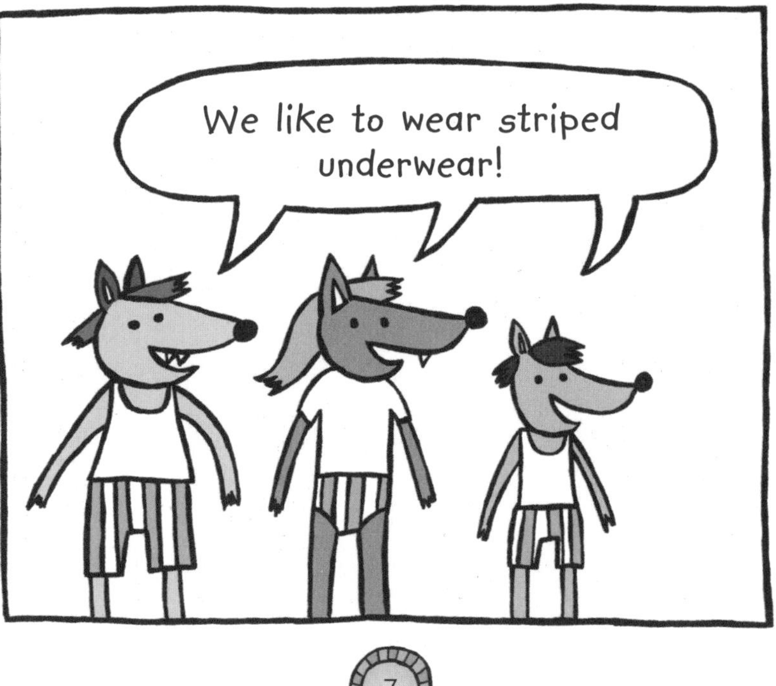
We like to wear striped underwear!

Father Kittie built Mousie a special smell-proof clubhouse in the closet in Kiki's room. Any time cats come over, Mousie runs into the clubhouse and locks the door.

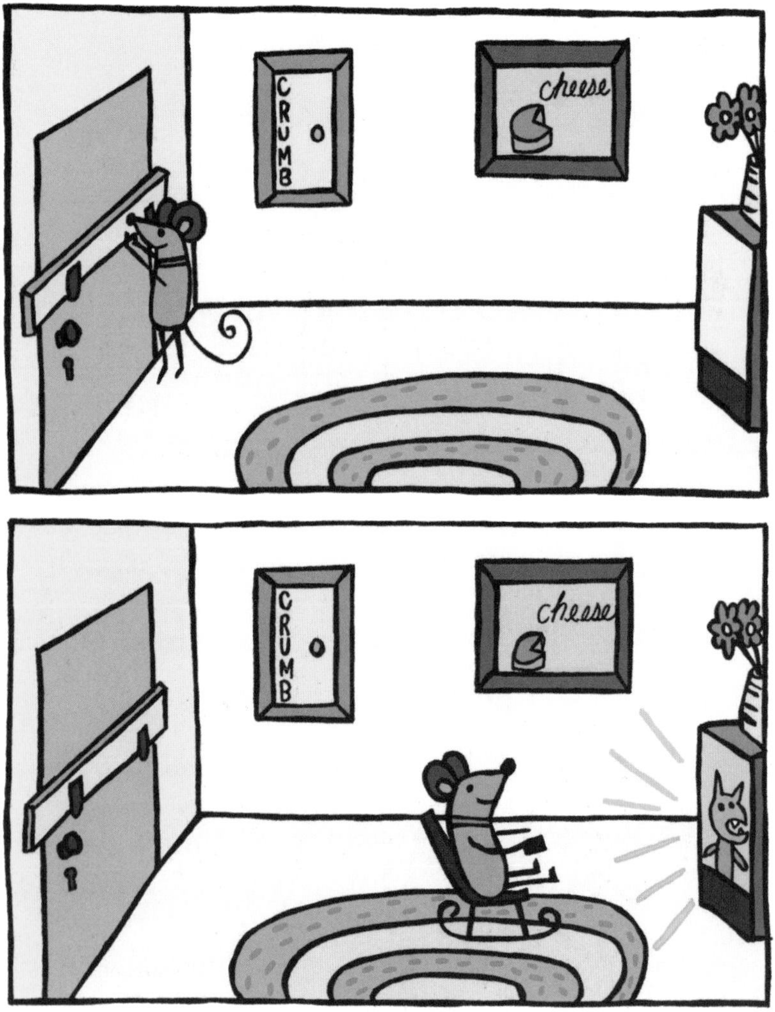
CRUMB
cheese
CRUMB
cheese

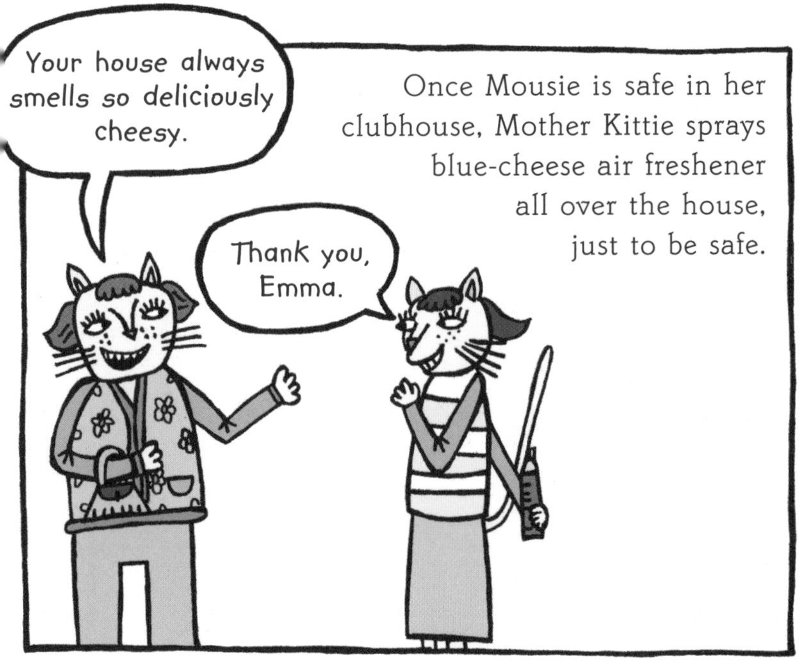
Your house always smells so deliciously cheesy.
Once Mousie is safe in her clubhouse, Mother Kittie sprays blue-cheese air freshener all over the house, just to be safe.
Thank you, Emma.

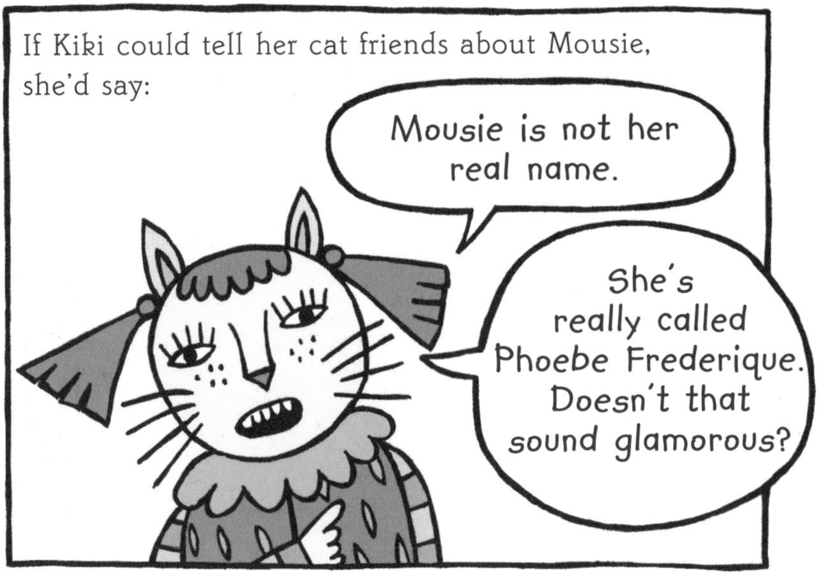
If Kiki could tell her cat friends about Mousie, she'd say:
Mousie is not her real name.
She's really called Phoebe Frederique. Doesn't that sound glamorous?

But she can't tell anybody Mousie's real name, not even her family, because six months ago . . .

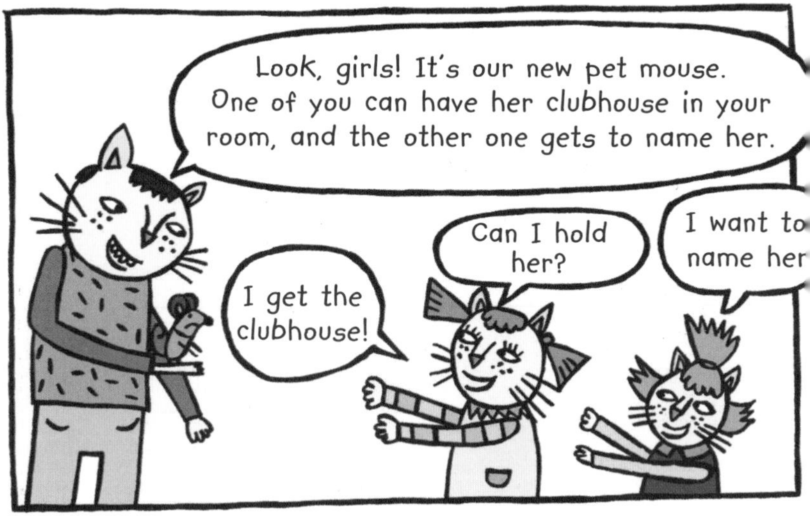
Look, girls! It's our new pet mouse. One of you can have her clubhouse in your room, and the other one gets to name her.
I get the clubhouse!
Can I hold her?
I want to name her

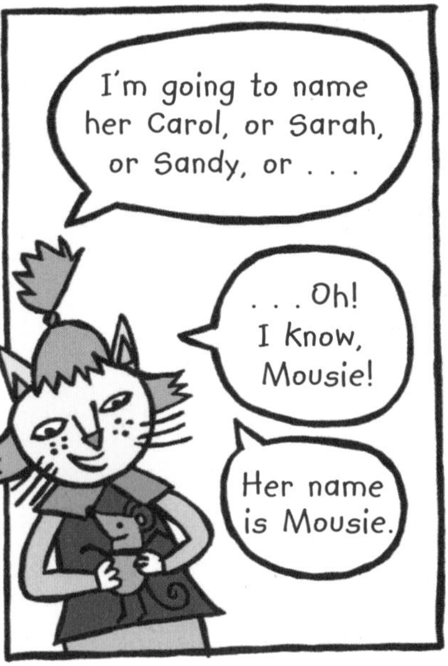
I'm going to name her Carol, or Sarah, or Sandy, or . . .
. . . Oh! I know, Mousie!
Her name is Mousie.

Which was no big surprise because . . .

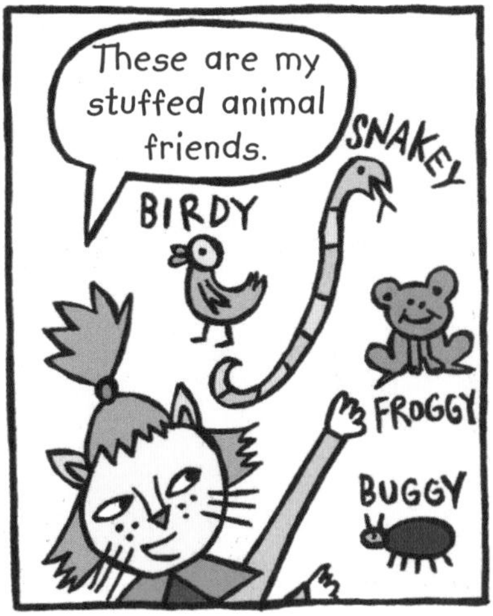
These are my stuffed animal friends.
SNAKEY
BIRDY
FROGGY
BUGGY

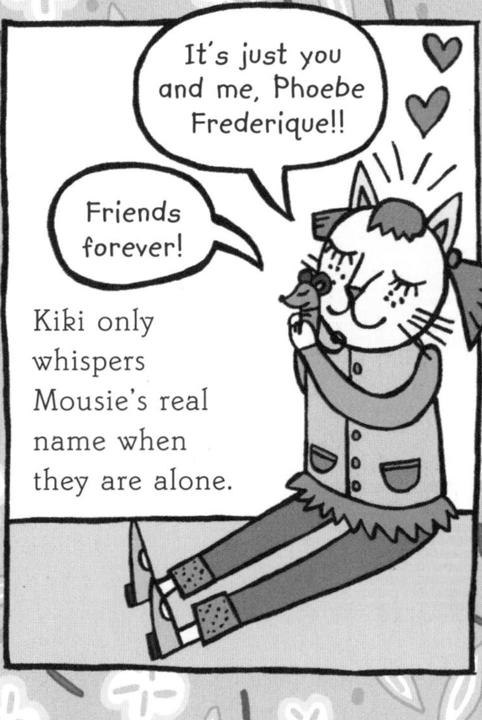
It's just you and me, Phoebe Frederique!!
Friends forever!
Kiki only whispers Mousie's real name when they are alone.

The second reason the Kittie family is unusual is that Mother Kittie believes in free fashion, which means she lets Kiki and Lana pick out all their own clothes. Most mothers don't do this because it upsets them when patterns like:

are displayed all together on one body.

This doesn't bother Mother Kittie. As long as Kiki and Lana wear jackets and hats in the wintertime, Mother Kittie is happy.

Kiki has a natural flair for fashion.
Everyone says so:

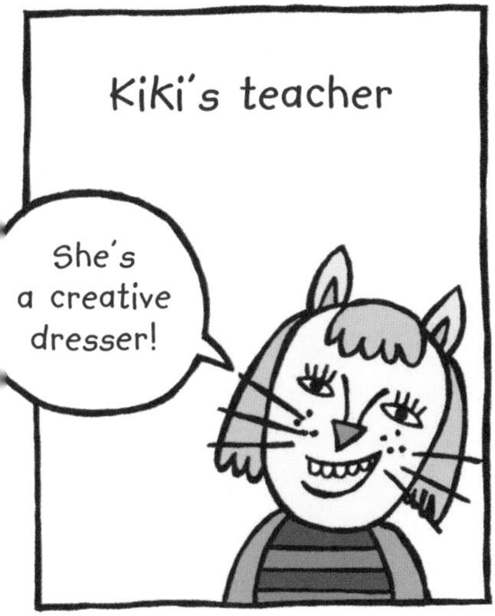
Kiki's teacher
She's a creative dresser!

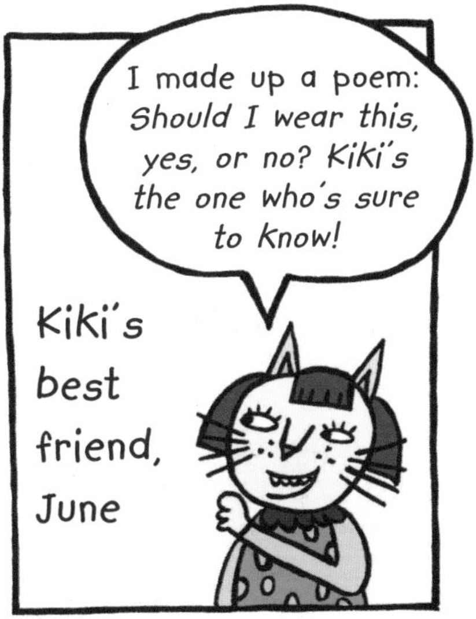
I made up a poem: *Should I wear this, yes, or no? Kiki's the one who's sure to know!*
Kiki's best friend, June

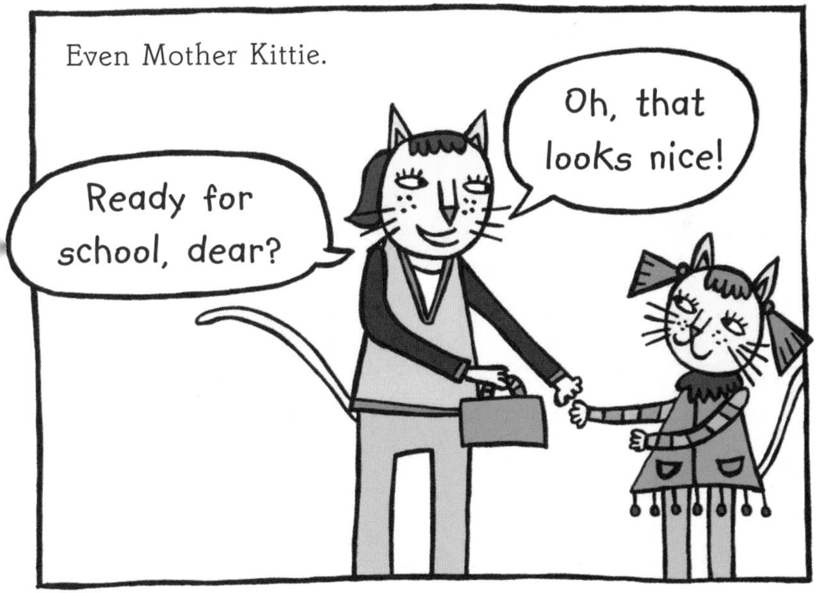
Even Mother Kittie.
Ready for school, dear?
Oh, that looks nice!

Lana, on the other hand, is a different story. She wears some very unusual clothing combinations.

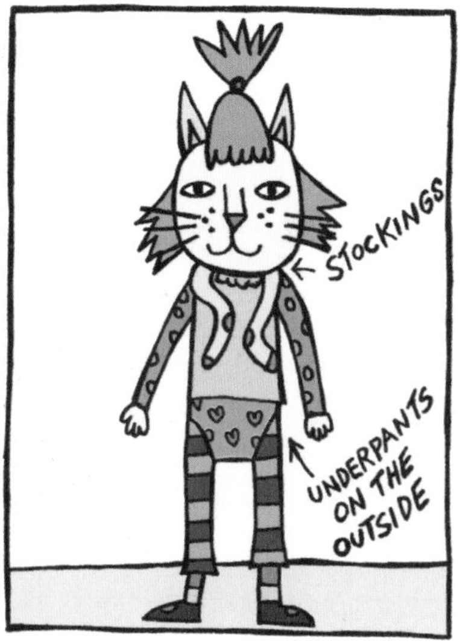
STOCKINGS
UNDERPANTS ON THE OUTSIDE

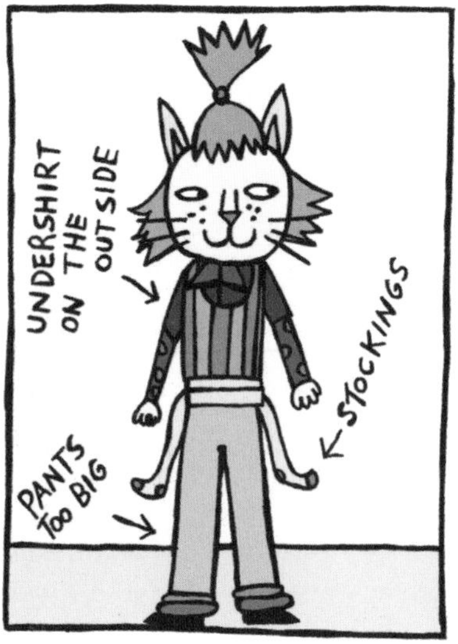
UNDERSHIRT ON THE OUTSIDE
STOCKINGS
PANTS TOO BIG

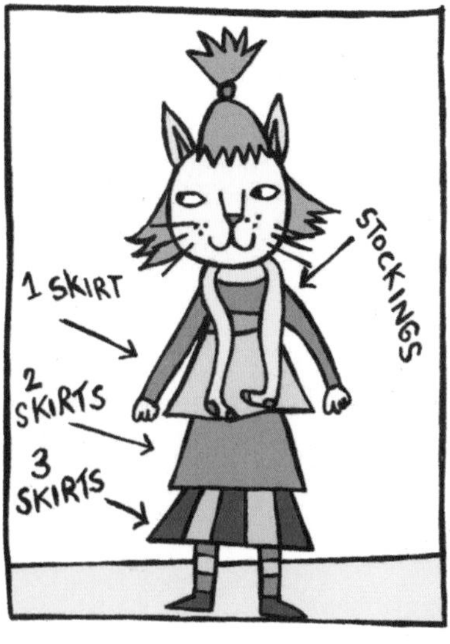
STOCKINGS
1 SKIRT
2 SKIRTS
3 SKIRTS

Sometimes Kiki just can't help herself and she says:

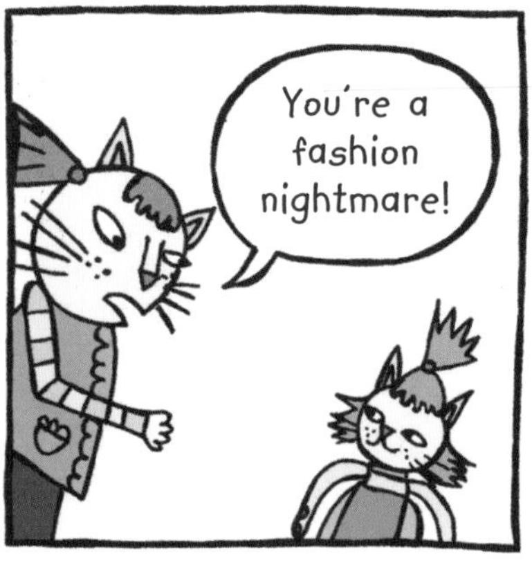
You're a fashion nightmare!

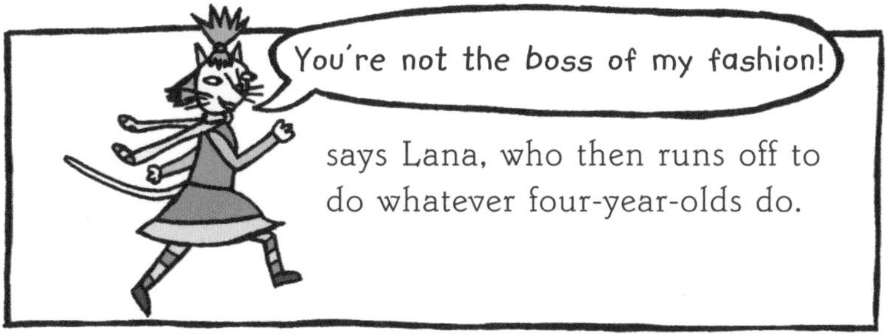
You're not the *boss* of my fashion!
says Lana, who then runs off to do whatever four-year-olds do.

Kiki is glad that Lana doesn't go to school yet. At least at home no one can see her.

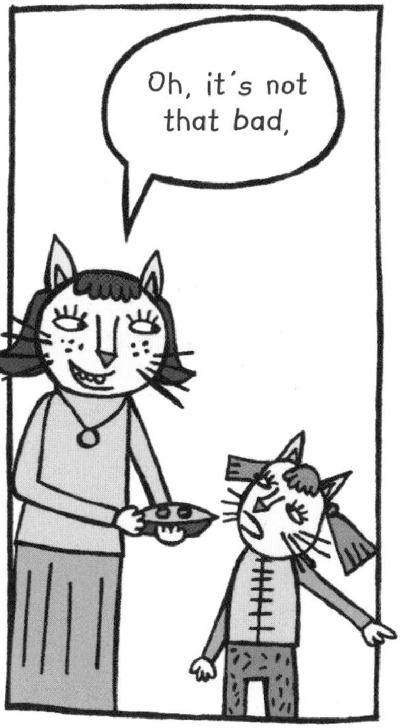
Oh, it's not that *bad*,

says Mother Kittie when Kiki complains.

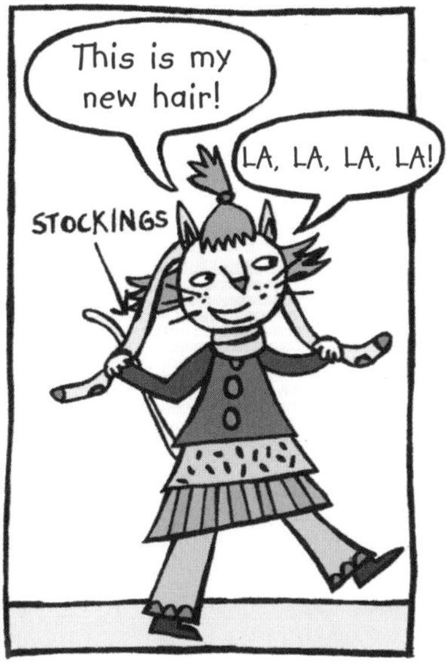
This is my new hair!
LA, LA, LA, LA!
STOCKINGS

But Kiki knows that mothers don't always see the truth about their children, and she secretly wonders if sometimes they are too nice.

The **THIRD** and most important reason the Kittie family is unusual is that they know the secret identity of Fashion Kitty.

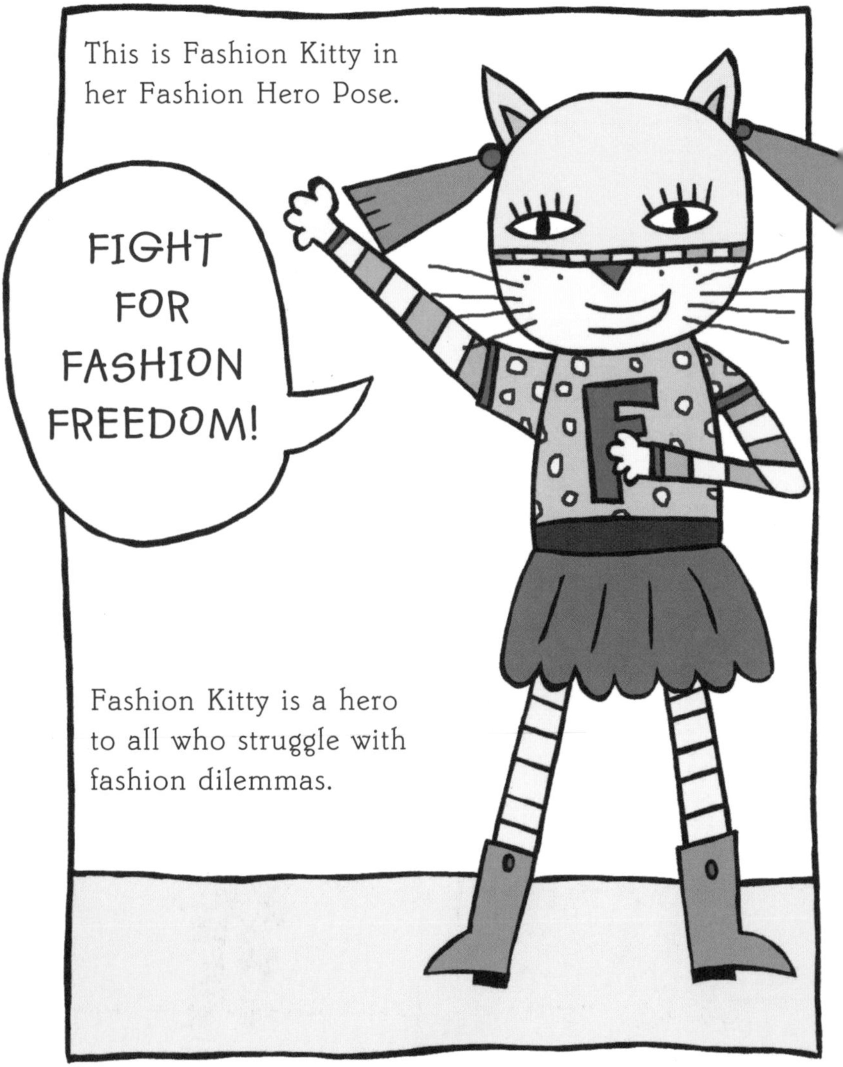
This is Fashion Kitty in her Fashion Hero Pose.
FIGHT FOR FASHION FREEDOM!
F
Fashion Kitty is a hero to all who struggle with fashion dilemmas.

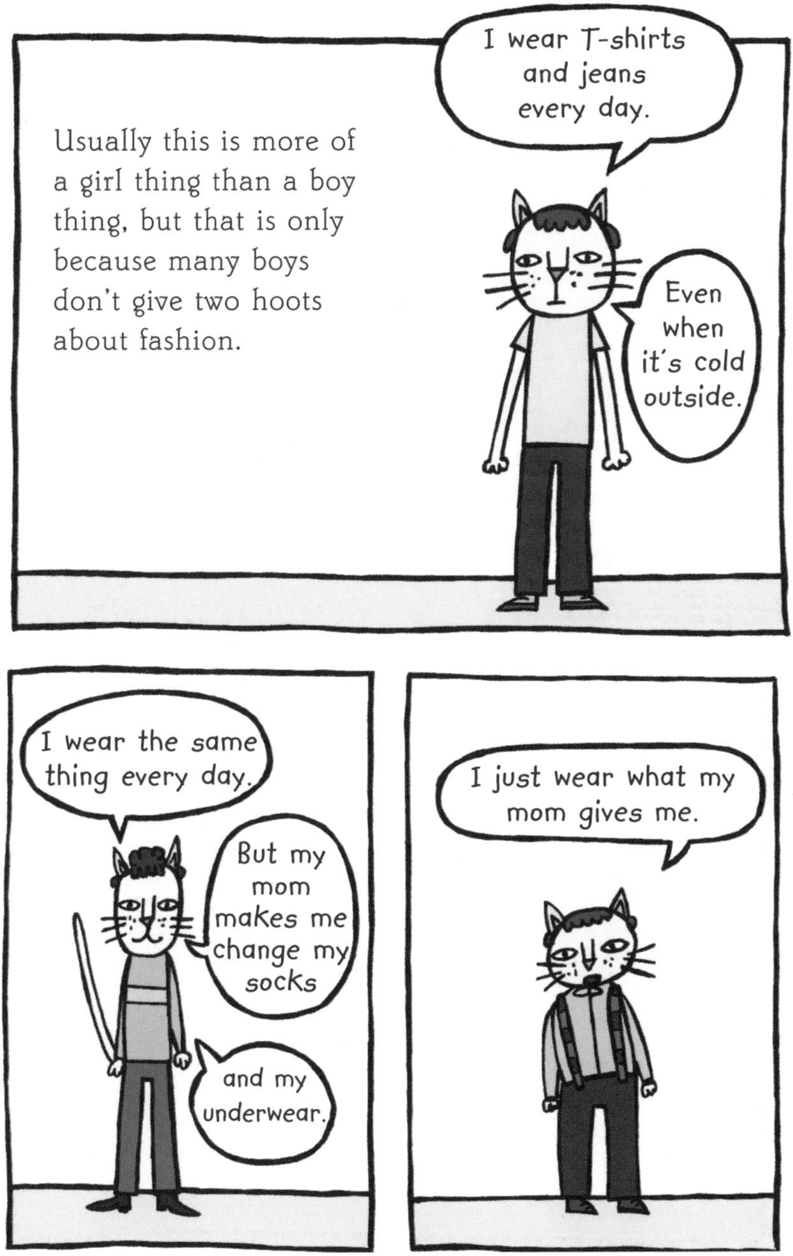
Usually this is more of a girl thing than a boy thing, but that is only because many boys don't give two hoots about fashion.
I wear T-shirts and jeans every day.
Even when it's cold outside.
I wear the same thing every day.
But my mom makes me change my socks
and my underwear.
I just wear what my mom gives me.

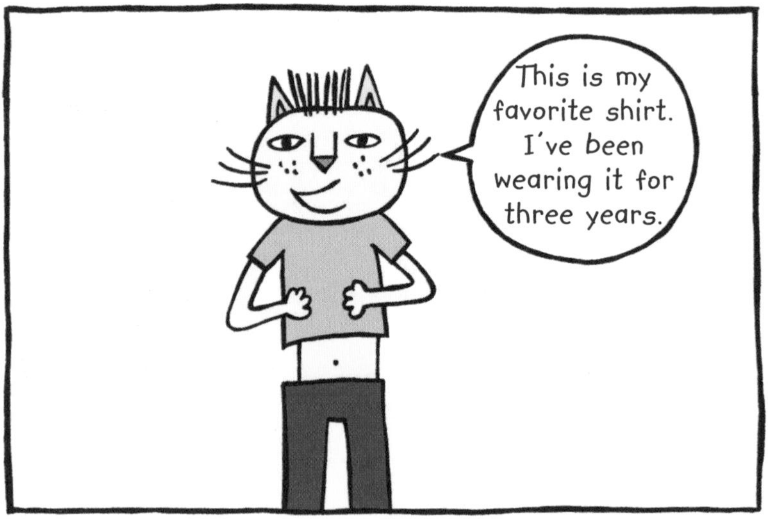
This is my favorite shirt. I've *been* wearing it for three years.

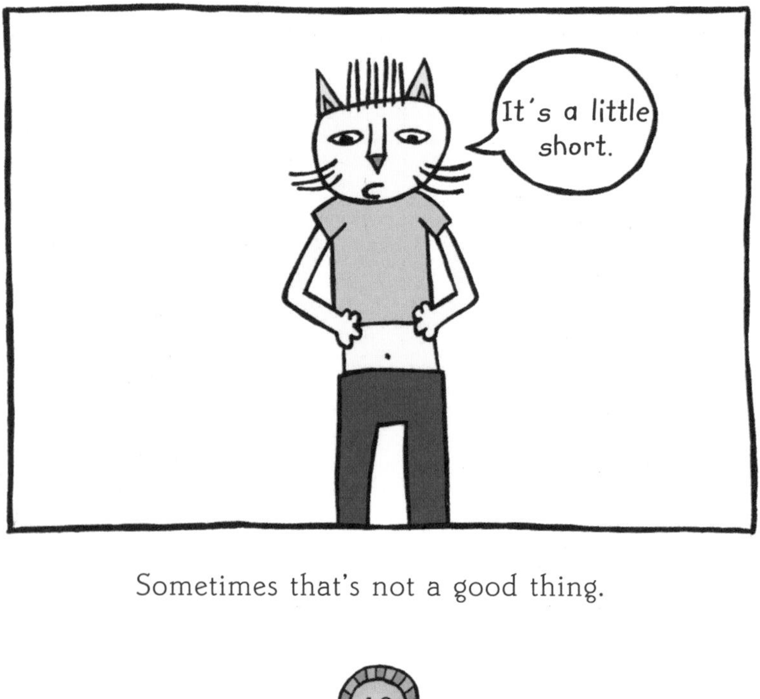
It's a little short.

Sometimes that's not a good thing.

Fashion Kitty doesn't live on top of a mountain,

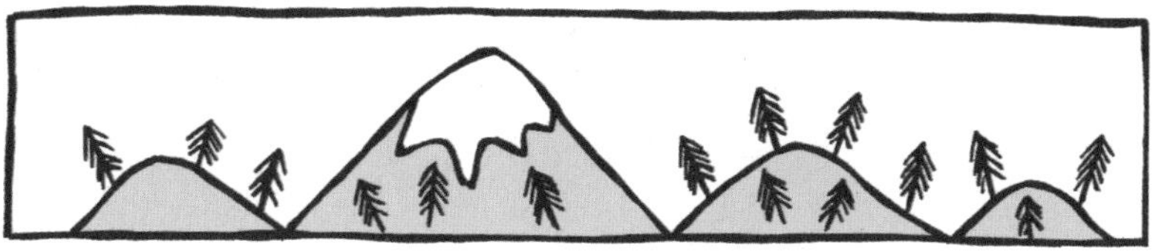

in a fancy apartment building,

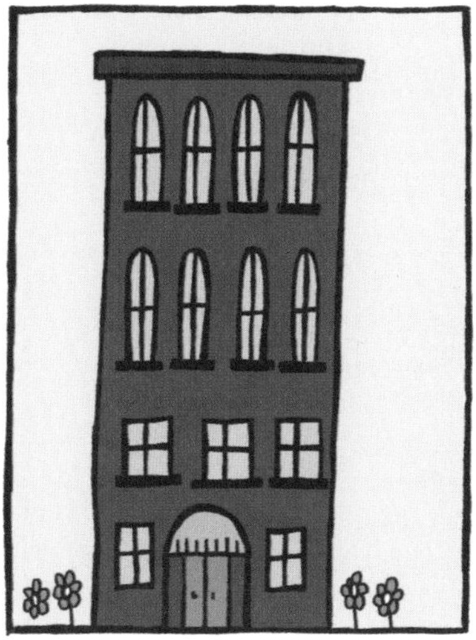

or even in a stylish secret superhero cave.

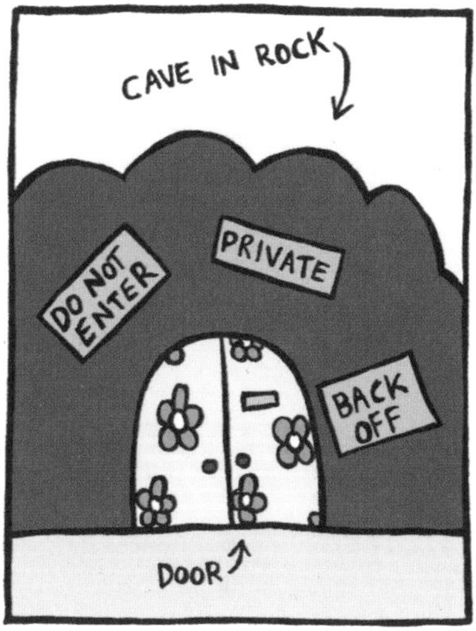
CAVE IN ROCK
PRIVATE
DO NOT ENTER
BACK OFF
DOOR

She lives with her mother, father, and little sister, Lana. That's right! Fashion Kitty is really Kiki Kittie. Kiki wasn't always a fashion hero. Right up until her birthday four months ago, Kiki Kittie was just her regular fashionable self. But on her birthday, something unexplainable happened.

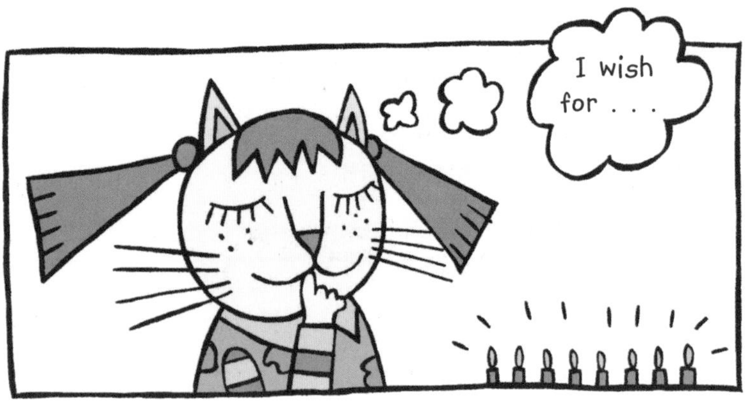
I wish
for . . .

Kiki was blowing out her candles on her birthday cake when a shelf above her broke and sent a pile of fashion magazines tumbling down on her head.

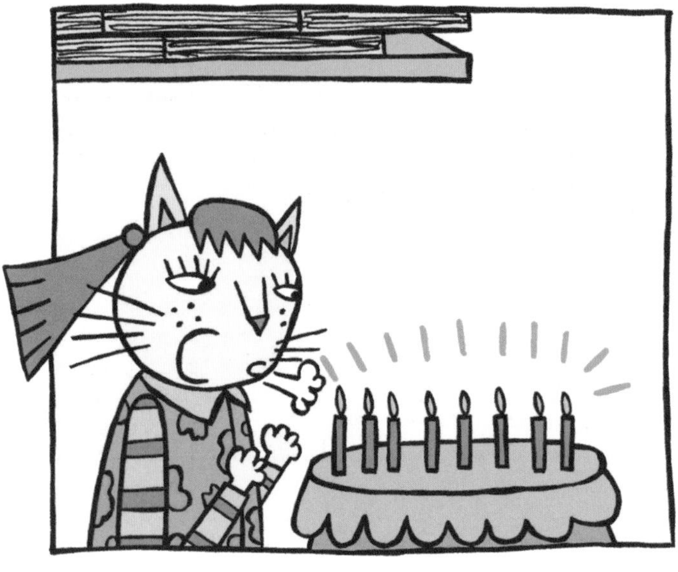

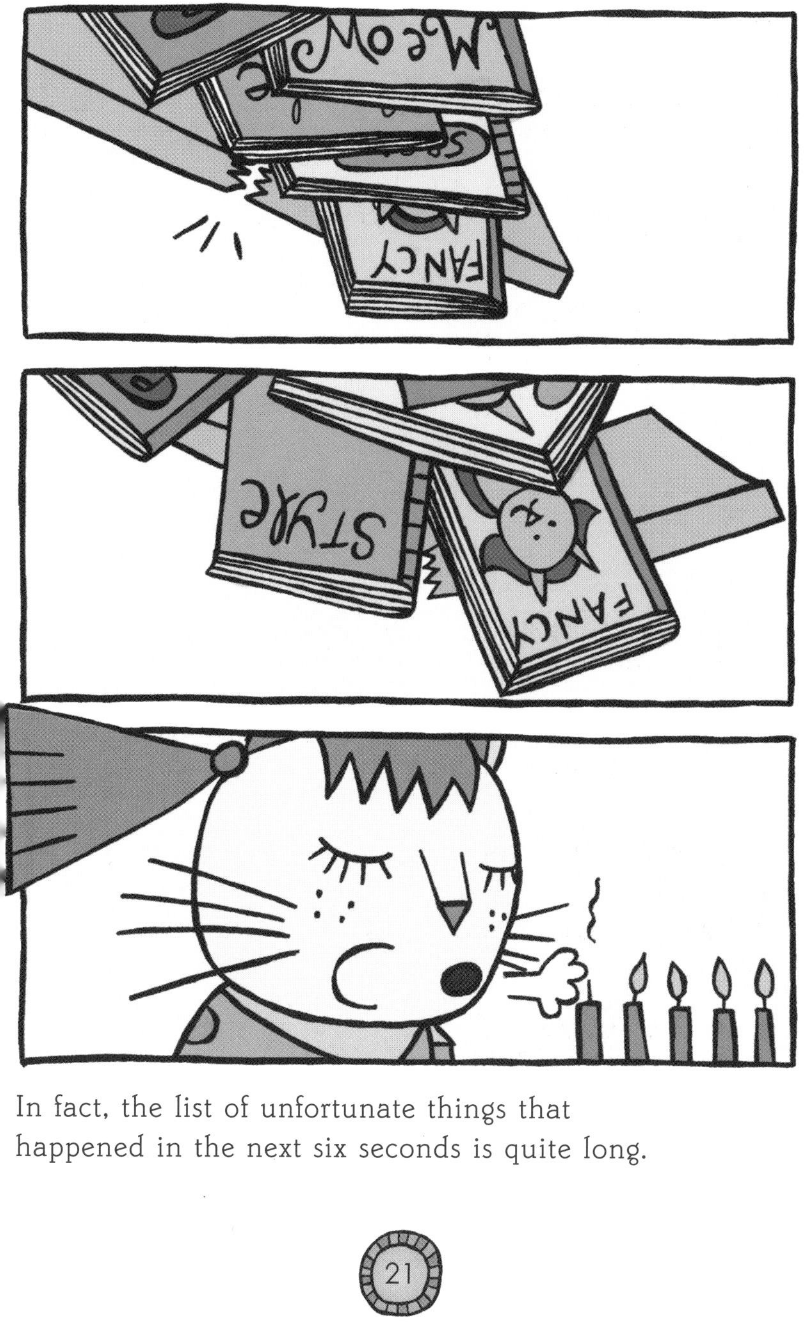
FANCY
STYLE
FANCY

In fact, the list of unfortunate things that happened in the next six seconds is quite long.

It was unfortunate that...

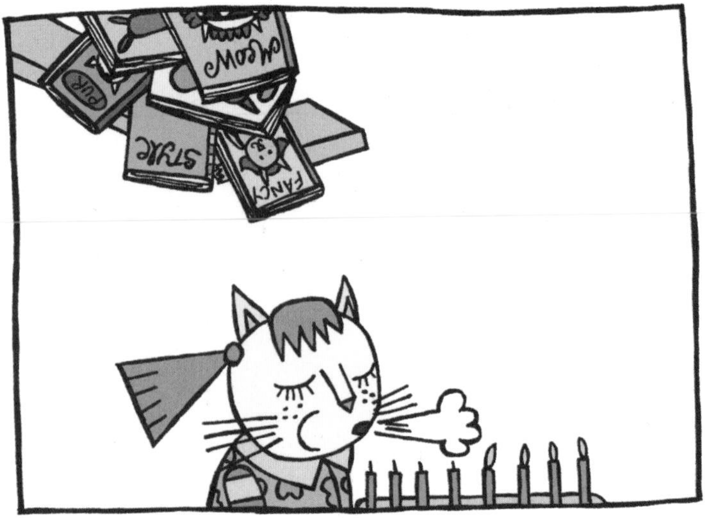
MEOW
PUR
STYLE
FANCY

the shelf broke when Kiki was directly underneath it blowing out the candles on her birthday cake;

the magazines hit Kiki on the head, causing her to fall down and knock over the table that held the birthday cake;

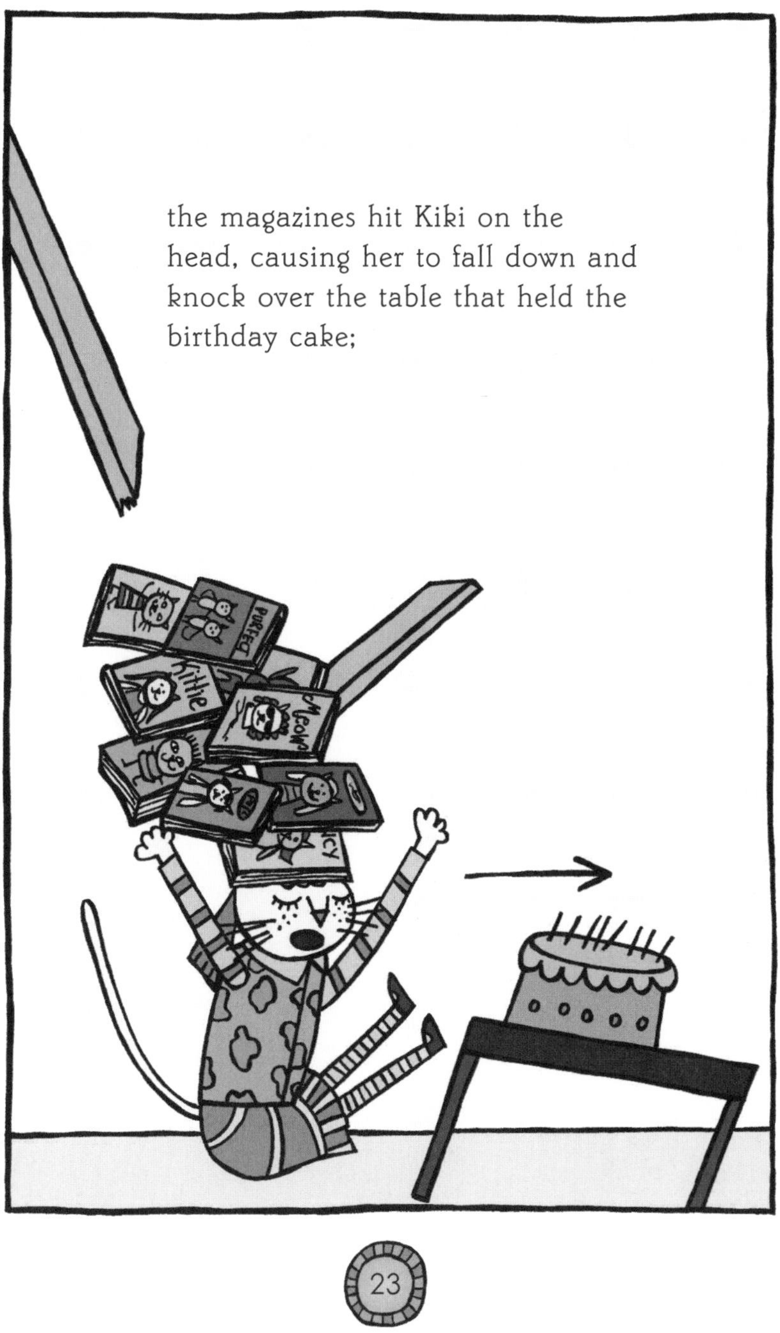
PURRFECT
Kittie
Meow

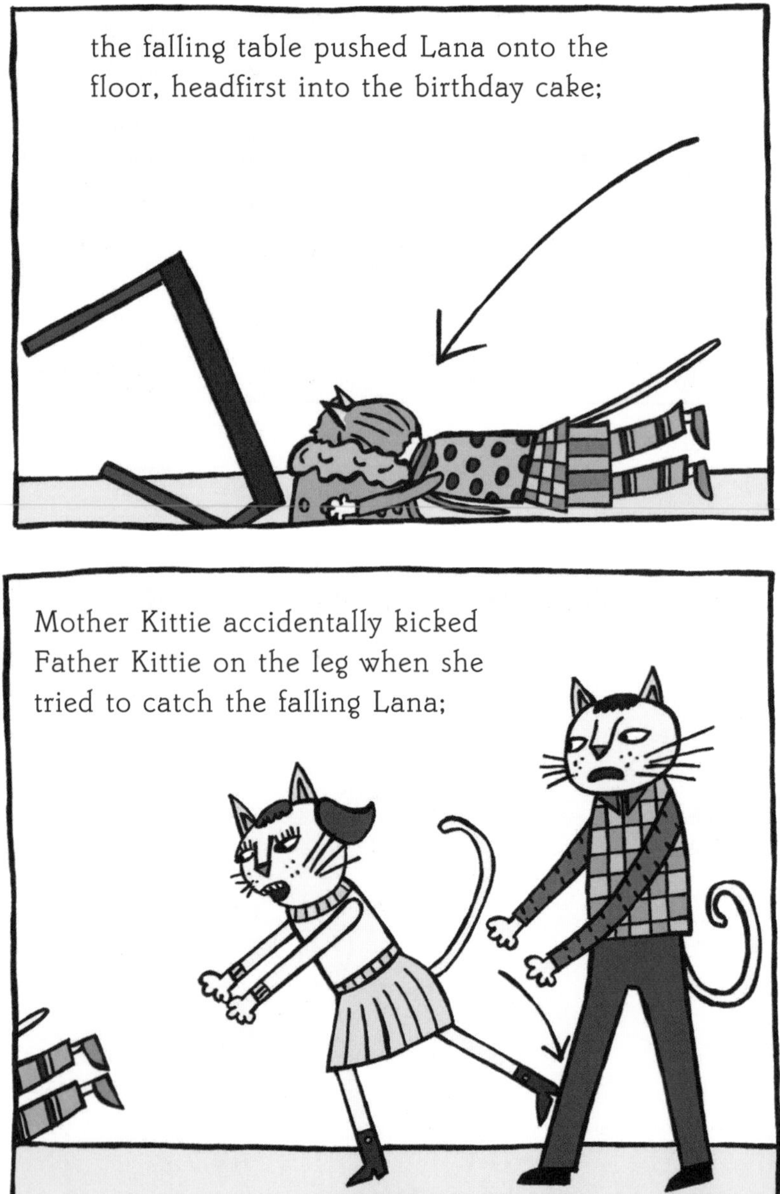
the falling table pushed Lana onto the floor, headfirst into the birthday cake;
Mother Kittie accidentally kicked Father Kittie on the leg when she tried to catch the falling Lana;

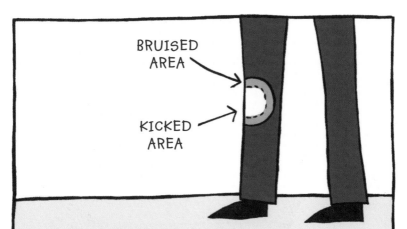

BRUISED AREA

KICKED AREA

the leg Mother Kittie kicked already had a big bruise on it from two days before, when Father Kittie had tripped on one of Lana's toys;

Father Kittie, while yelling and grabbing his sore leg, knocked over a prized antique vase that was his and Mrs. Kittie's favorite wedding present;

and the vase broke.

But the most unfortunate thing was that Kiki Kittie was lying very still on the floor, with her eyes closed, and she was not sleeping.

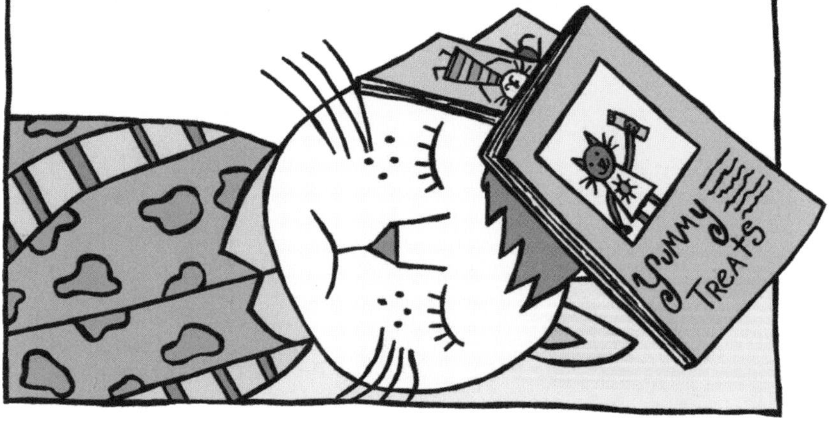
YUMMY TREATS

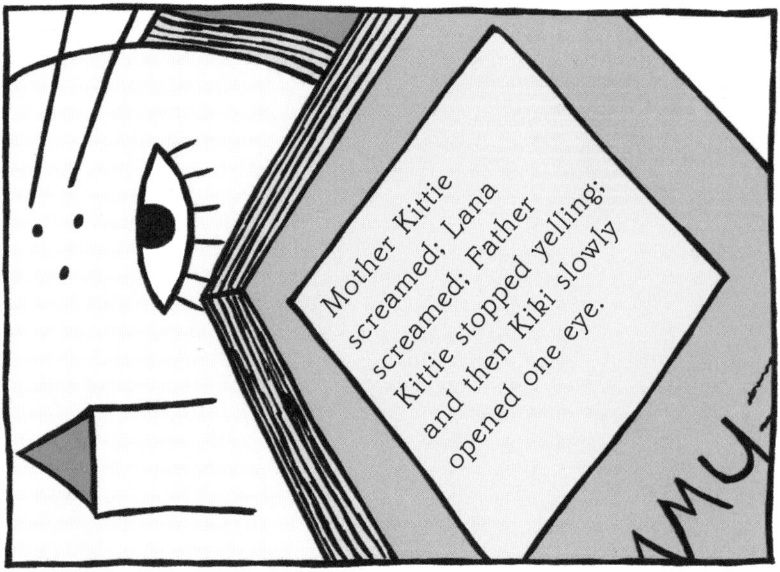
Mother Kittie screamed; Lana screamed; Father Kittie stopped yelling; and then Kiki slowly opened one eye.

Often, when bad things happen, it is comforting to make a silent list of how it could have been worse.

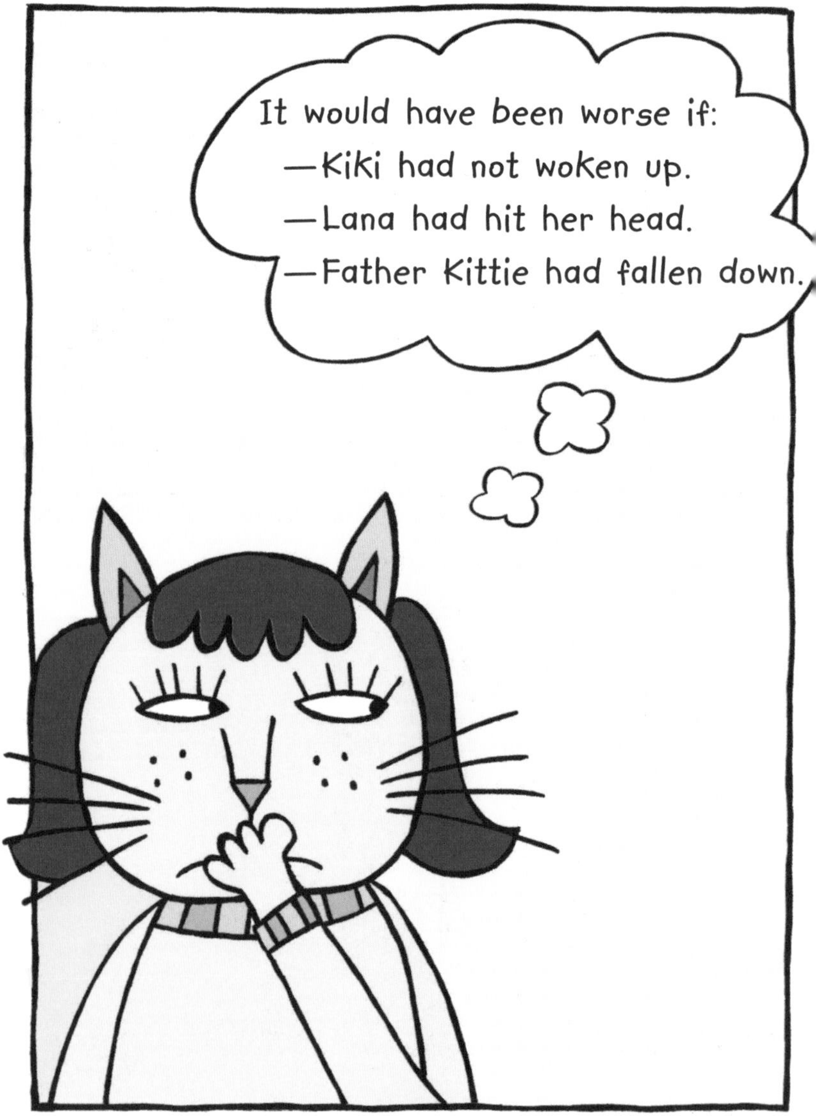
It would have been worse if:
—Kiki had not woken up.
—Lana had hit her head.
—Father Kittie had fallen down.

Looking at the mess, Mother Kittie said:

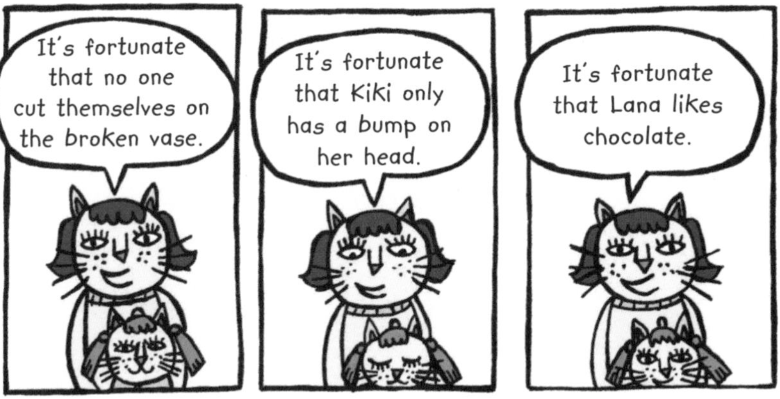
It's fortunate that no one cut themselves on the broken vase.
It's fortunate that Kiki only has a bump on her head.
It's fortunate that Lana likes chocolate.

And then they laughed, because Lana was covered with chocolate cake.

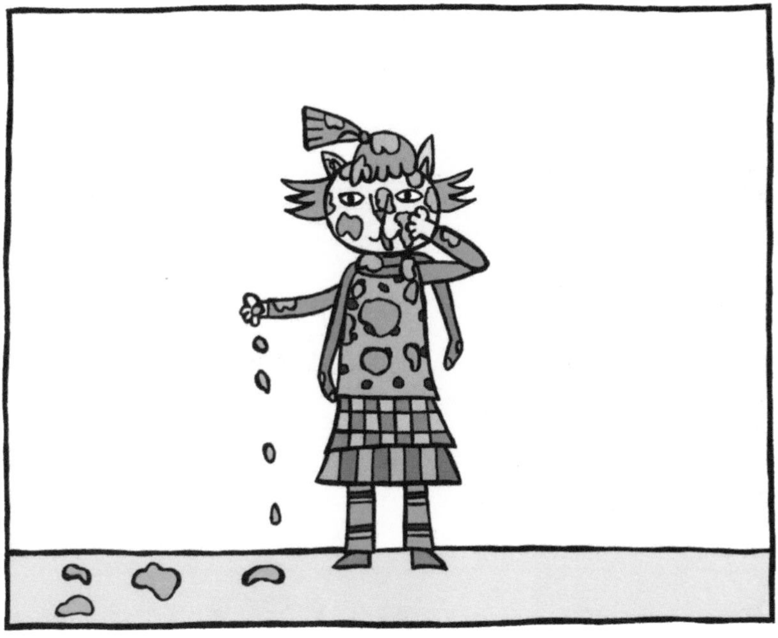

Later, when everything was almost cleaned up and everyone was getting ready to go out to Tom's Treats, the most fancy and delicious cake-and-ice-cream restaurant in town, Lana said:

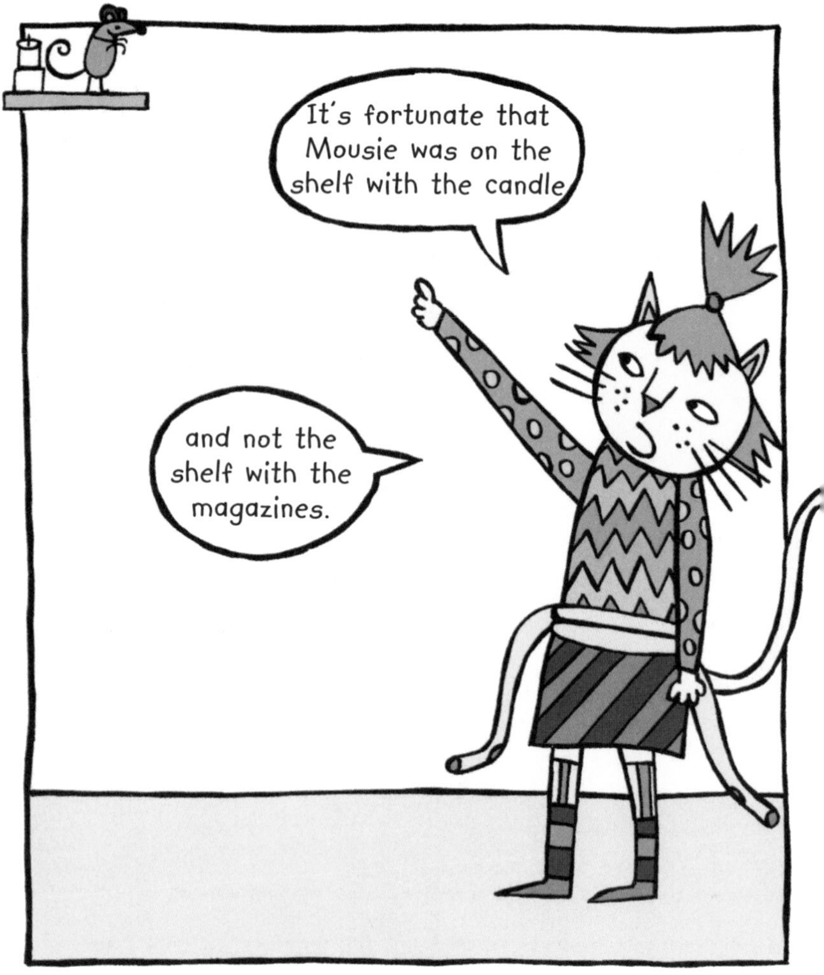
It's fortunate that Mousie was on the shelf with the candle
and not the shelf with the magazines.

And everyone agreed it was.

And then, right when everything seemed almost normal, the unexplainable thing happened. Kiki screamed and fell to the floor. Mother and Father Kittie rushed over, thinking the same horrible thought:

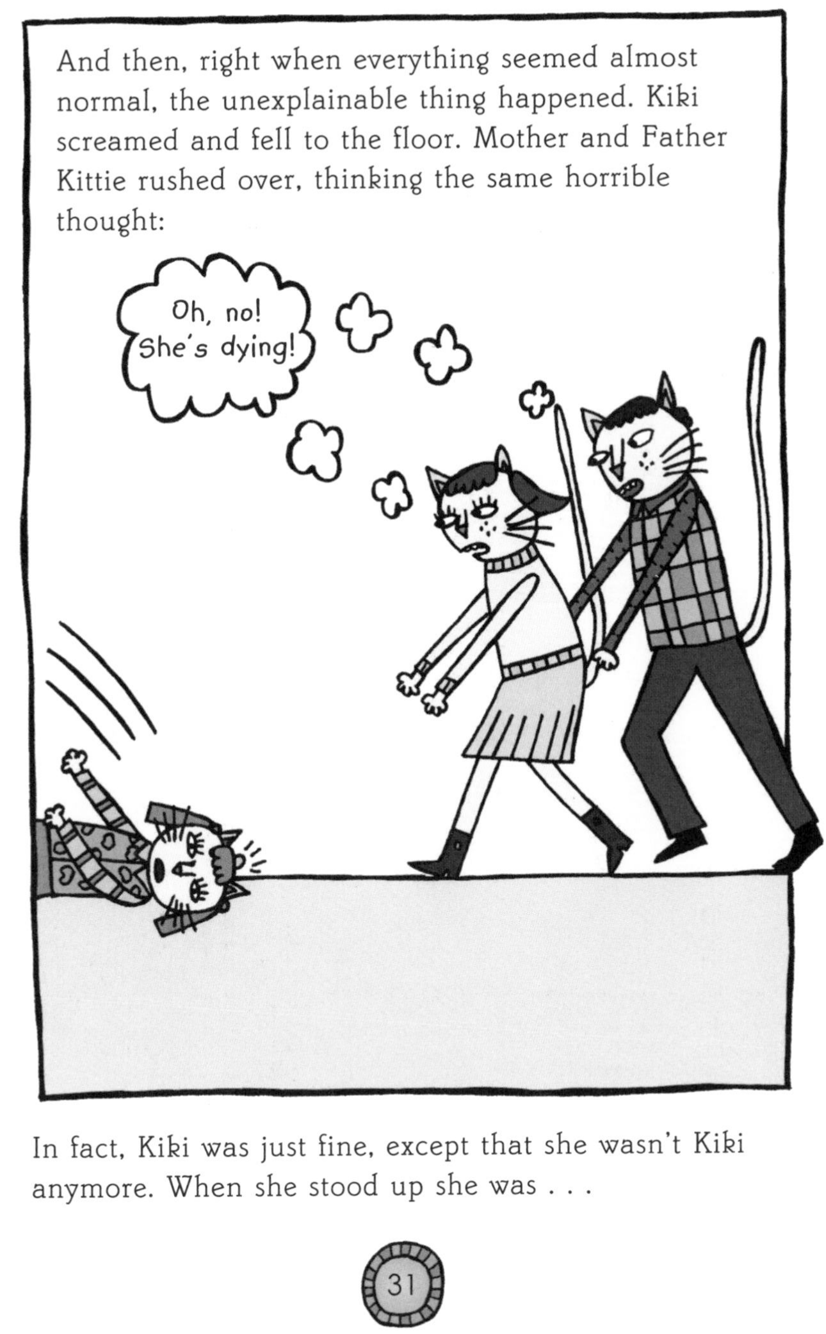

Oh, no! She's dying!

In fact, Kiki was just fine, except that she wasn't Kiki anymore. When she stood up she was . . .

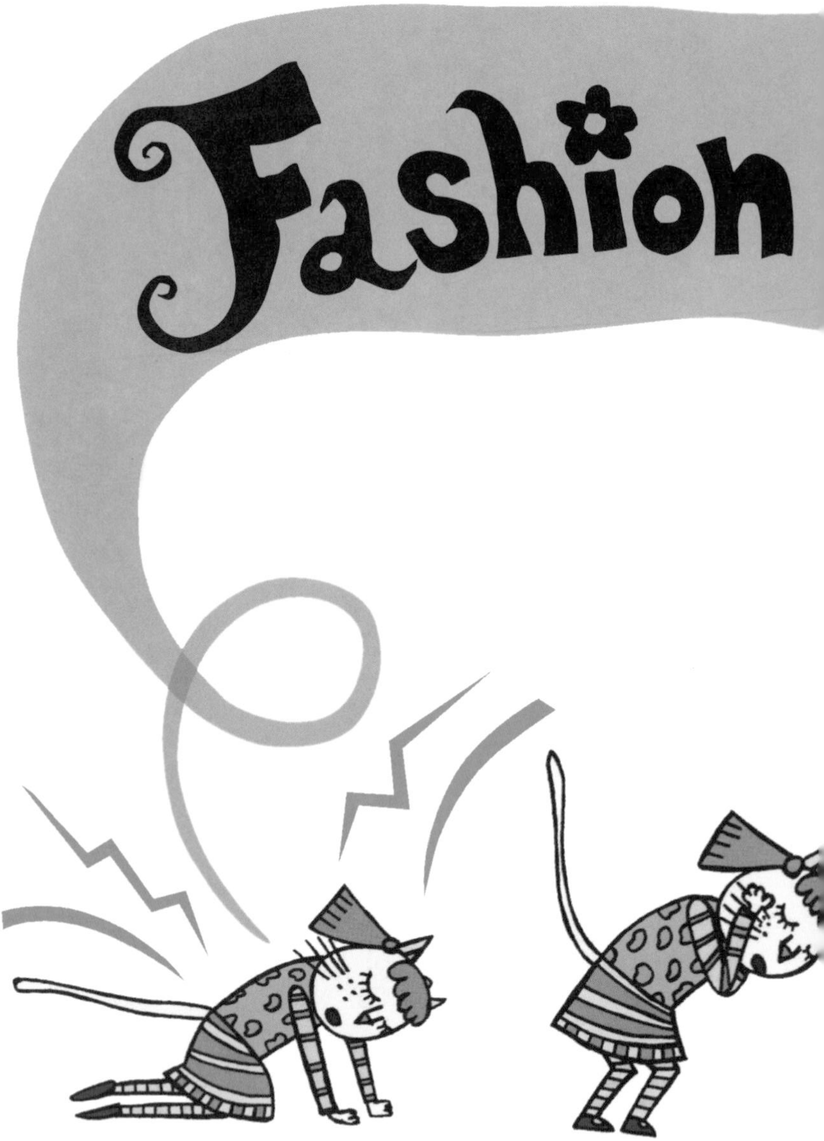
Fashion

Kitty

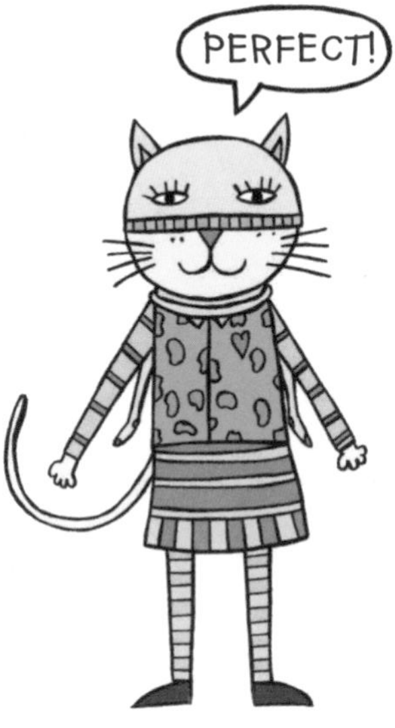
PERFECT!

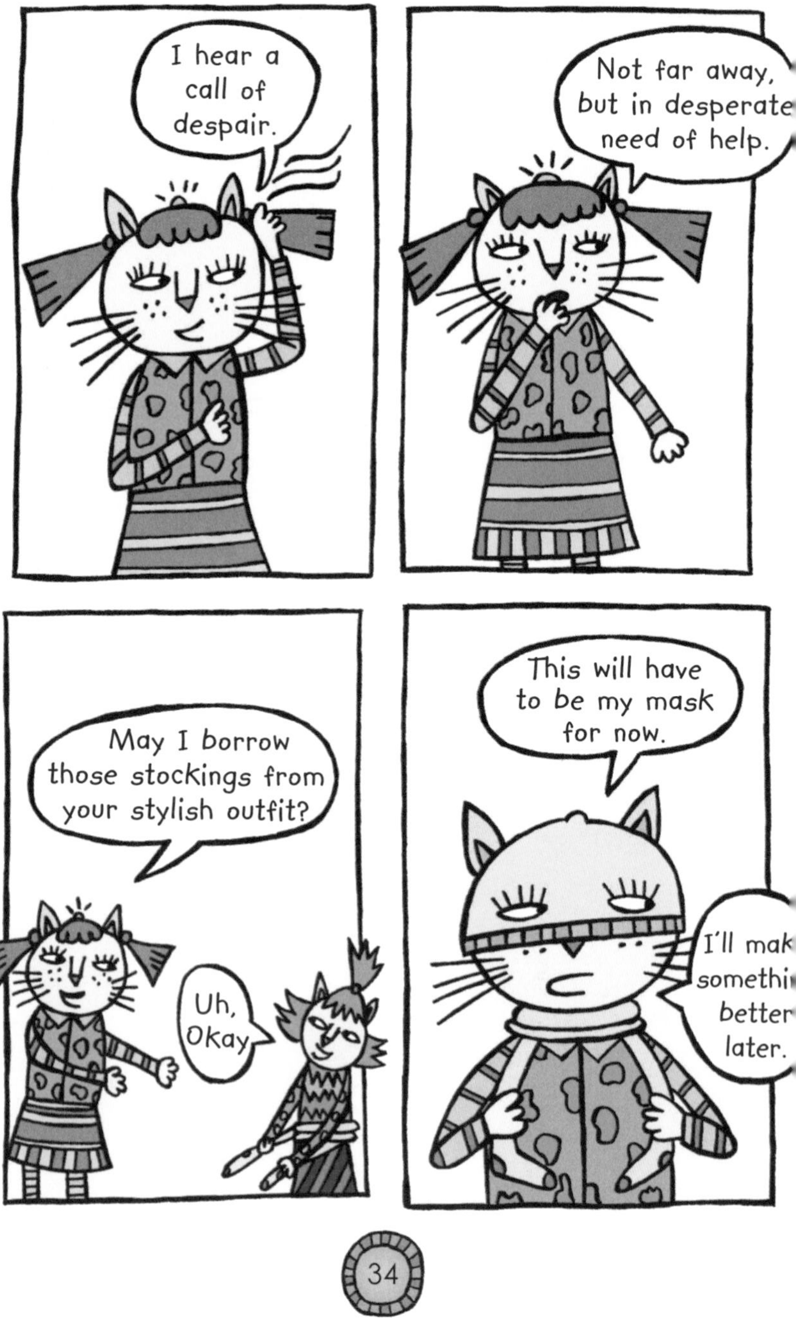
I hear a call of despair.
Not far away, but in desperate need of help.
May I borrow those stockings from your stylish outfit?
Uh, Okay.
This will have to be my mask for now.
I'll mak somethi better later.

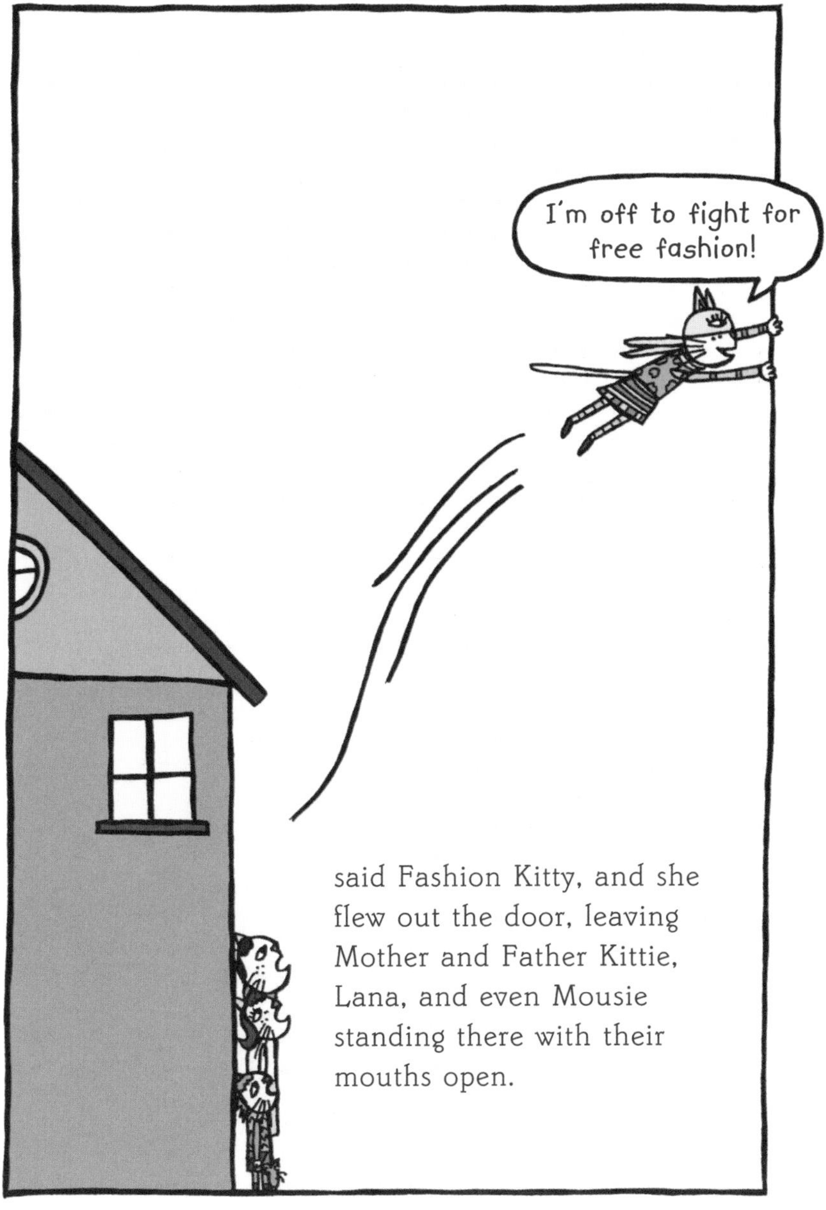
I'm off to fight for free fashion!

said Fashion Kitty, and she flew out the door, leaving Mother and Father Kittie, Lana, and even Mousie standing there with their mouths open.

Super Abilities of Fashion Kitty

Brain that can mix and match hundreds of outfits in a second

Ears that hear the distress call of someone in need of fashion help

X-ray eyes that can see through buildings or anything else that's in the way

Heart, mostly good

Tail of comfort. One touch of the tail makes everything seem all right

Supersonic feet that make Fashion Kitty really bounce

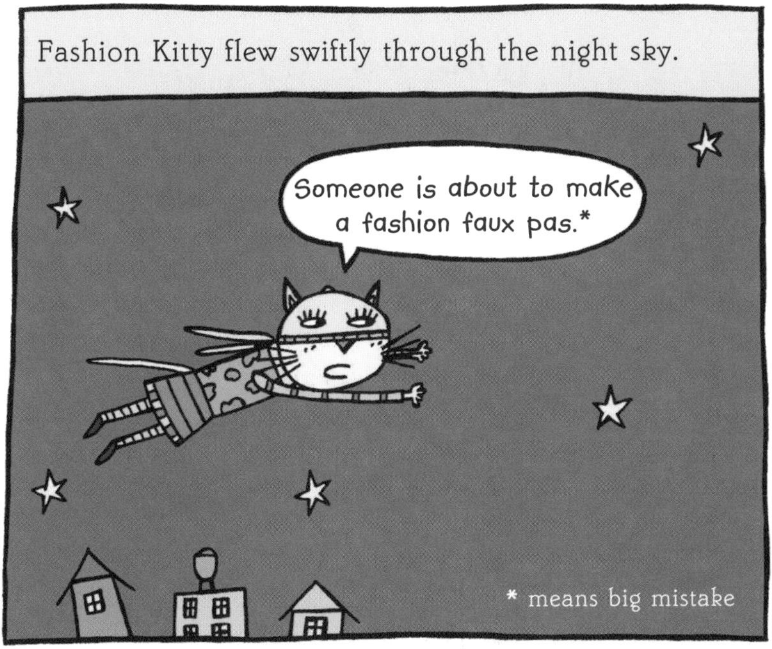
Fashion Kitty flew swiftly through the night sky.
Someone is about to make a fashion faux pas.*
* means big mistake

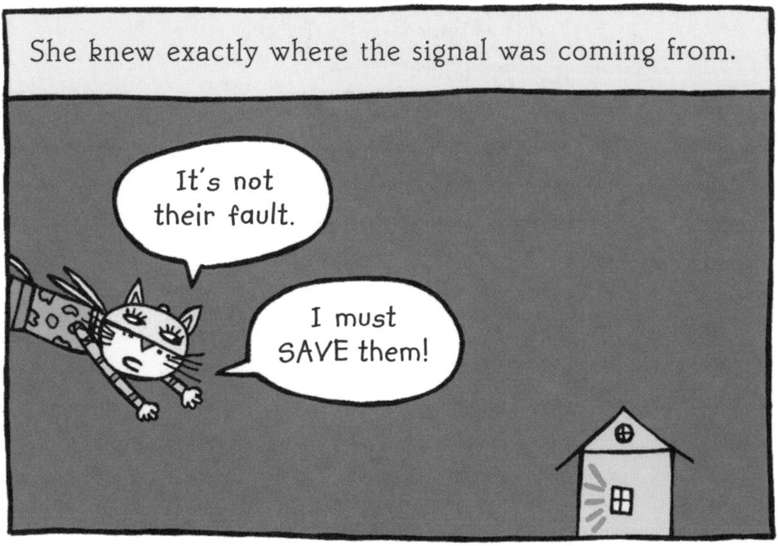
She knew exactly where the signal was coming from.
It's not their fault.
I must SAVE them!

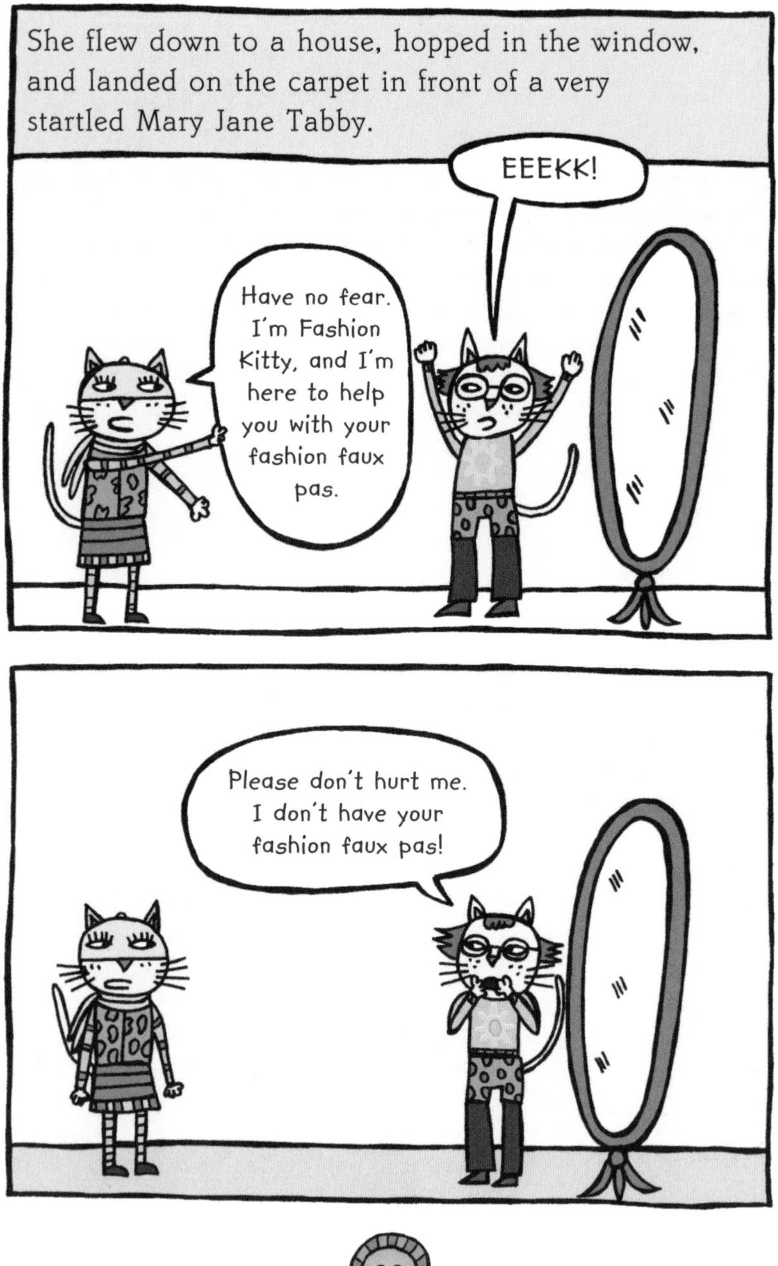
She flew down to a house, hopped in the window, and landed on the carpet in front of a very startled Mary Jane Tabby.
EEEKK!
Have no fear. I'm Fashion Kitty, and I'm here to help you with your fashion faux pas.
Please don't hurt me. I don't have your fashion faux pas!

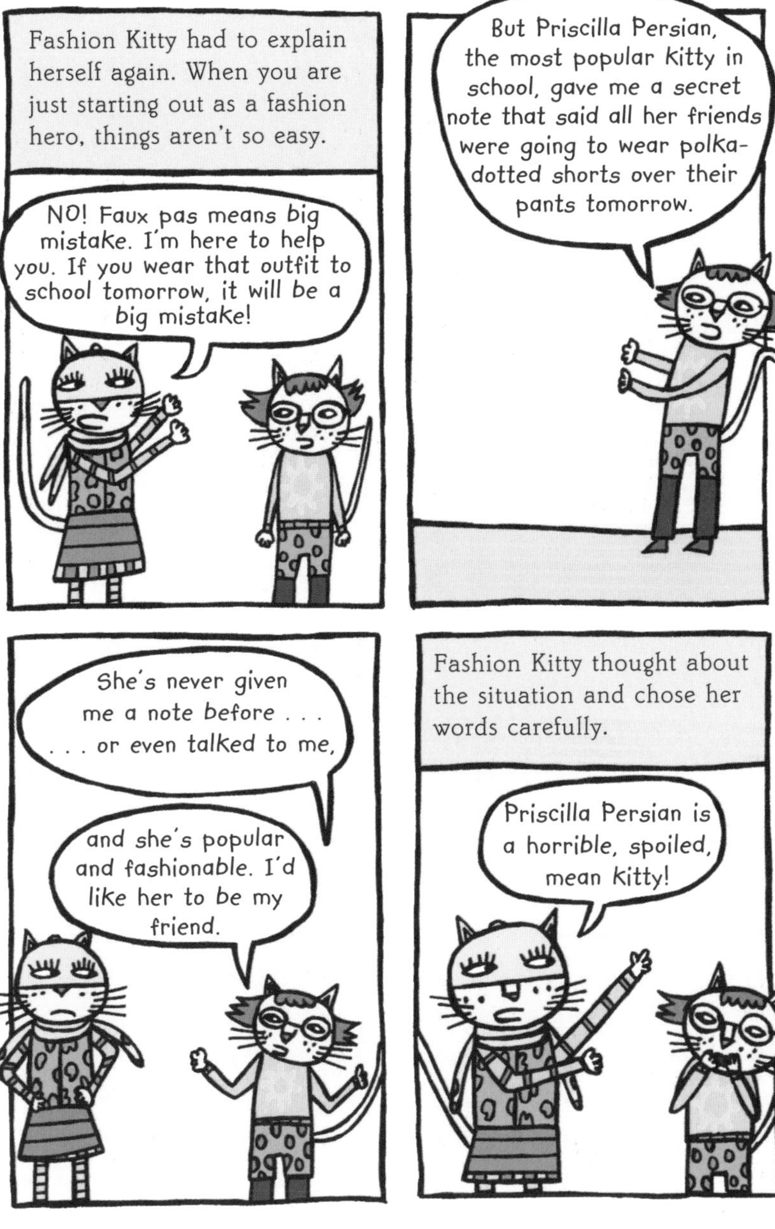
Fashion Kitty had to explain herself again. When you are just starting out as a fashion hero, things aren't so easy.
NO! Faux pas means big mistake. I'm here to help you. If you wear that outfit to school tomorrow, it will be a big mistake!
But Priscilla Persian, the most popular kitty in school, gave me a secret note that said all her friends were going to wear polka-dotted shorts over their pants tomorrow.
She's never given me a note before . . .
. . . or even talked to me,
and she's popular and fashionable. I'd like her to be my friend.
Fashion Kitty thought about the situation and chose her words carefully.
Priscilla Persian is a horrible, spoiled, mean kitty!

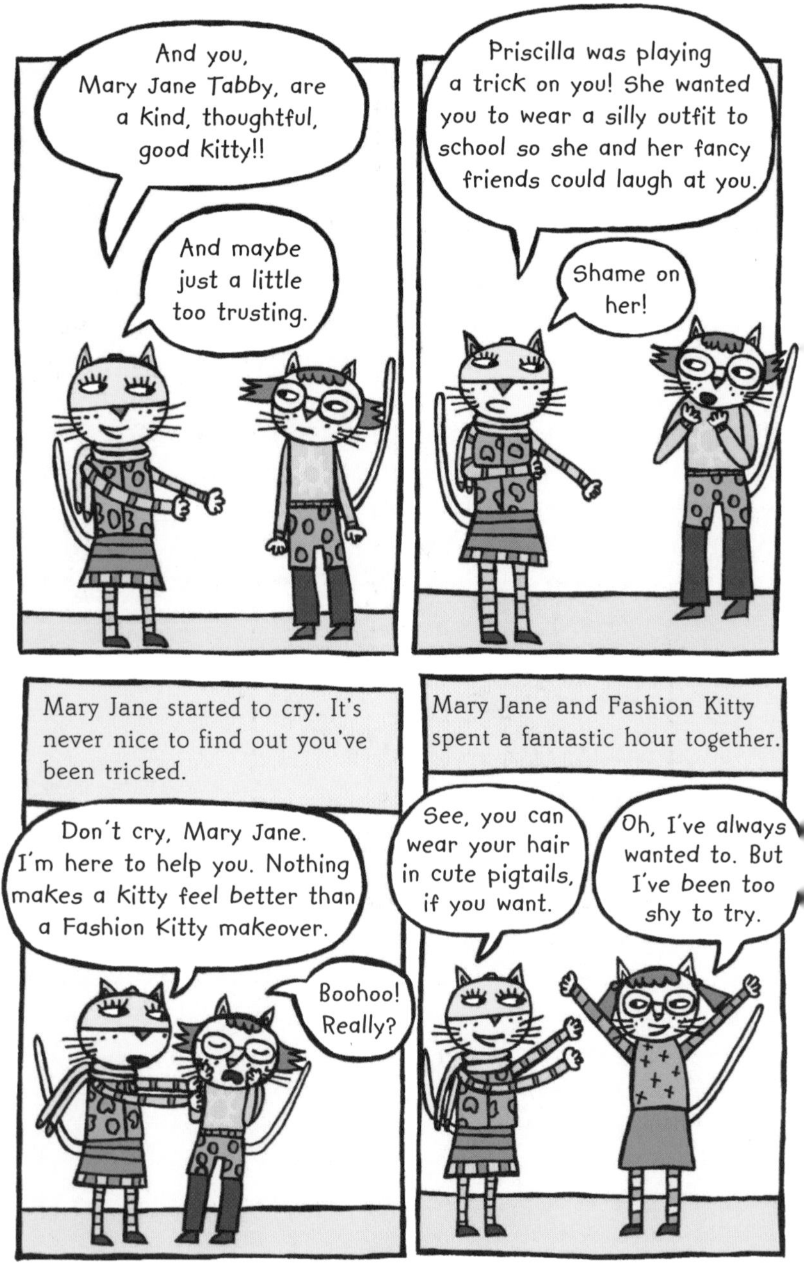
And you, Mary Jane Tabby, are a kind, thoughtful, good kitty!!
And maybe just a little too trusting.
Priscilla was playing a trick on you! She wanted you to wear a silly outfit to school so she and her fancy friends could laugh at you.
Shame on her!
Mary Jane started to cry. It's never nice to find out you've been tricked.
Don't cry, Mary Jane. I'm here to help you. Nothing makes a kitty feel better than a Fashion Kitty makeover.
Boohoo! Really?
Mary Jane and Fashion Kitty spent a fantastic hour together.
See, you can wear your hair in cute pigtails, if you want.
Oh, I've always wanted to. But I've been too shy to try.

Fashion Kitty says ...

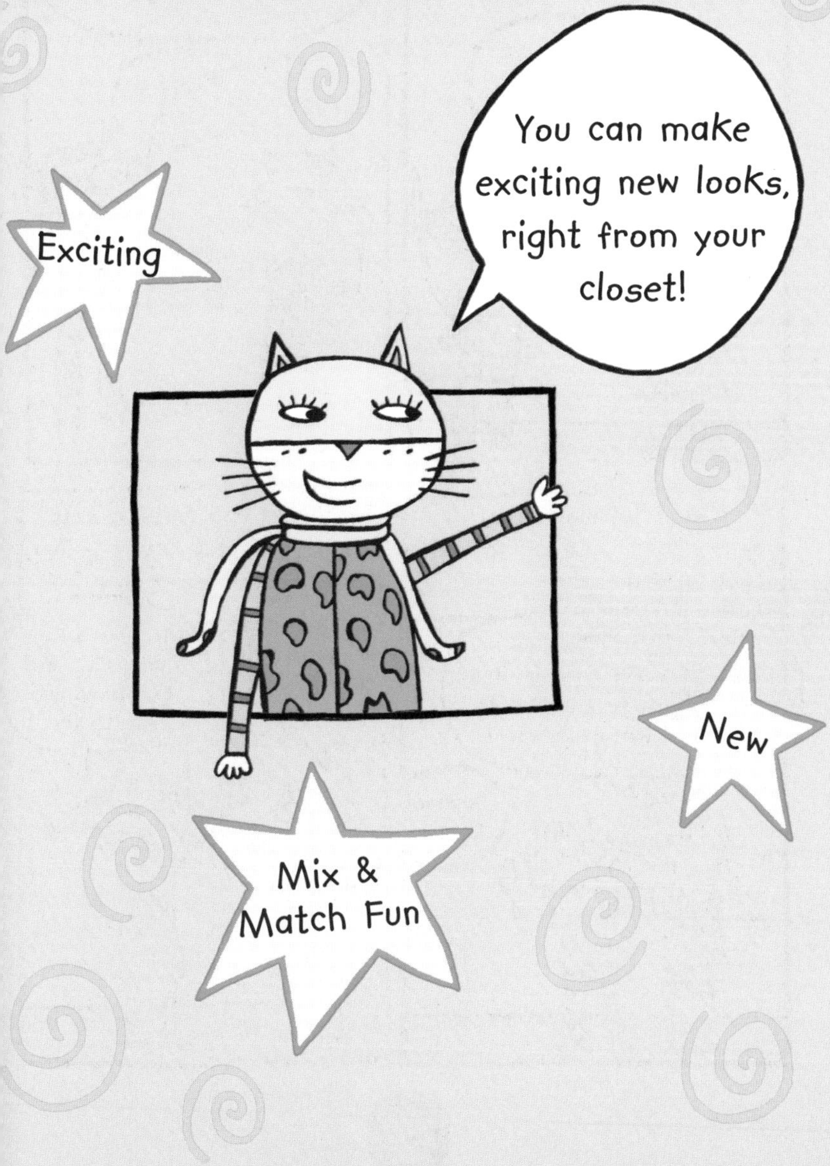

You can make exciting new looks, right from your closet!
Exciting
New
Mix & Match Fun

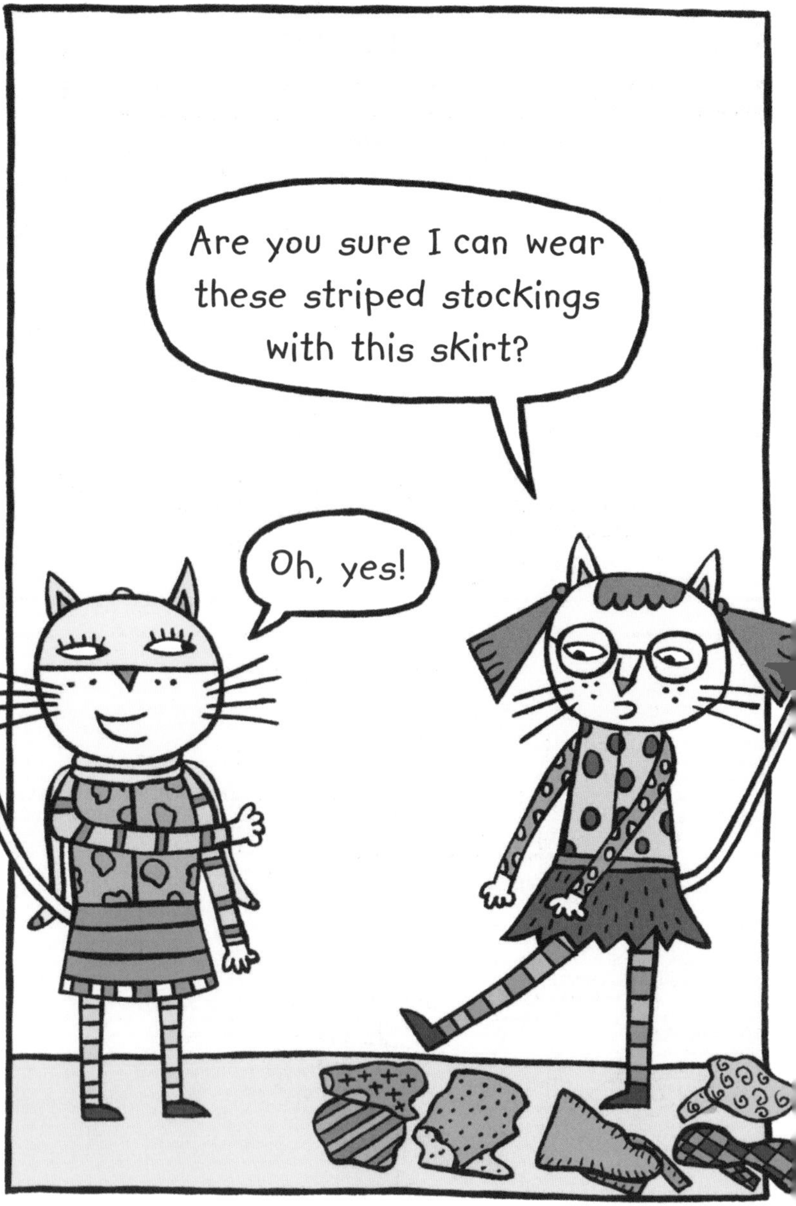
Are you sure I can wear these striped stockings with this skirt?
Oh, yes!

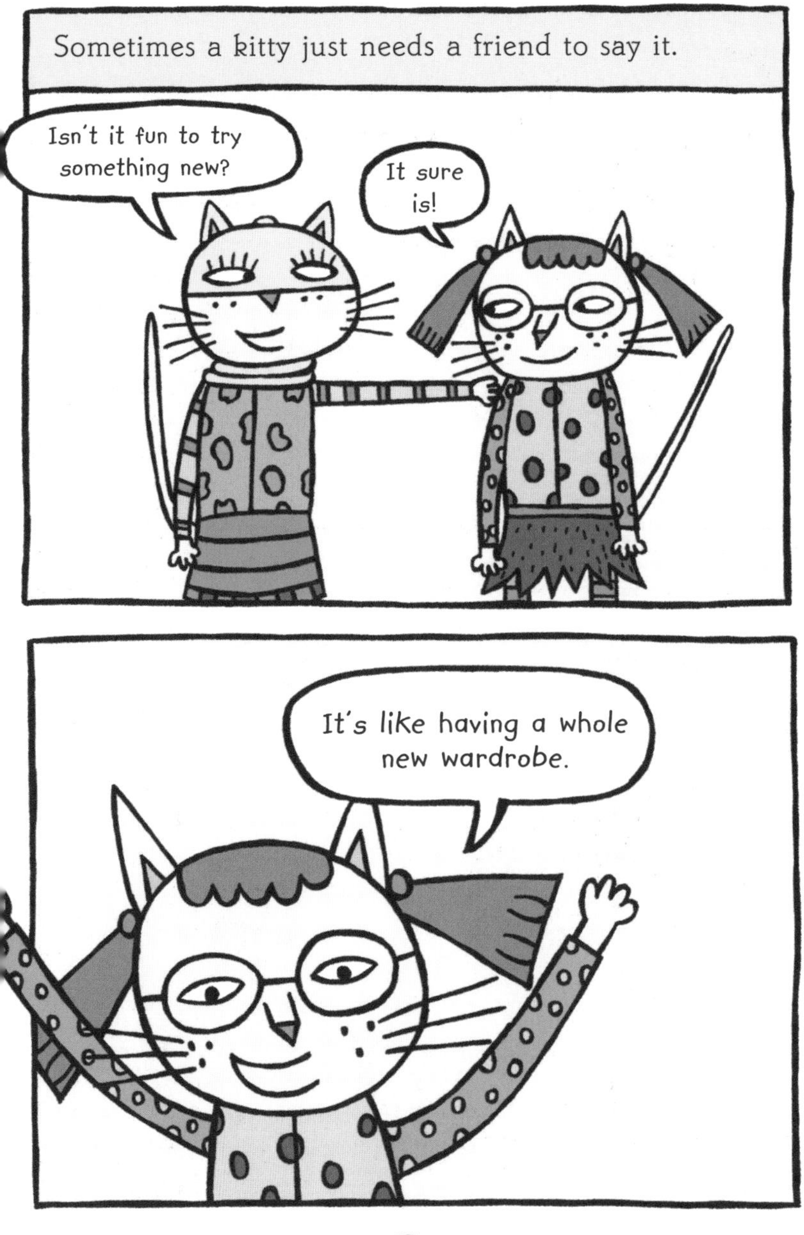
Sometimes a kitty just needs a friend to say it.
Isn't it fun to try something new?
It sure is!
It's like having a whole new wardrobe.

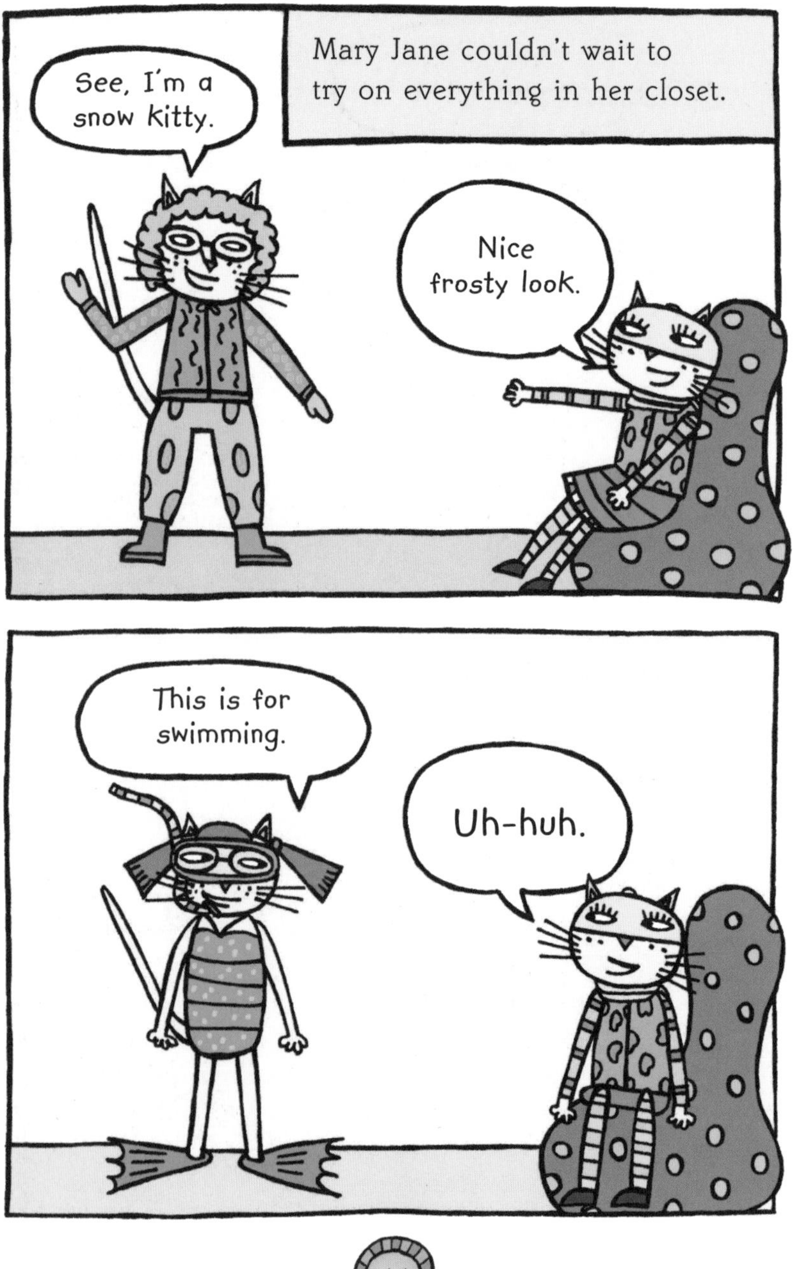
Mary Jane couldn't wait to try on everything in her closet.
See, I'm a snow kitty.
Nice frosty look.
This is for swimming.
Uh-huh.

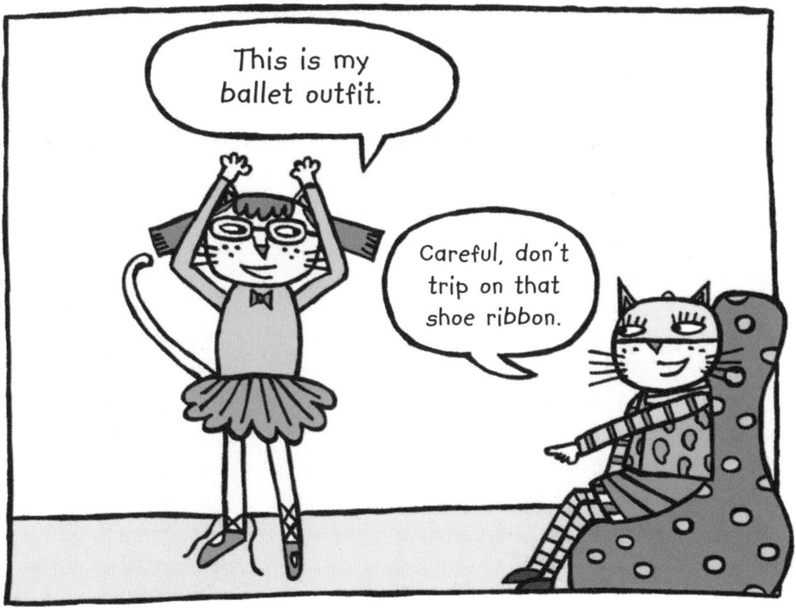
This is my ballet outfit.
Careful, don't trip on that shoe ribbon.

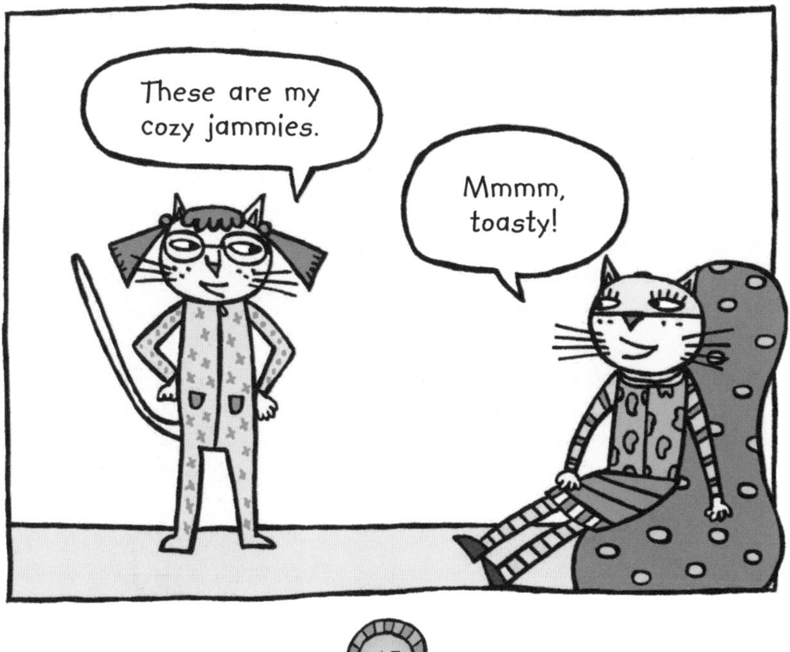
These are my cozy jammies.
Mmmm, toasty!

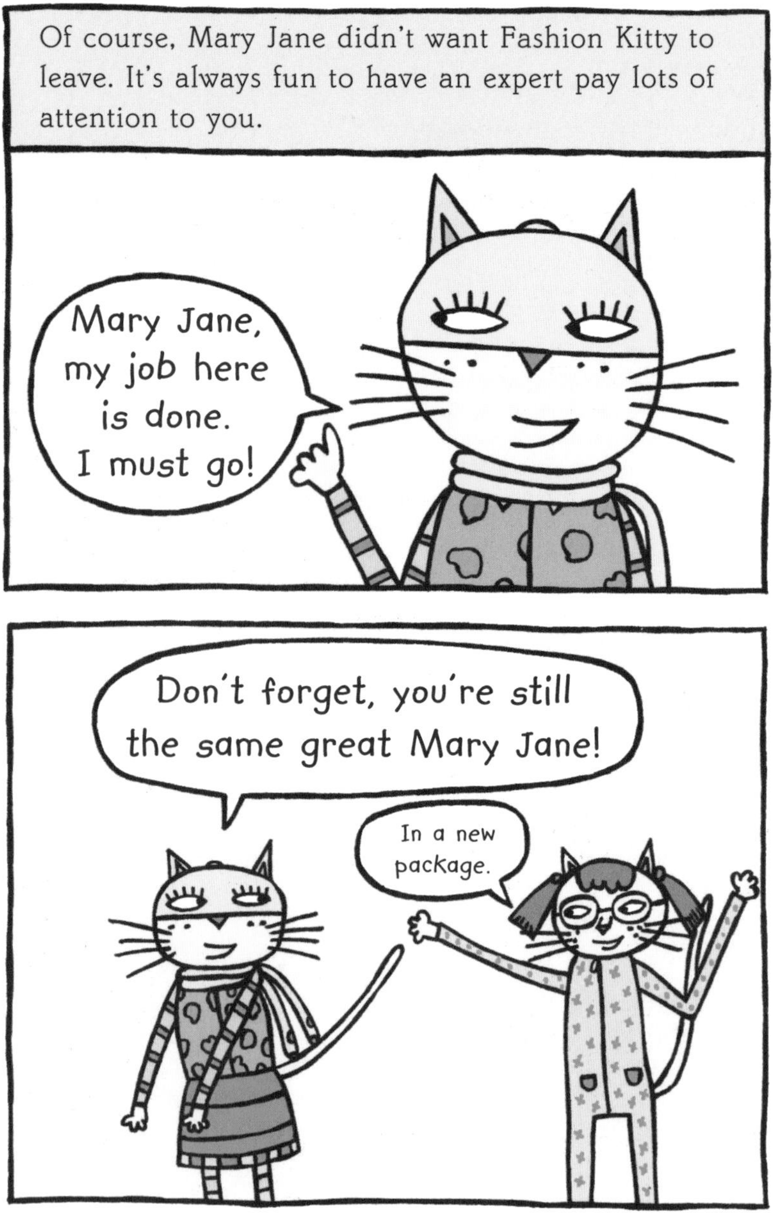
Of course, Mary Jane didn't want Fashion Kitty to leave. It's always fun to have an expert pay lots of attention to you.
Mary Jane, my job here is done. I must go!
Don't forget, you're still the same great Mary Jane!
In a new package.

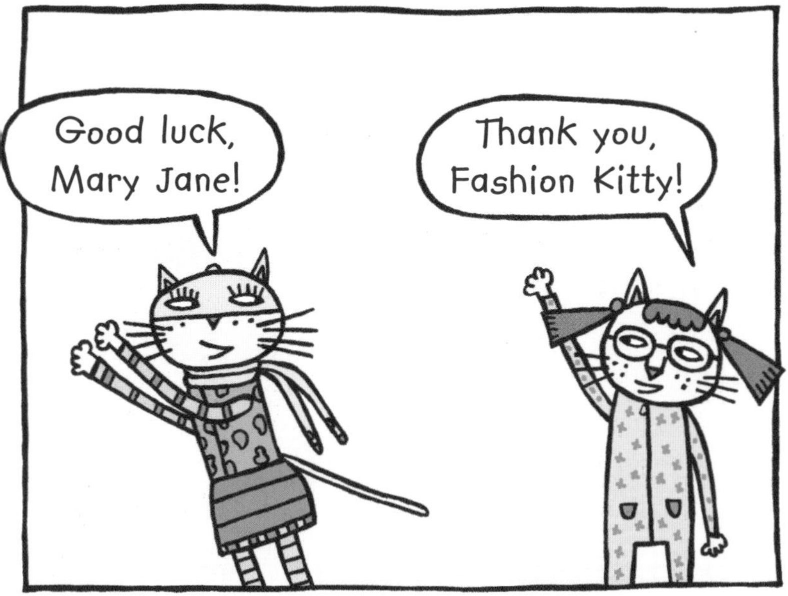
Good luck, Mary Jane!
Thank you, Fashion Kitty!

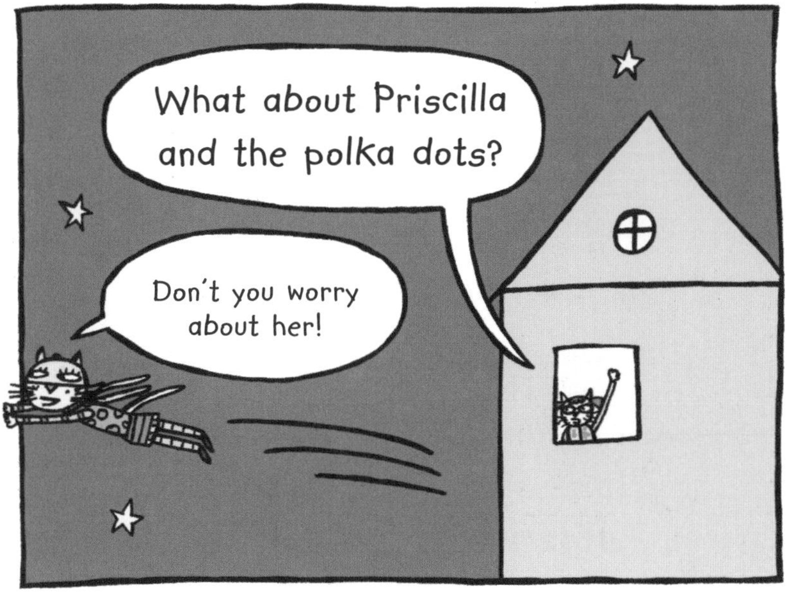
What about Priscilla and the polka dots?
Don't you worry about her!

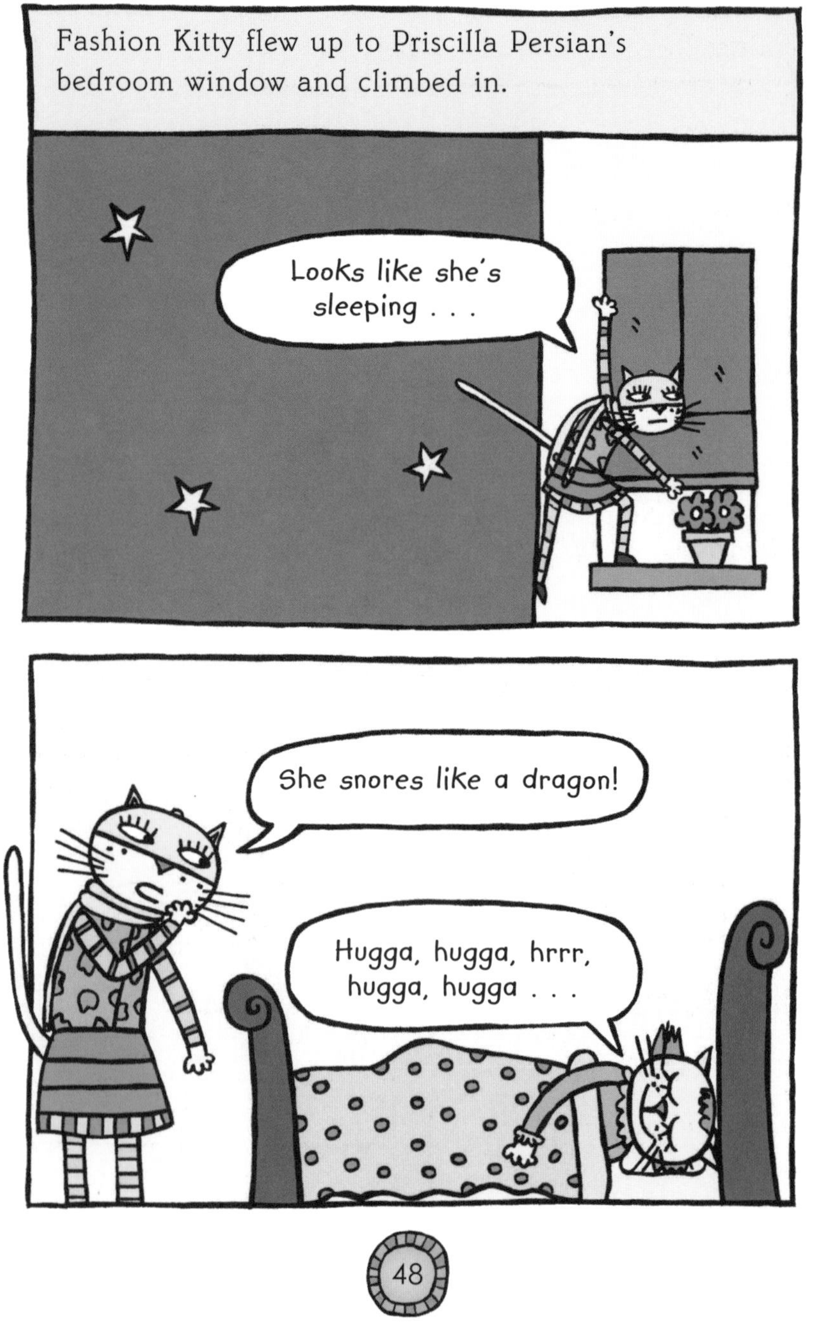
Fashion Kitty flew up to Priscilla Persian's bedroom window and climbed in.
Looks like she's sleeping . . .
She snores like a dragon!
Hugga, hugga, hrrr, hugga, hugga . . .

Priscilla was a slave to fashion magazines.

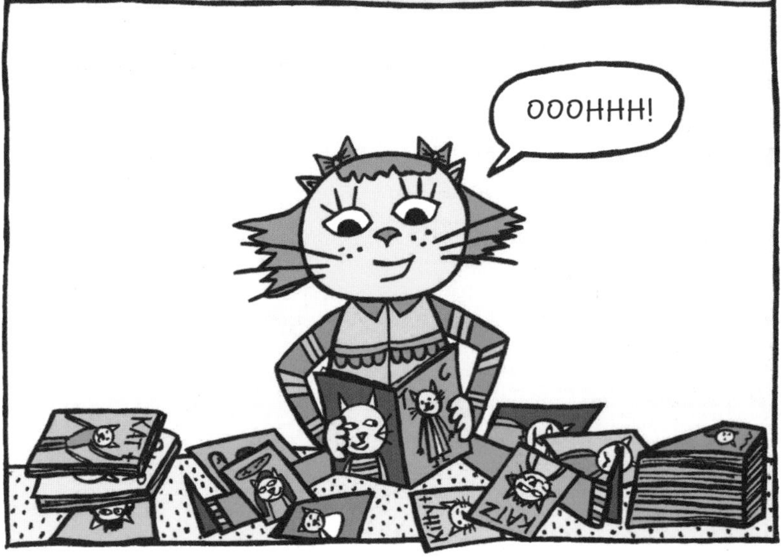

OOOHHH!
KATZ
Kitty

That means she didn't have her own style.

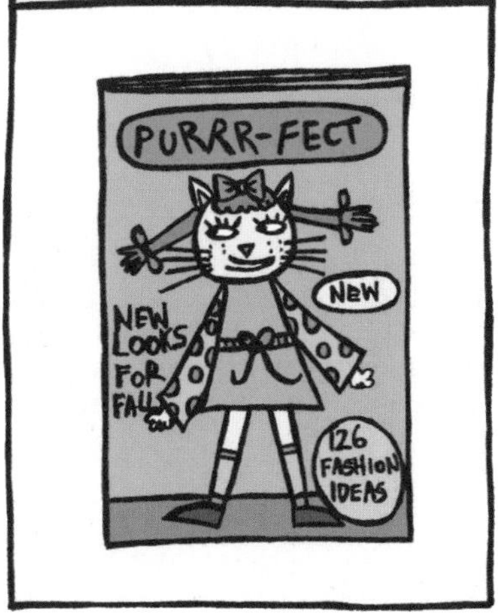

PURRR-FECT
NEW
NEW LOOKS FOR FALL
126 FASHION IDEAS

She just copied whatever she saw.

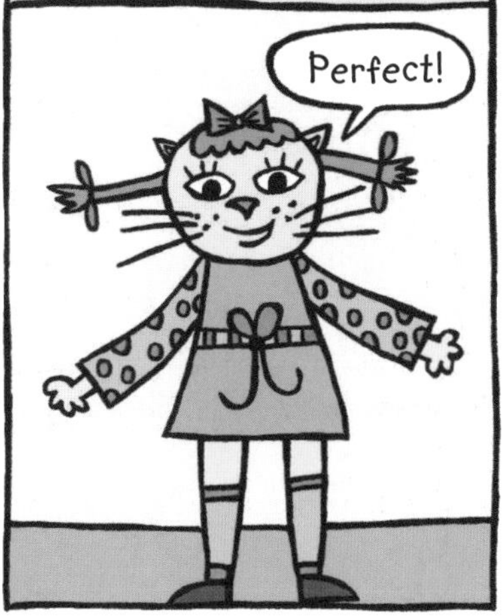

Perfect!

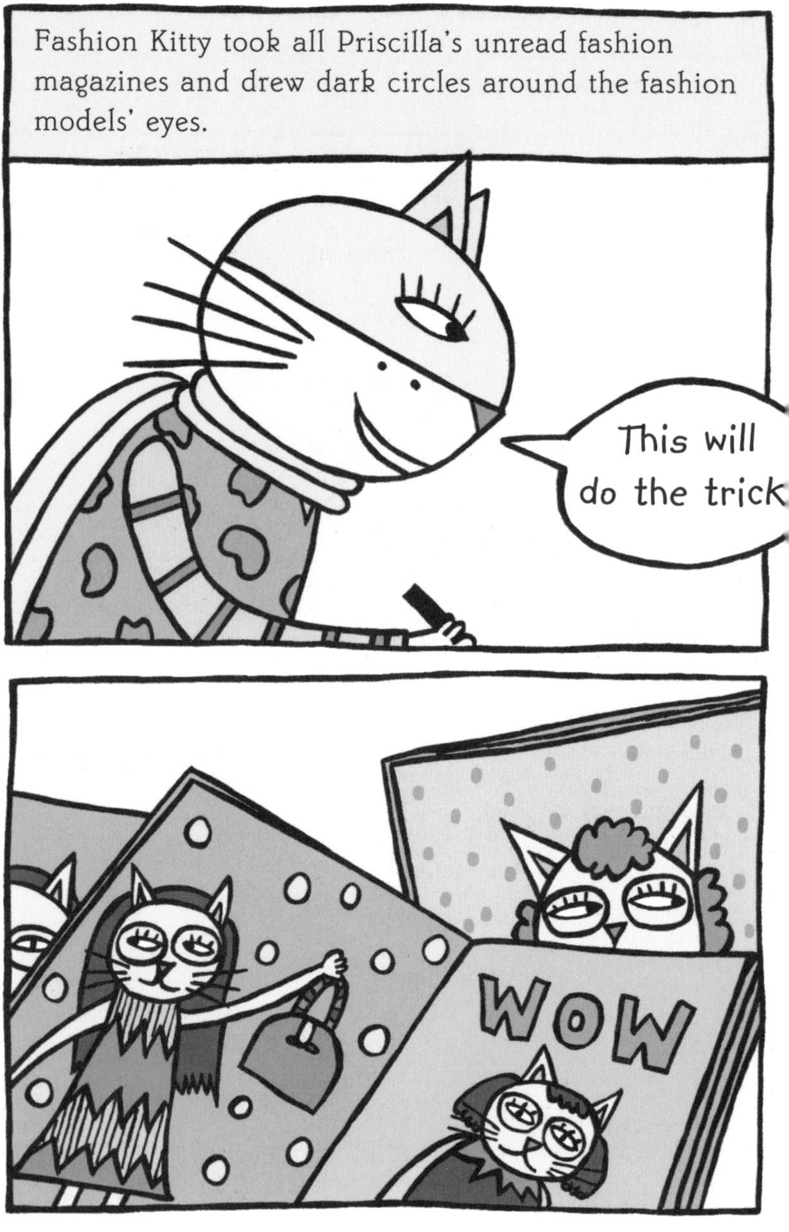
Fashion Kitty took all Priscilla's unread fashion magazines and drew dark circles around the fashion models' eyes.
This will do the trick
WOW

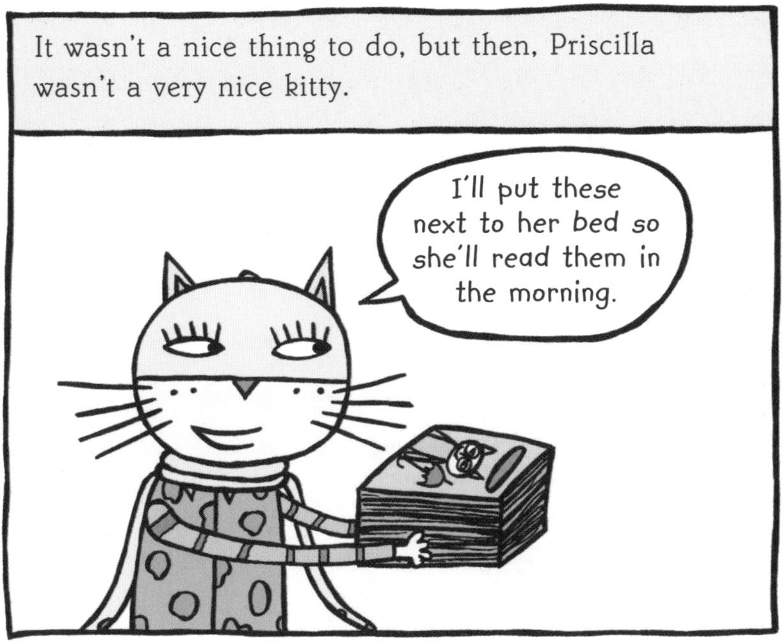
It wasn't a nice thing to do, but then, Priscilla wasn't a very nice kitty.
I'll put these next to her *bed* so she'll read them in the morning.

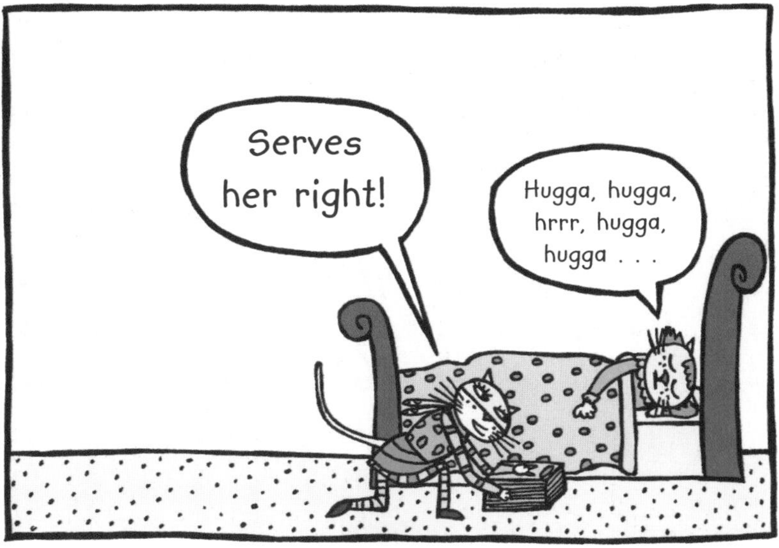
Serves her right!
Hugga, hugga, hrrr, hugga, hugga . . .

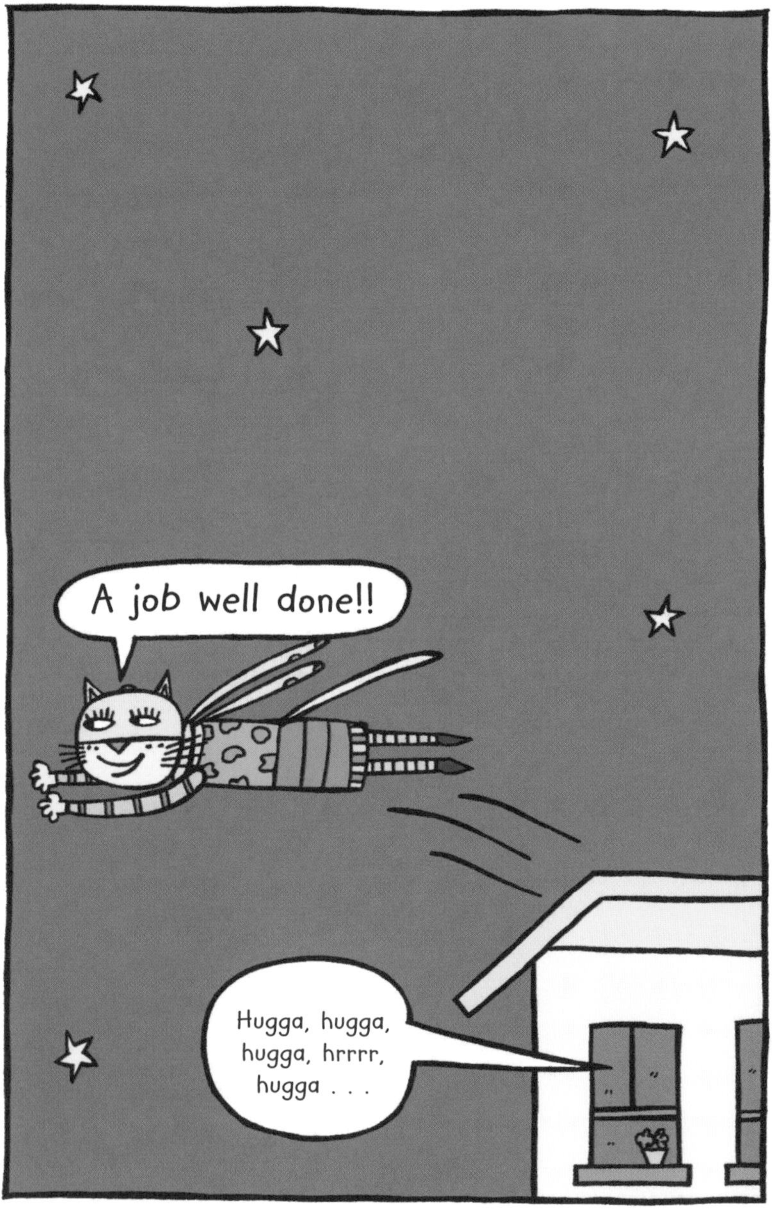
A job well done!!
Hugga, hugga,
hugga, hrrrr,
hugga . . .

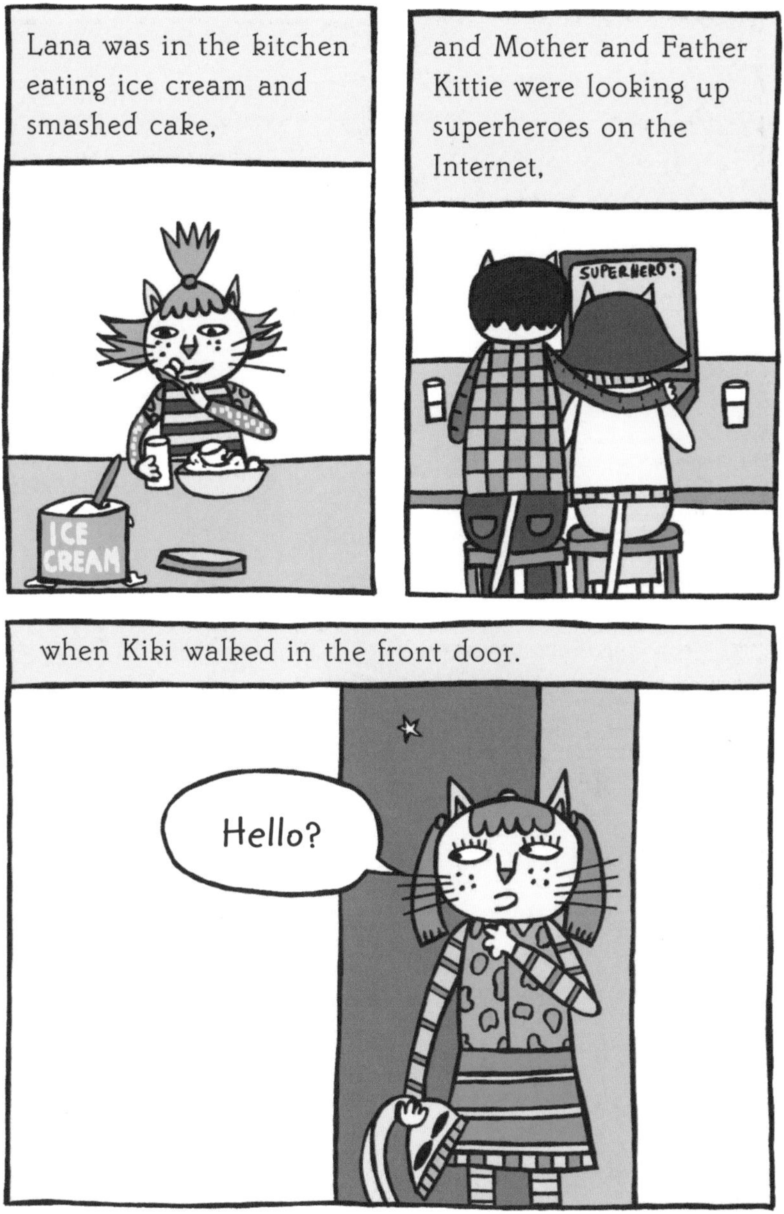
Lana was in the kitchen eating ice cream and smashed cake,
ICE CREAM
and Mother and Father Kittie were looking up superheroes on the Internet,
SUPERHERO:
when Kiki walked in the front door.
Hello?

As soon as Mother and Father Kittie saw her, they asked all the important "W" and "H" questions.

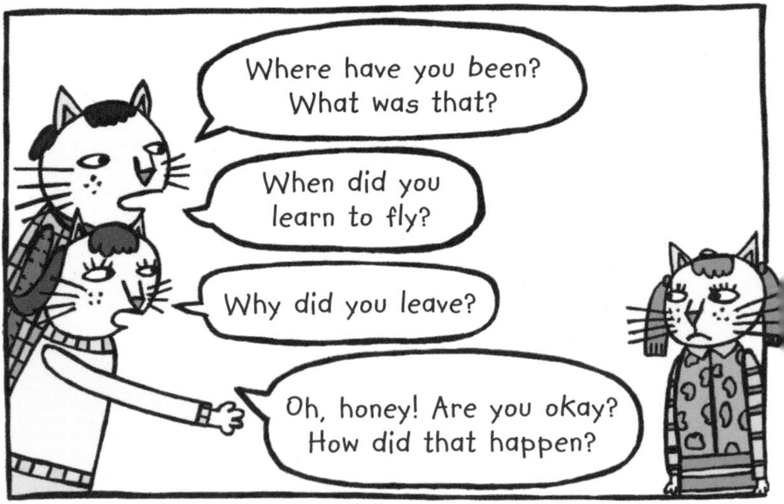
Where have you been? What was that?
When did you learn to fly?
Why did you leave?
Oh, honey! Are you okay? How did that happen?

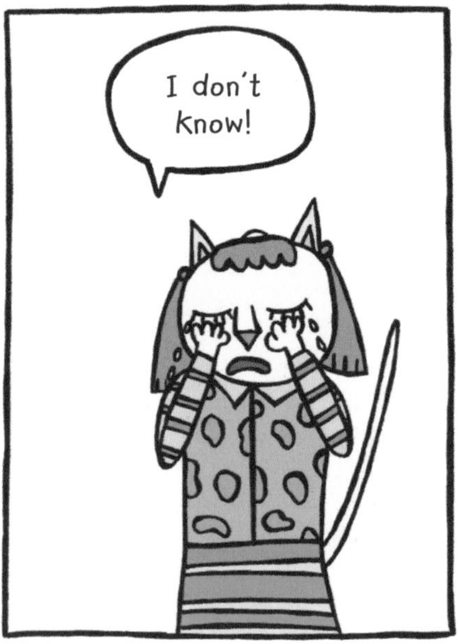
I don't know!

answered Kiki, and she began to cry. Her head hurt, and she wasn't sure she wanted to be a fashion hero.

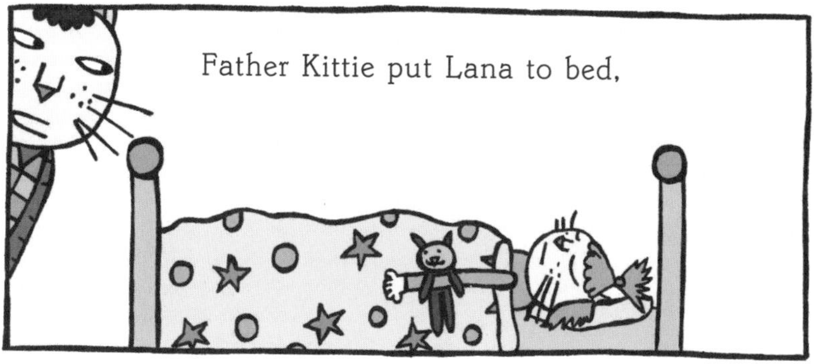
Father Kittie put Lana to bed,

and then he and Mother Kittie sat with Kiki while she ate ice cream and three pieces of new birthday cake.

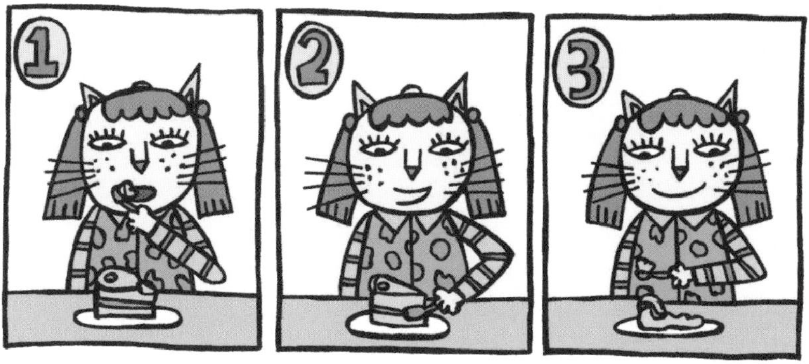
1
2
3

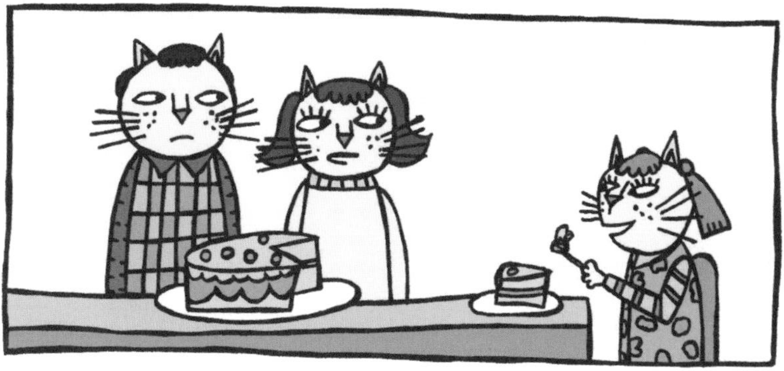

She was surprisingly hungry.

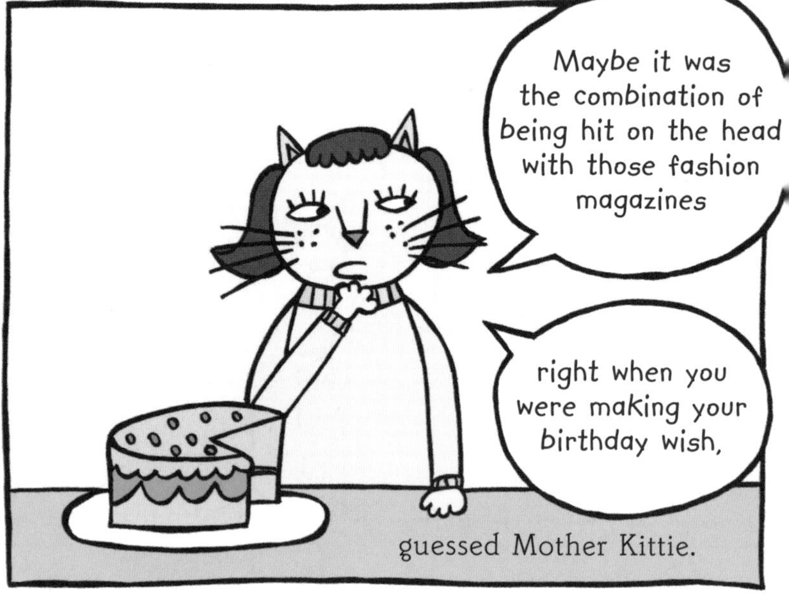
Maybe it was the combination of being hit on the head with those fashion magazines
right when you were making your birthday wish,
guessed Mother Kittie.

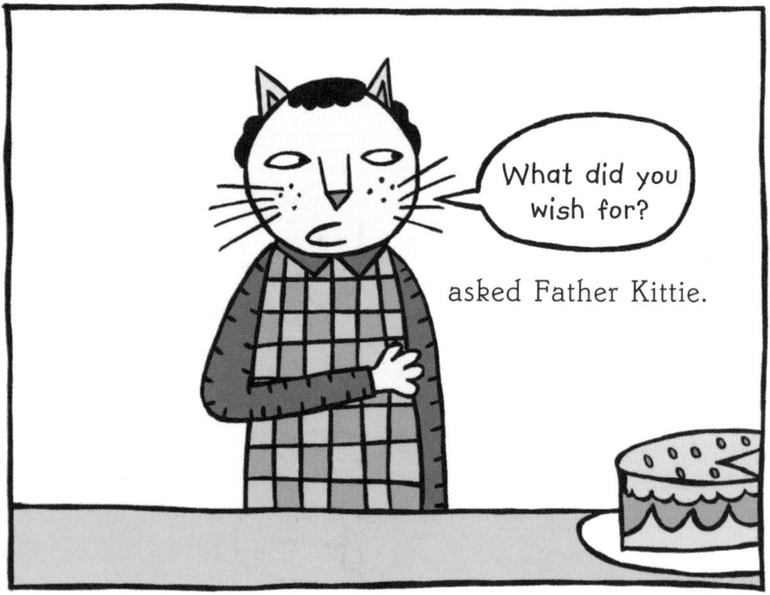
What did you wish for?
asked Father Kittie.

But Kiki just rubbed her lumpy head and said:

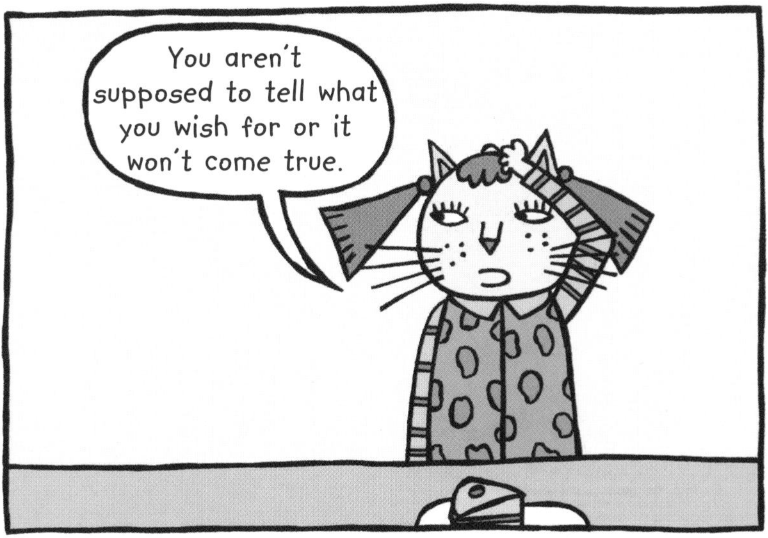
You aren't supposed to tell what you wish for or it won't come true.

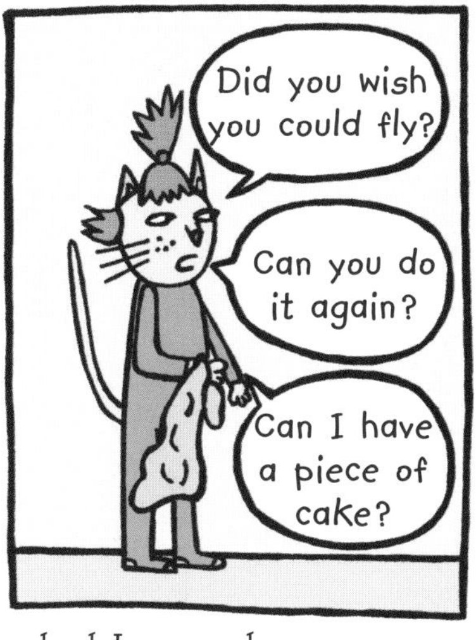
Did you wish you could fly?
Can you do it again?
Can I have a piece of cake?

asked Lana, who was standing in the doorway.

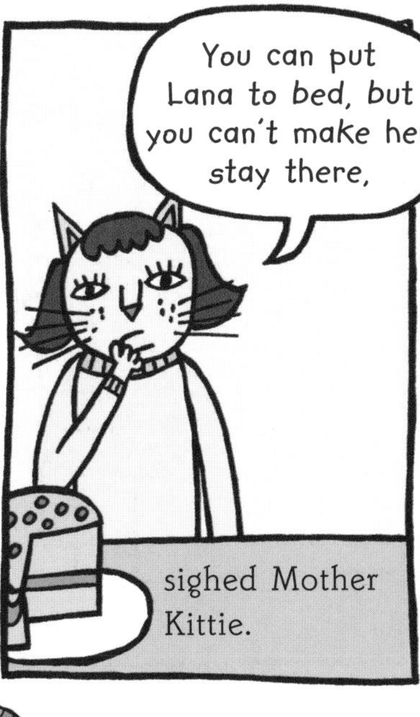
You can put Lana to bed, but you can't make her stay there,

sighed Mother Kittie.

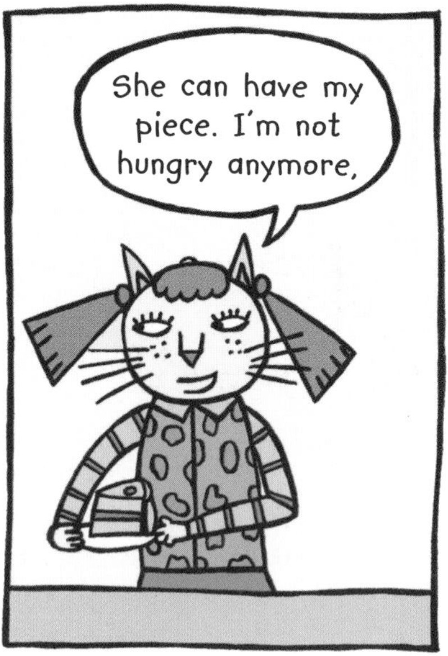
She can have my piece. I'm not hungry anymore,

said Kiki.

This was a very unusual thing for Kiki to say. It wasn't like her to be generous with Lana; but then this had been an unusual day.

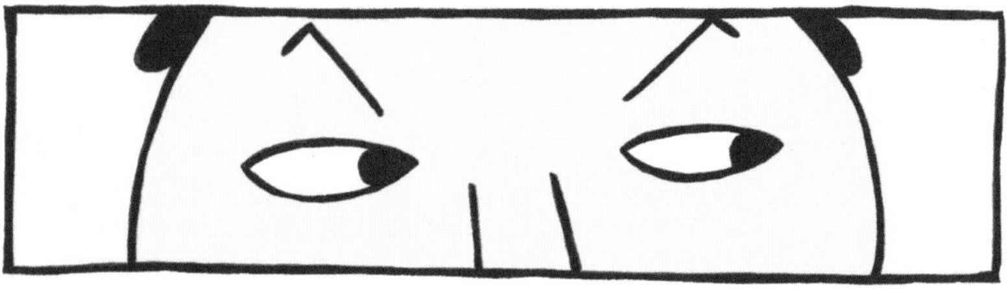

Mother and Father Kittie looked at each other

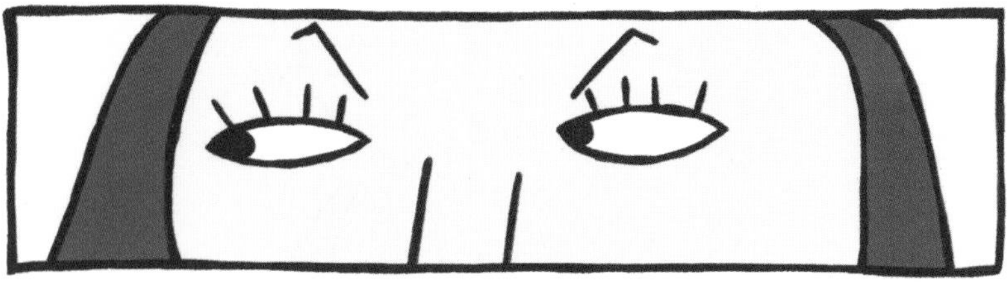

and quietly raised their eyebrows.

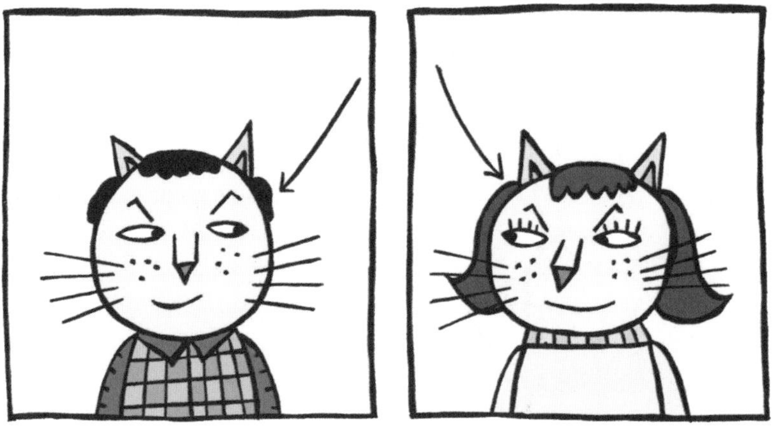

This is something adults do when they want to say, "Hey, look at that, isn't that nice?" but don't want their children to hear it.

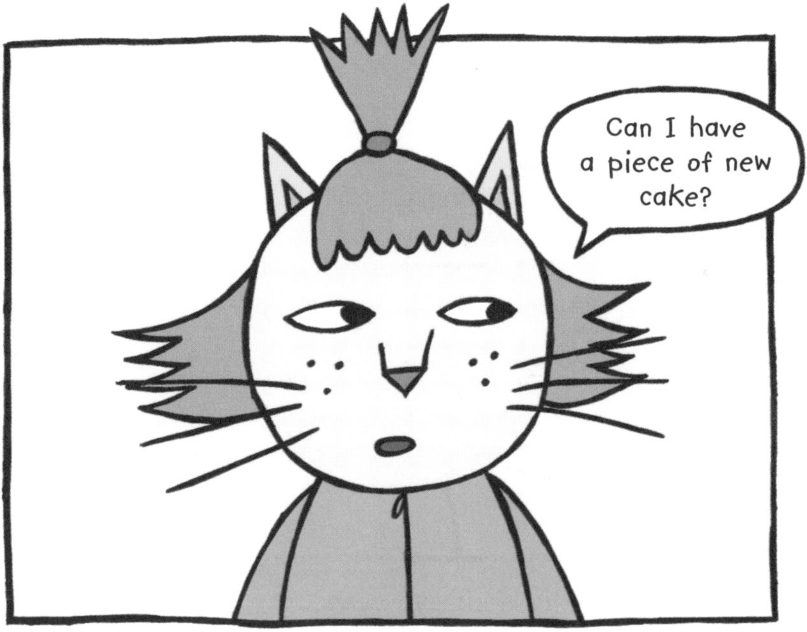
Can I have a piece of new cake?

Lana was full of questions and her mouth was full of chocolate cake, but Mother Kittie didn't say anything about chewing with your mouth open. On a normal day she would have.

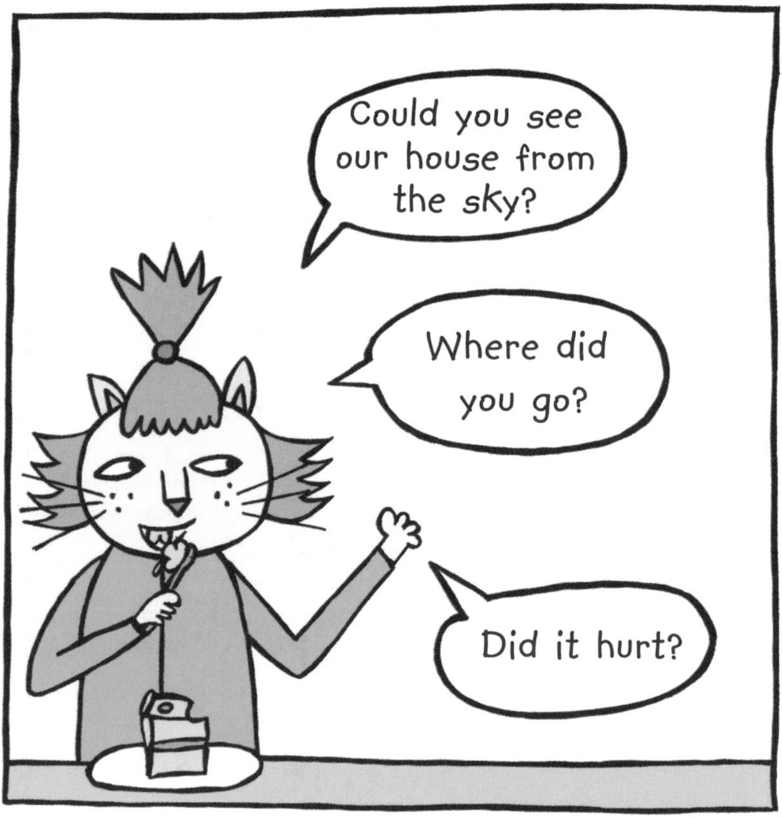
Could you see our house from the sky?
Where did you go?
Did it hurt?

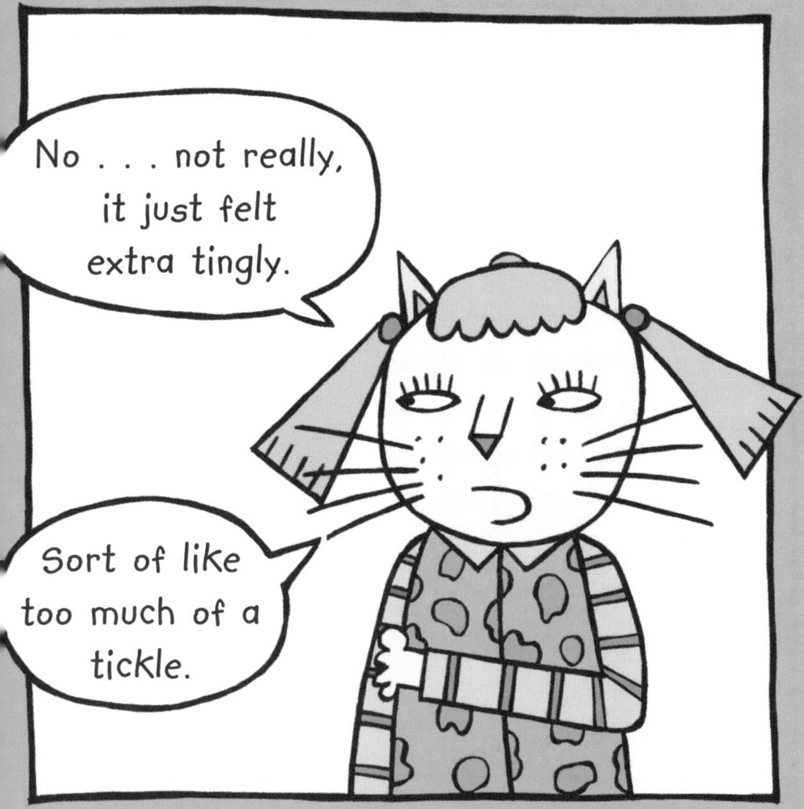
No . . . not really, it just felt extra tingly.
Sort of like too much of a tickle.

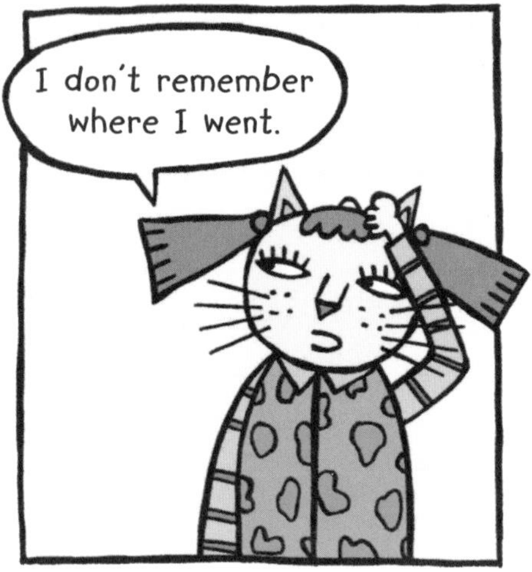
I don't remember
where I went.

Kiki wasn't sure why she felt she should keep her adventures as Fashion Kitty a secret.

She was too tired to talk about it anyway.

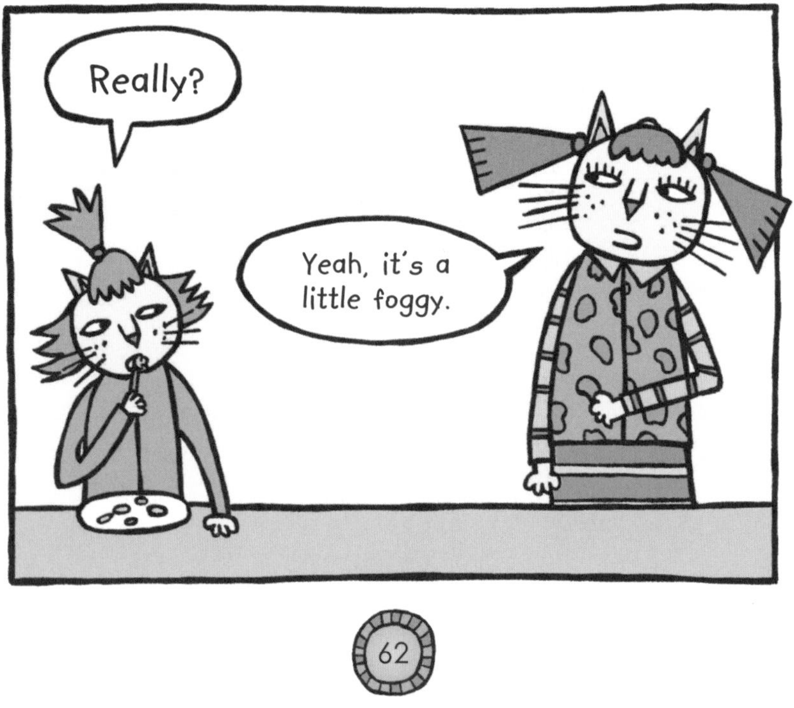
Really?
Yeah, it's a
little foggy.

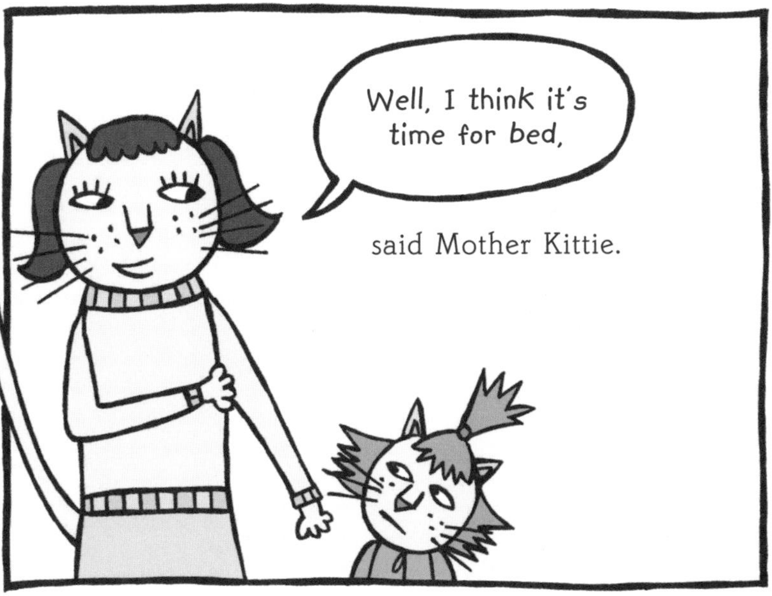
Well, I think it's time for bed,
said Mother Kittie.

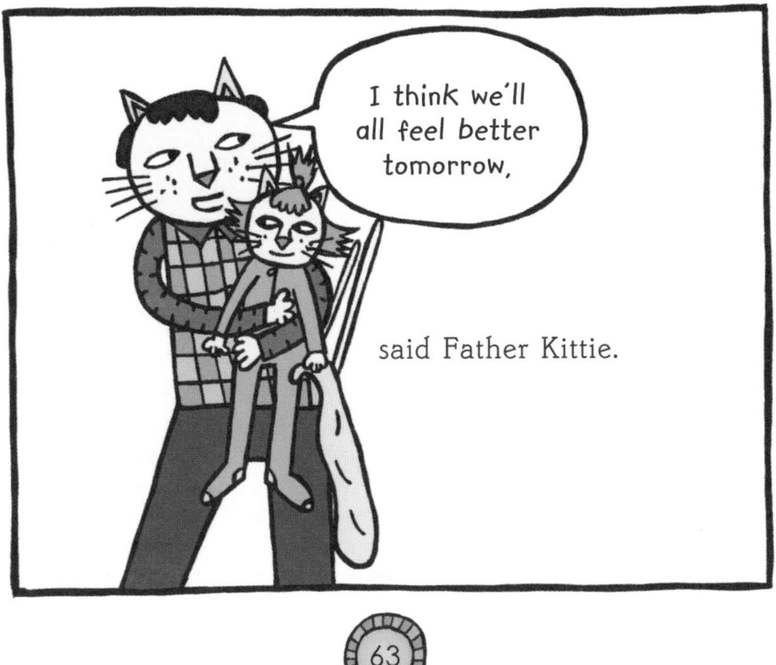
I think we'll all feel better tomorrow,
said Father Kittie.

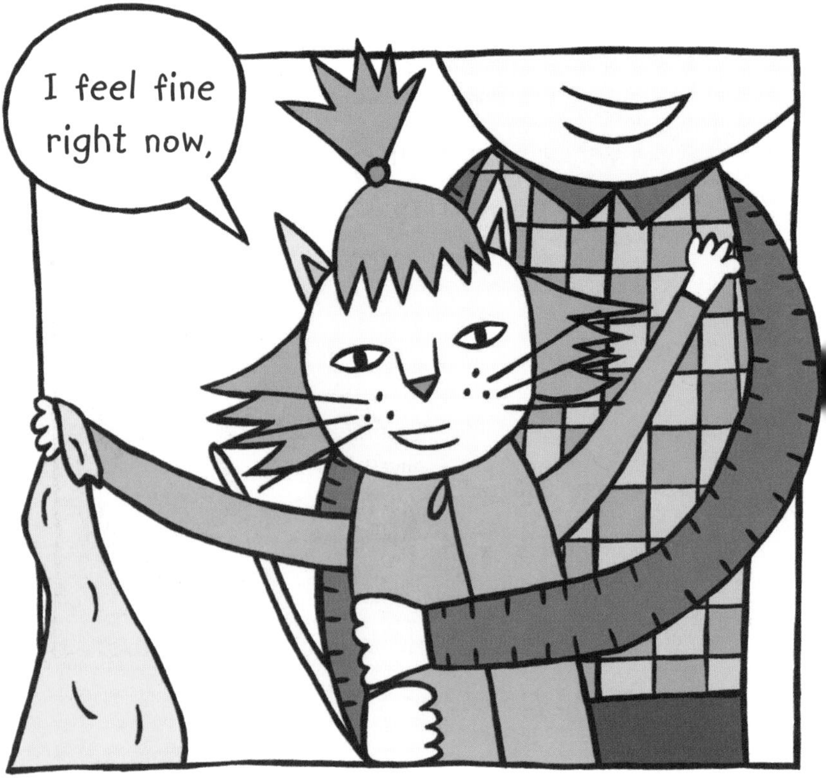
I feel fine right now,

said Lana. And with that, the whole family went right to bed without washing their faces or brushing their teeth . . . It was that kind of day.

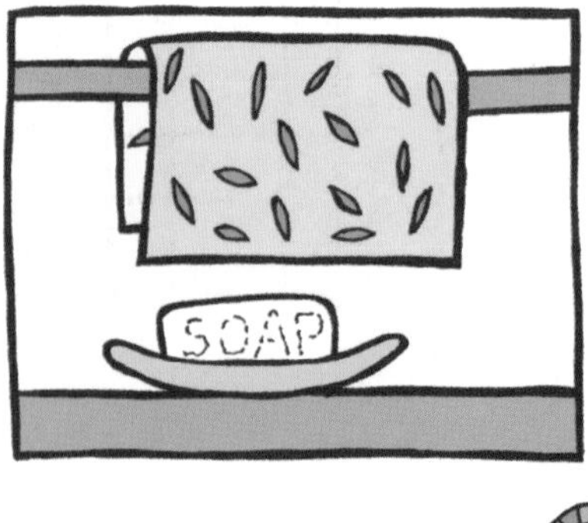
SOAP

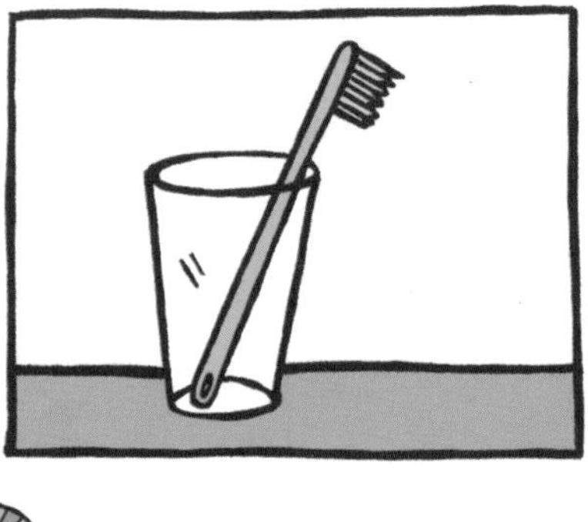

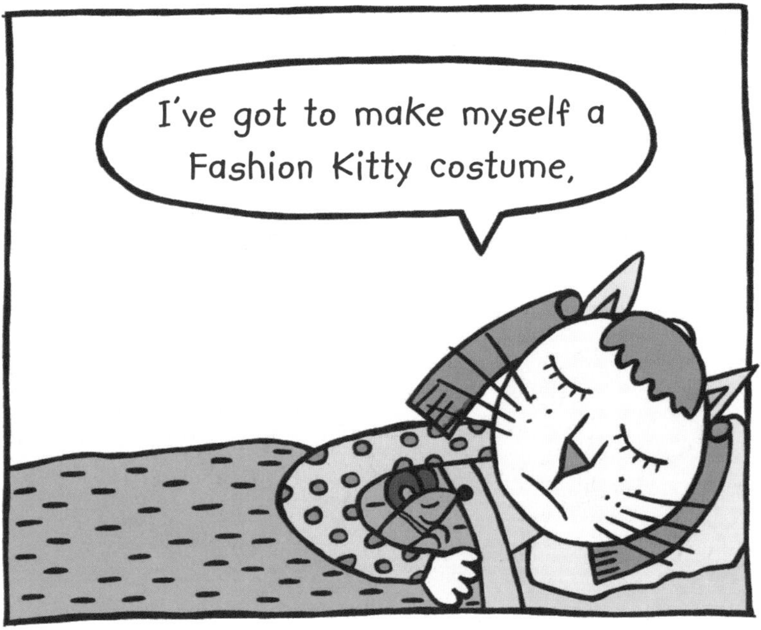
I've got to make myself a Fashion Kitty costume,

whispered Kiki to Mousie, and she mumbled words like:

stripes polka dots and checks

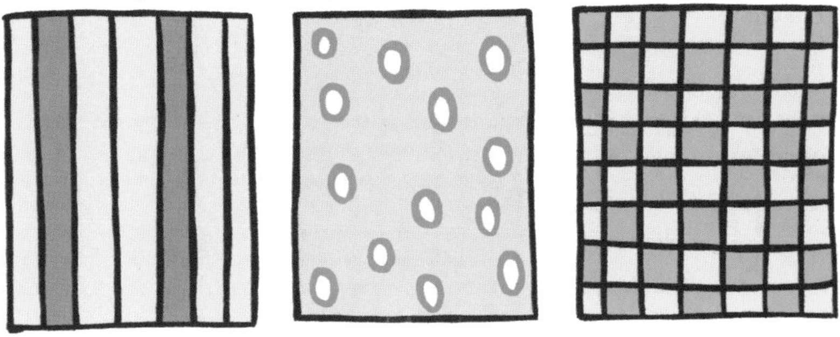

until she fell asleep.

The next morning, while the family was eating breakfast and Kiki was opening her birthday presents from the day before, Kiki said:

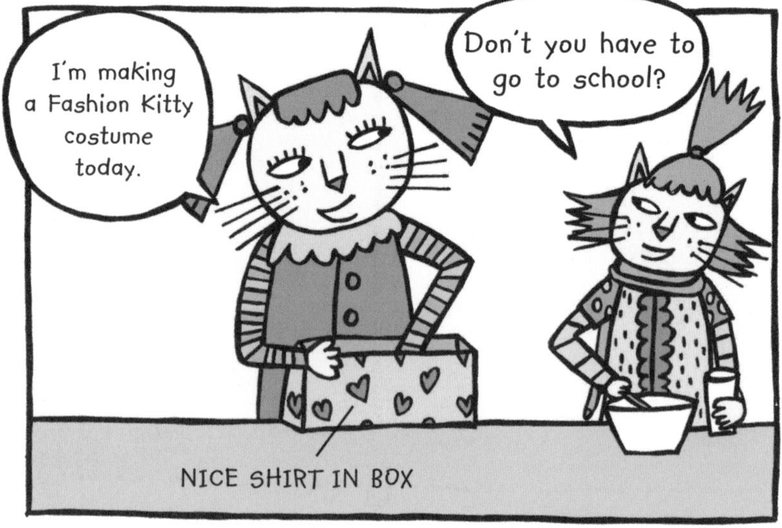
I'm making a Fashion Kitty costume today.
Don't you have to go to school?
NICE SHIRT IN BOX

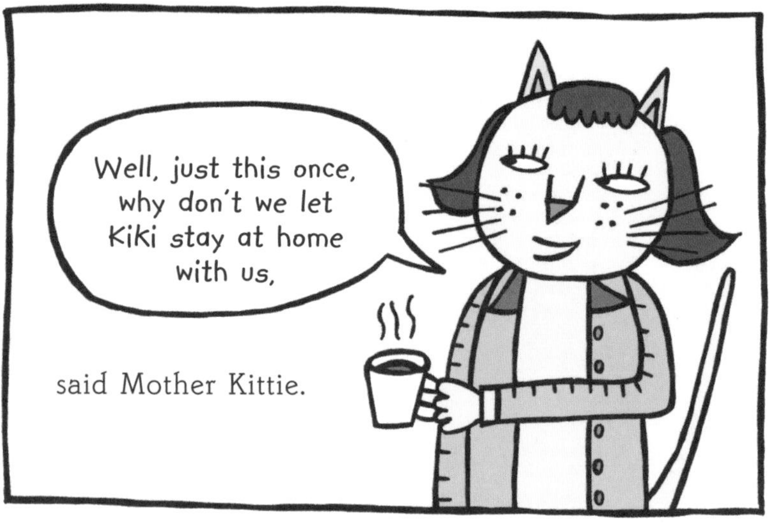
Well, just this once, why don't we let Kiki stay at home with us,

said Mother Kittie.

Kiki spent the day trying various costume looks.

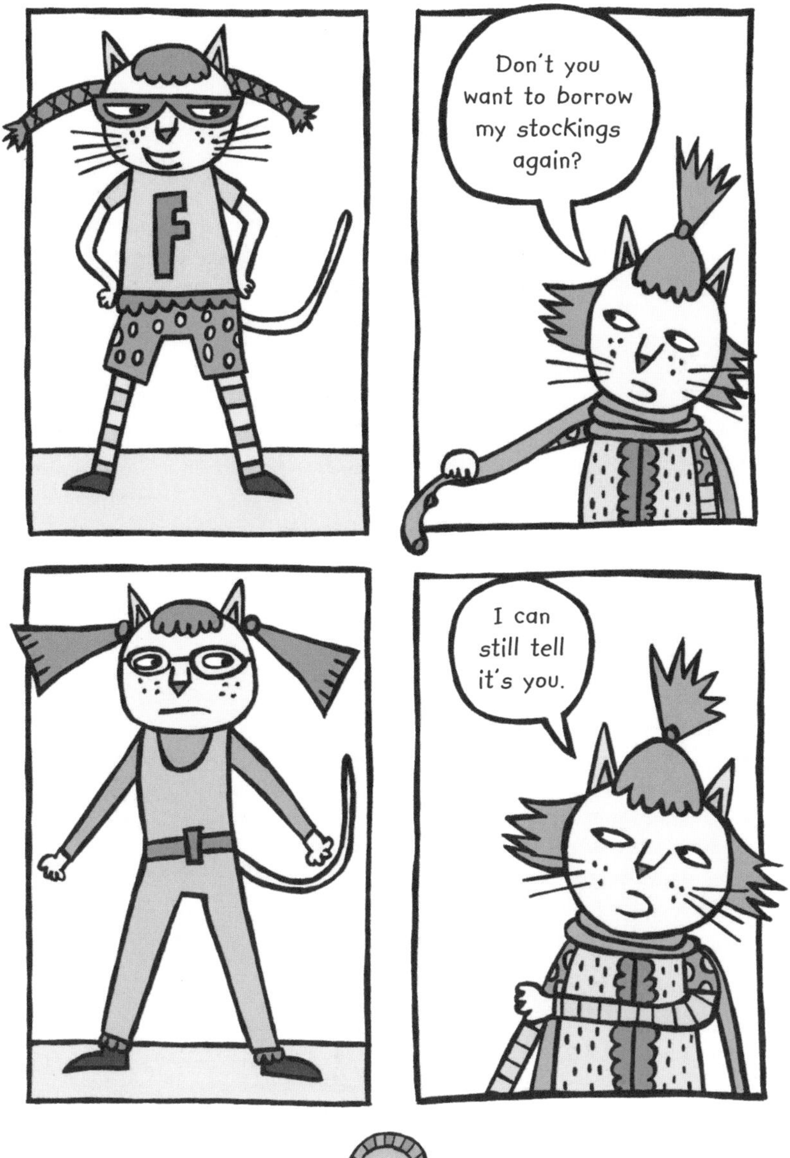
Don't you want to borrow my stockings again?
I can still tell it's you.

Lana, of course, had an opinion about everything.

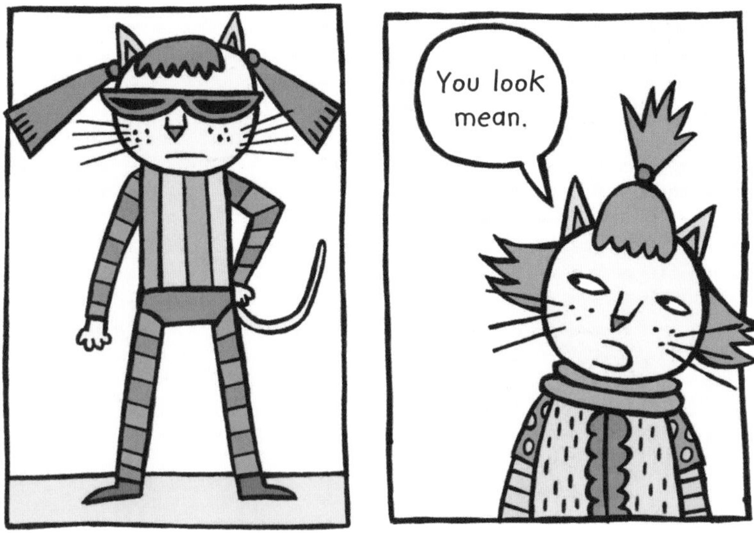
You look mean.

Kiki didn't pay any attention to her until Lana said:

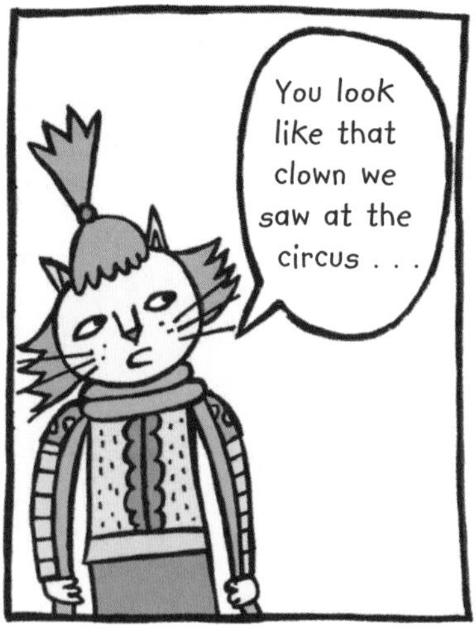
You look like that clown we saw at the circus . . .

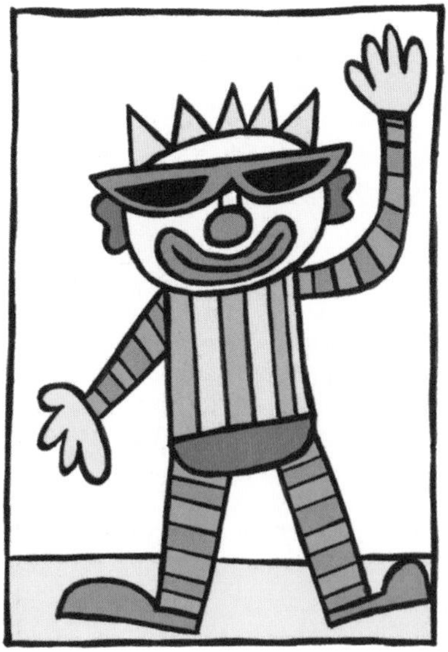

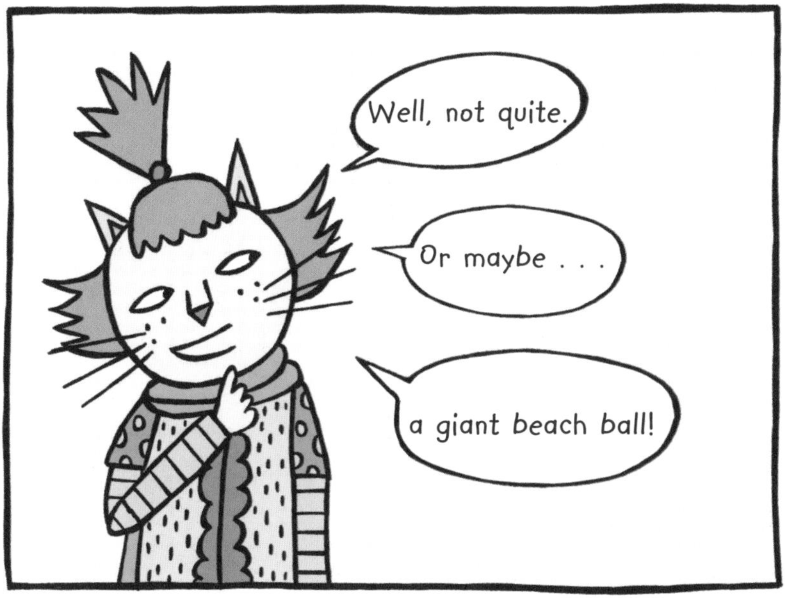
Well, not quite.
Or maybe . . .
a giant beach ball!

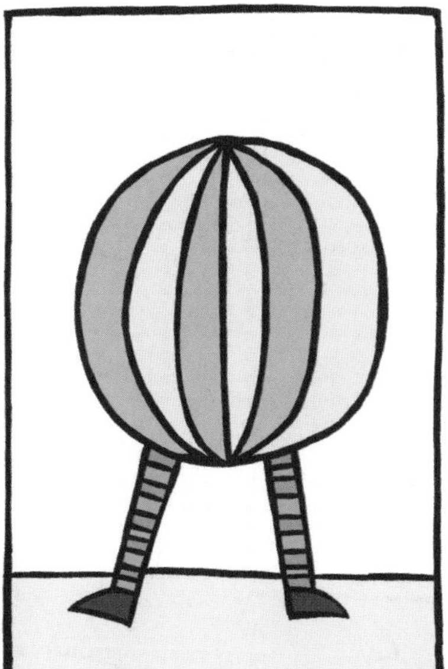

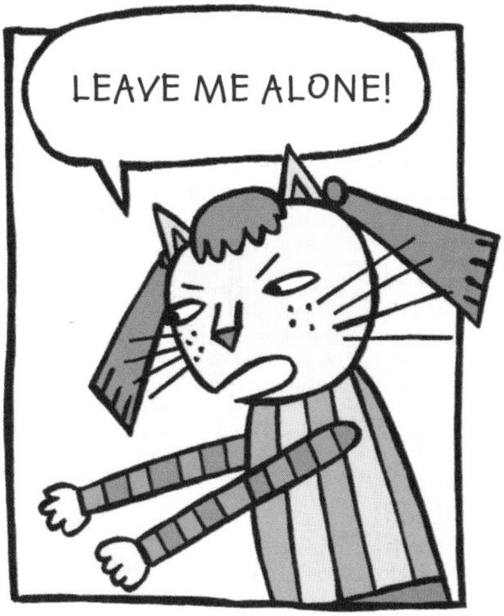
LEAVE ME ALONE!

yelled Kiki. She couldn't help herself. After all, a kitty can only take so much.

Lana looked upset for about five seconds, then she said:

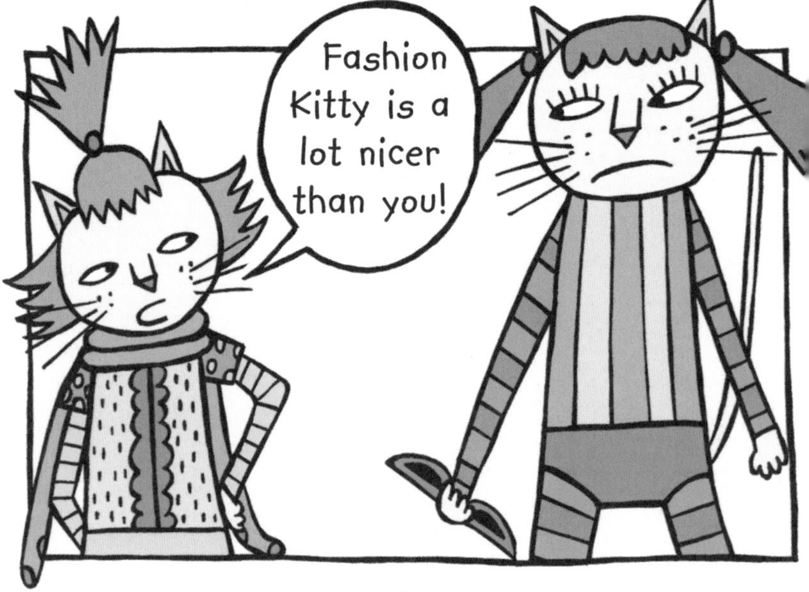
Fashion Kitty is a lot nicer than you!

Then she skipped off, singing a song that only a four-year-old would like.

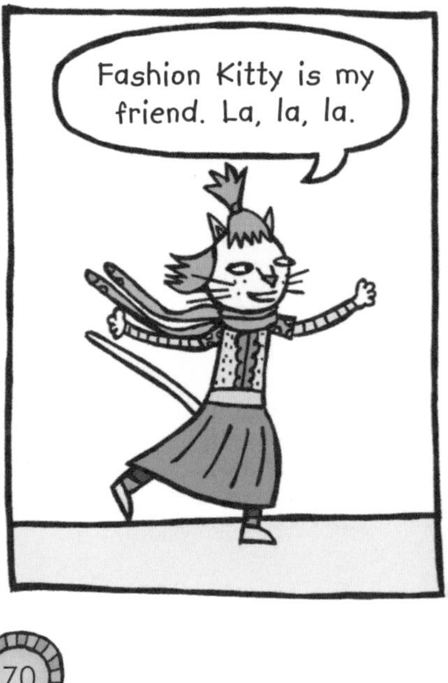
Fashion Kitty is my friend. La, la, la.

Kiki quickly changed out of the beach-ball outfit, and after only twenty minutes more of fashion work, had a costume she was happy with.

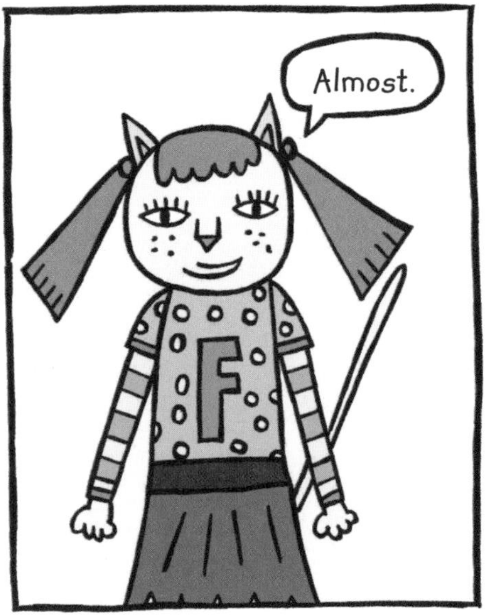
Almost.

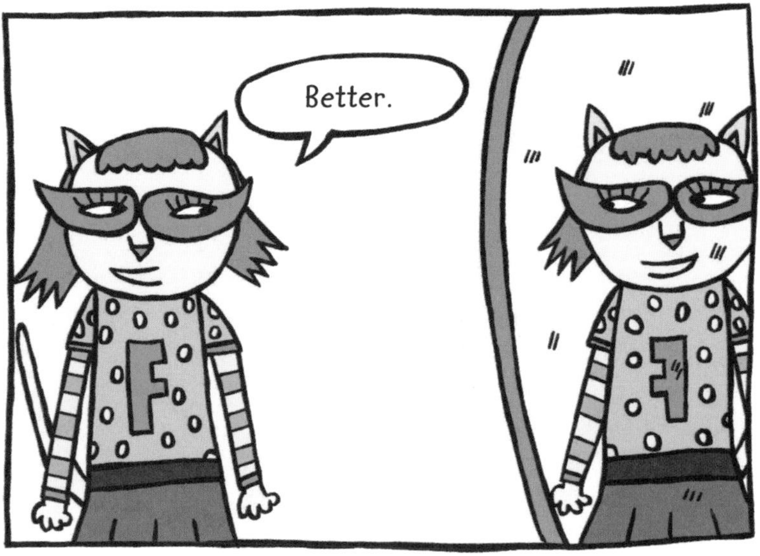
Better.

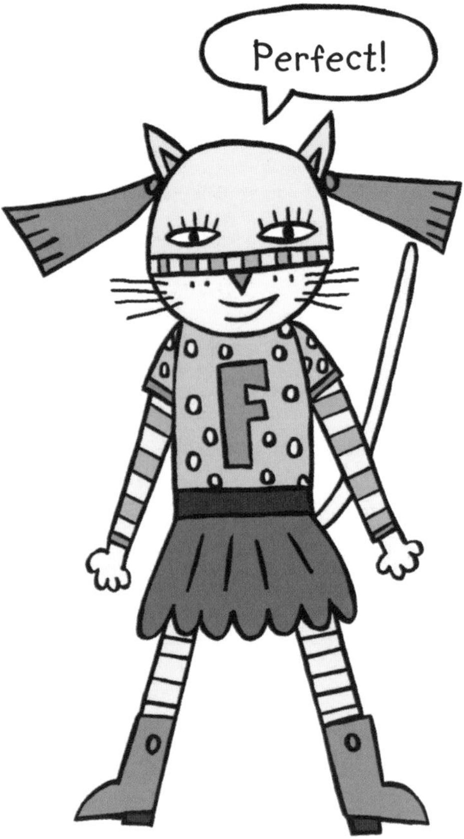
Perfect!

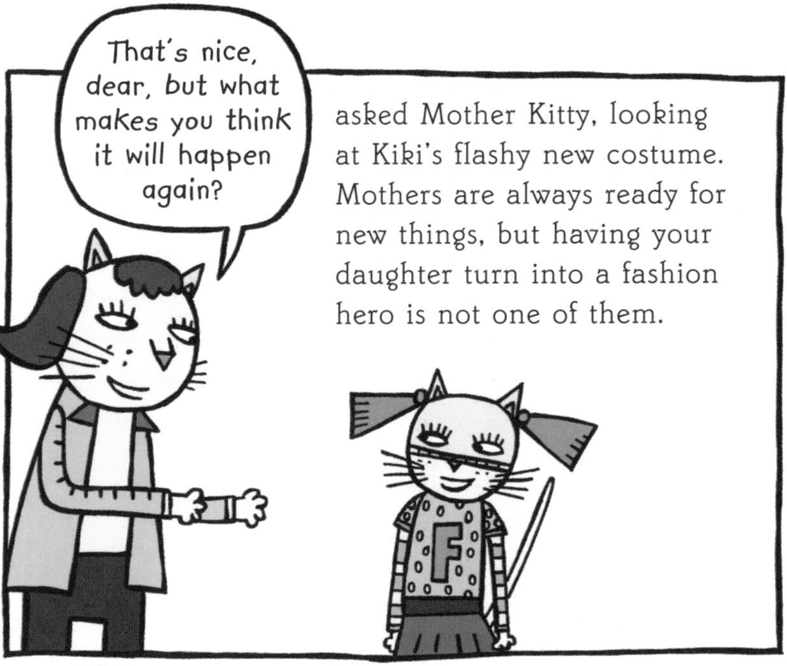
That's nice, dear, but what makes you think it will happen again?

asked Mother Kitty, looking at Kiki's flashy new costume. Mothers are always ready for new things, but having your daughter turn into a fashion hero is not one of them.

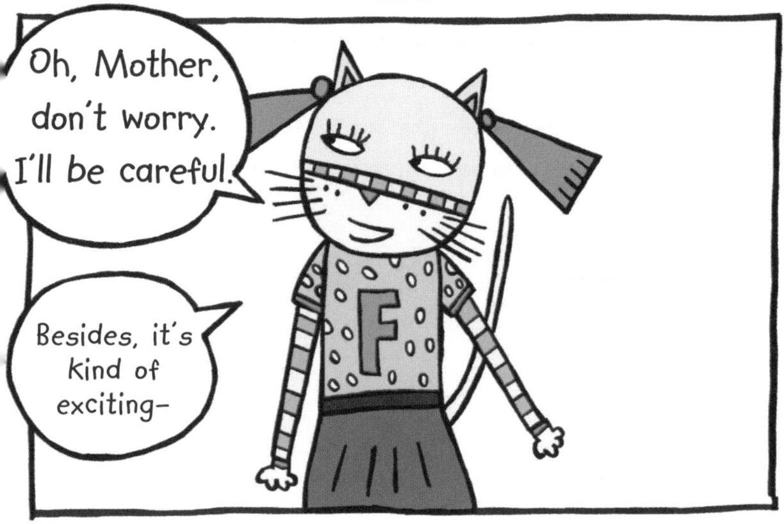
Oh, Mother, don't worry. I'll be careful.
Besides, it's kind of exciting–

said Kiki, because she knew it would happen again, and it would be very soon . . .

Epilogue

(which means this is
what happened
at the end.)

Early the next morning, Priscilla Persian looked at her magazines as soon as she got up.

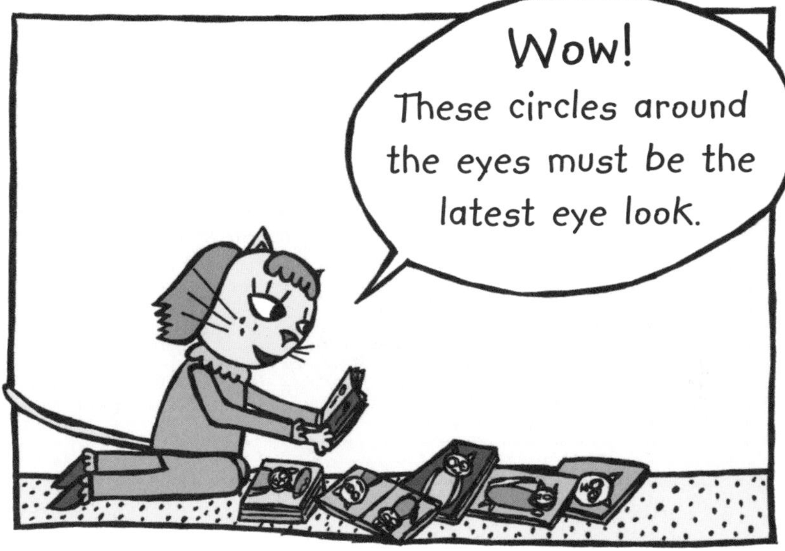
Wow!
These circles around the eyes must be the latest eye look.

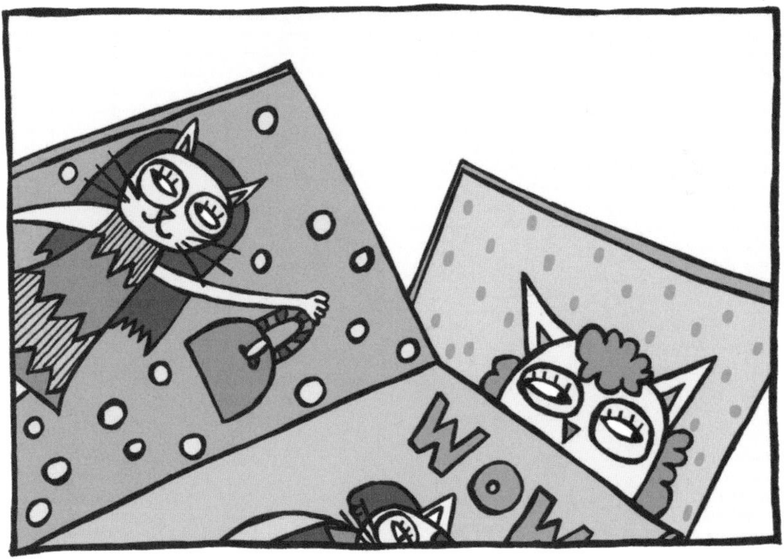
WOW

She picked out her outfit for the day.

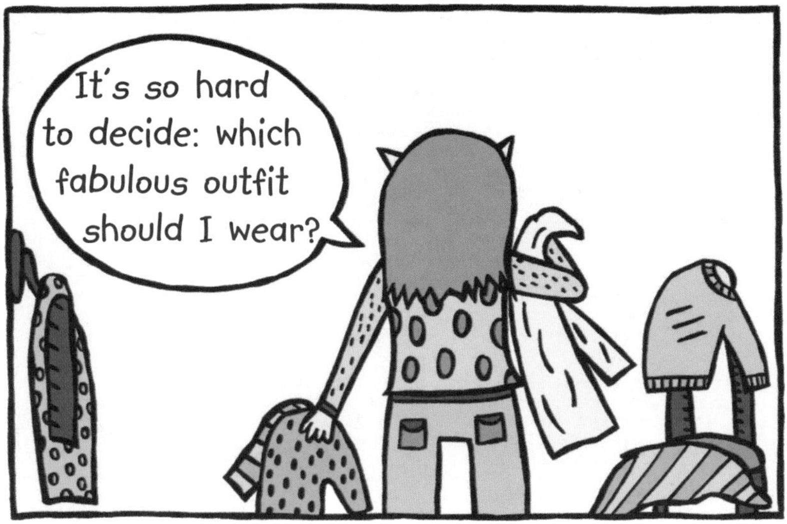
It's so hard to decide: which fabulous outfit should I wear?

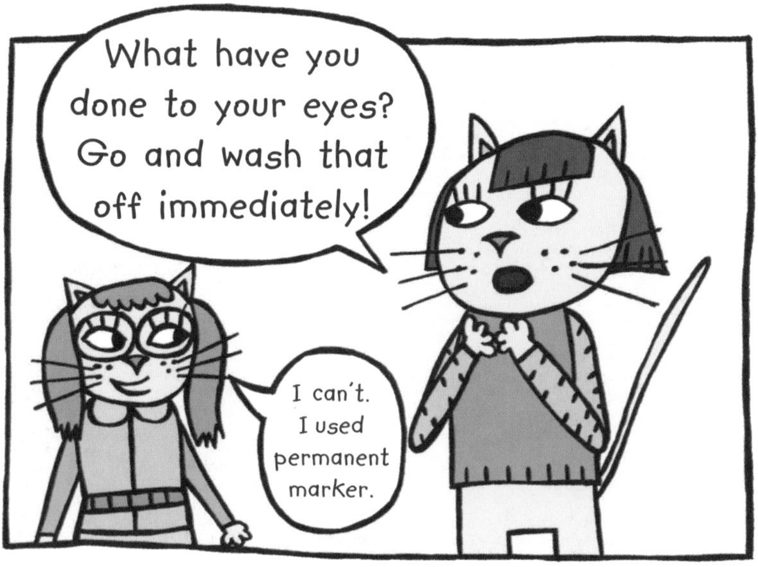
What have you done to your eyes? Go and wash that off immediately!
I can't. I used permanent marker.

After breakfast, Priscilla walked to school.

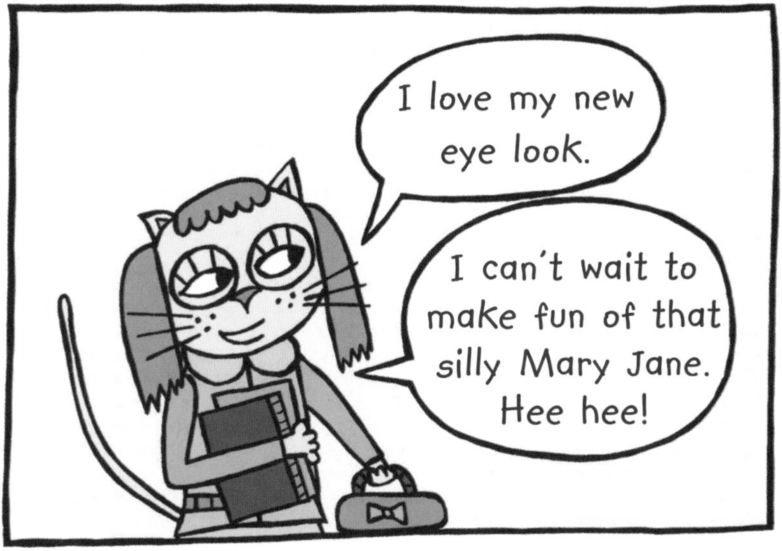
I love my new eye look.
I can't wait to make fun of that silly Mary Jane. Hee hee!

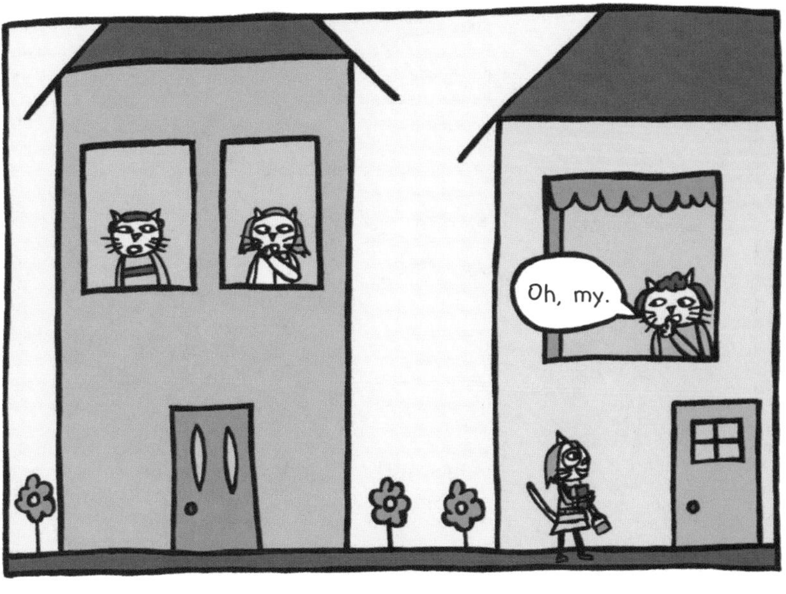
Oh, my.

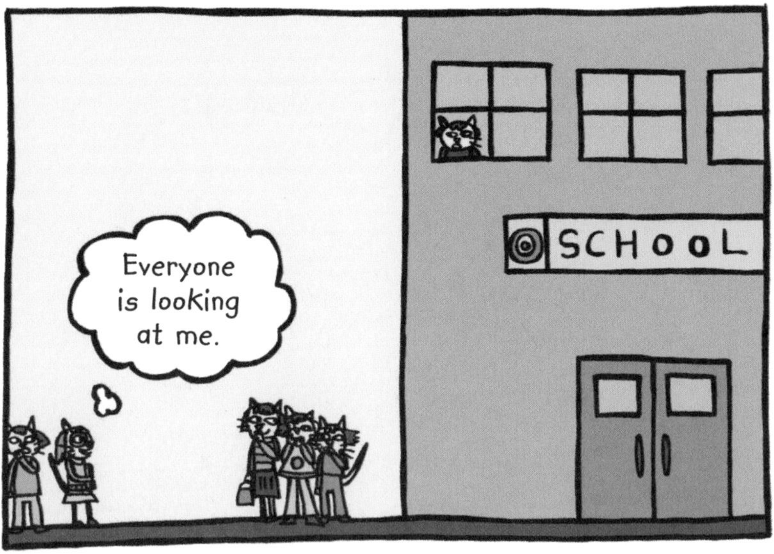
SCHOOL
Everyone is looking at me.

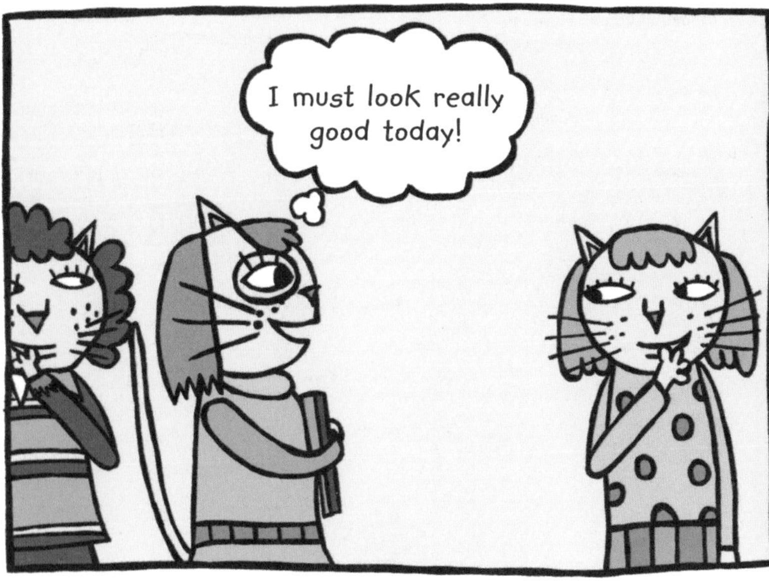
I must look really good today!

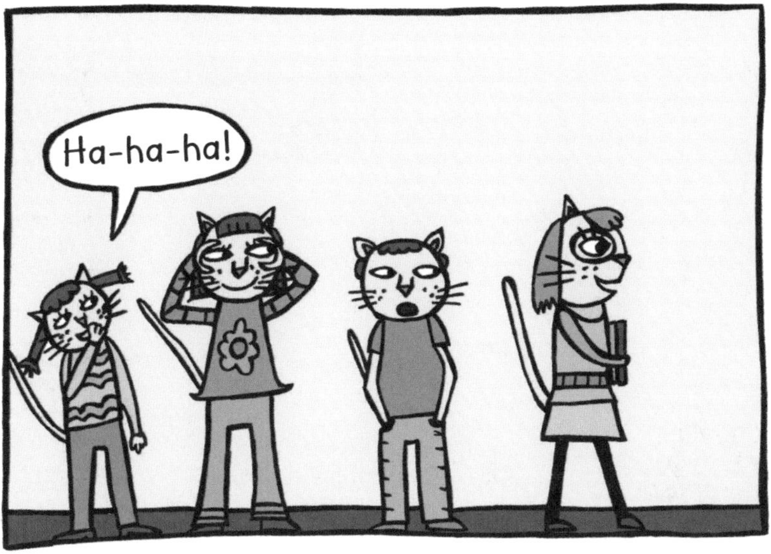
Ha-ha-ha!

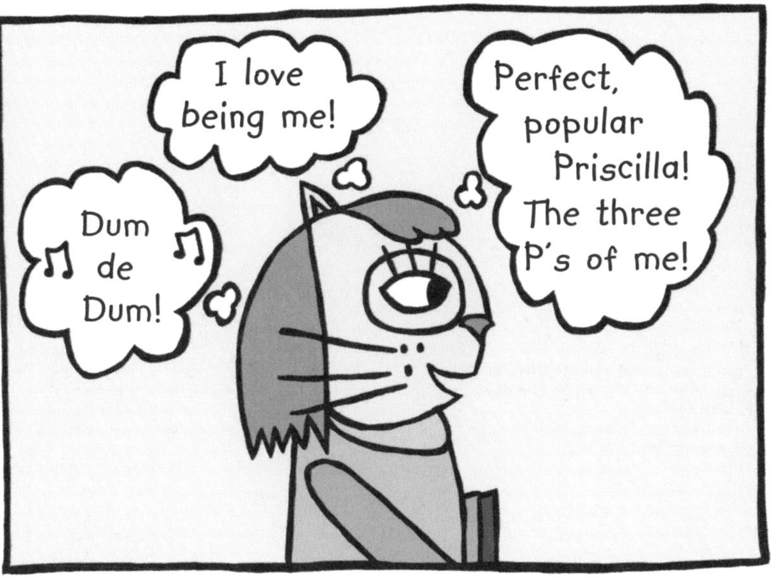
I love being me!
Perfect, popular Priscilla! The three P's of me!
Dum de Dum!

Outside, in the school yard, she met her friend Sally.

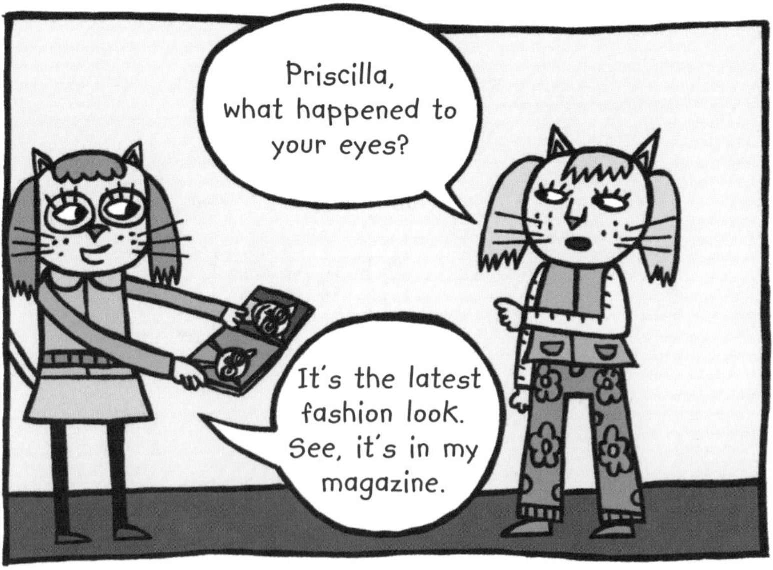
Priscilla, what happened to your eyes?
It's the latest fashion look. See, it's in my magazine.

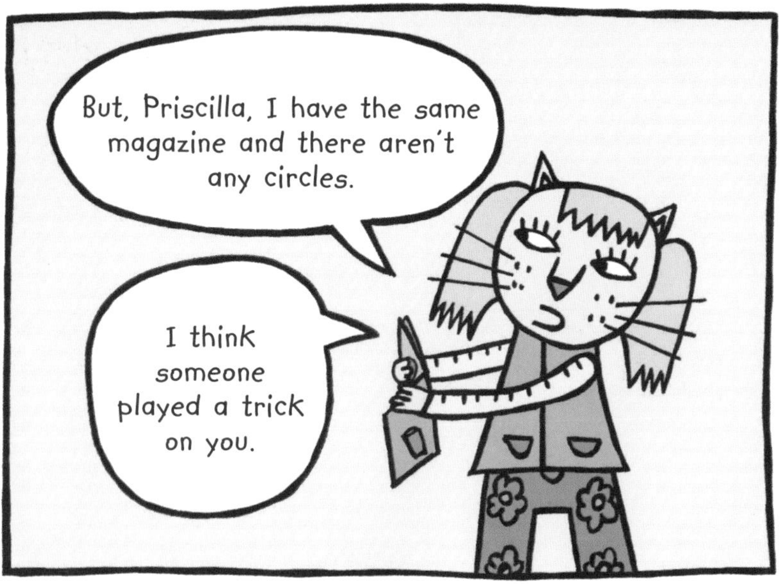
But, Priscilla, I have the same magazine and there aren't any circles.
I think someone played a trick on you.

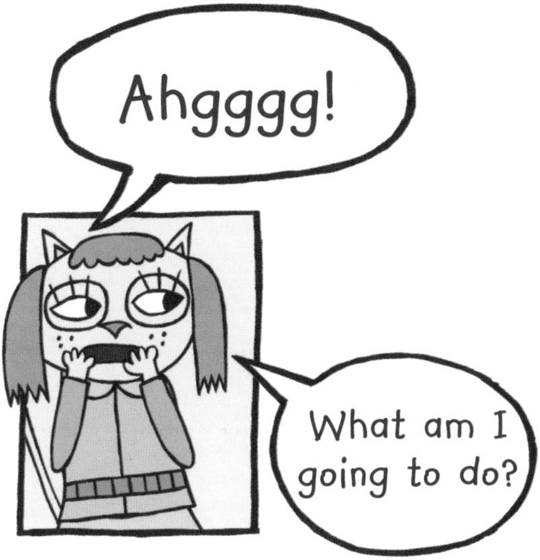
Ahgggg!
What am I going to do?

Priscilla ran screaming
into the bathroom.

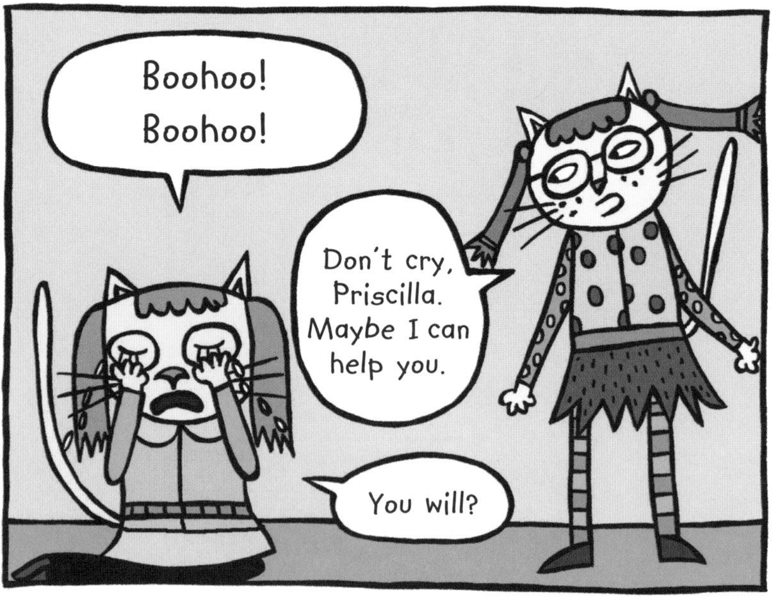
Boohoo!
Boohoo!
Don't cry, Priscilla. Maybe I can help you.
You will?

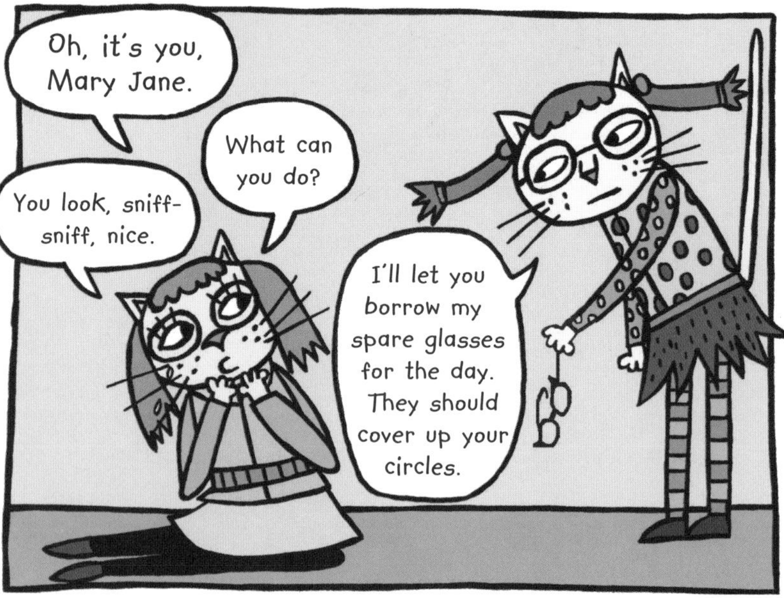
Oh, it's you, Mary Jane.
What can you do?
You look, sniff-sniff, nice.
I'll let you borrow my spare glasses for the day. They should cover up your circles.

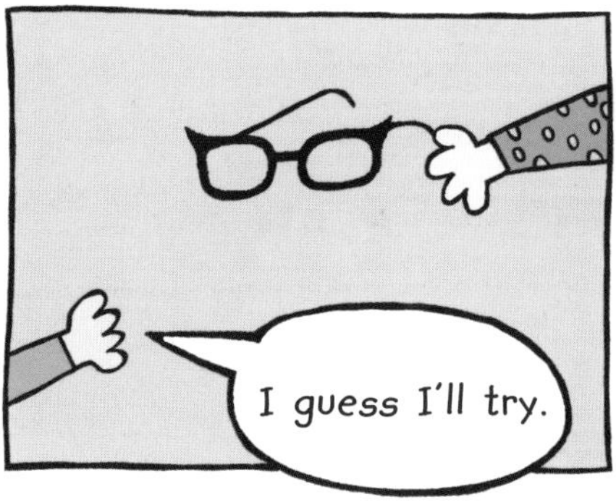
I guess I'll try.

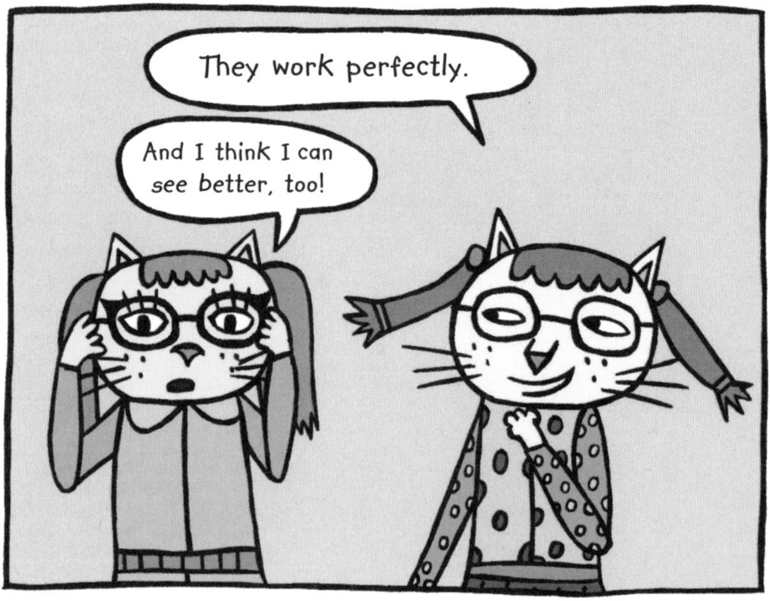
They work perfectly.
And I think I can see better, too!

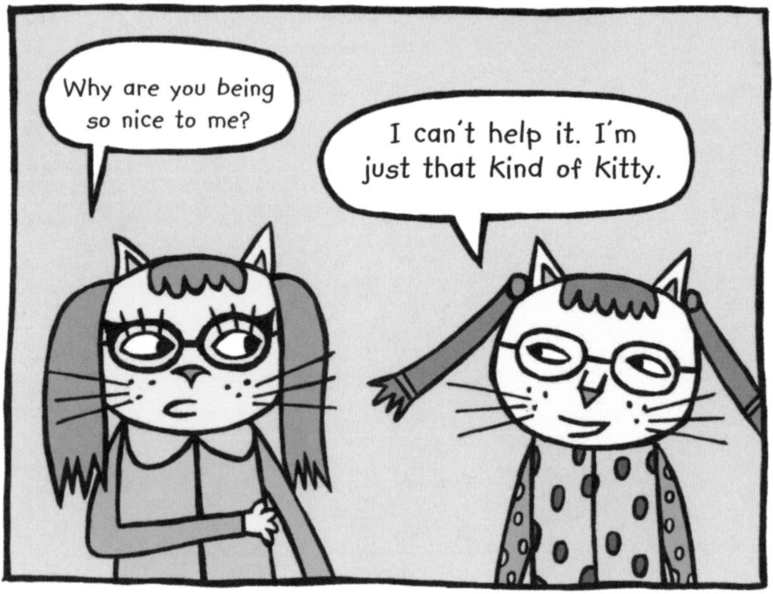
Why are you being so nice to me?
I can't help it. I'm just that kind of kitty.

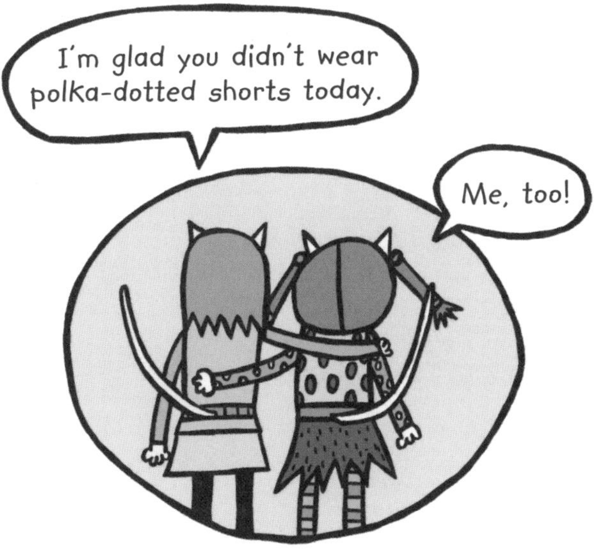
I'm glad you didn't wear polka-dotted shorts today.
Me, too!

The End

Book Two

Fashion Kitty

versus

the Fashion Queen

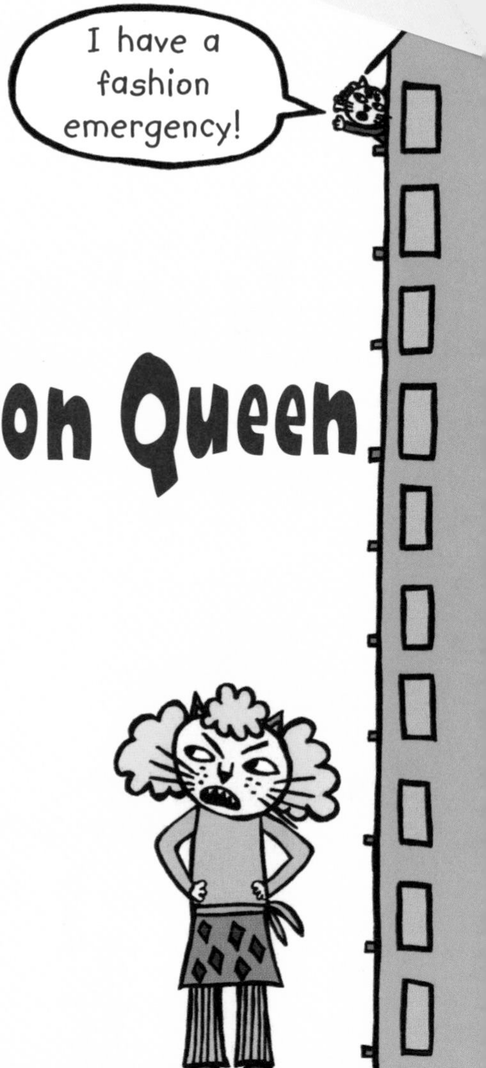
I have a fashion emergency!

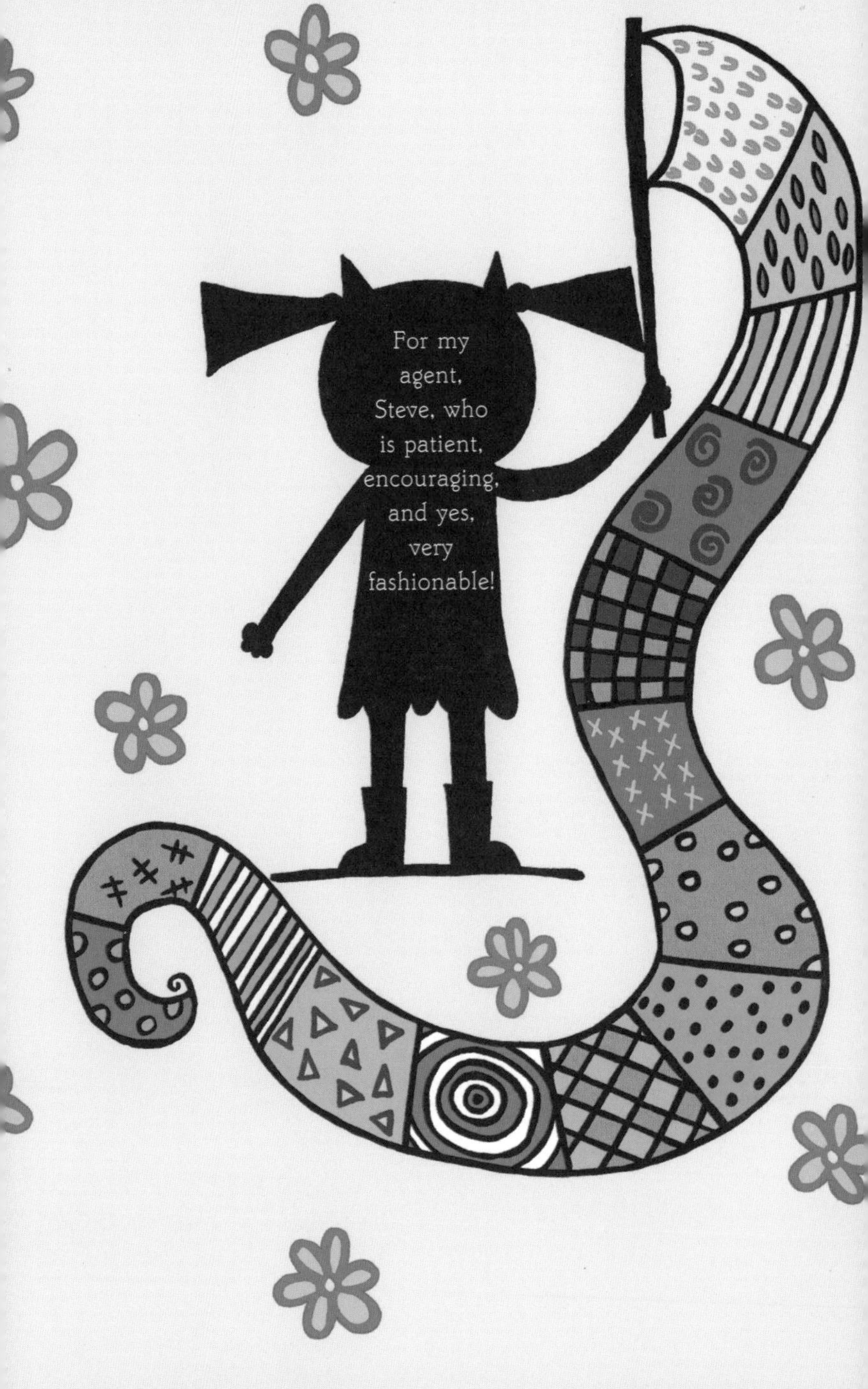
For my
agent,
Steve, who
is patient,
encouraging,
and yes,
very
fashionable!

This is Kiki Kittie.

And this is Fashion Kitty,
her secret identity.

Kiki Kittie mixes stripes, solids, patterns, and colors with style.

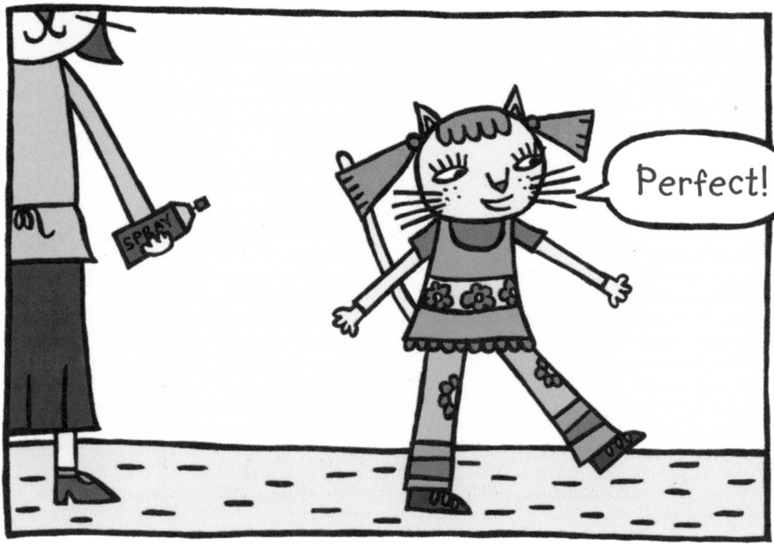
SPRAY
Perfect!

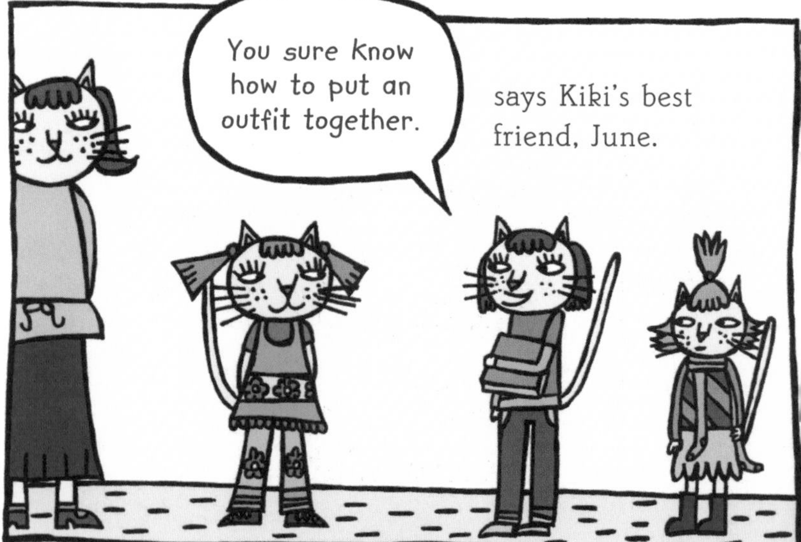
You sure know how to put an outfit together.
says Kiki's best friend, June.

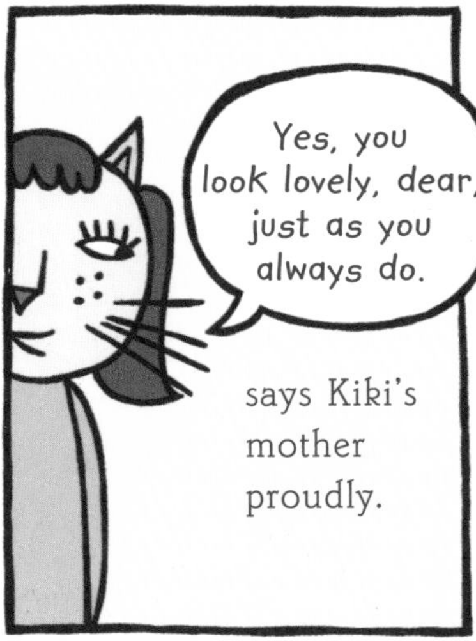
Yes, you look lovely, dear, just as you always do.
says Kiki's mother proudly.

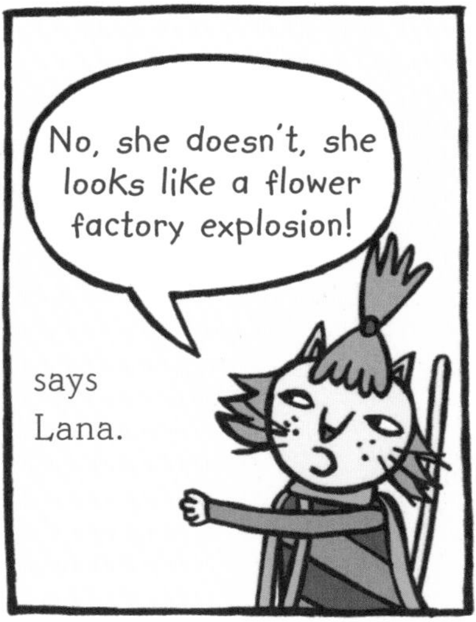
No, she doesn't, she looks like a flower factory explosion!
says Lana.

Lana is Kiki's little sister. Lana has her own fashion style.

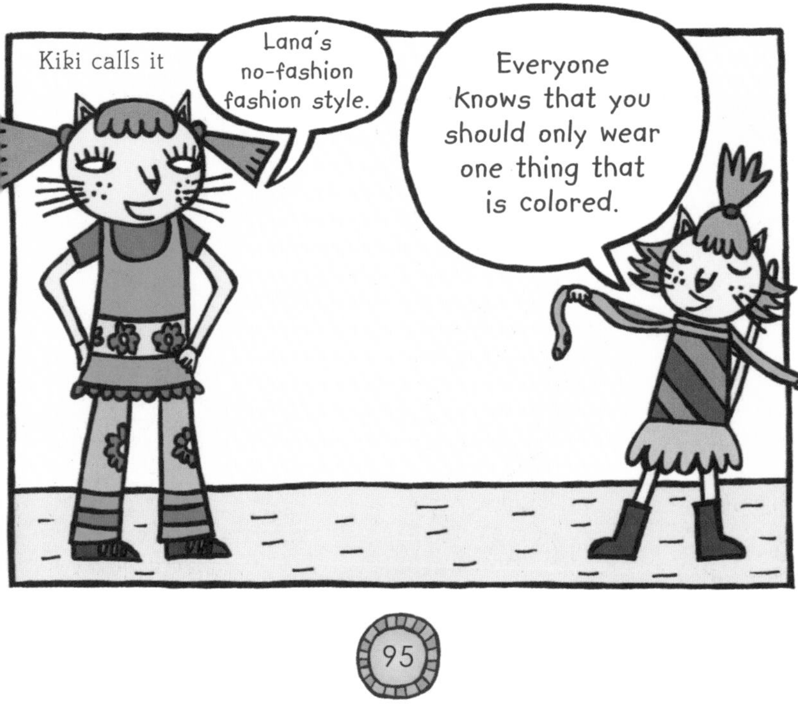
Kiki calls it
Lana's no-fashion fashion style.
Everyone knows that you should only wear one thing that is colored.

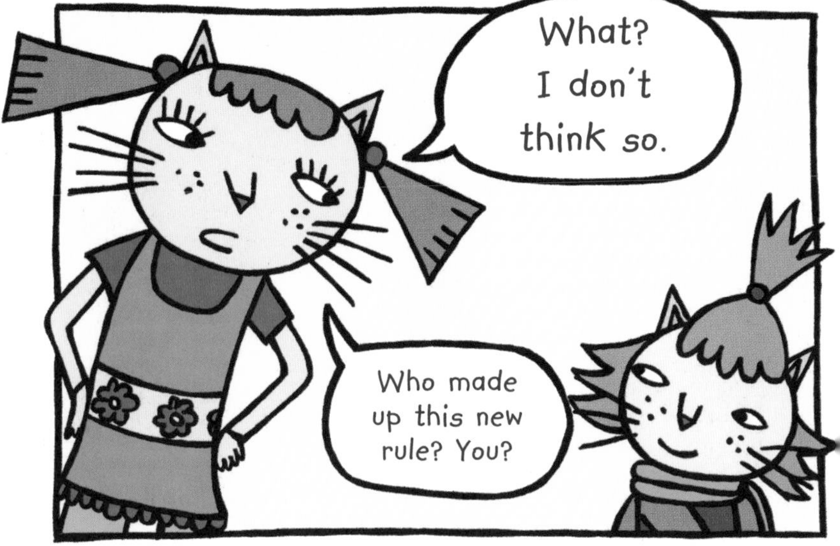
What? I don't think so.
Who made up this new rule? You?

Sometimes Kiki thinks that Lana is more annoying than other times, and this was definitely one of those "sometimes."

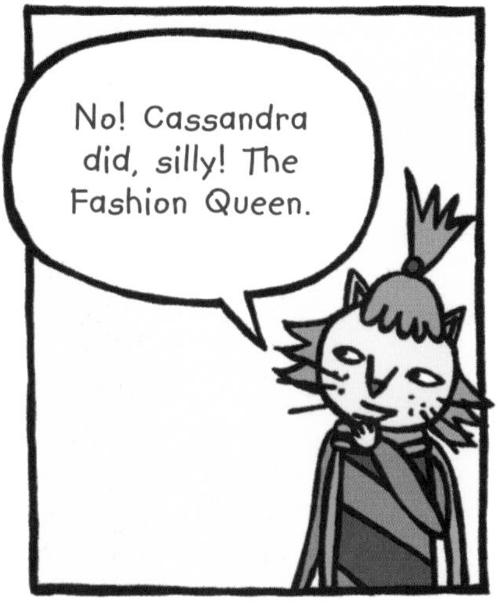
No! Cassandra did, silly! The Fashion Queen.

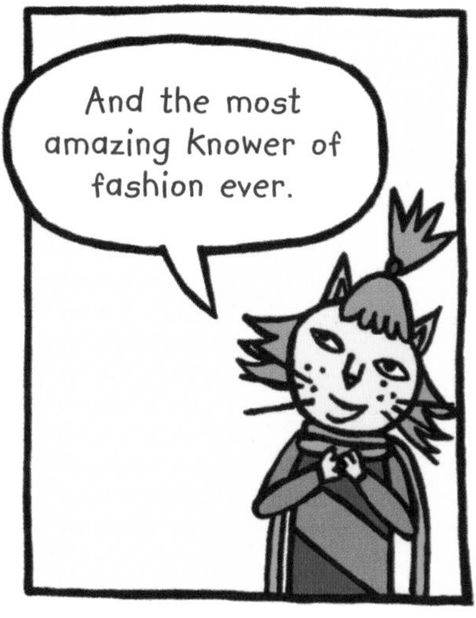
And the most amazing knower of fashion ever.

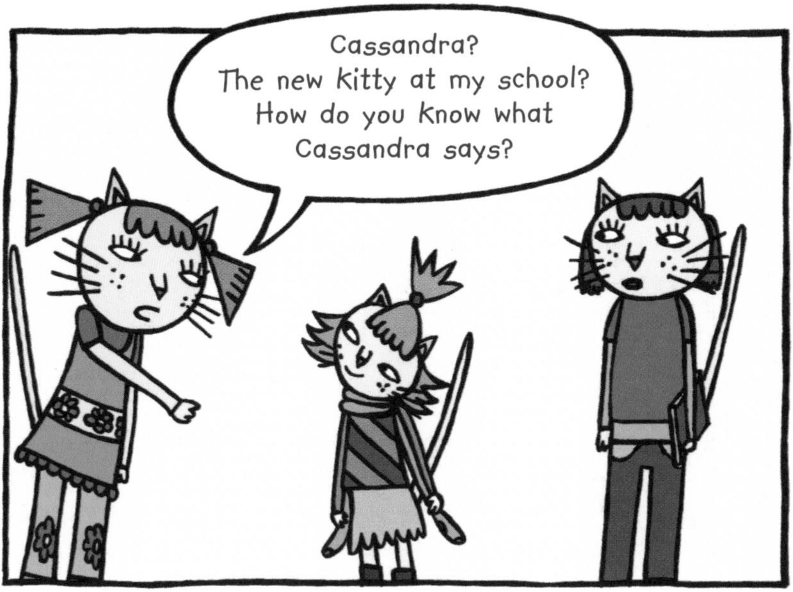
Cassandra? The new kitty at my school? How do you know what Cassandra says?

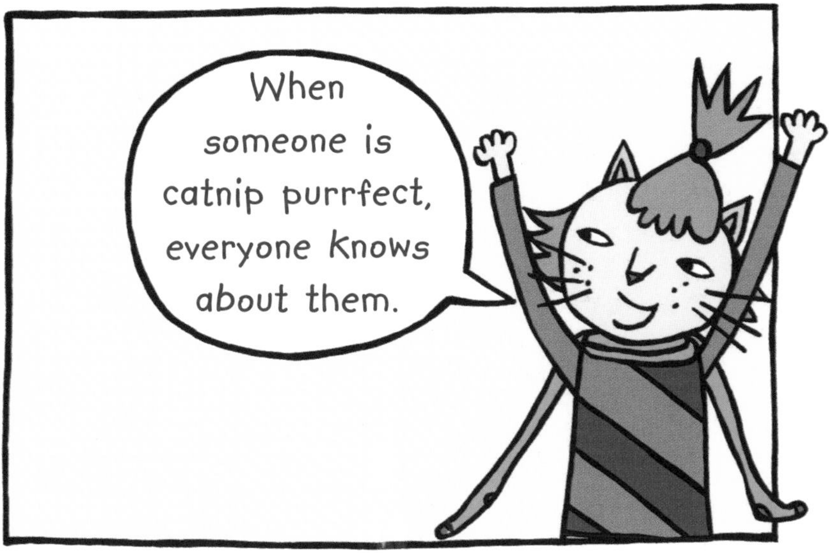
When someone is catnip purrfect, everyone knows about them.

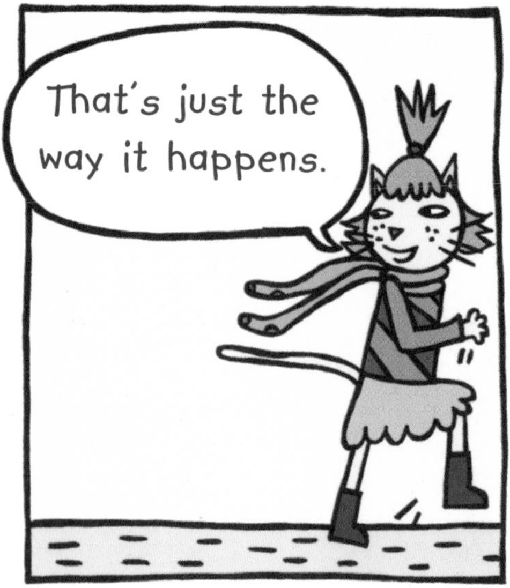
That's just the way it happens.

And then Lana skipped off so fast she didn't hear another word Kiki said.

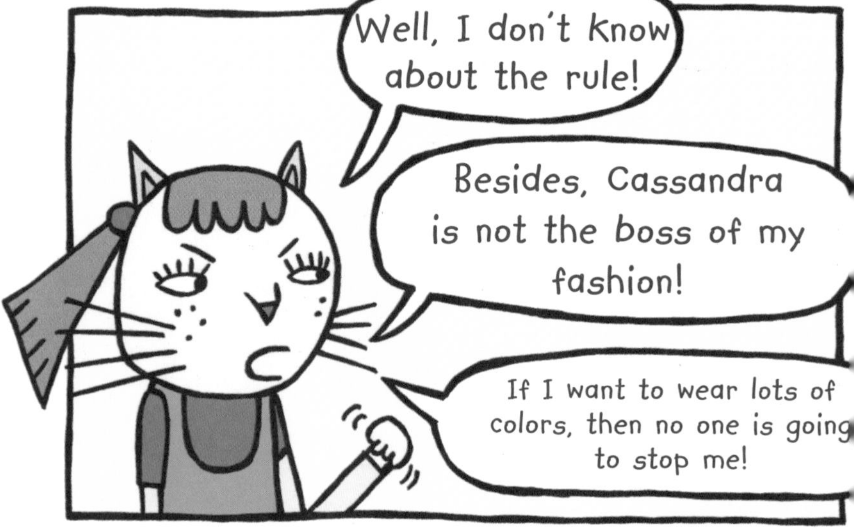
Well, I don't know about the rule!
Besides, Cassandra is not the boss of my fashion!
If I want to wear lots of colors, then no one is going to stop me!

It is not very satisfying to do lots of arguing first thing in the morning before breakfast.

And it is especially not very
satisfying to do lots of arguing
with a four-year-old who
thinks she is always right.

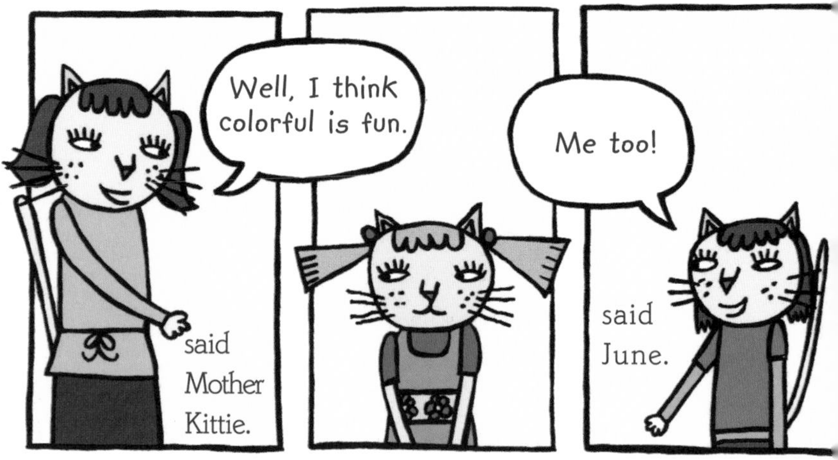
Well, I think colorful is fun.
said Mother Kittie.
Me too!
said June.

Kiki tried to smile and make herself feel better, but inside her head she was thinking about the two things she knew about Cassandra . . .

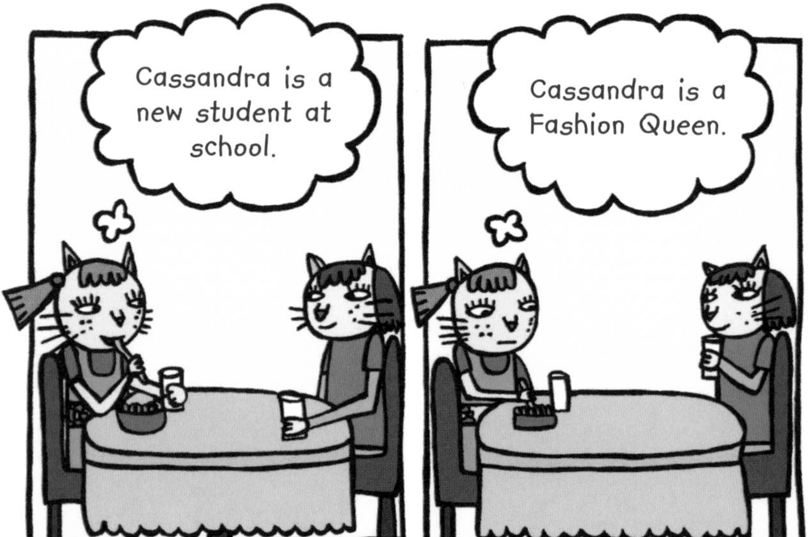
Cassandra is a new student at school.
Cassandra is a Fashion Queen.

and the one thing she didn't know
but was probably going to find out.

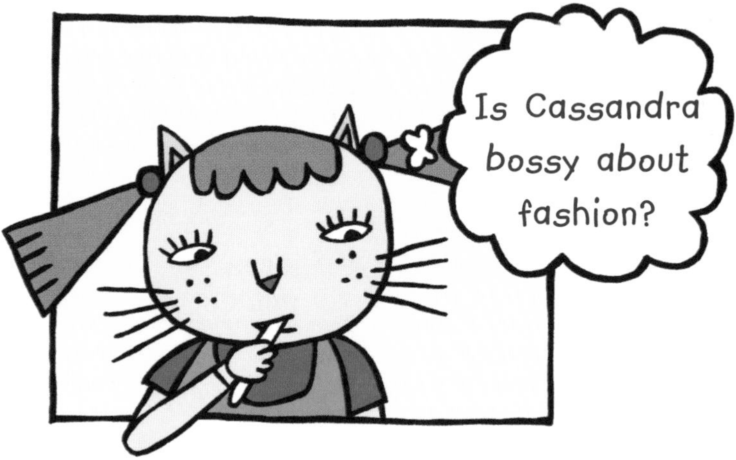
Is Cassandra bossy about fashion?

It's not a good thing to decide you don't like someone before you even meet them, but it can happen.

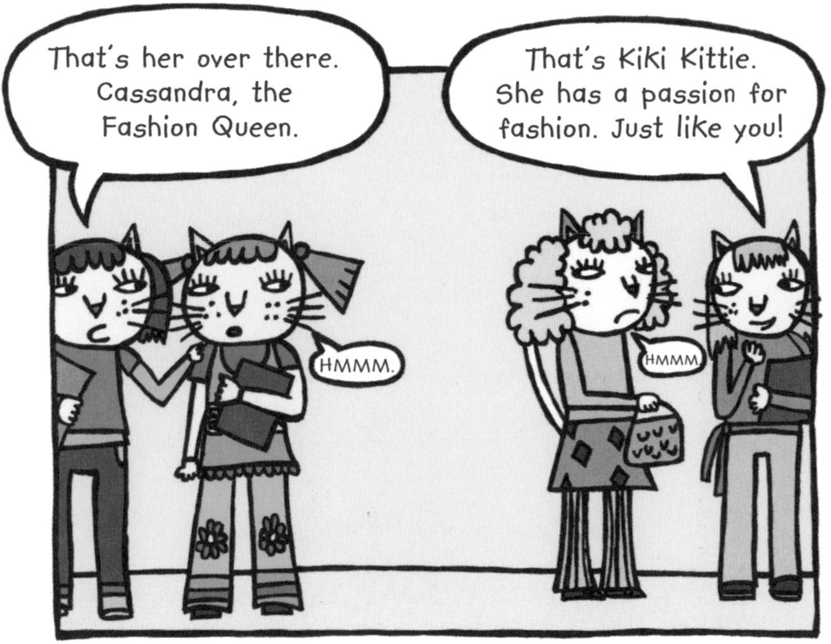
That's her over there.
Cassandra, the
Fashion Queen.
That's KiKi Kittie.
She has a passion for
fashion. Just like you!
HMMM.
HMMM

And sometimes once you do meet them it only takes a few words to decide that yes, you were right, you do not like them even one little bit.

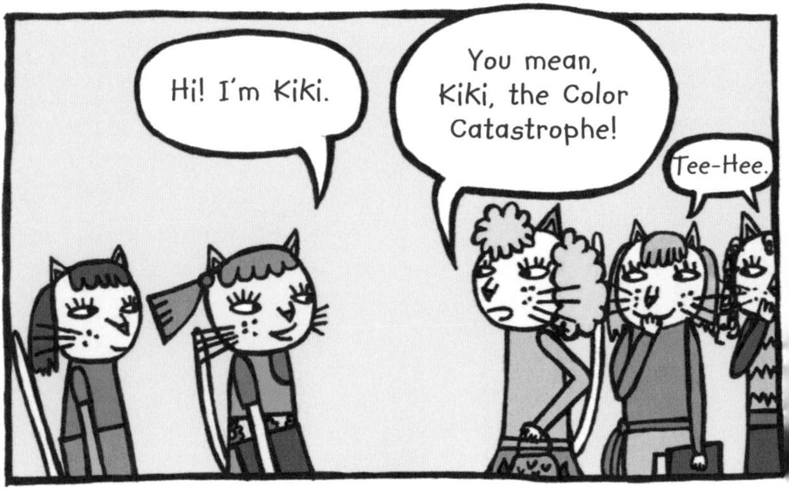
Hi! I'm KiKi.
You mean,
KiKi, the Color
Catastrophe!
Tee-Hee.

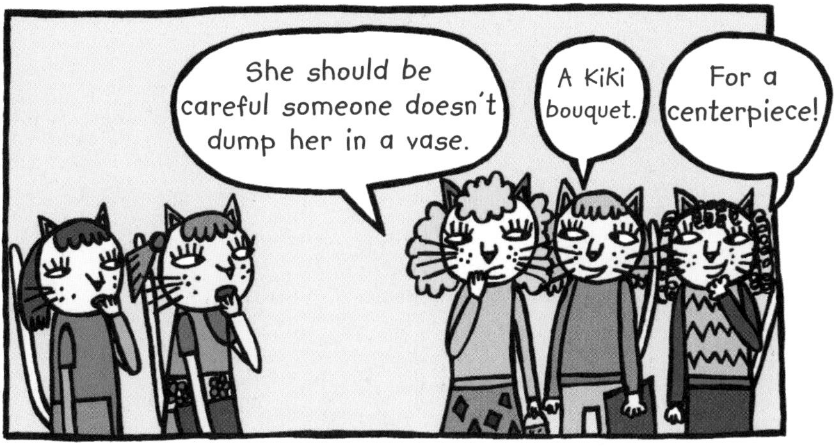
She should be careful someone doesn't dump her in a vase.
A Kiki bouquet.
For a centerpiece!

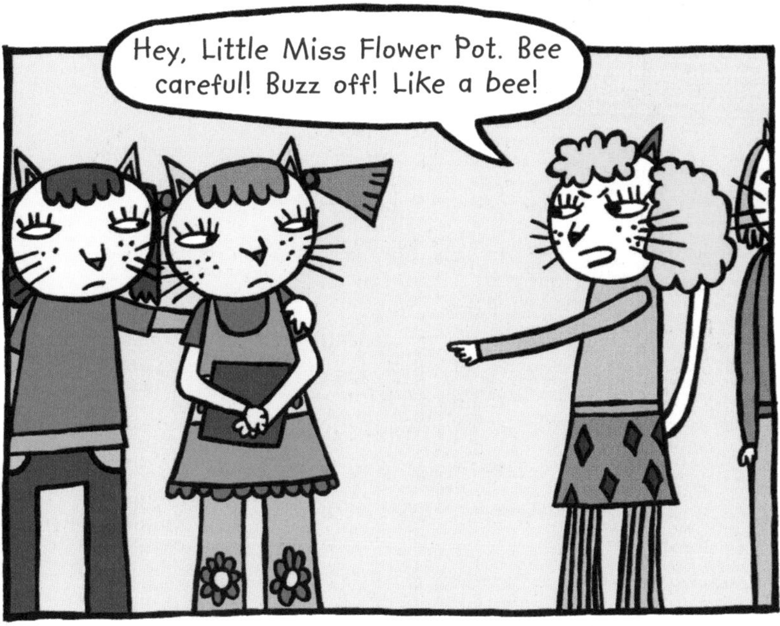
Hey, Little Miss Flower Pot. Bee careful! Buzz off! Like a bee!

Kiki was mad on the outside, sad on the inside, and wishing for the one thing that was not going to happen.

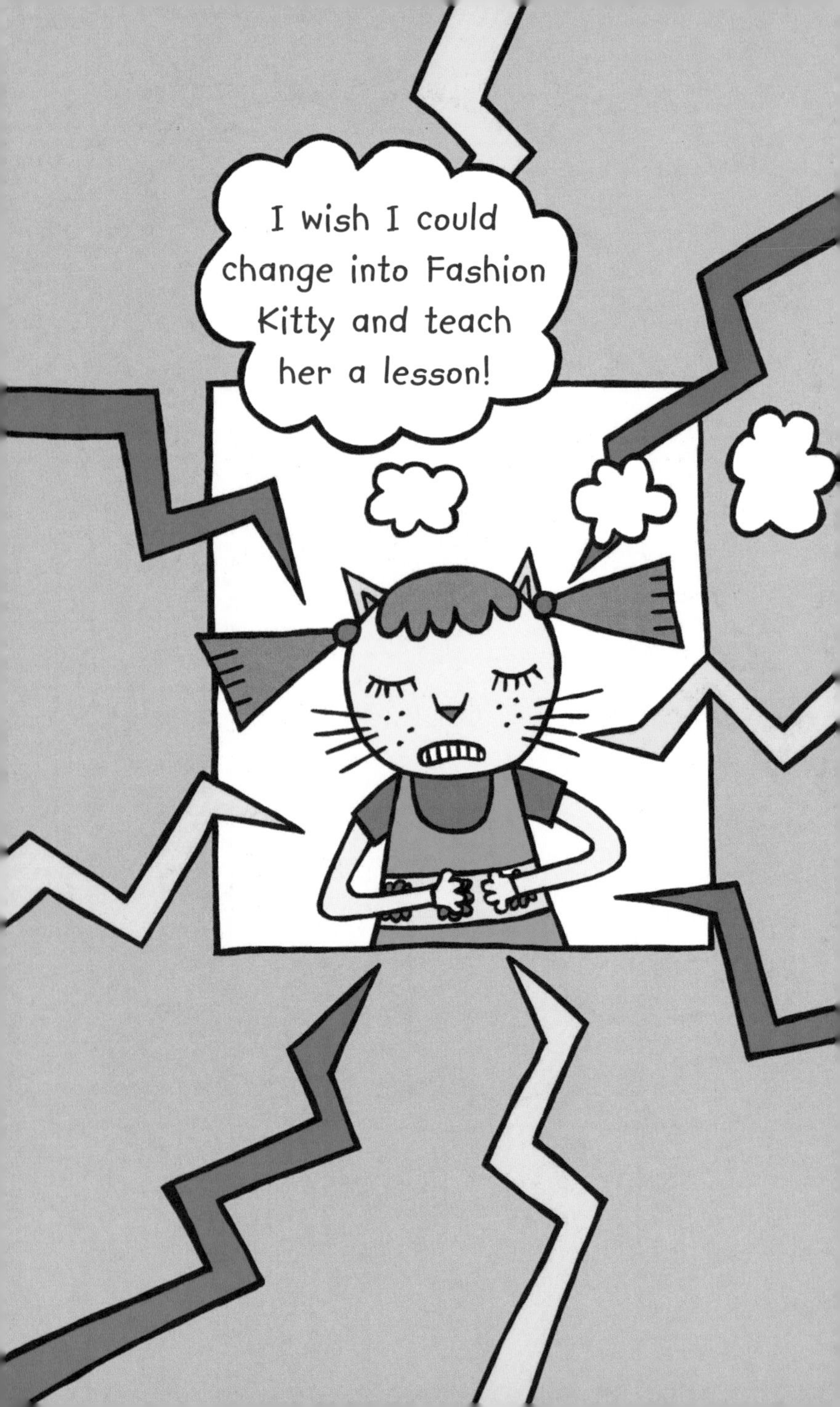
I wish I could change into Fashion Kitty and teach her a lesson!

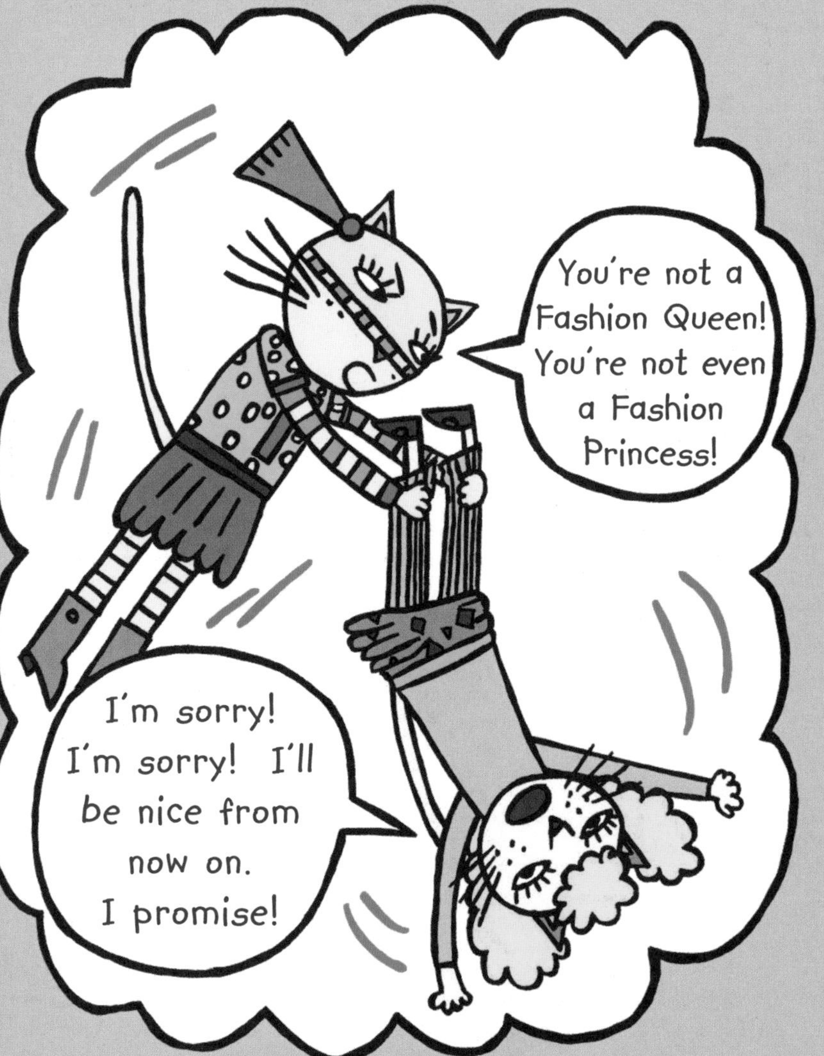
You're not a Fashion Queen! You're not even a Fashion Princess!
I'm sorry! I'm sorry! I'll be nice from now on. I promise!

It's not easy to keep a super power a secret. Especially when you'd like to use it to help yourself.

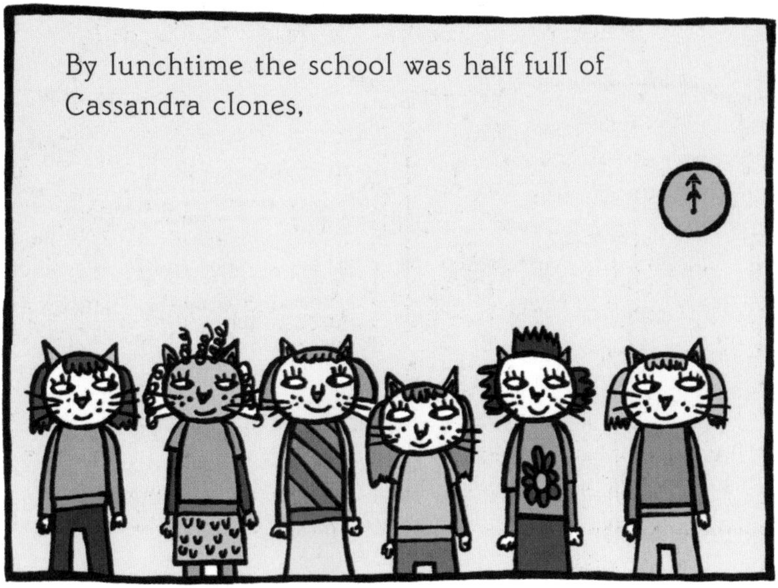
By lunchtime the school was half full of Cassandra clones,

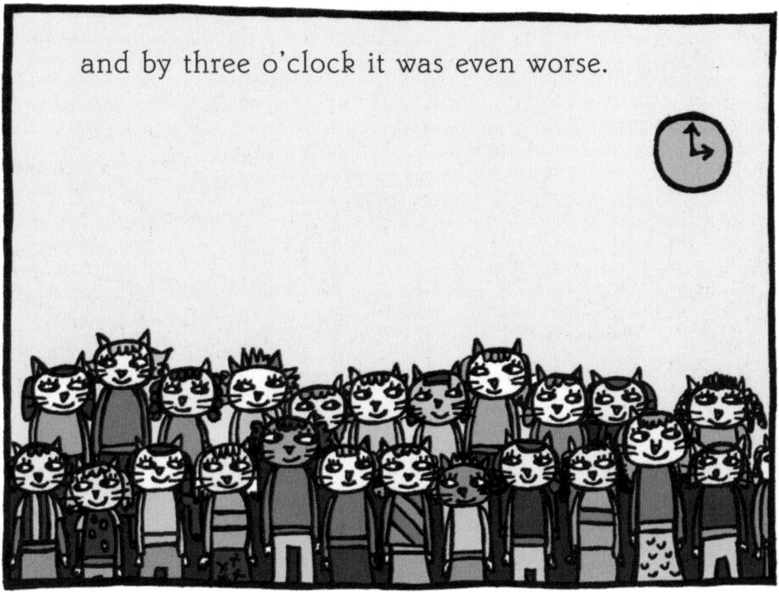
and by three o'clock it was even worse.

Kiki could not believe that someone so new

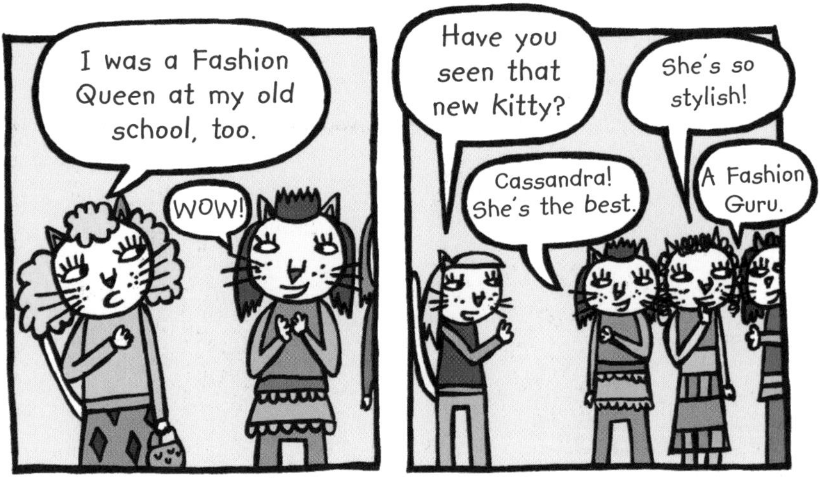
I was a Fashion Queen at my old school, too.
WOW!
Have you seen that new kitty?
Cassandra! She's the best.
She's so stylish!
A Fashion Guru.

could become popular so fast.

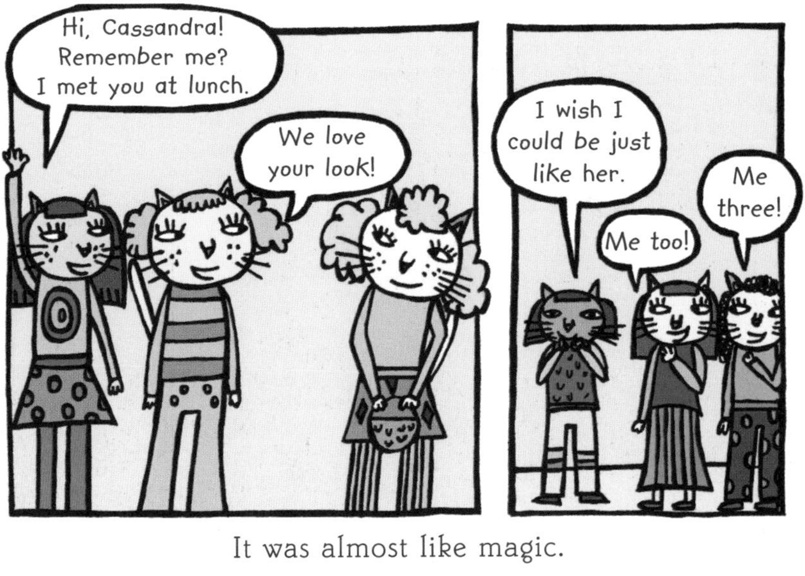
Hi, Cassandra! Remember me? I met you at lunch.
We love your look!
I wish I could be just like her.
Me too!
Me three!

It was almost like magic.

It was like a kitty having a pet mouse. Or a kitty changing into a fashion superhero. It was unbelievable.

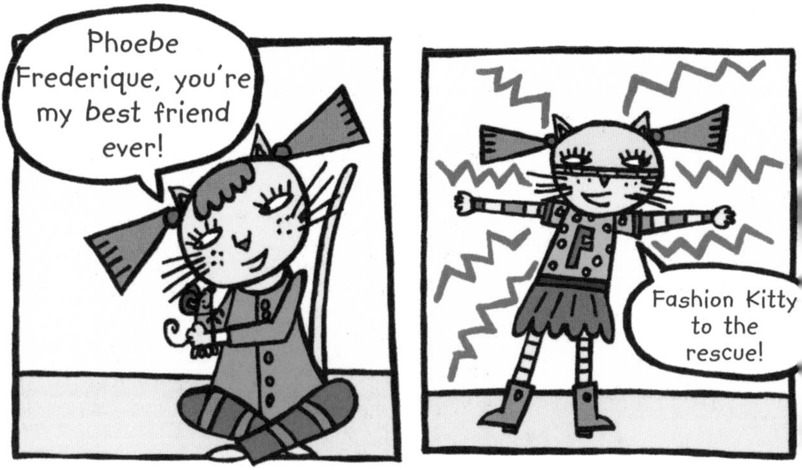
Phoebe Frederique, you're my best friend ever!
Fashion Kitty to the rescue!

And everyone was talking about it.

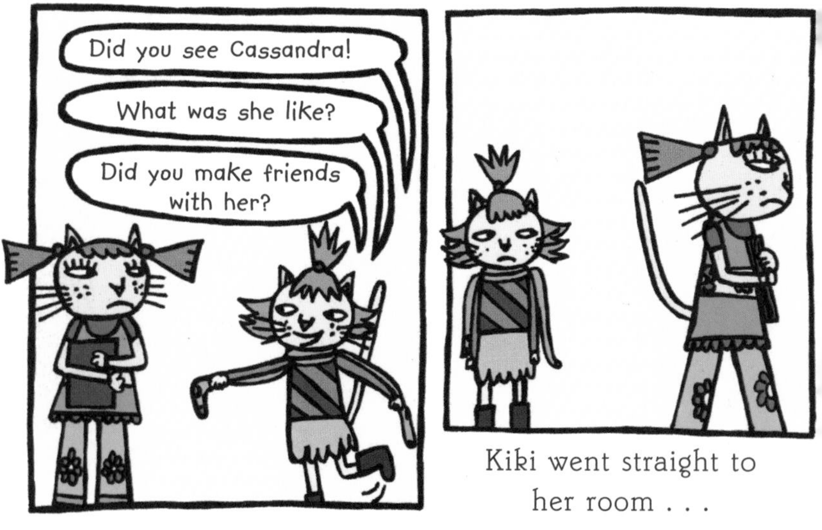
Did you see Cassandra!
What was she like?
Did you make friends with her?

Kiki went straight to her room . . .

and slammed the door!

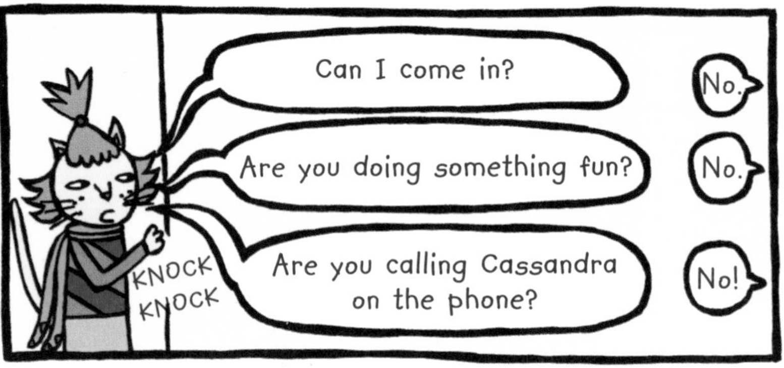
Can I come in?
No.
Are you doing something fun?
No.
KNOCK
KNOCK
Are you calling Cassandra on the phone?
No!

Sometimes, when she is feeling blue, Kiki flips through her Fashion Kitty scrapbook. She has saved every mention Fashion Kitty has ever gotten in the local newspaper.

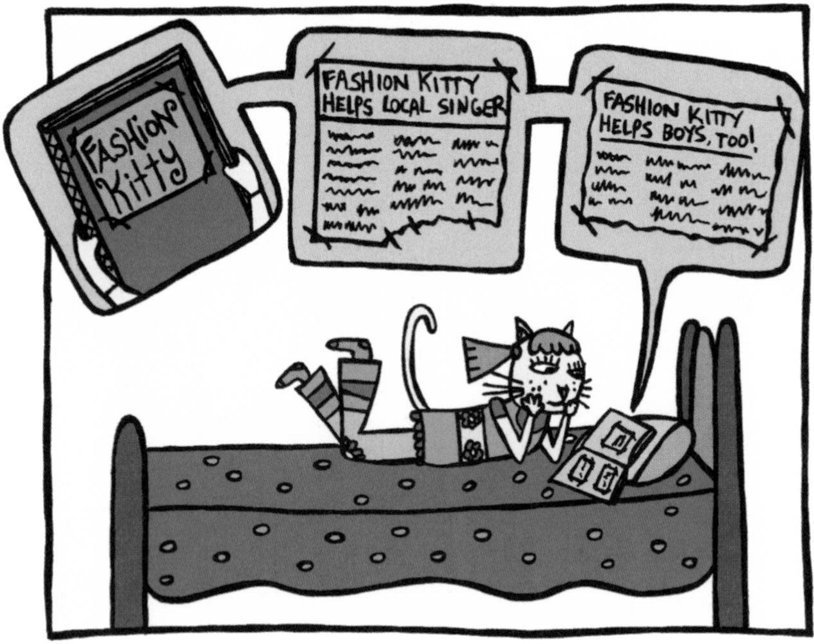
FASHION Kitty
FASHION KITTY HELPS LOCAL SINGER
FASHION KITTY HELPS BOYS, TOO!

Kiki was still feeling a little depressed, which is a word that means sad, yucky, and blah all mixed together, when she heard a fashion distress call.

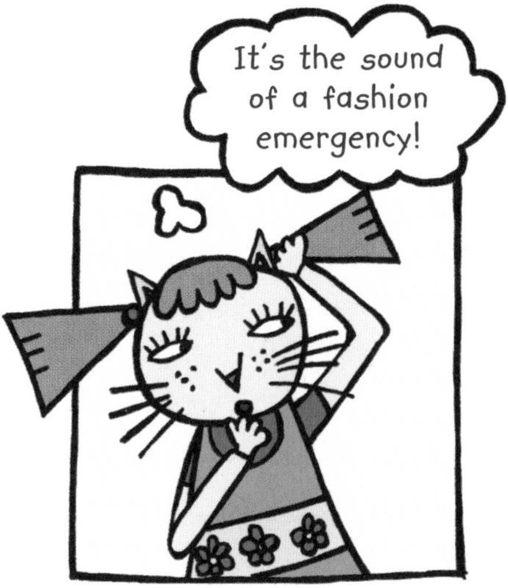
It's the sound of a fashion emergency!

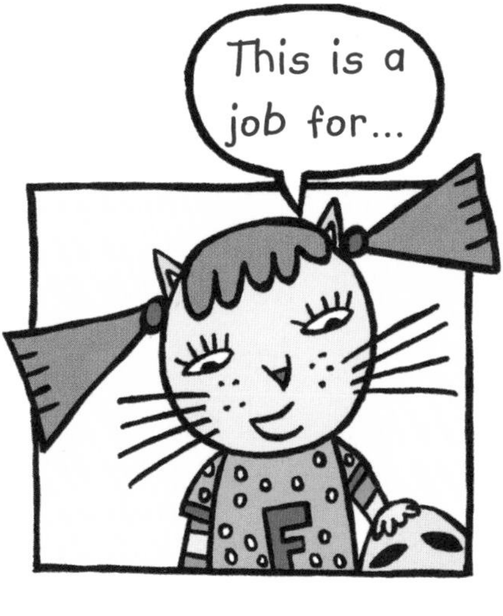
This is a job for...
F

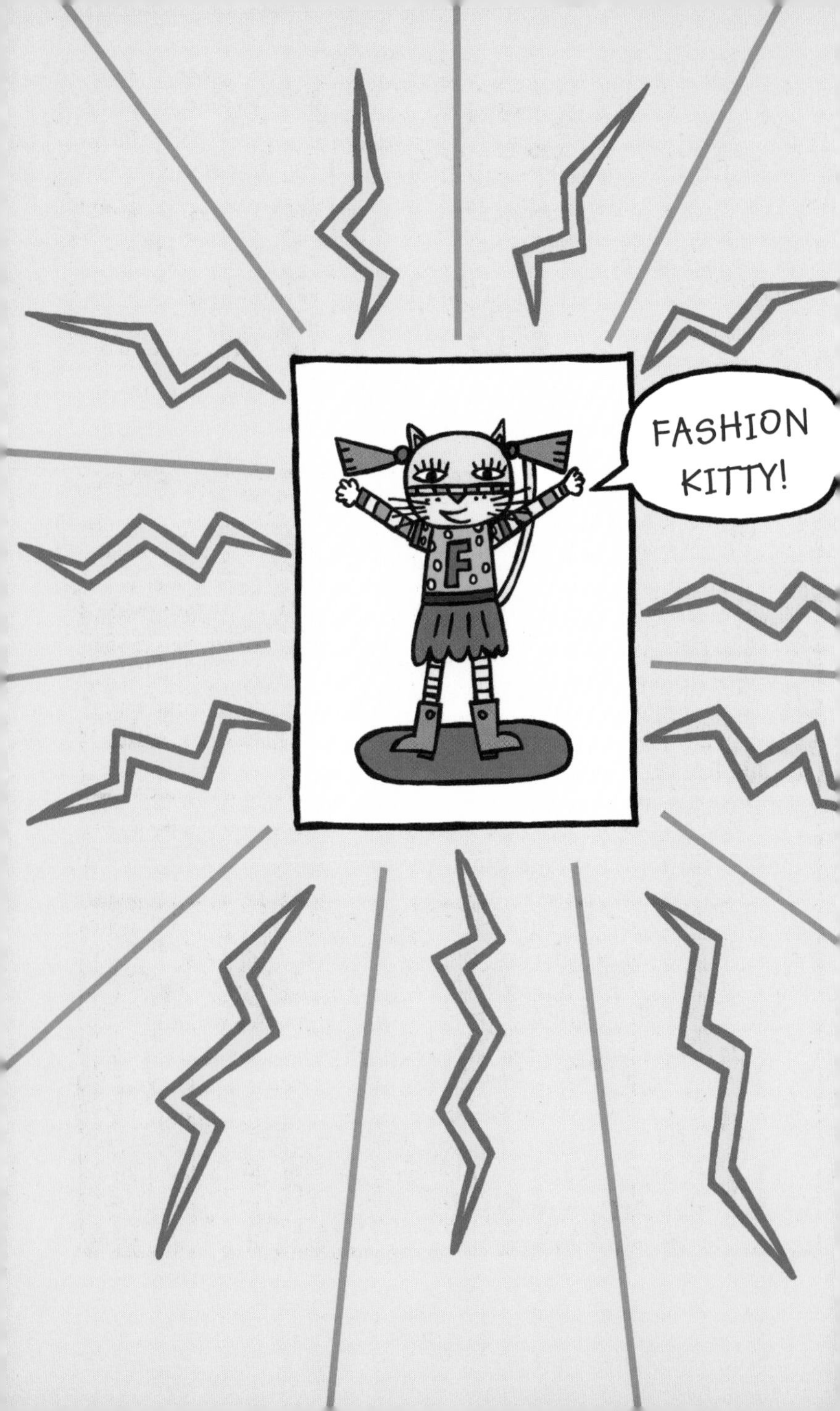
FASHION KITTY!

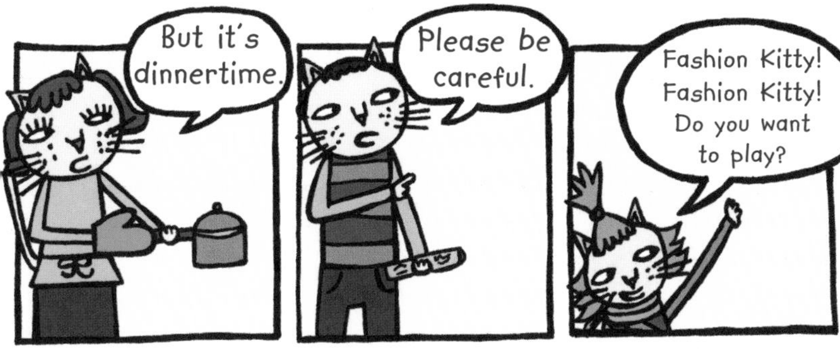
But it's dinnertime.
Please be careful.
Fashion Kitty! Fashion Kitty! Do you want to play?

said Mother, Father, and Lana Kittie all at once when they saw her.

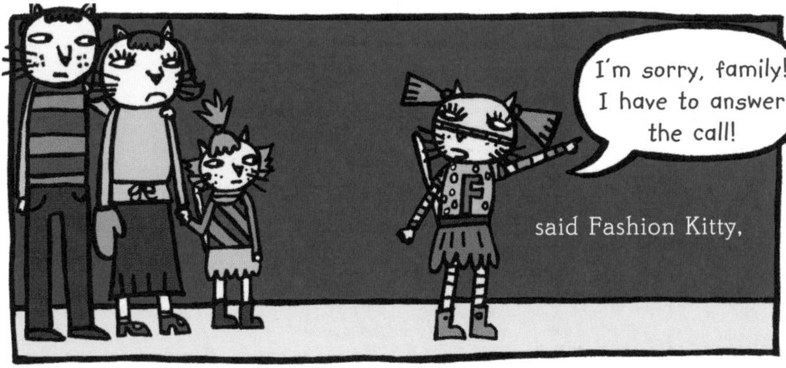
I'm sorry, family! I have to answer the call!
said Fashion Kitty,

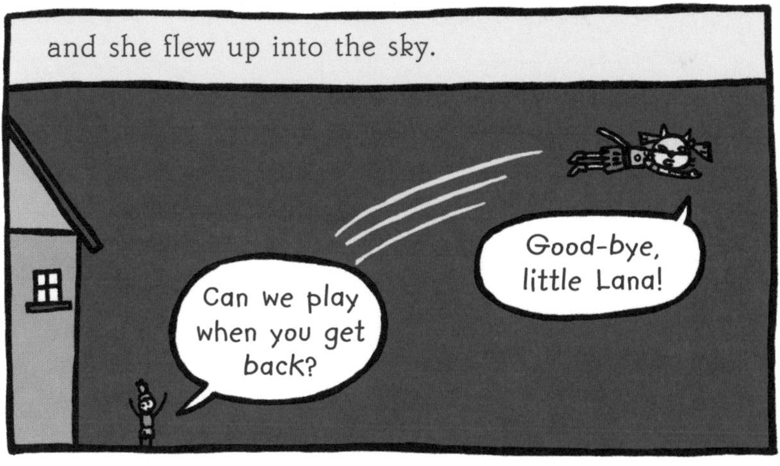
and she flew up into the sky.
Good-bye, little Lana!
Can we play when you get back?

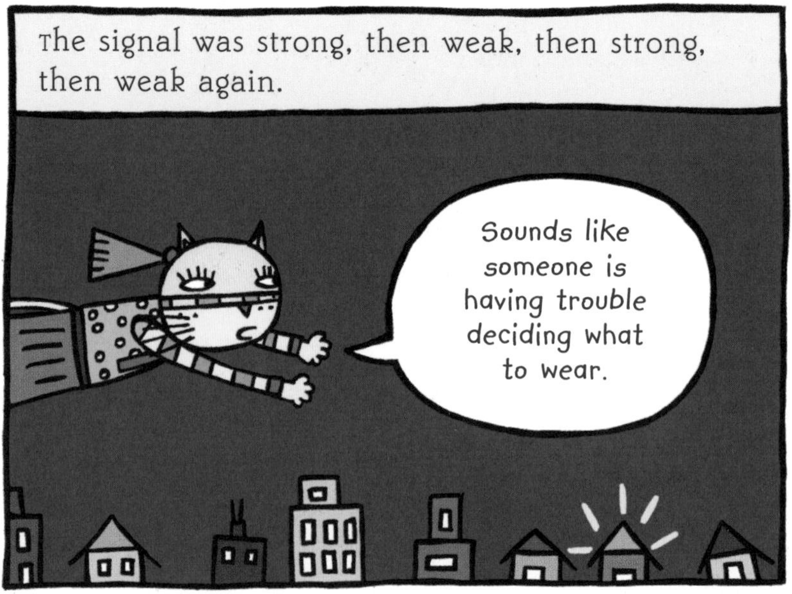
The signal was strong, then weak, then strong, then weak again.
Sounds like someone is having trouble deciding what to wear.

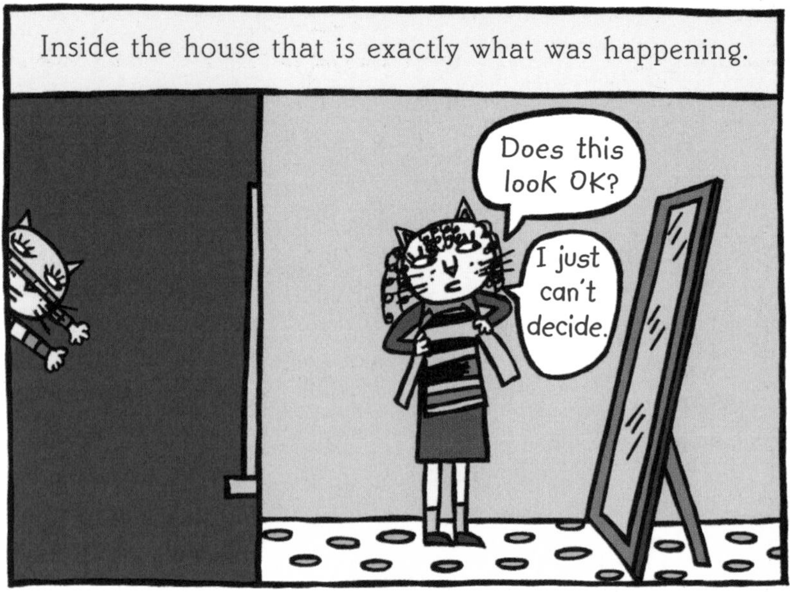
Inside the house that is exactly what was happening.
Does this look OK?
I just can't decide.

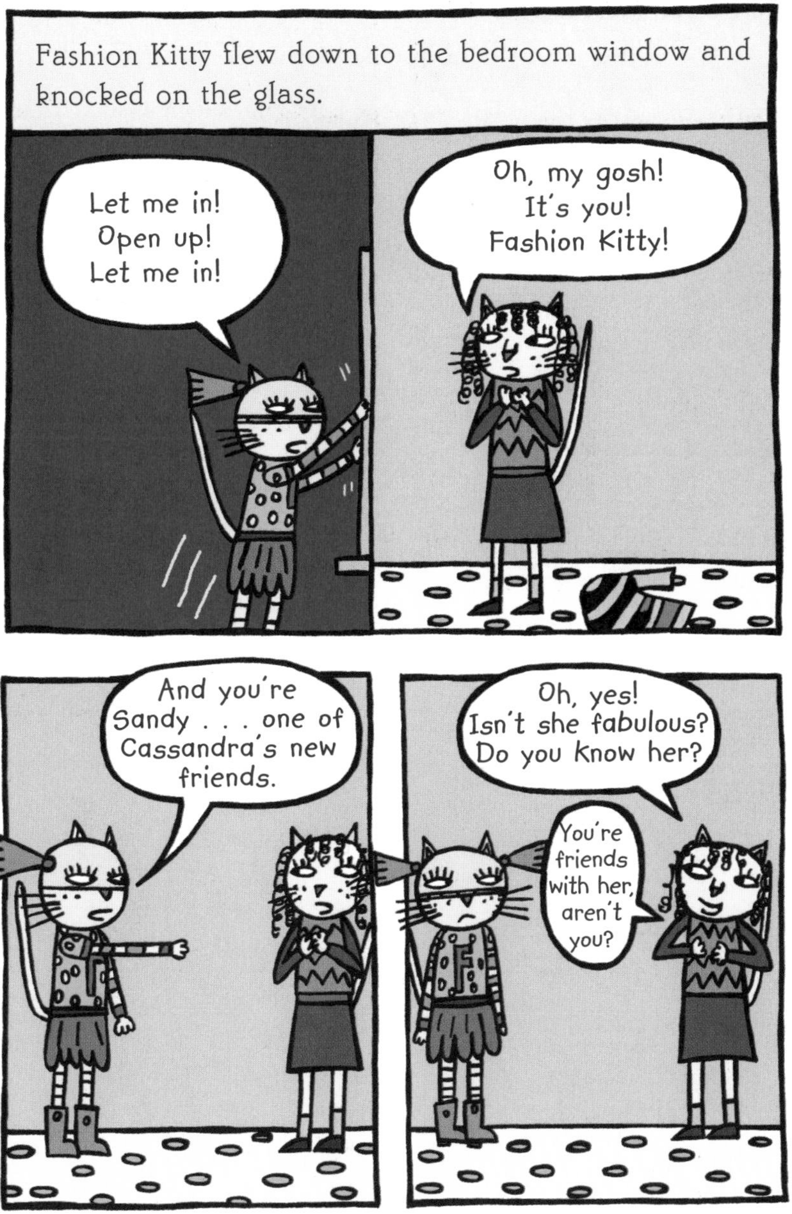
Fashion Kitty flew down to the bedroom window and knocked on the glass.
Let me in! Open up! Let me in!
Oh, my gosh! It's you! Fashion Kitty!
And you're Sandy . . . one of Cassandra's new friends.
Oh, yes! Isn't she fabulous? Do you know her?
You're friends with her, aren't you?

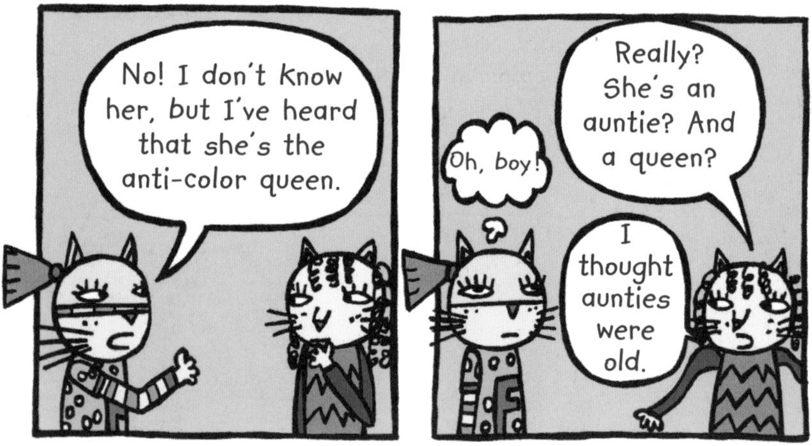
No! I don't know her, but I've heard that she's the anti-color queen.
Oh, boy!
Really? She's an auntie? And a queen?
I thought aunties were old.

Fashion Kitty had to explain the difference between "anti" (which means against) and "auntie" (which is someone who is related to you and hopefully gives you nice presents on your birthday).

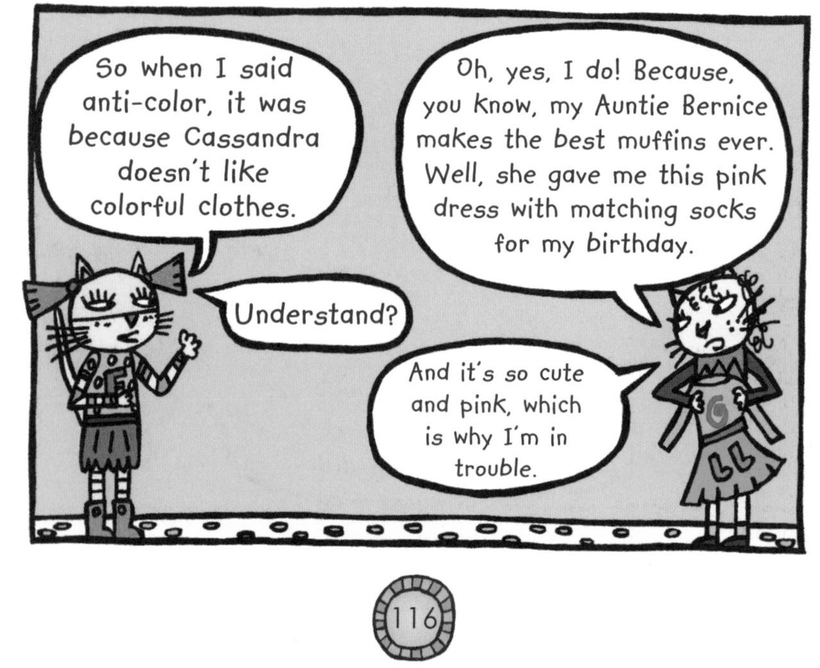
So when I said anti-color, it was because Cassandra doesn't like colorful clothes.
Understand?
Oh, yes, I do! Because, you know, my Auntie Bernice makes the best muffins ever. Well, she gave me this pink dress with matching socks for my birthday.
And it's so cute and pink, which is why I'm in trouble.

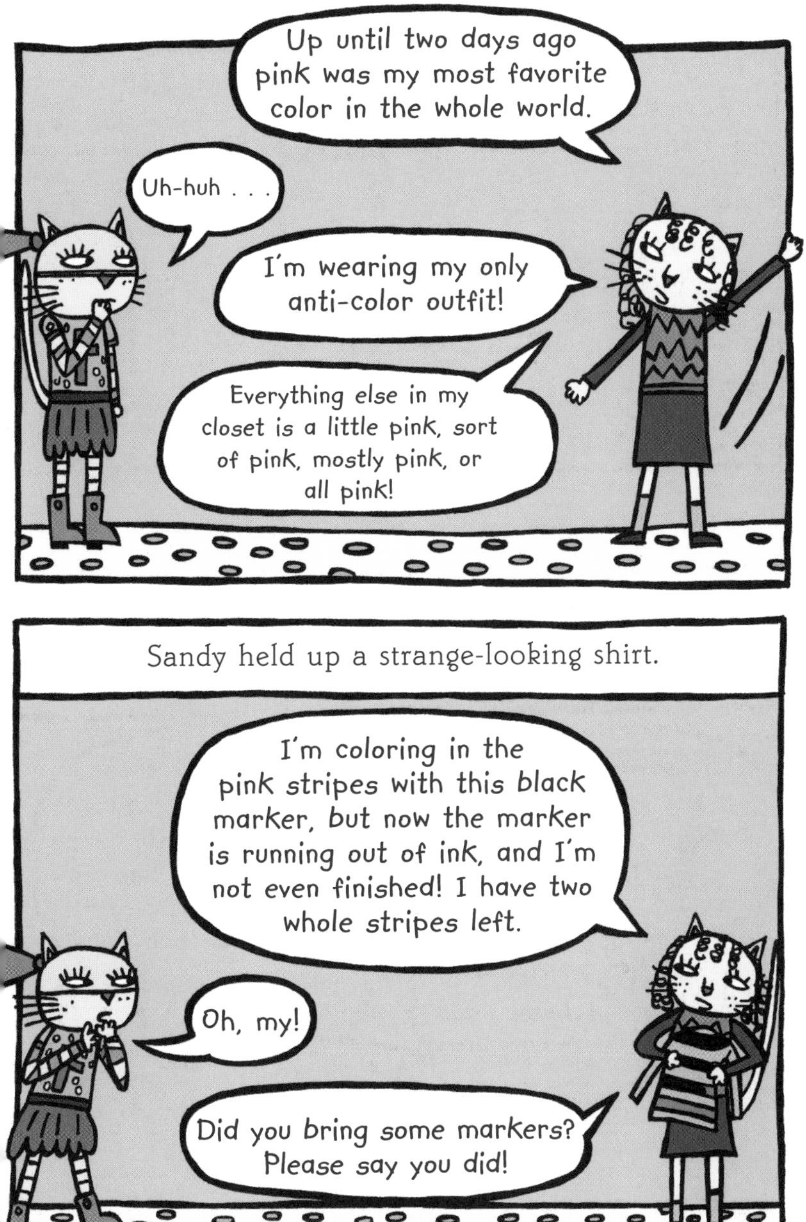
Up until two days ago pink was my most favorite color in the whole world.
Uh-huh . . .
I'm wearing my only anti-color outfit!
Everything else in my closet is a little pink, sort of pink, mostly pink, or all pink!
Sandy held up a strange-looking shirt.
I'm coloring in the pink stripes with this *black* marker, *but* now the marker is running out of ink, and I'm not even finished! I have two whole stripes left.
Oh, my!
Did you bring some markers? Please say you did!

Fashion Kitty had never met anyone who talked as much as Sandy.

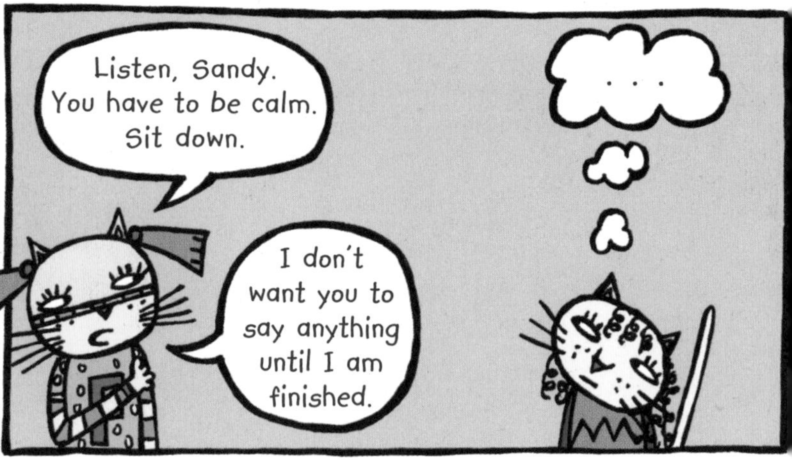
Listen, Sandy. You have to be calm. Sit down.
I don't want you to say anything until I am finished.
. . .

Fashion Kitty paused. Because a fashion hero should mostly try to be kind, even if it is not the easy thing to do.

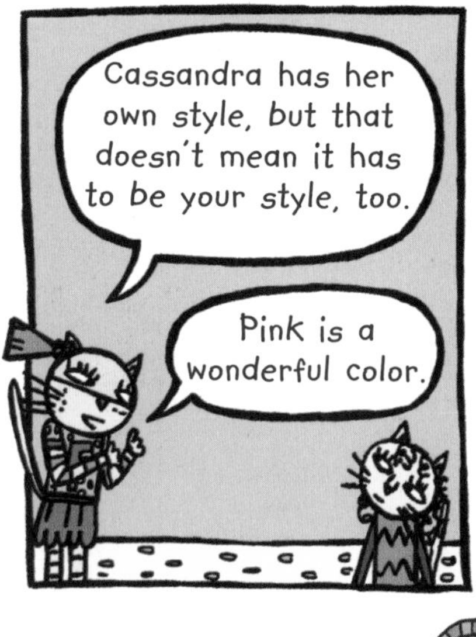
Cassandra has her own style, but that doesn't mean it has to be your style, too.
Pink is a wonderful color.

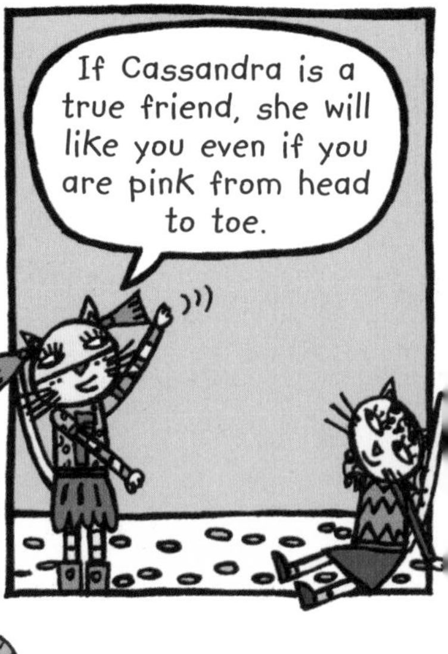
If Cassandra is a true friend, she will like you even if you are pink from head to toe.

Fashion Kitty waited, and Sandy waited, and Fashion Kitty waited, and Sandy waited.

Then Fashion Kitty remembered and said:

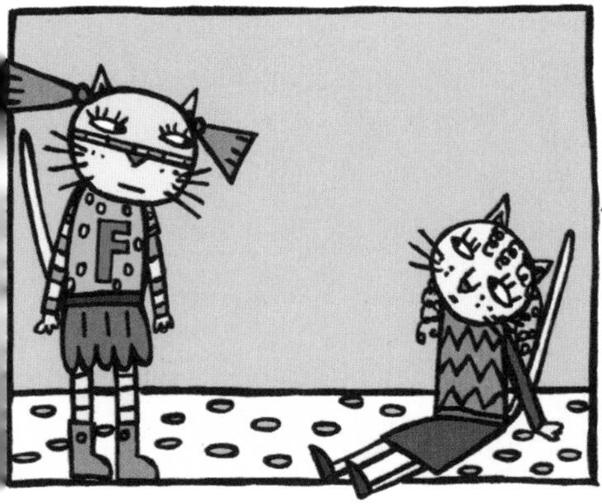

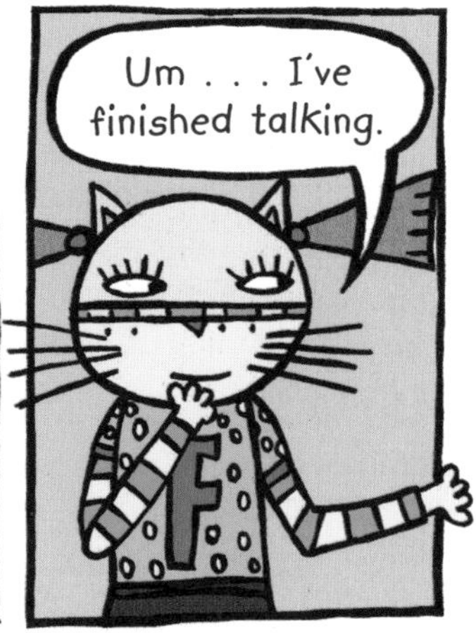
Um . . . I've finished talking.

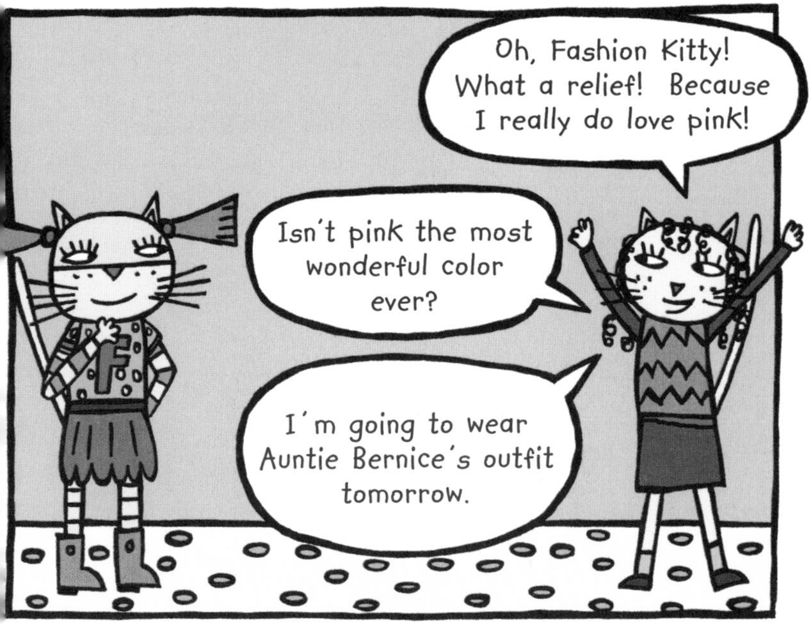
Oh, Fashion Kitty! What a relief! Because I really do love pink!
Isn't pink the most wonderful color ever?
I'm going to wear Auntie Bernice's outfit tomorrow.

Fashion Kitty thought carefully about what to say next.

Pink has always been *one* of my favorite colors, and you can tell Cassandra I said so.

Then Sandy threw her black marker out the window.

I don't need you anymore.

Luckily it landed right in a trash can, because nobody likes a litterbug, even a cute pink one.

When Kiki walked in the front door, Mother, Father, and Lana Kittie said:

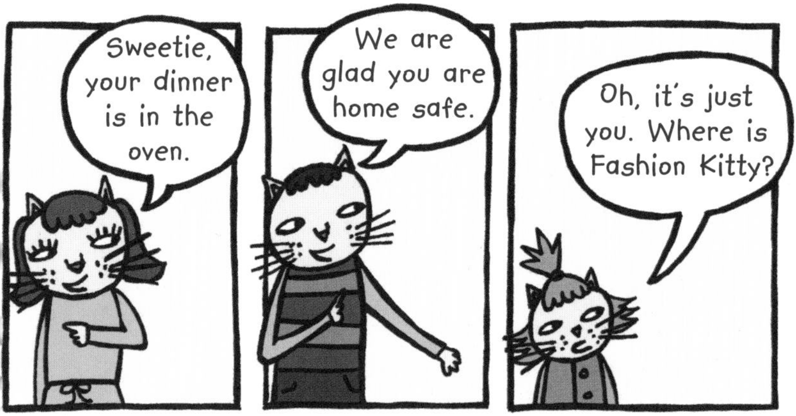
Sweetie, your dinner is in the oven.
We are glad you are home safe.
Oh, it's just you. Where is Fashion Kitty?

all at the same time.

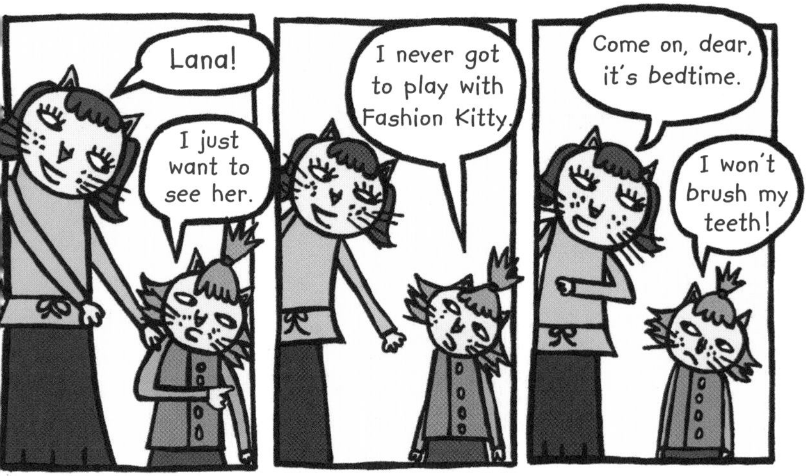
Lana!
I just want to see her.
I never got to play with Fashion Kitty.
Come on, dear, it's bedtime.
I won't brush my teeth!

iki liked to have some quiet time after a big Fashion itty adventure, so the family left her alone to eat her inner. This was hard for Lana.

After dinner, Kiki went straight to bed.
She knew three things about tomorrow.

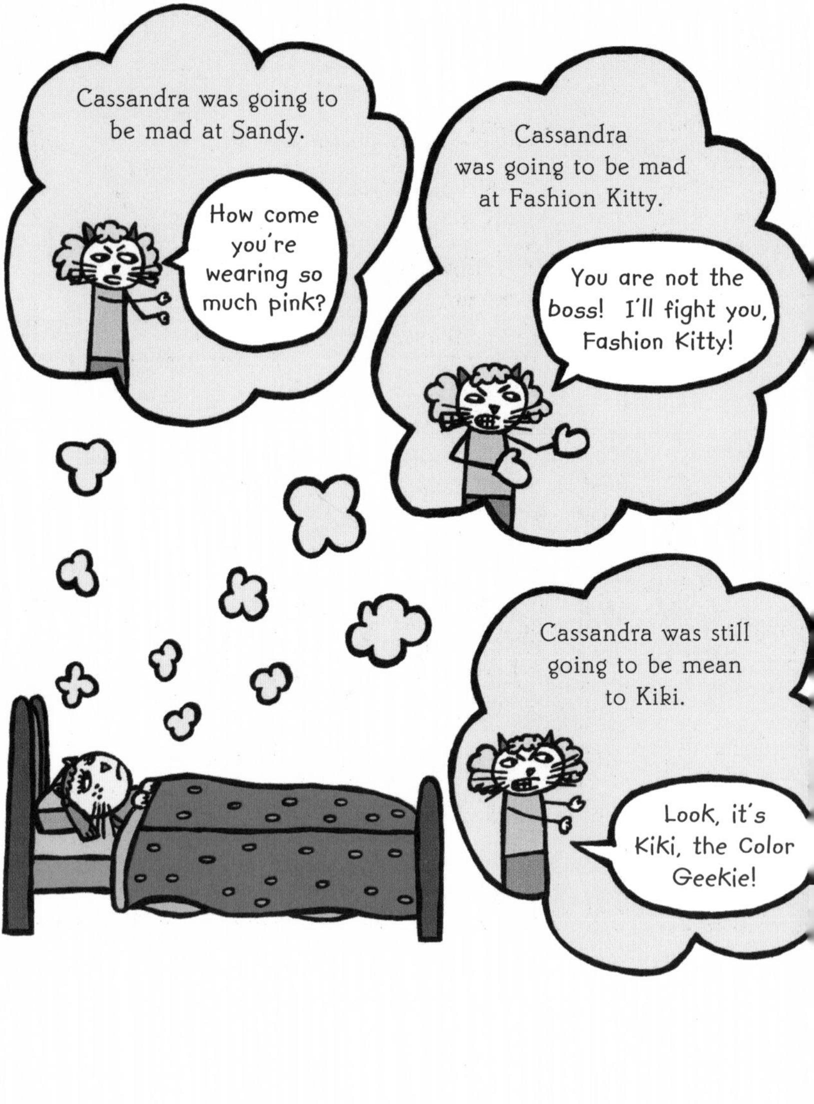

Cassandra was going to be mad at Sandy.
How come you're wearing so much pink?
Cassandra was going to be mad at Fashion Kitty.
You are not the boss! I'll fight you, Fashion Kitty!
Cassandra was still going to be mean to Kiki.
Look, it's Kiki, the Color Geekie!

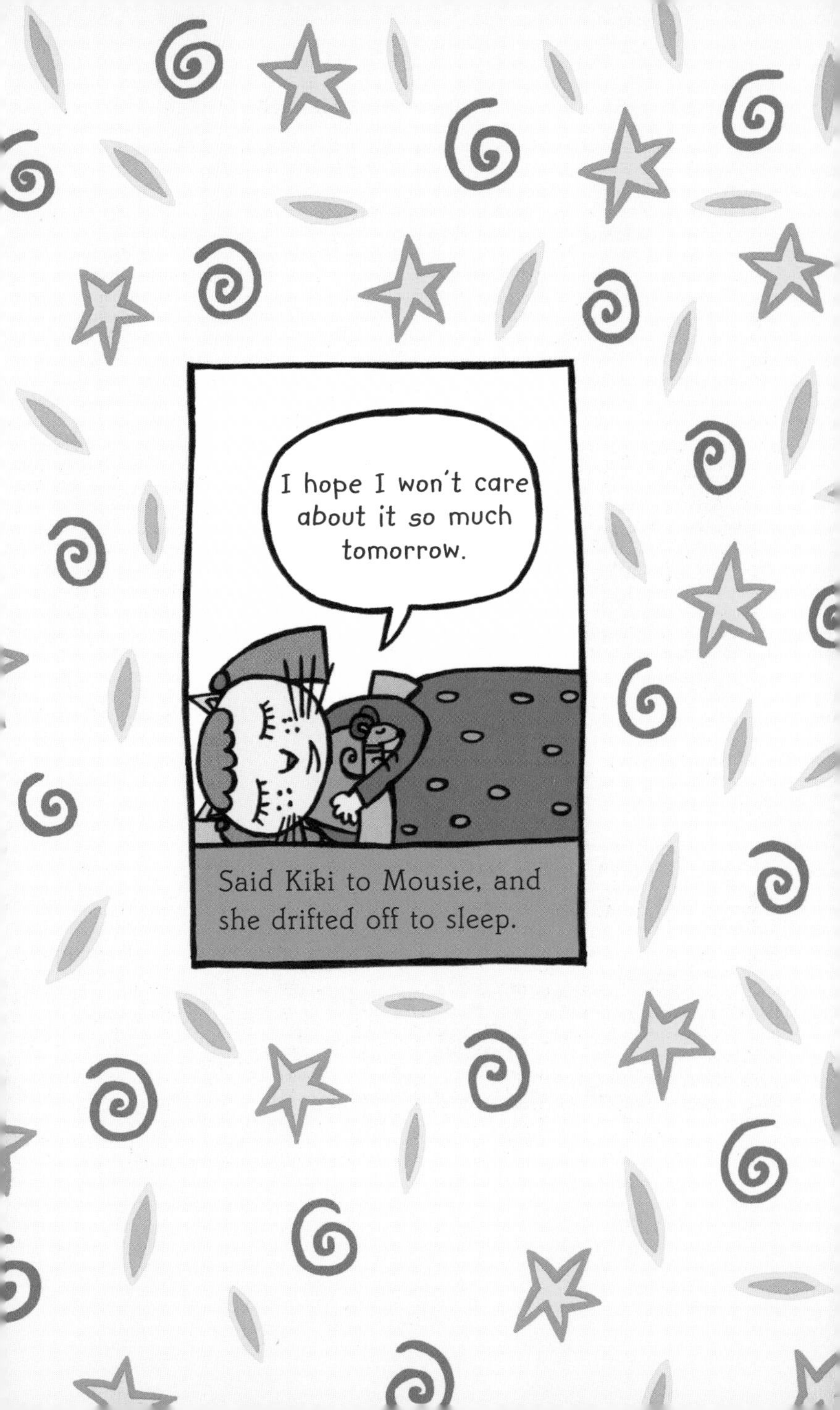
I hope I won't care about it so much tomorrow.
Said Kiki to Mousie, and she drifted off to sleep.

It's nice to be right, but somehow not that satisfying if you are right about something bad.

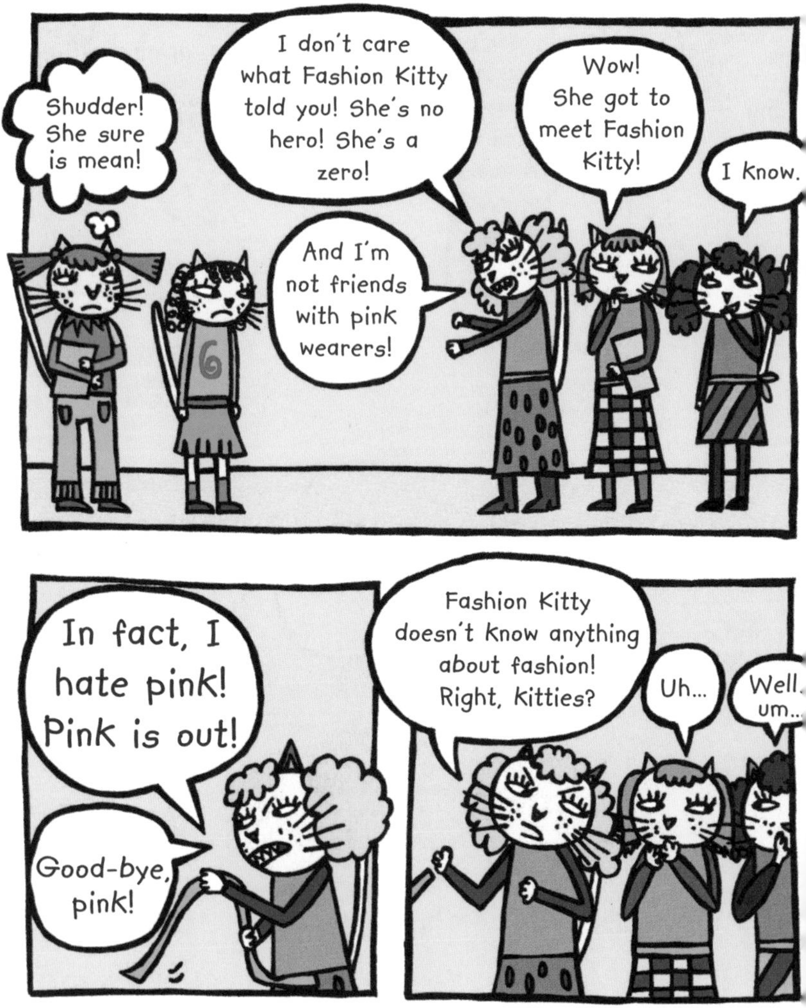
Shudder! She sure is mean!
I don't care what Fashion Kitty told you! She's no hero! She's a zero!
And I'm not friends with pink wearers!
Wow! She got to meet Fashion Kitty!
I know.
In fact, I hate pink! Pink is out!
Good-bye, pink!
Fashion Kitty doesn't know anything about fashion! Right, kitties?
Uh...
Well, um...

And then Cassandra and her mumbling kitty clones walked off.

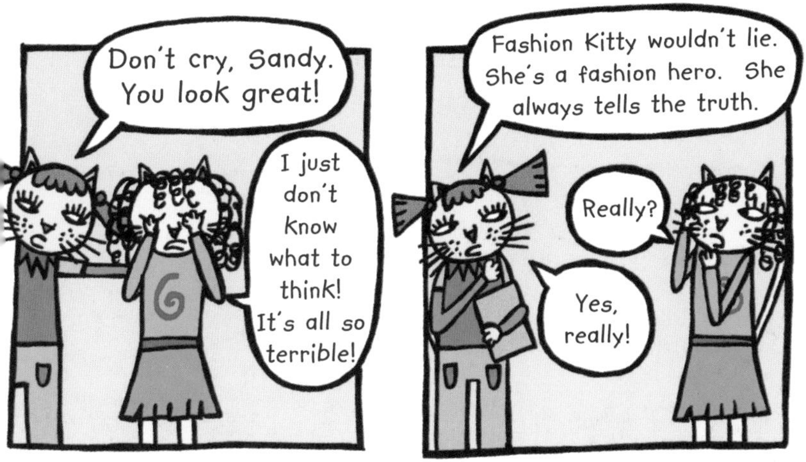
Don't cry, Sandy. You look great!
I just don't know what to think! It's all so terrible!
Fashion Kitty wouldn't lie. She's a fashion hero. She always tells the truth.
Really?
Yes, really!

But Kiki didn't feel much better, so she guessed that Sandy wasn't feeling much better, either. And she was right.

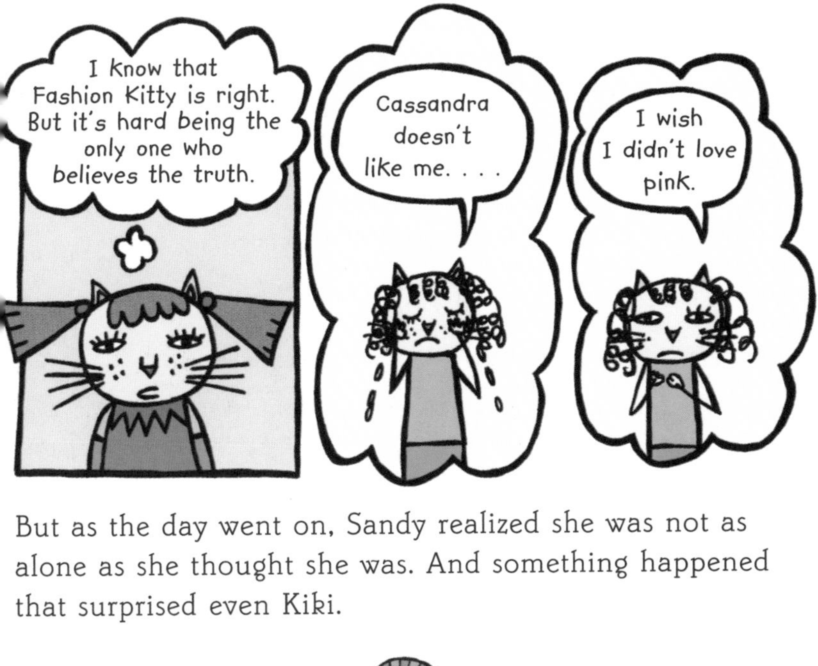
I know that Fashion Kitty is right. But it's hard being the only one who believes the truth.
Cassandra doesn't like me. . . .
I wish I didn't love pink.

But as the day went on, Sandy realized she was not as alone as she thought she was. And something happened that surprised even Kiki.

It started with some thinking,

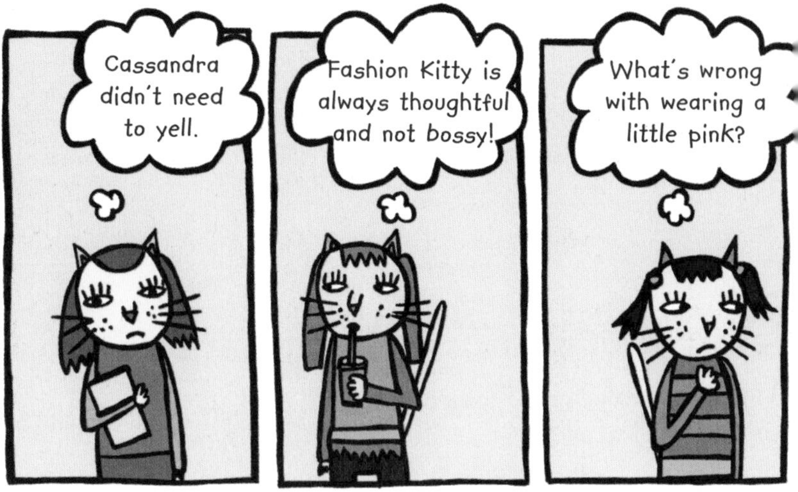

Cassandra didn't need to yell.
Fashion Kitty is always thoughtful and not bossy!
What's wrong with wearing a little pink?

and then some talking,

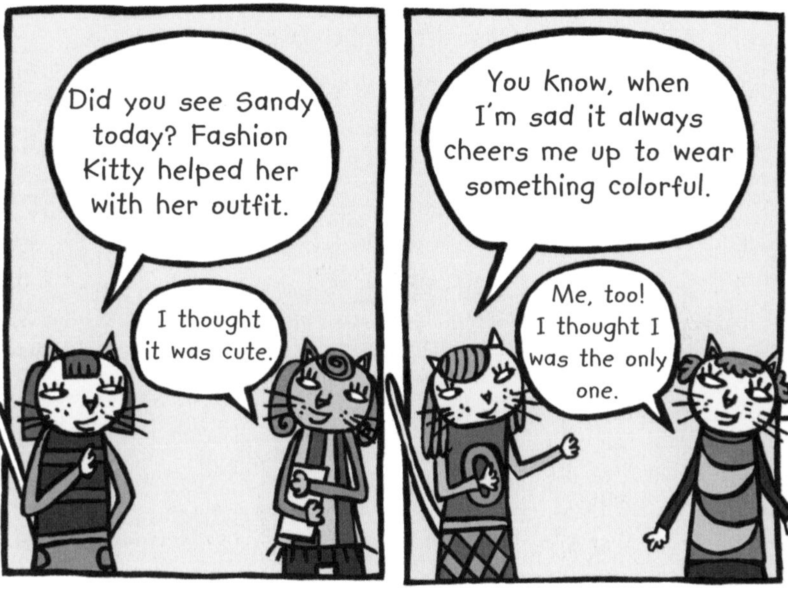

Did you see Sandy today? Fashion Kitty helped her with her outfit.
I thought it was cute.
You know, when I'm sad it always cheers me up to wear something colorful.
Me, too! I thought I was the only one.

and then some friendly support,

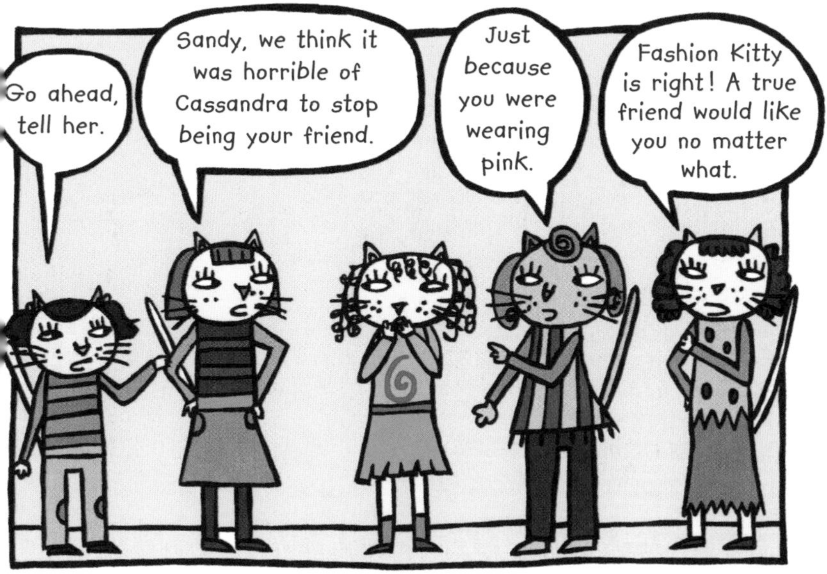
Go ahead, tell her.
Sandy, we think it was horrible of Cassandra to stop being your friend.
Just because you were wearing pink.
Fashion Kitty is right! A true friend would like you no matter what.

and finally some doing.

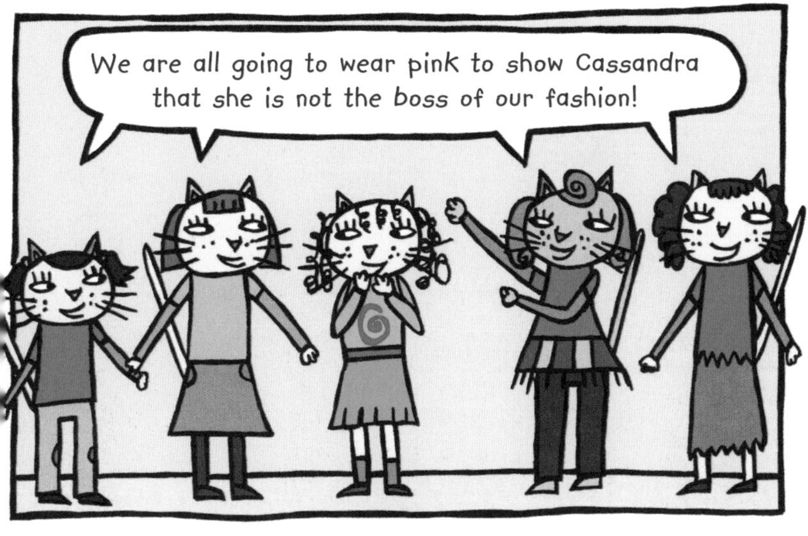
We are all going to wear pink to show Cassandra that she is not the *boss* of our fashion!

It was a movement in pink.

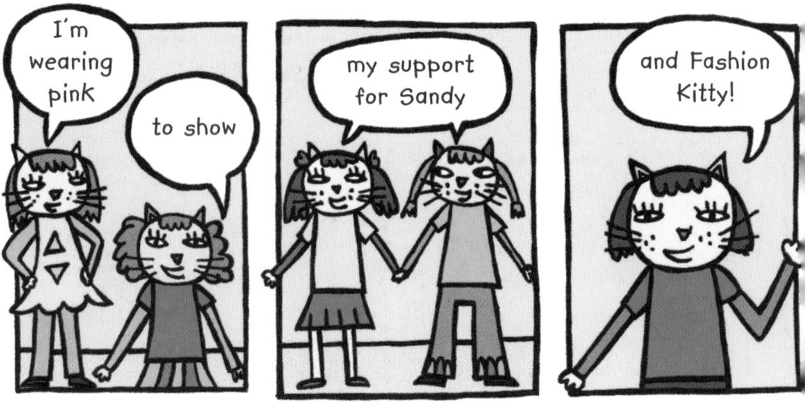
I'm wearing pink
to show
my support for Sandy
and Fashion Kitty!

Almost everyone joined in, even some of the boys.

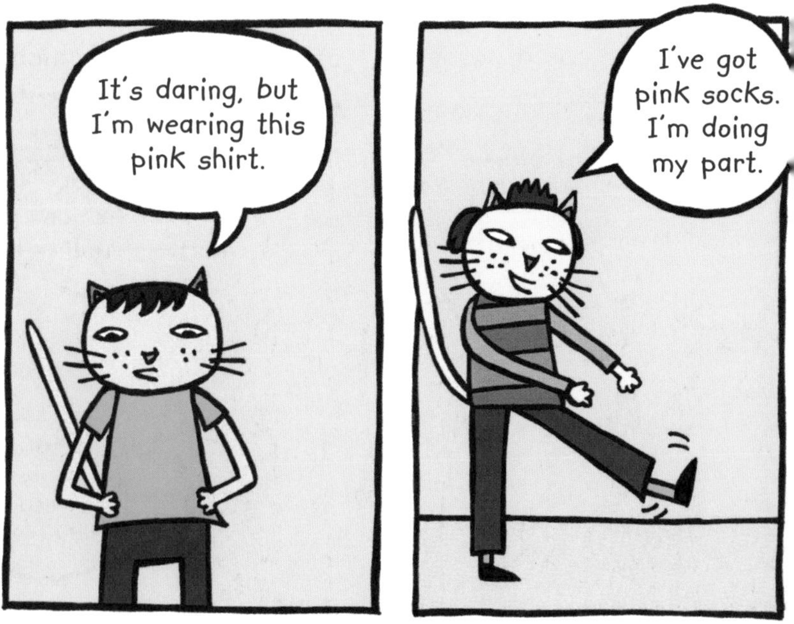
It's daring, but I'm wearing this pink shirt.
I've got pink socks. I'm doing my part.

Kiki could not believe it.

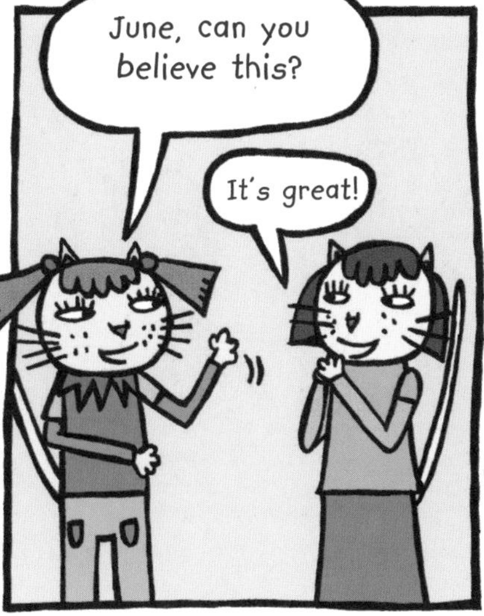
June, can you believe this?
It's great!

She was overjoyed, which means, happy, happy, happy!

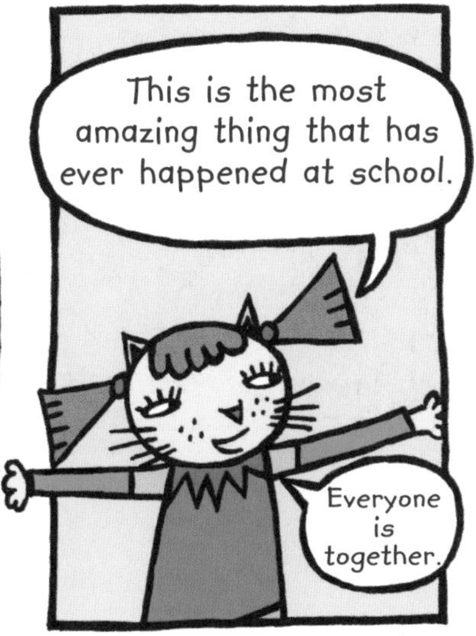
This is the most amazing thing that has ever happened at school.
Everyone is together.

Cassandra could not believe it, either.

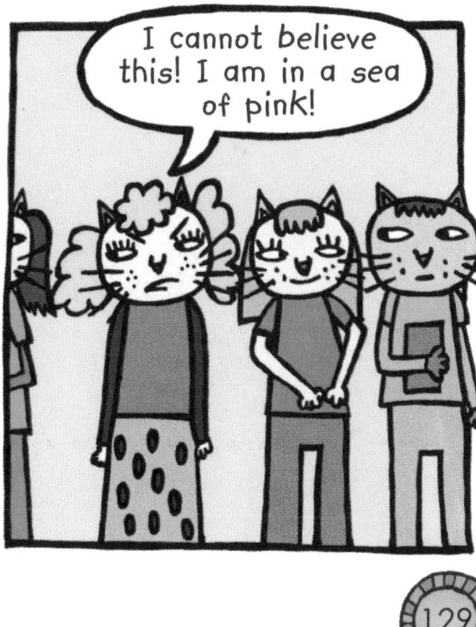
I cannot *believe* this! I am in a *sea* of pink!

She was incensed, which means, mad, mad, mad!

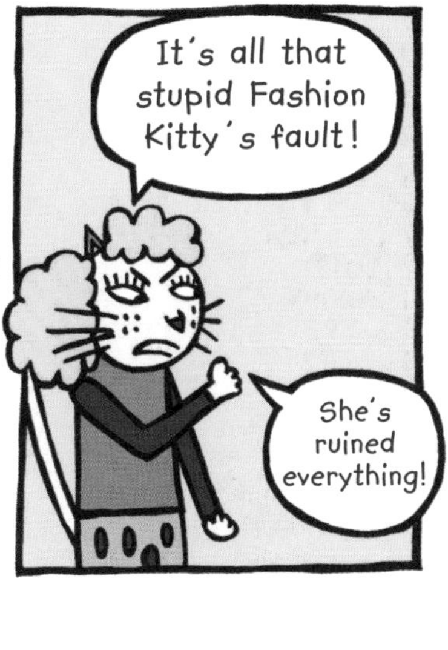
It's all that stupid Fashion Kitty's fault!
She's ruined everything!

When you have the fashion popularity spotlight all to yourself,

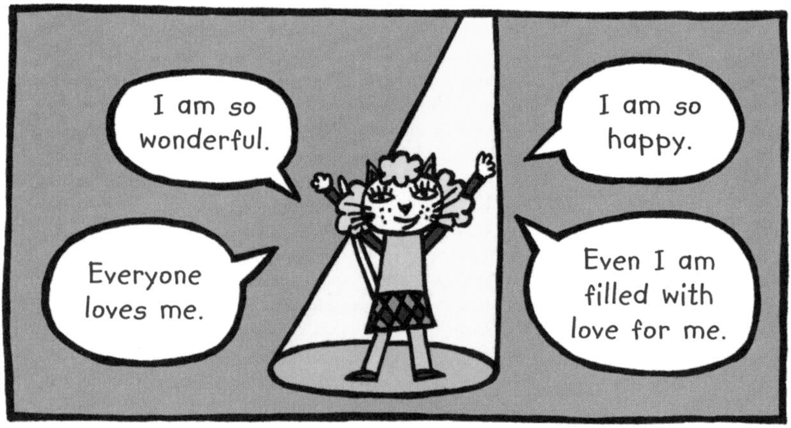

I am so wonderful.
Everyone loves me.
I am so happy.
Even I am filled with love for me.

it's not easy to give it up,

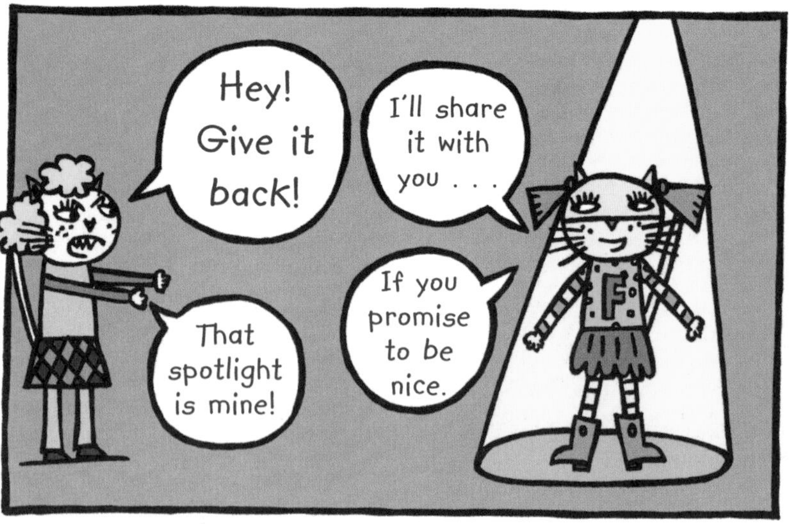

Hey! Give it back!
That spotlight is mine!
I'll share it with you . . .
If you promise to be nice.

even if you don't deserve it anymore.

For days it seemed like all everyone could talk about was Fashion Kitty . . .

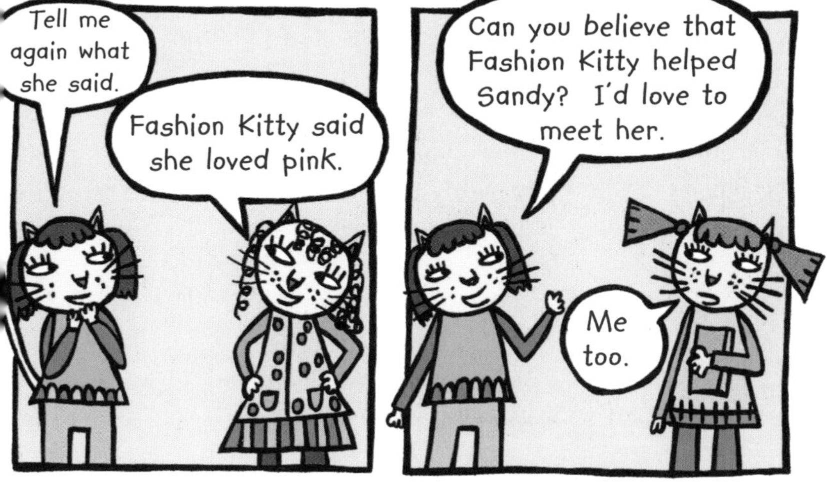
Tell me again what she said.
Fashion Kitty said she loved pink.
Can you believe that Fashion Kitty helped Sandy? I'd love to meet her.
Me too.

Fashion Kitty, and more Fashion Kitty.

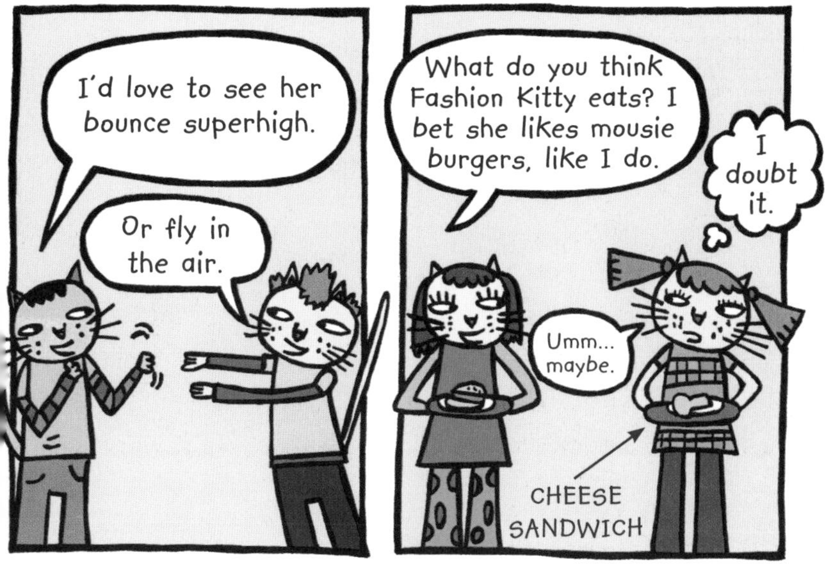
I'd love to see her bounce superhigh.
Or fly in the air.
What do you think Fashion Kitty eats? I bet she likes mousie burgers, like I do.
I doubt it.
Umm... maybe.
CHEESE SANDWICH

Even Kiki was getting a little tired of it.

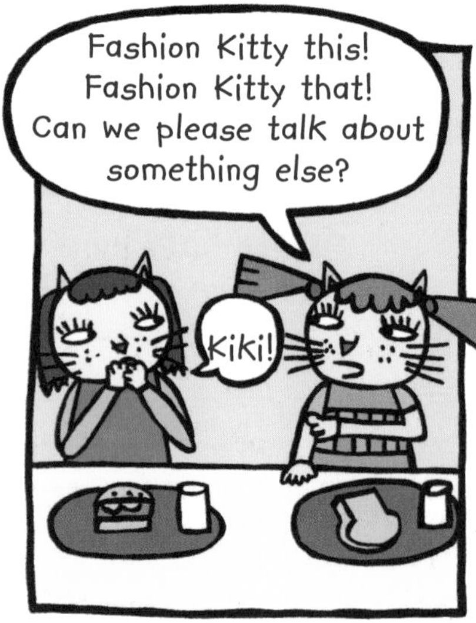
Fashion Kitty this!
Fashion Kitty that!
Can we please talk about
something else?
Kiki!

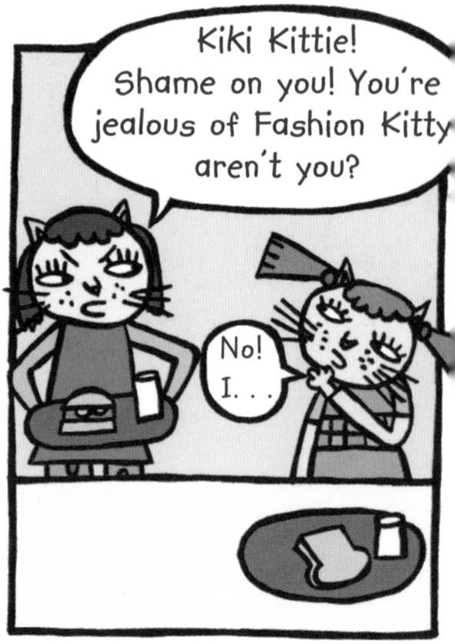
Kiki Kittie!
Shame on you! You're
jealous of Fashion Kitty
aren't you?
No!
I. . .

It's not easy to keep two big secrets from your best kitty friend in the whole world.

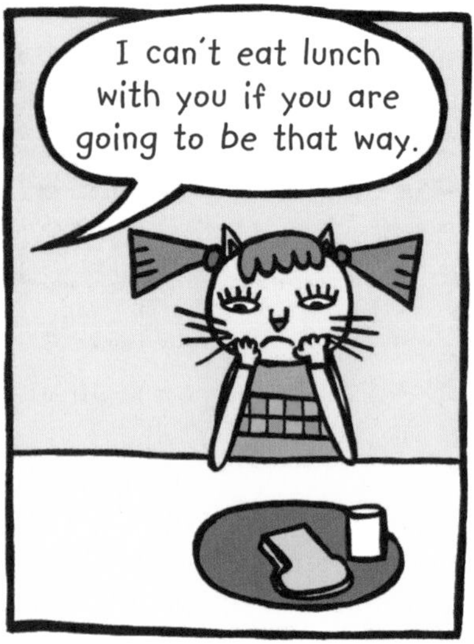
I can't eat lunch
with you if you are
going to be that way.

Kiki tried not to think about Mousie or Fashion Kitty

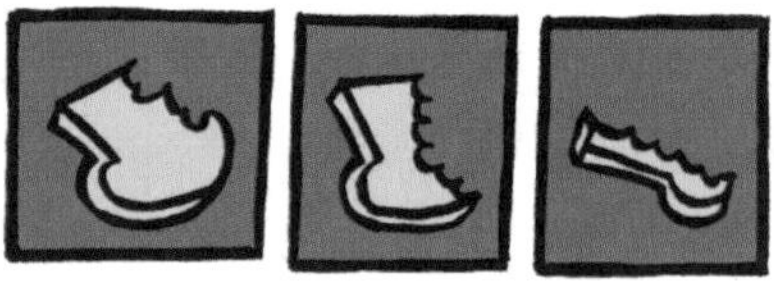

as she ate her lunch.

Not far away, someone else was wishing she didn't have to think about Fashion Kitty, either.

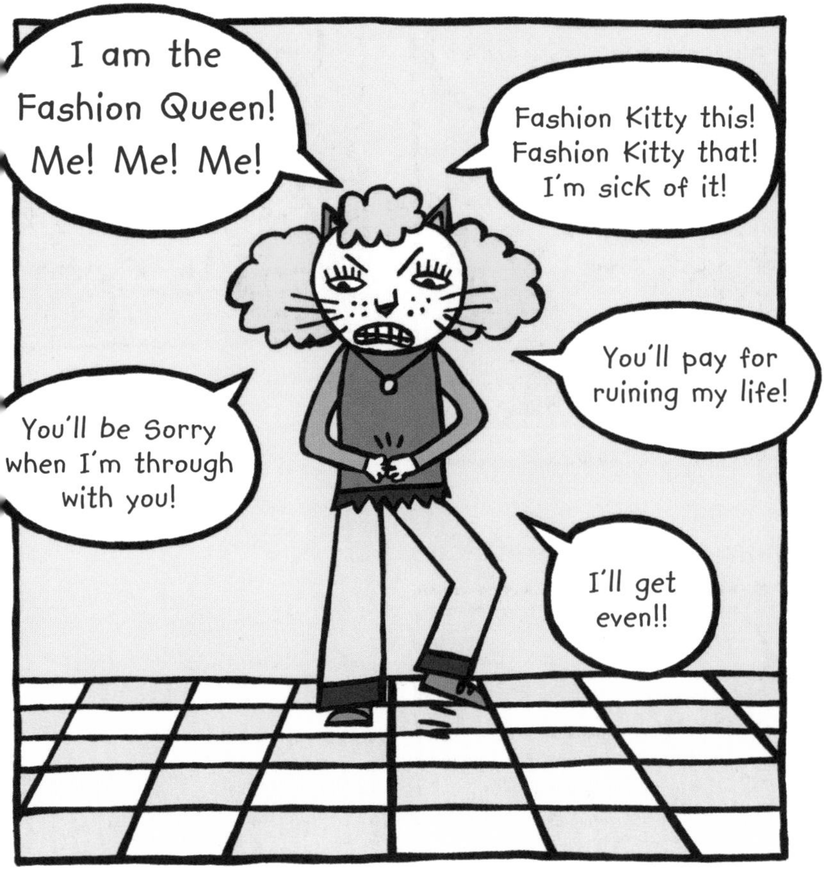
I am the Fashion Queen! Me! Me! Me!
Fashion Kitty this! Fashion Kitty that! I'm sick of it!
You'll be Sorry when I'm through with you!
You'll pay for ruining my life!
I'll get even!!

And that someone was stamping her foot on the ground,

because that was what she did when

she was really

mad.

Cassandra imagined all the ways she could make Fashion Kitty look silly, and all the things she wished she could hear Fashion Kitty say. These imaginings made her smile a very wicked smile.

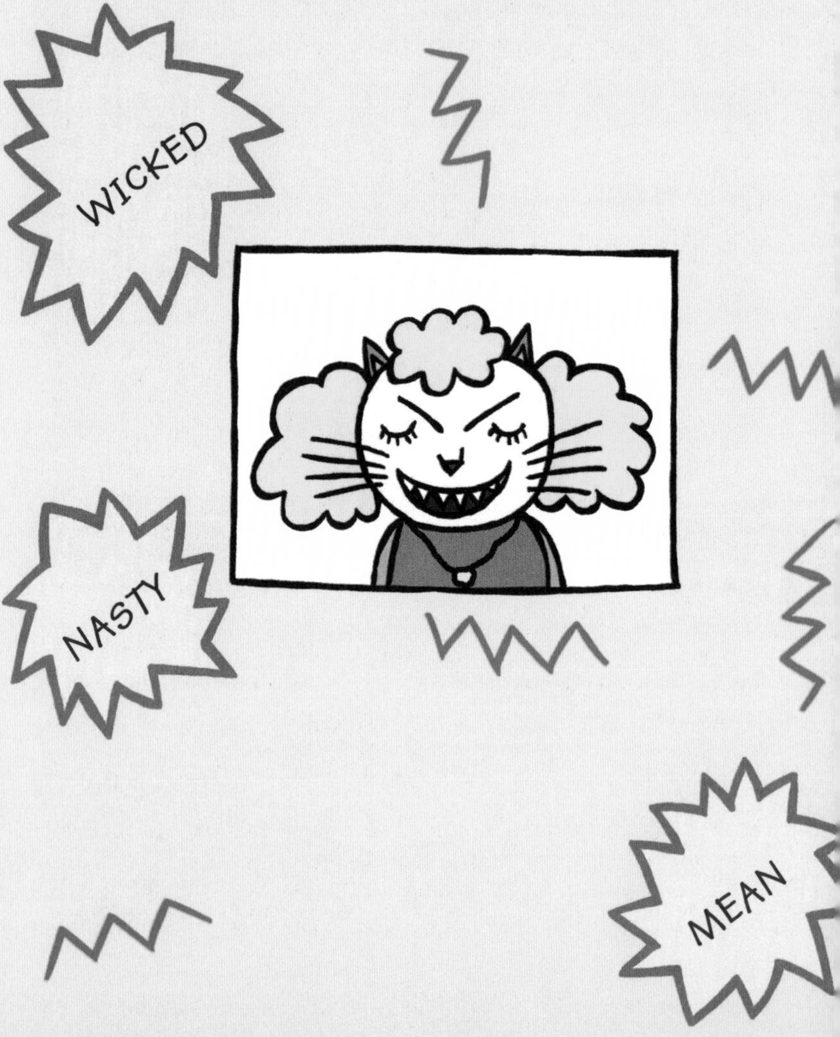
WICKED
NASTY
MEAN

She didn't know that Fashion Kitty (MOKA* Kiki Kittie) was already suffering, but not quite in the way Cassandra had imagined.

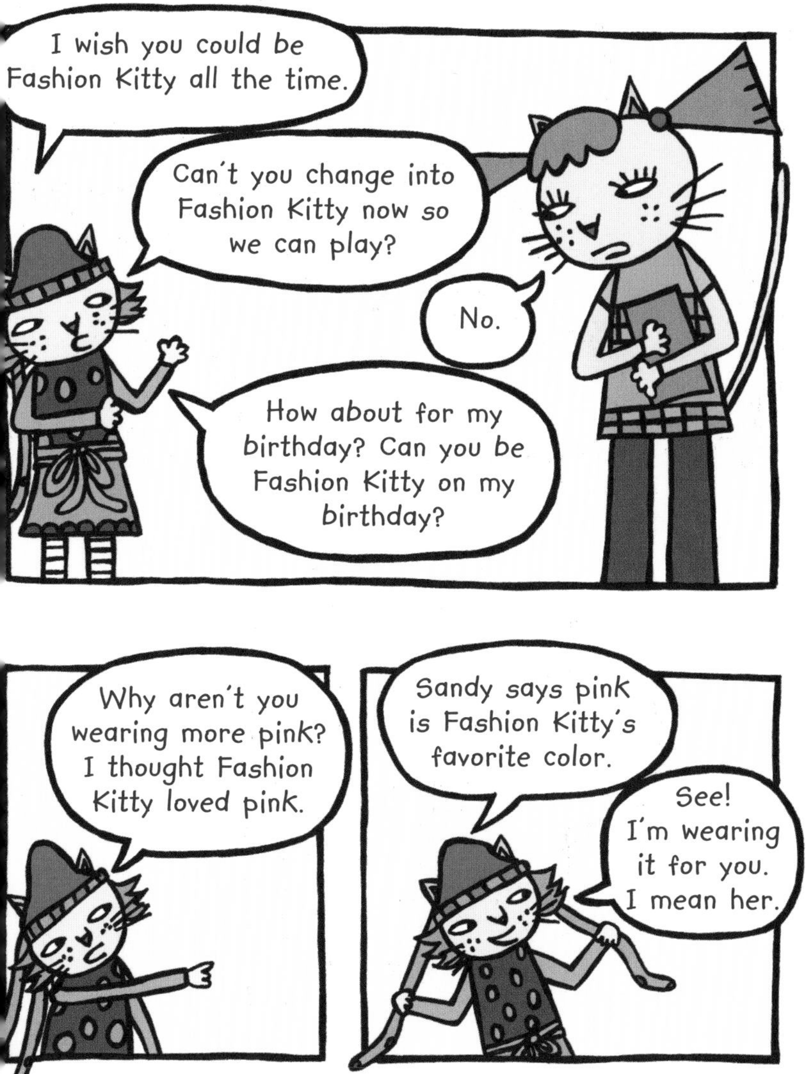
I wish you could be Fashion Kitty all the time.
Can't you change into Fashion Kitty now so we can play?
No.
How about for my birthday? Can you be Fashion Kitty on my birthday?
Why aren't you wearing more pink? I thought Fashion Kitty loved pink.
Sandy says pink is Fashion Kitty's favorite color.
See! I'm wearing it for you. I mean her.

*MOKA (most often known as)

This was almost too much Fashion Kitty, even for Kiki.

Fashion Kitty told Sandy that pink was *one* of her favorite colors! Not her *only* favorite color.

She likes other colors, too!

See! Fashion Kitty wouldn't yell at me like you do! That's why I like her.

Unfortunately, it did not end well.

Don't bother me!

KIKI's ROOM

SLAM

Kiki just couldn't help it.

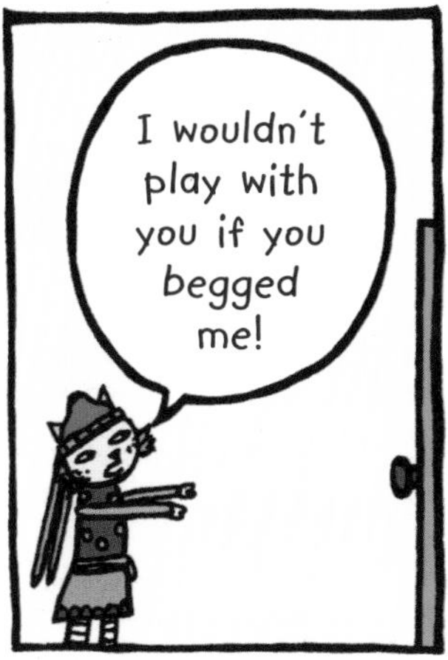
I wouldn't play with you if you begged me!

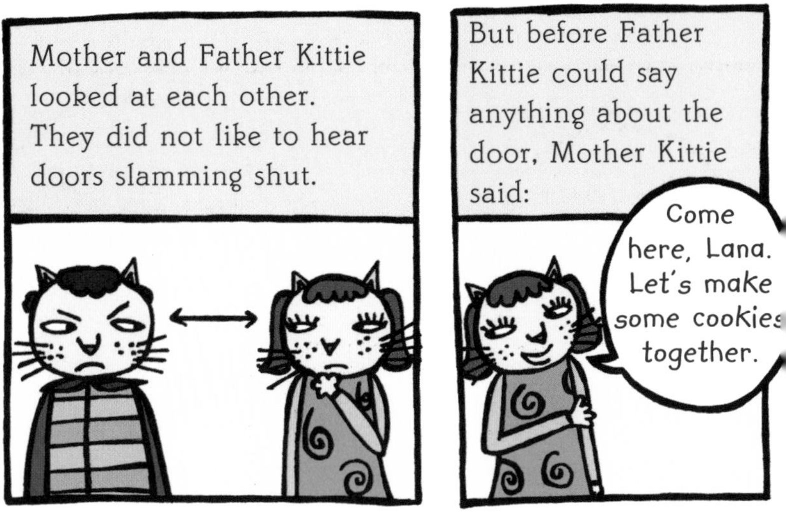
Mother and Father Kittie looked at each other. They did not like to hear doors slamming shut.
But before Father Kittie could say anything about the door, Mother Kittie said:
Come here, Lana. Let's make some cookies together.

Sometimes mothers know the exact right thing to say and when to say it.

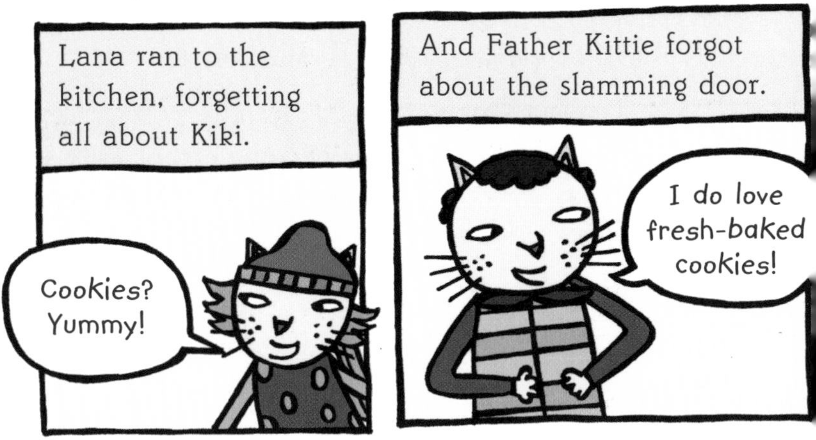
Lana ran to the kitchen, forgetting all about Kiki.
Cookies? Yummy!
And Father Kittie forgot about the slamming door.
I do love fresh-baked cookies!

Mother Kittie could tell that Kiki was having a hard tim being a fashion hero, and it would not make things one bit better if she got in trouble for slamming her door.

Across town, Cassandra was up to no good.

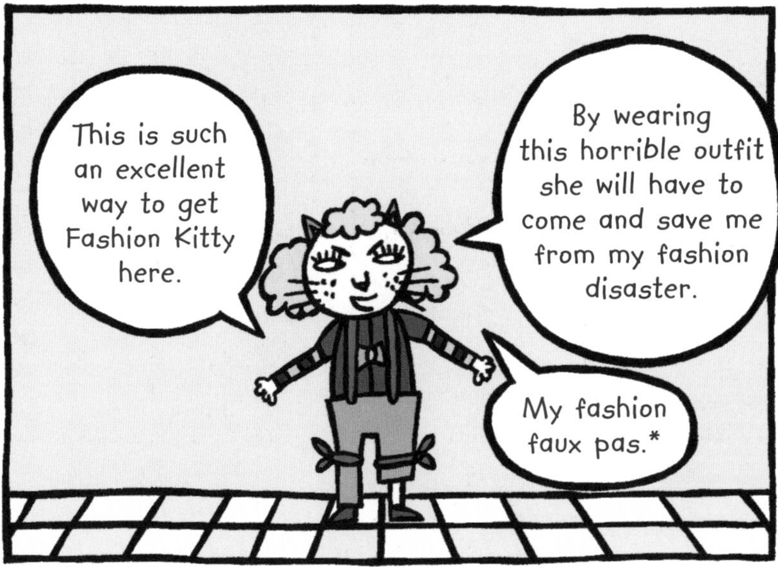
This is such an excellent way to get Fashion Kitty here.
By wearing this horrible outfit she will have to come and save me from my fashion disaster.
My fashion faux pas.*

Cassandra waited, waited, and waited,

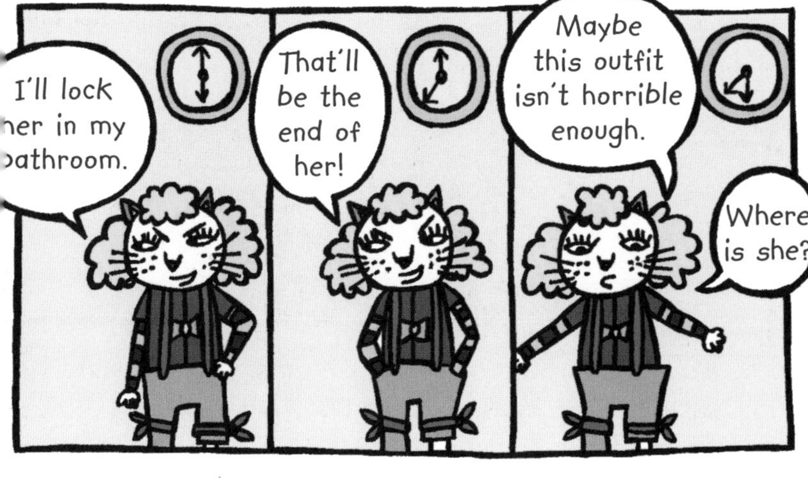
I'll lock
ner in my
bathroom.
That'll be the end of her!
Maybe this outfit isn't horrible enough.
Where is she?

*mistake

but still no Fashion Kitty.

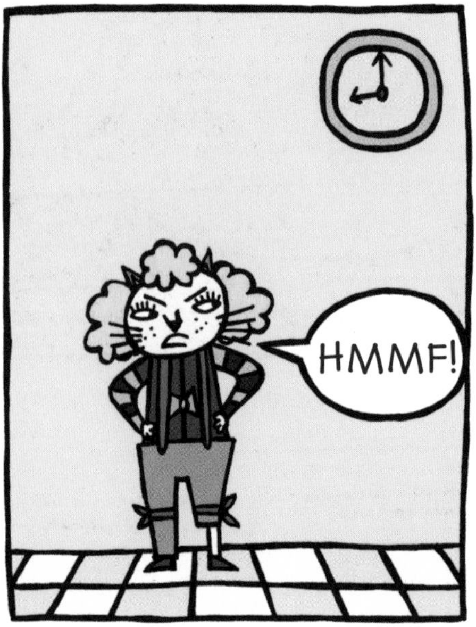
HMMF!

She didn't know that Fashion Kitty could only respond to real fashion emergencies, and not a fake fashion faux pas.

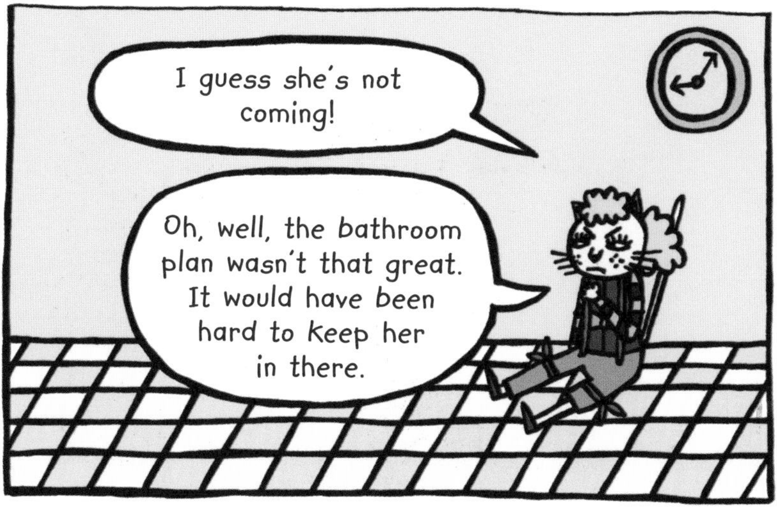
I guess she's not coming!
Oh, well, the bathroom plan wasn't that great. It would have been hard to keep her in there.

That night two very different kitties went to sleep with smiles on their lips.

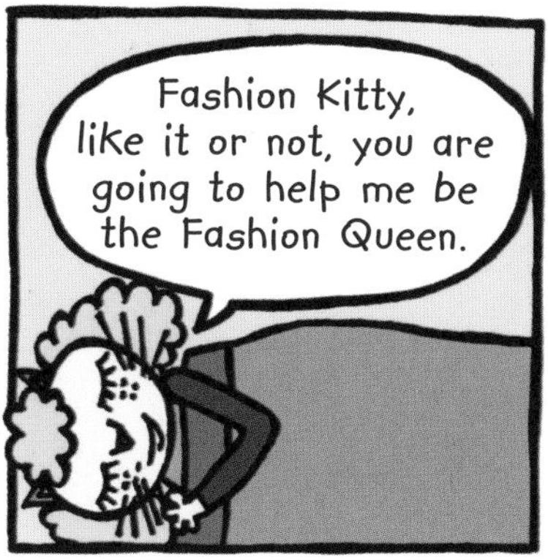
Fashion Kitty, like it or not, you are going to help me be the Fashion Queen.

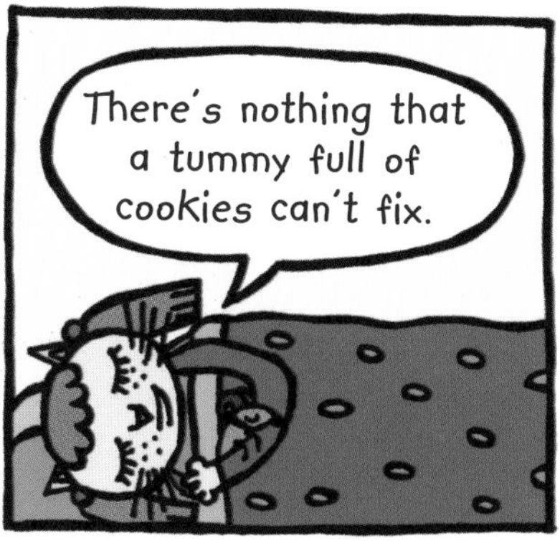
There's nothing that a tummy full of cookies can't fix.

One kitty was right, and the other kitty was wrong. Very wrong!

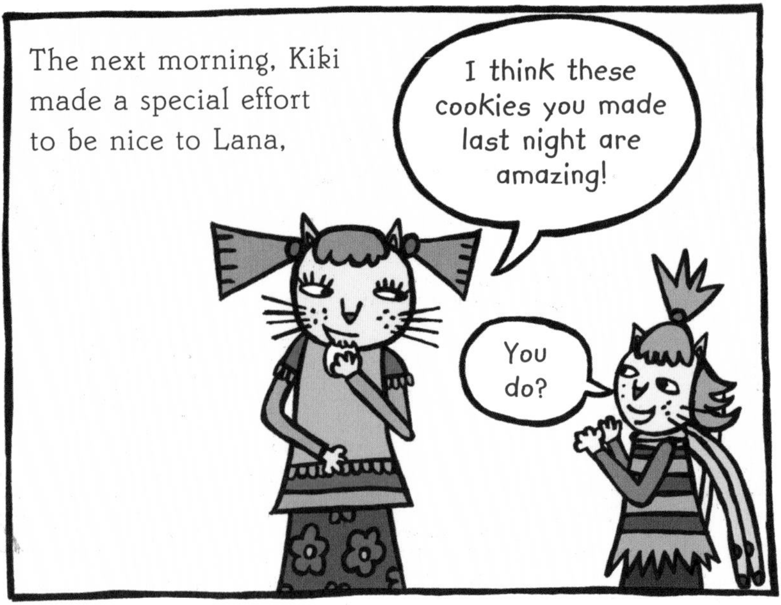
The next morning, Kiki made a special effort to be nice to Lana,
I think these cookies you made last night are amazing!
You do?

and on the way to school she made a promise to herself.

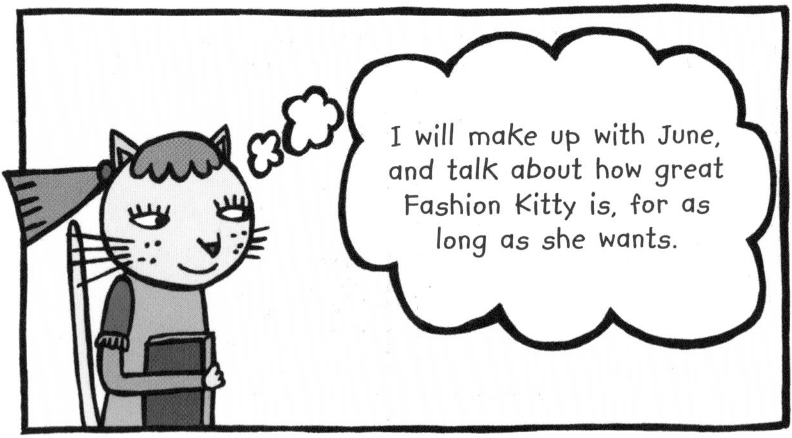
I will make up with June, and talk about how great Fashion Kitty is, for as long as she wants.

She felt very good.

Very good until . . .

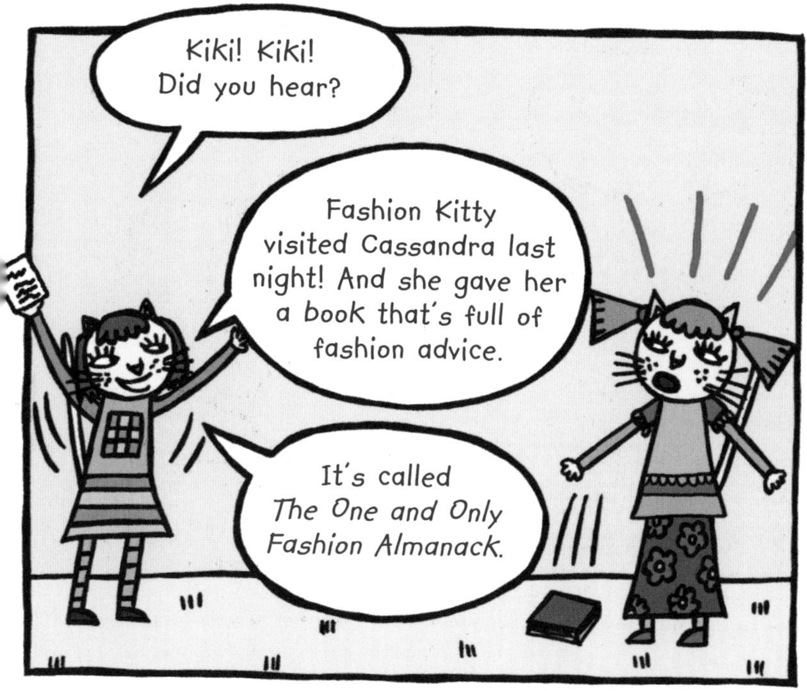

Kiki! Kiki! Did you hear?
Fashion Kitty visited Cassandra last night! And she gave her a *book* that's full of fashion advice.
It's called *The One and Only Fashion Almanack.*

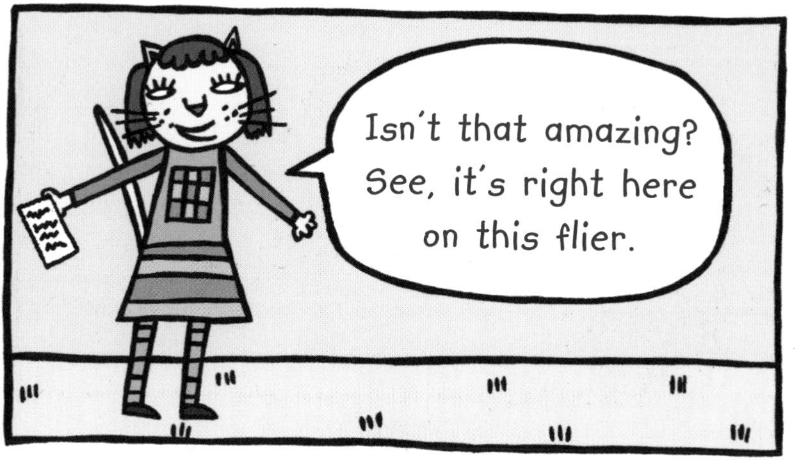

Isn't that amazing? See, it's right here on this flier.

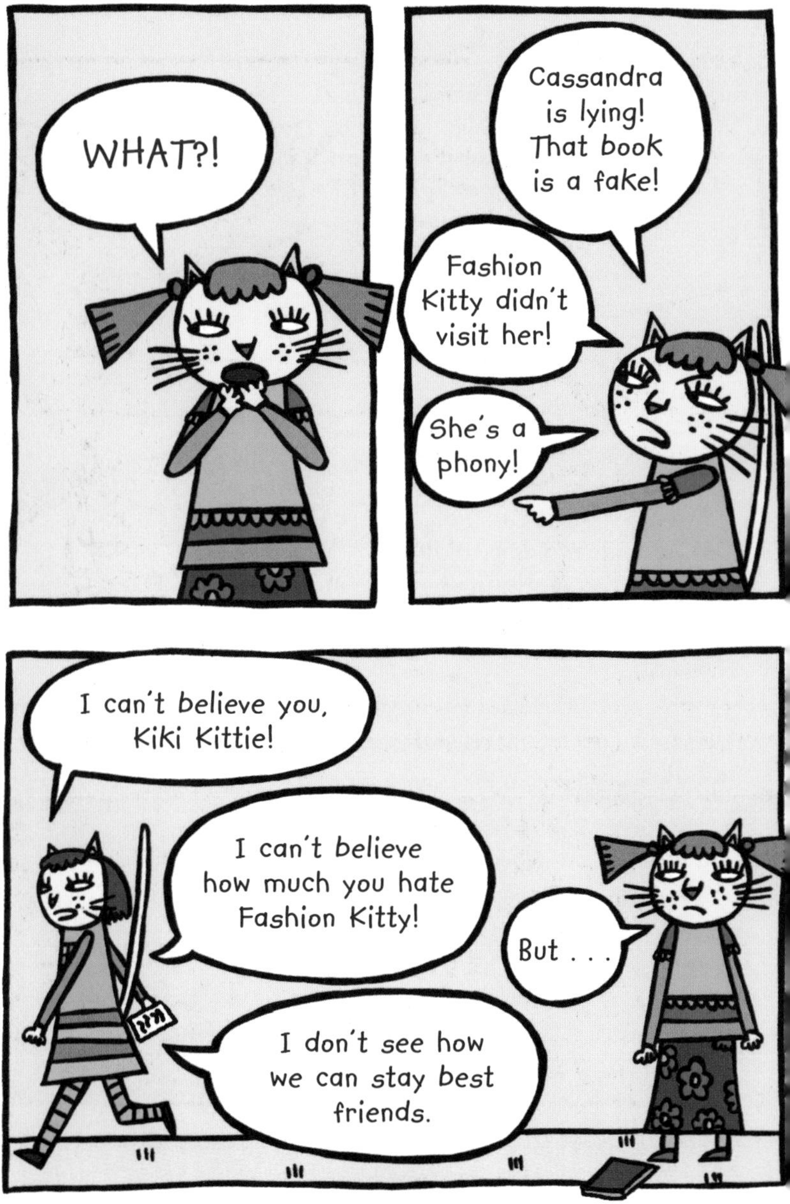
WHAT?!
Cassandra is lying! That book is a fake!
Fashion Kitty didn't visit her!
She's a phony!
I can't believe you, Kiki Kittie!
I can't believe how much you hate Fashion Kitty!
But . . .
I don't see how we can stay best friends.

"But" was a big word for Kiki that day.

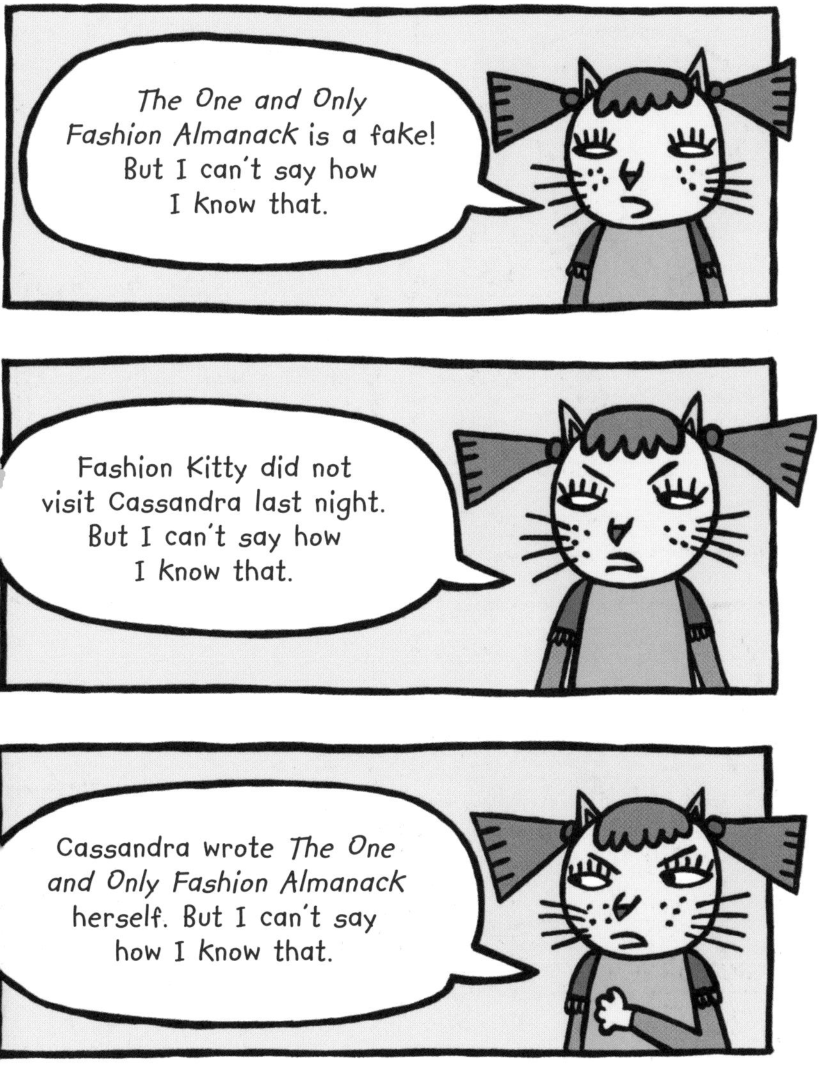
The One and Only Fashion Almanack is a fake! But I can't say how I know that.
Fashion Kitty did not visit Cassandra last night. But I can't say how I know that.
Cassandra wrote *The One and Only Fashion Almanack* herself. But I can't say how I know that.

By the end of the day she felt very angry.

On the way home from school, Kiki thought about all the things that bothered her.

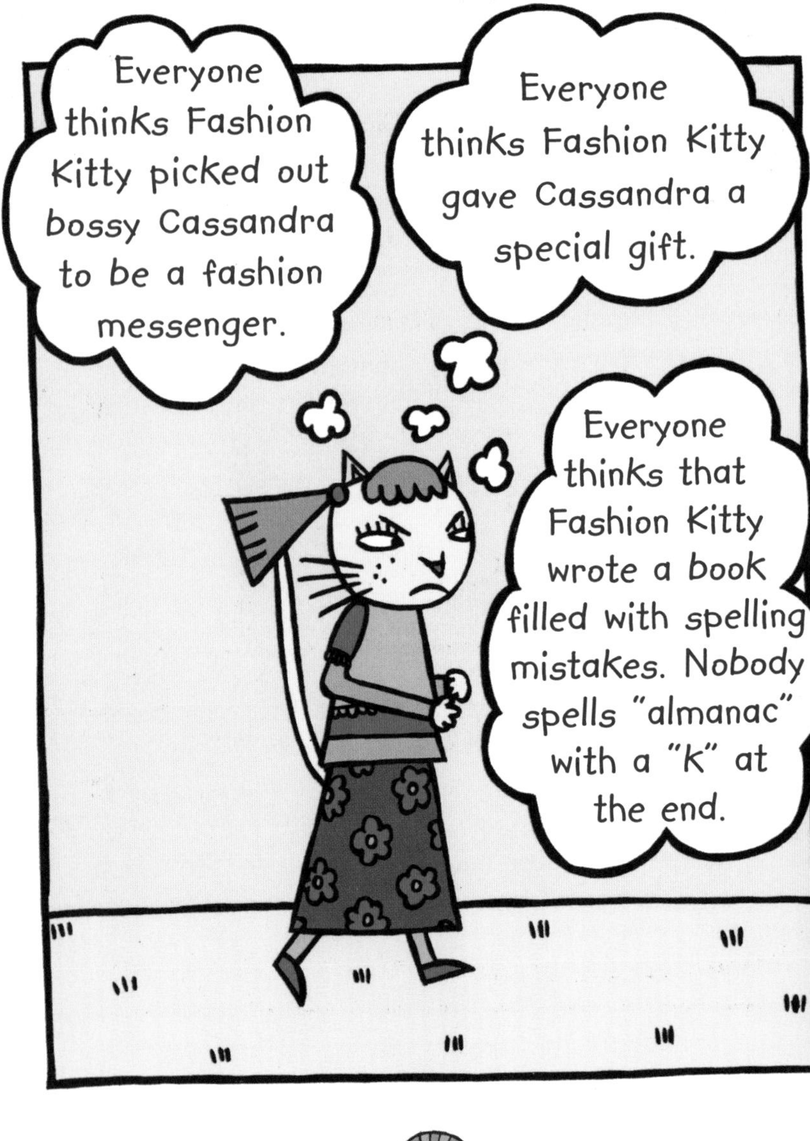

Everyone thinks Fashion Kitty picked out bossy Cassandra to be a fashion messenger.
Everyone thinks Fashion Kitty gave Cassandra a special gift.
Everyone thinks that Fashion Kitty wrote a book filled with spelling mistakes. Nobody spells "almanac" with a "K" at the end.

But the thing that bothered her the most was:

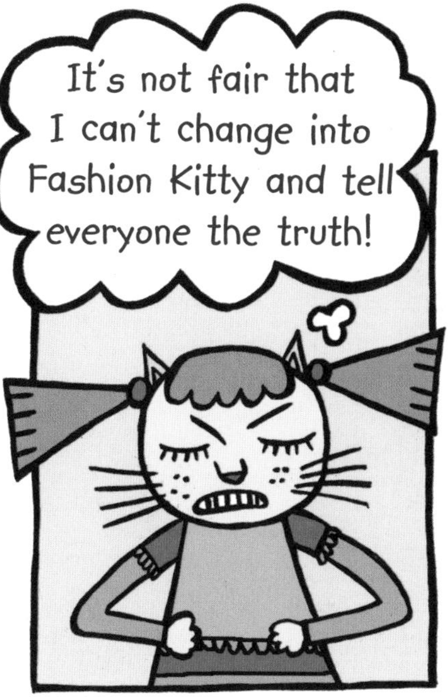
It's not fair that I can't change into Fashion Kitty and tell everyone the truth!

And really, if you thought about it, she was right. It wasn't fair at all.

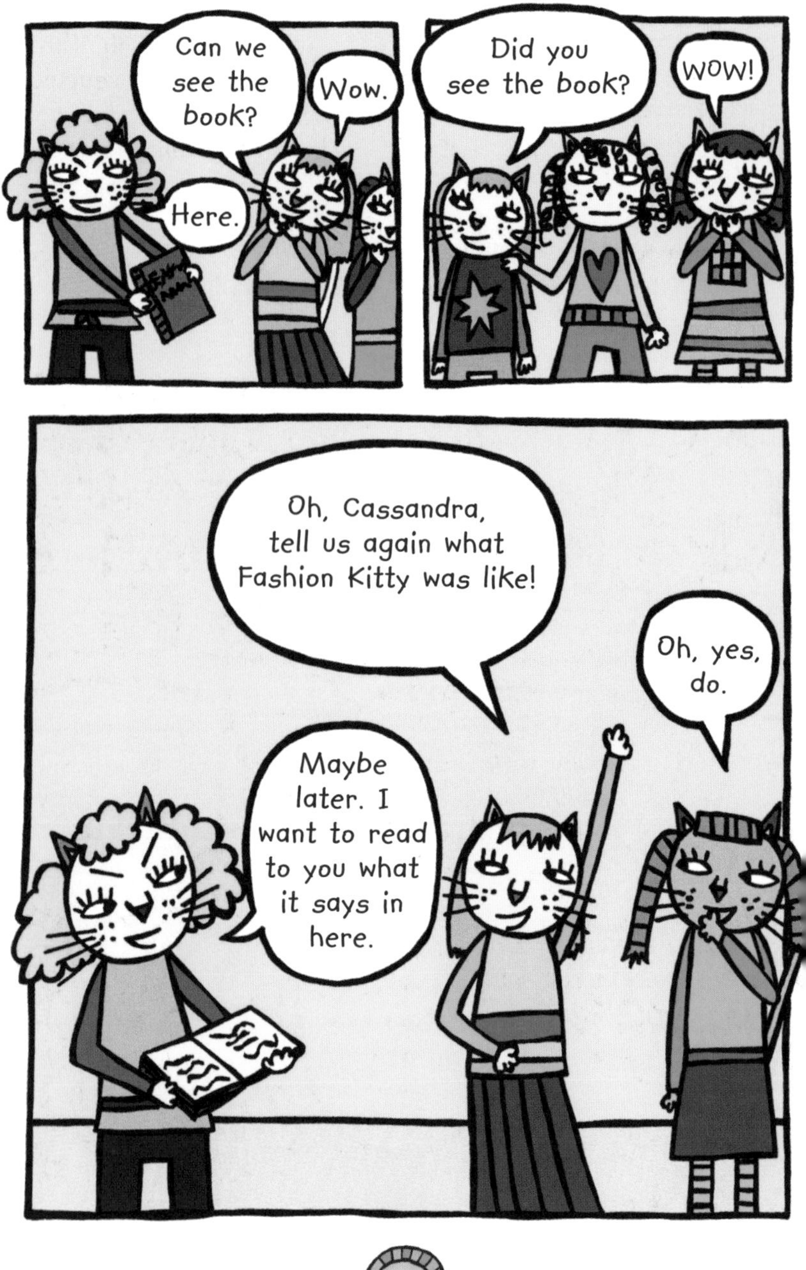
Can we see the book?
Here.
Wow.
Did you see the book?
WOW!
Oh, Cassandra, tell us again what Fashion Kitty was like!
Oh, yes, do.
Maybe later. I want to read to you what it says in here.

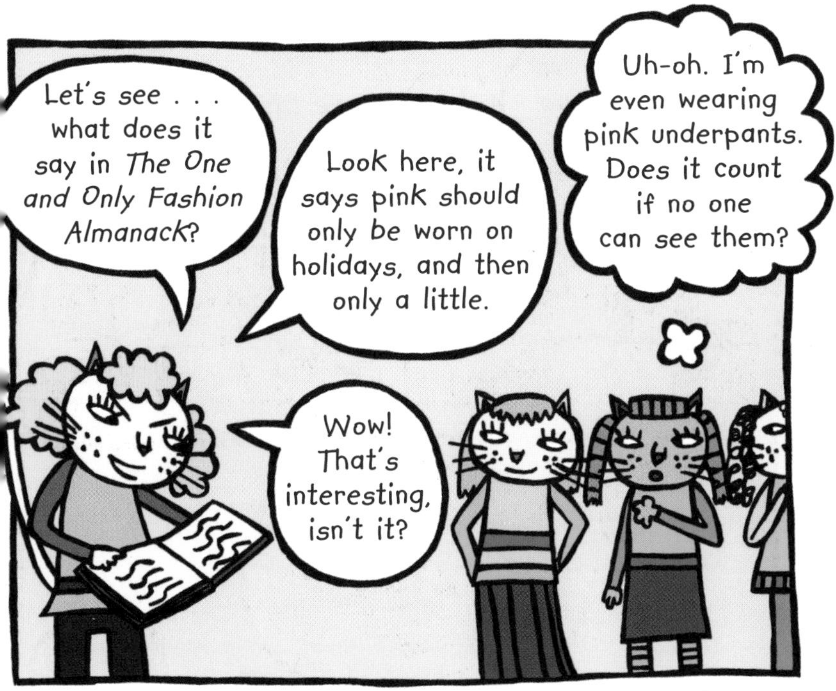
Let's see . . . what does it say in *The One and Only Fashion Almanack*?
Look here, it says pink should only be worn on holidays, and then only a little.
Uh-oh. I'm even wearing pink underpants. Does it count if no one can see them?
Wow! That's interesting, isn't it?

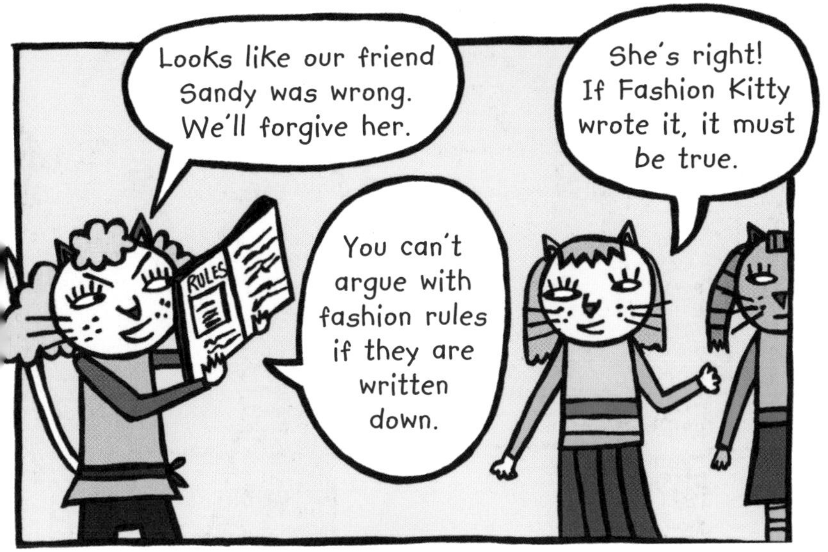
Looks like our friend Sandy was wrong. We'll forgive her.
She's right! If Fashion Kitty wrote it, it must be true.
You can't argue with fashion rules if they are written down.
RULES

Cassandra was so happy she skipped all the way home.

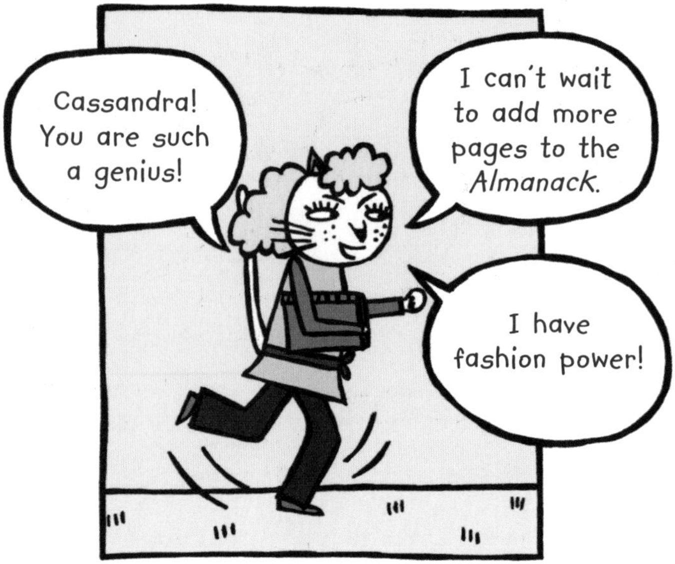
Cassandra! You are such a genius!
I can't wait to add more pages to the *Almanack*.
I have fashion power!

And though she didn't look any different, Cassandra certainly seemed to be the Fashion Queen once again.

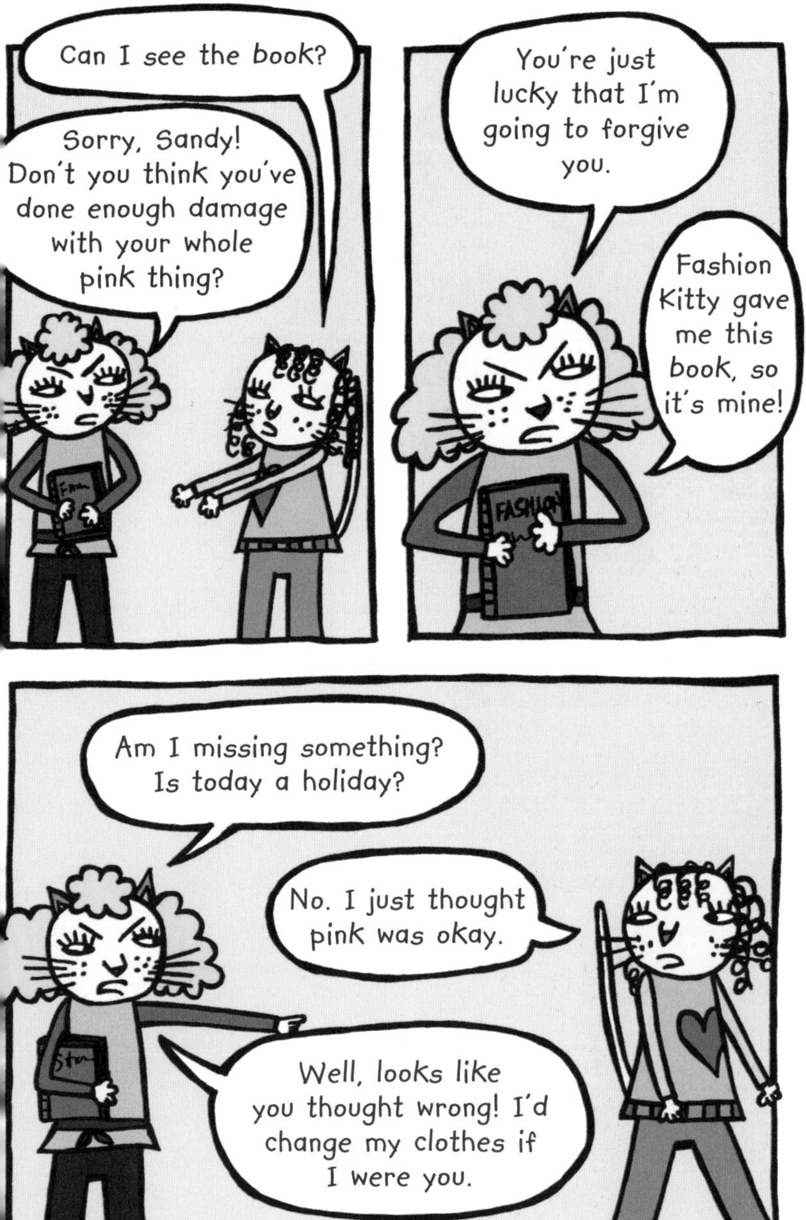
Can I see the book?
Sorry, Sandy! Don't you think you've done enough damage with your whole pink thing?
You're just lucky that I'm going to forgive you.
Fashion Kitty gave me this *book*, so it's mine!
Am I missing something? Is today a holiday?
No. I just thought pink was okay.
Well, looks like you thought wrong! I'd change my clothes if I were you.

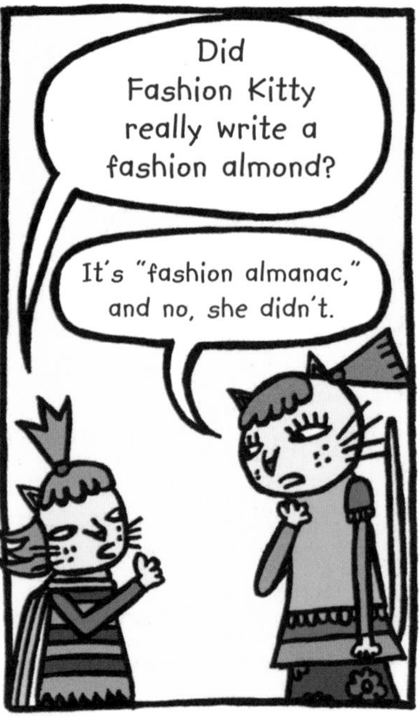
Did Fashion Kitty really write a fashion almond?
It's "fashion almanac," and no, she didn't.

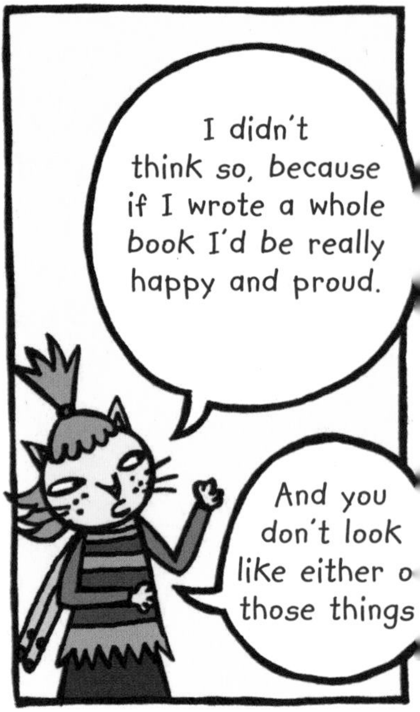
I didn't think so, because if I wrote a whole book I'd be really happy and proud.
And you don't look like either o
those things

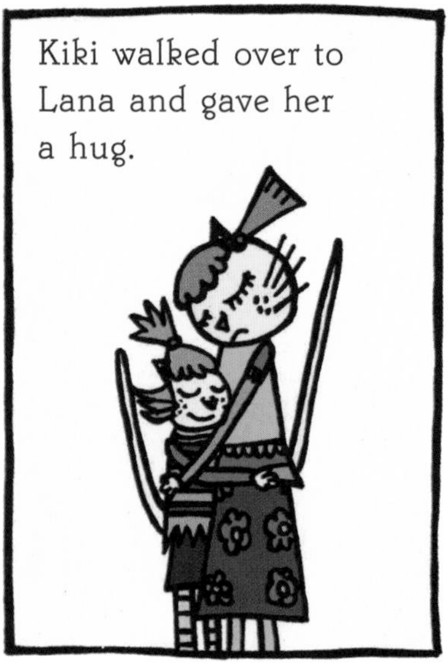
Kiki walked over to Lana and gave her a hug.

Sometimes Lana was much smarter than a normal four-year-old, and that was what made her special.

The next day, Cassandra was ready for everyone, with some new fashion rules.

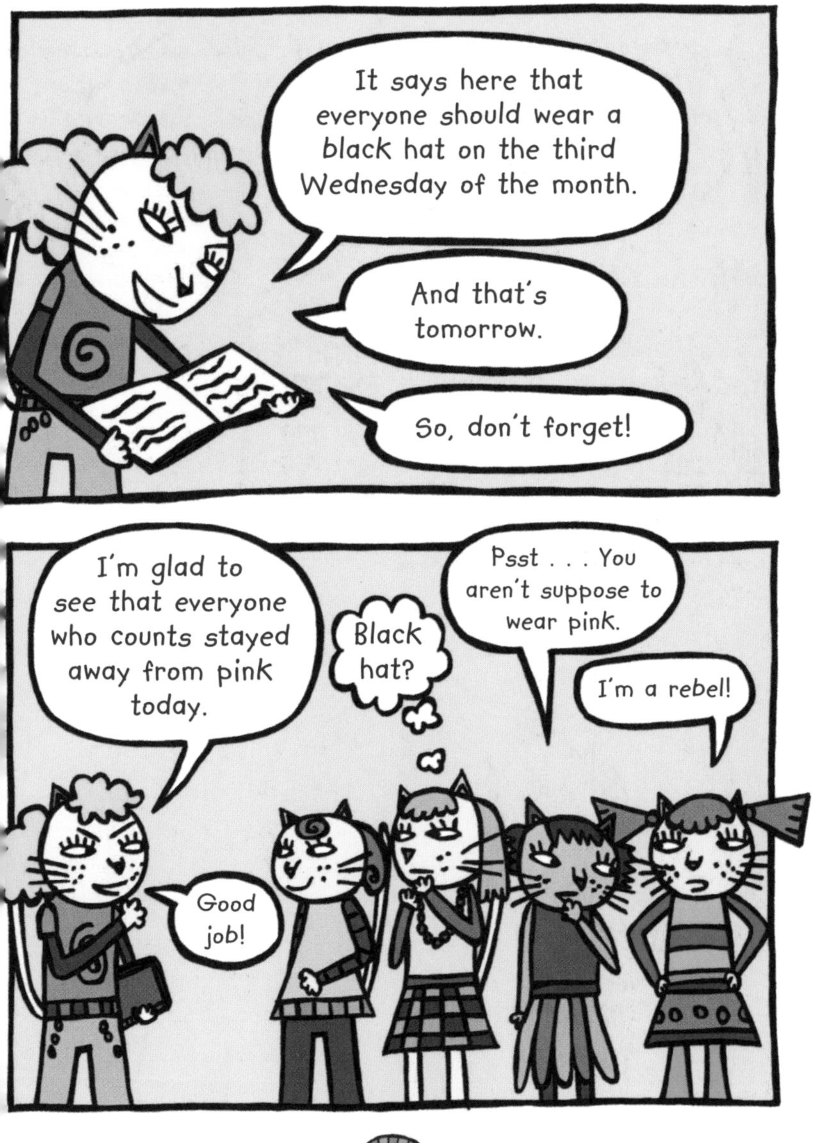
It says here that everyone should wear a black hat on the third Wednesday of the month.
And that's tomorrow.
So, don't forget!
I'm glad to see that everyone who counts stayed away from pink today.
Good job!
Black hat?
Psst . . . You aren't suppose to wear pink.
I'm a rebel!

Cassandra was using her fashion almanac to make everyone wear exactly what she wanted.
She was abusing her fashion power.

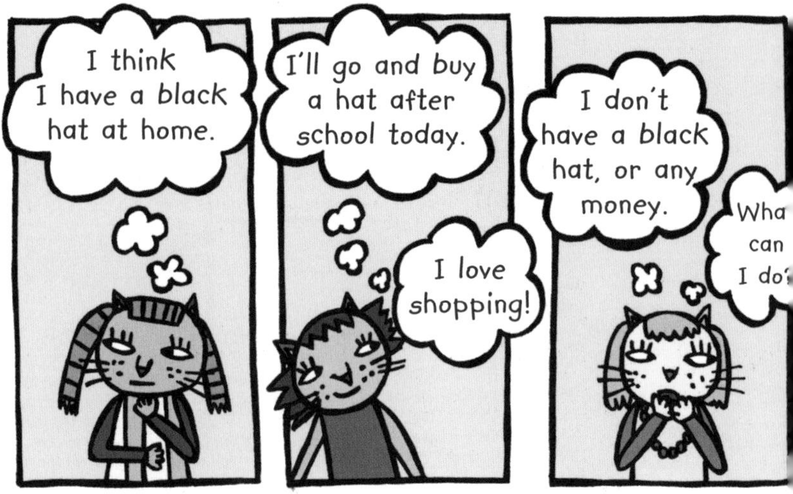
I think I have a *black* hat at home.
I'll go and buy a hat after school today.
I love shopping!
I don't have a *black* hat, or any money.

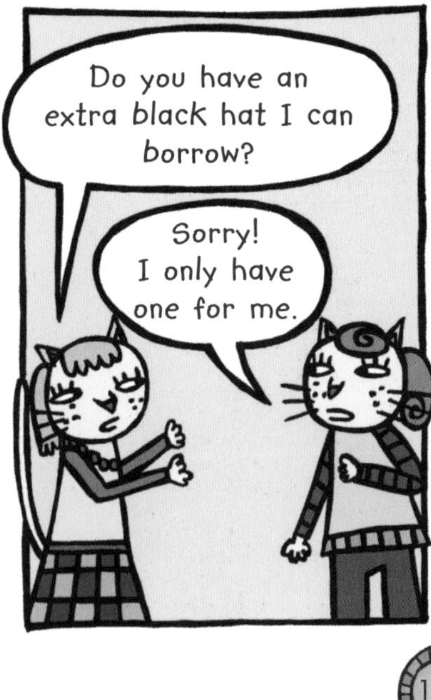
Do you have an extra *black* hat I can borrow?
Sorry! I only have one for me.

Sometimes when a kitty is desperate she might decide to do the wrong thing.

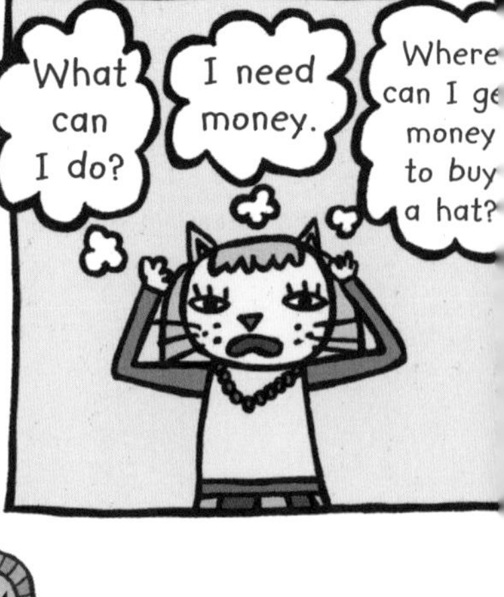
What can I do?
I need money.
Where can I ge money to buy a hat?

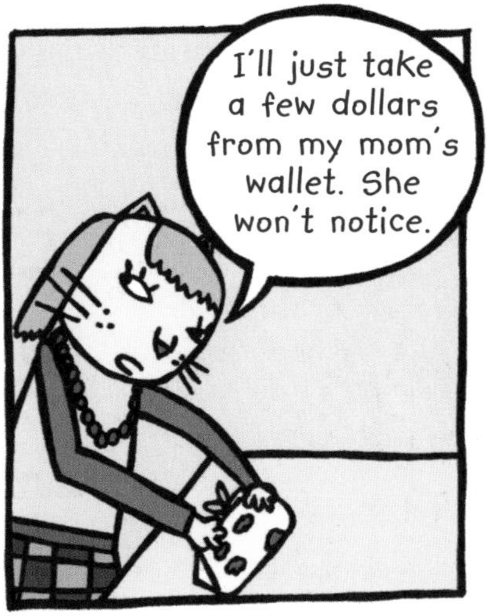
I'll just take a few dollars from my mom's wallet. She won't notice.

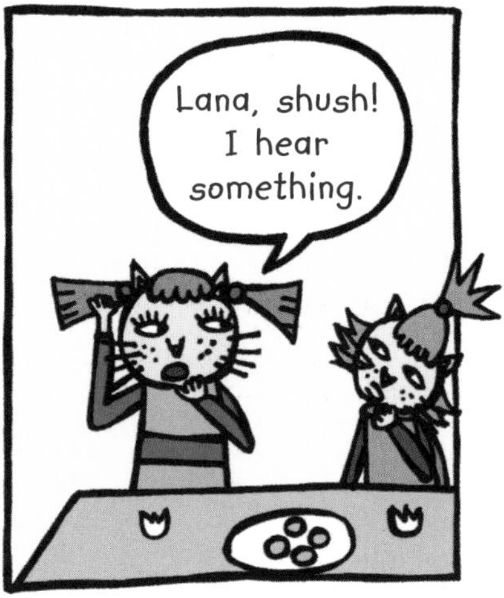
Lana, shush! I hear something.

It wasn't a fashion emergency, but it was an emergency for the sake of fashion, and that was good enough.

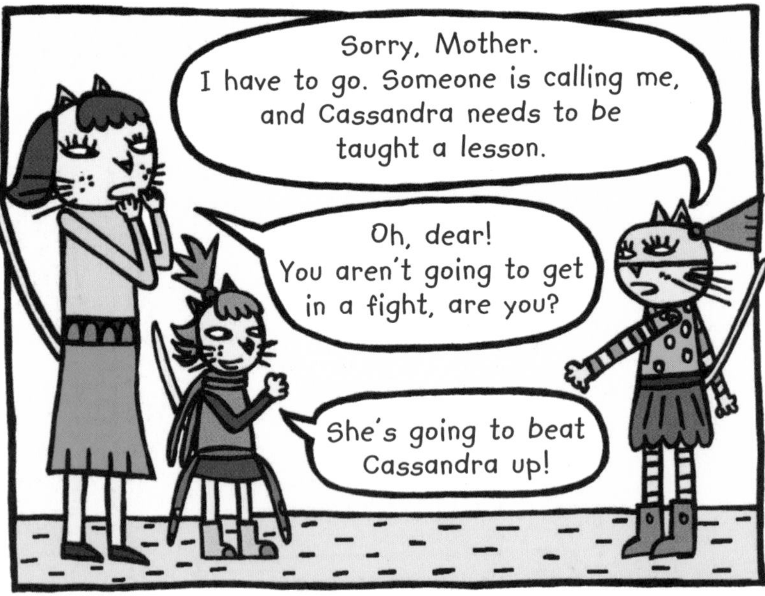
Sorry, Mother.
I have to go. Someone is calling me, and Cassandra needs to be taught a lesson.
Oh, dear!
You aren't going to get in a fight, are you?
She's going to beat Cassandra up!

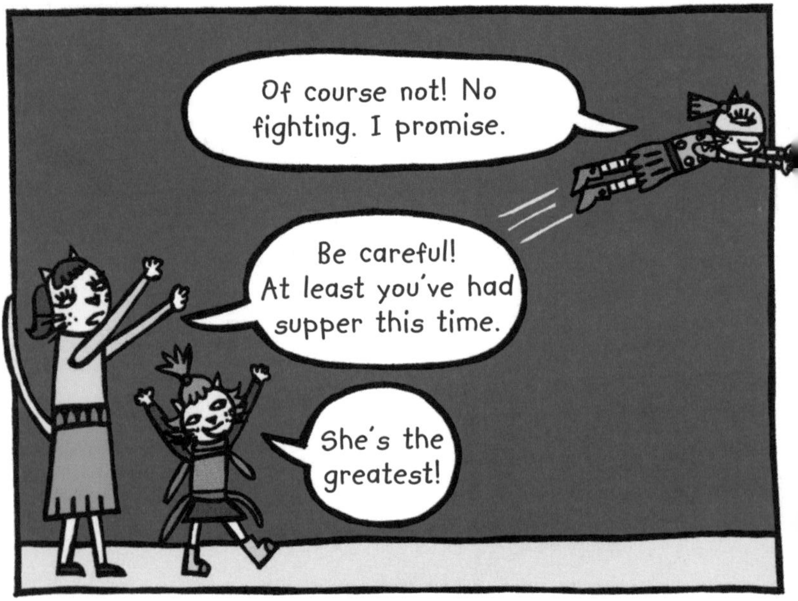
Of course not! No fighting. I promise.
Be careful!
At least you've had supper this time.
She's the greatest!

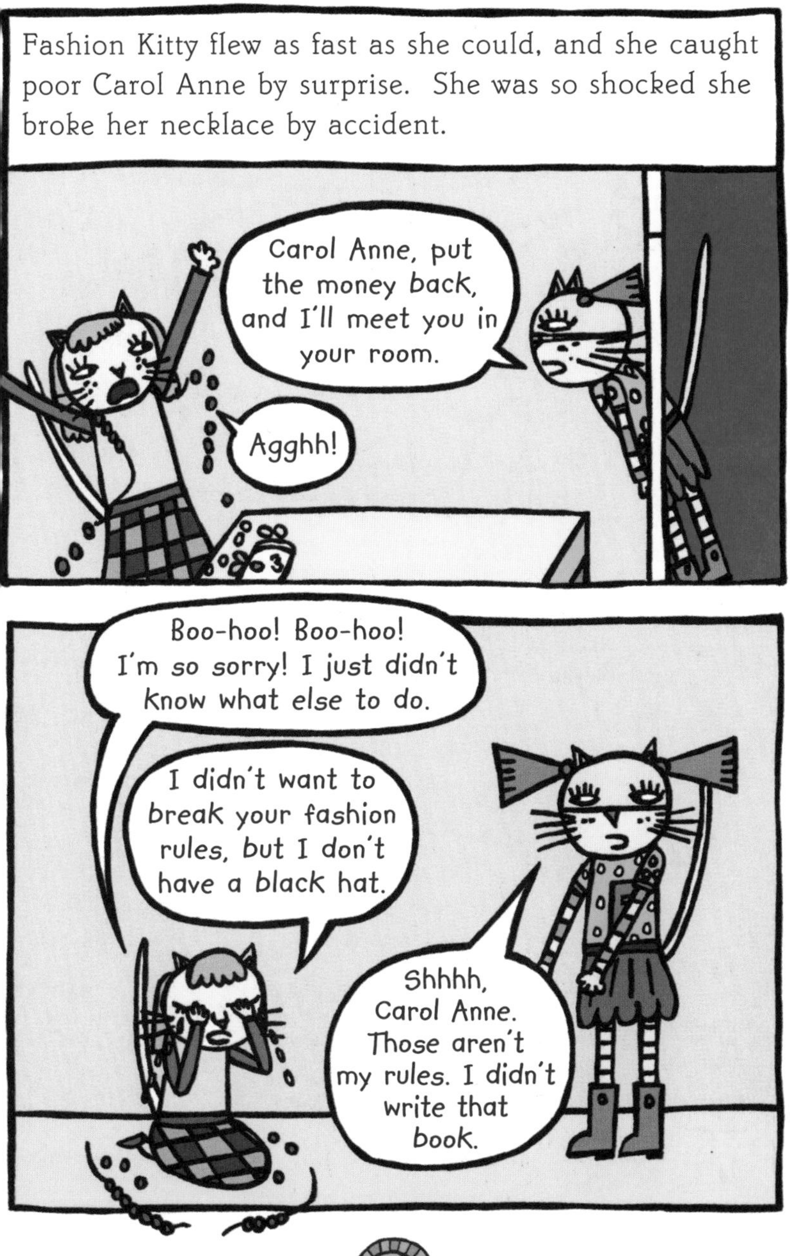
Fashion Kitty flew as fast as she could, and she caught poor Carol Anne by surprise. She was so shocked she broke her necklace by accident.
Carol Anne, put the money back, and I'll meet you in your room.
Agghh!
Boo-hoo! Boo-hoo! I'm so sorry! I just didn't know what else to do.
I didn't want to break your fashion rules, but I don't have a black hat.
Shhhh, Carol Anne. Those aren't my rules. I didn't write that book.

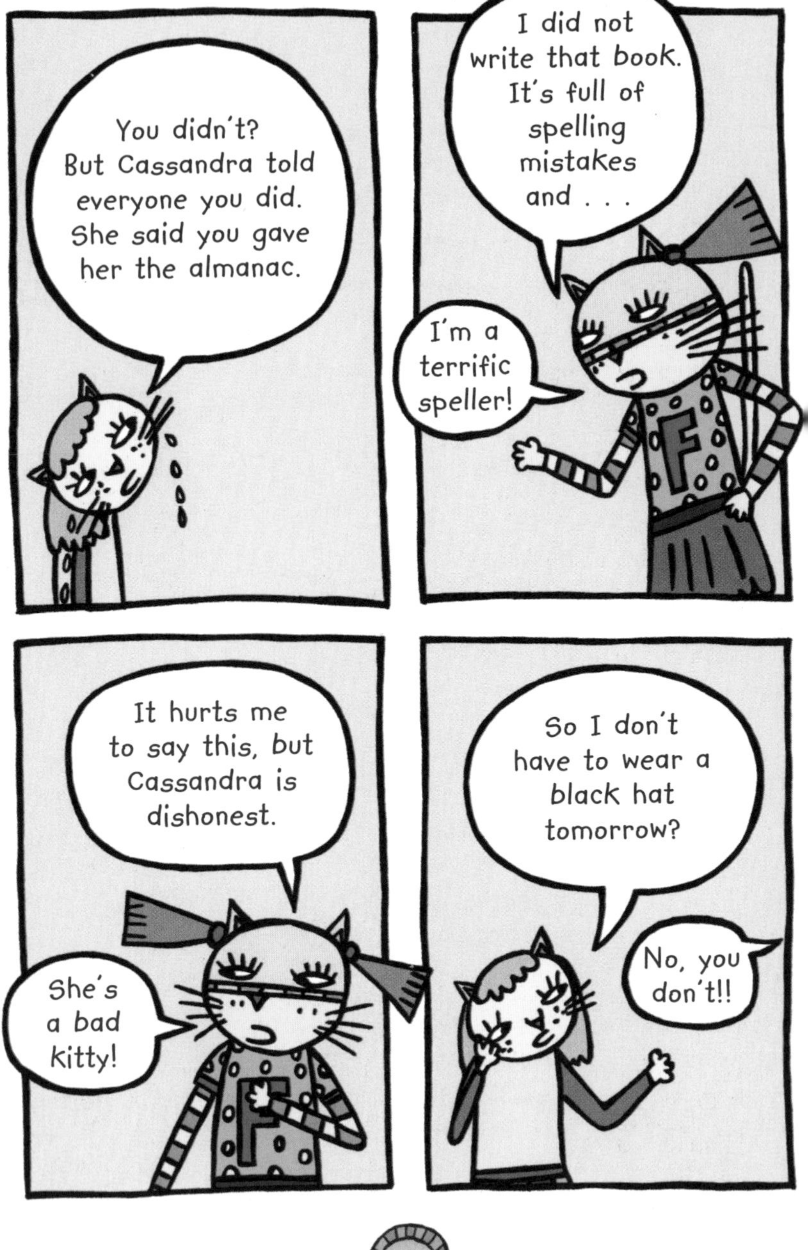
You didn't? But Cassandra told everyone you did. She said you gave her the almanac.
I did not write that book. It's full of spelling mistakes and . . .
I'm a terrific speller!
It hurts me to say this, but Cassandra is dishonest.
She's a bad kitty!
So I don't have to wear a black hat tomorrow?
No, you don't!!

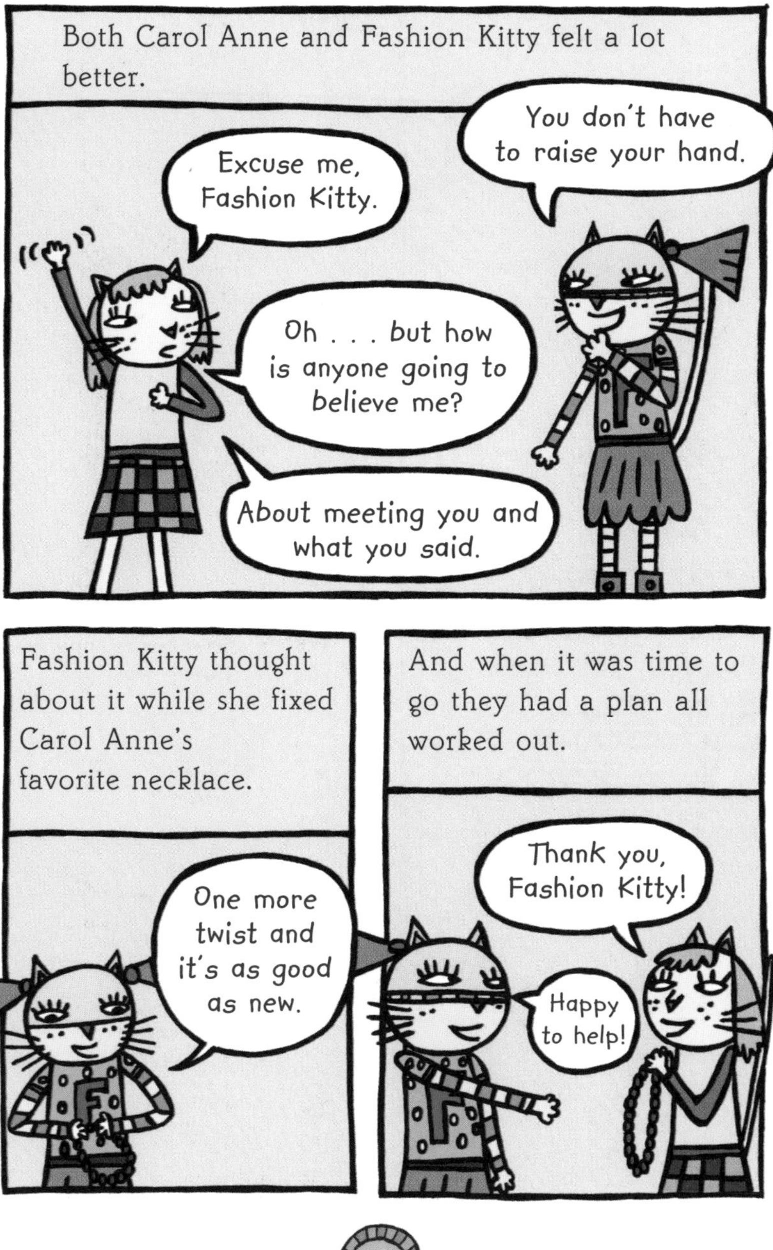
Both Carol Anne and Fashion Kitty felt a lot better.
Excuse me, Fashion Kitty.
You don't have to raise your hand.
Oh . . . but how is anyone going to believe me?
About meeting you and what you said.
Fashion Kitty thought about it while she fixed Carol Anne's favorite necklace.
One more twist and it's as good as new.
And when it was time to go they had a plan all worked out.
Thank you, Fashion Kitty!
Happy to help!

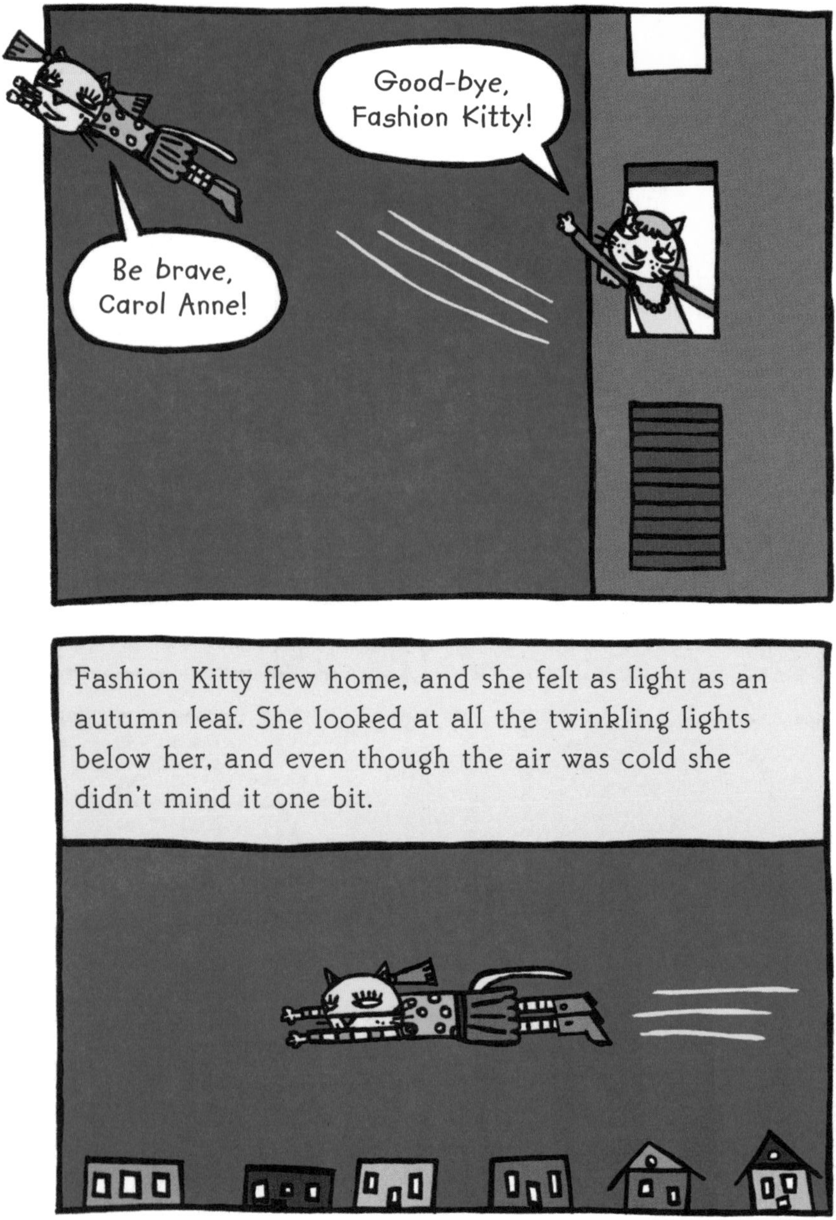
Good-bye, Fashion Kitty!
Be brave, Carol Anne!
Fashion Kitty flew home, and she felt as light as an autumn leaf. She looked at all the twinkling lights below her, and even though the air was cold she didn't mind it one bit.

Lana was still up when Kiki walked in the door. She was full of questions.

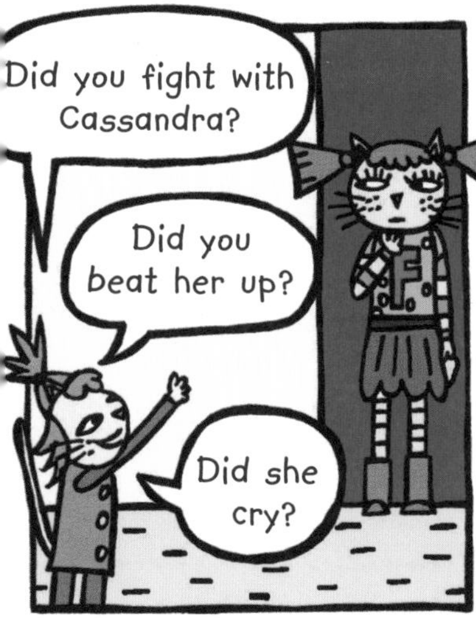
Did you fight with Cassandra?
Did you beat her up?
Did she cry?

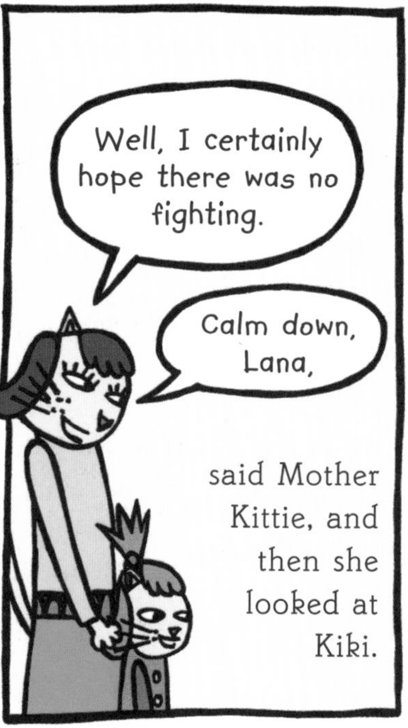
Well, I certainly hope there was no fighting.
Calm down, Lana,
said Mother Kittie, and then she looked at Kiki.

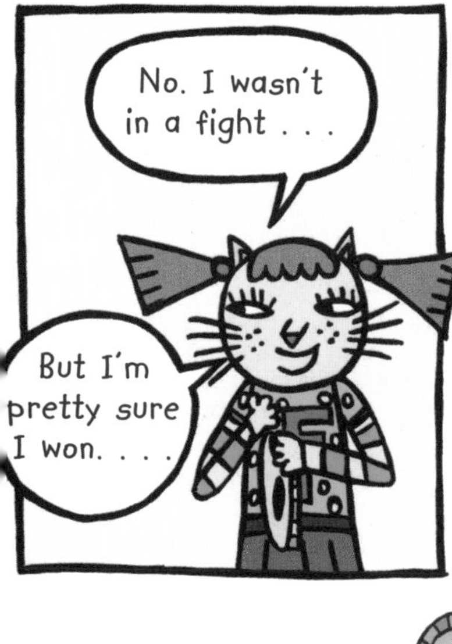
No. I wasn't in a fight . . .
But I'm pretty sure I won. . . .

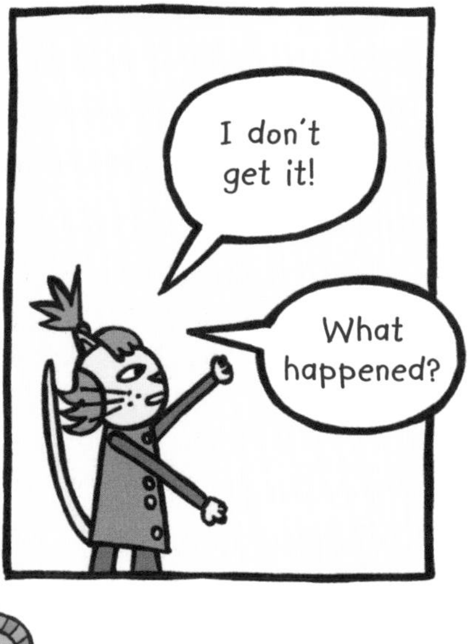
I don't get it!
What happened?

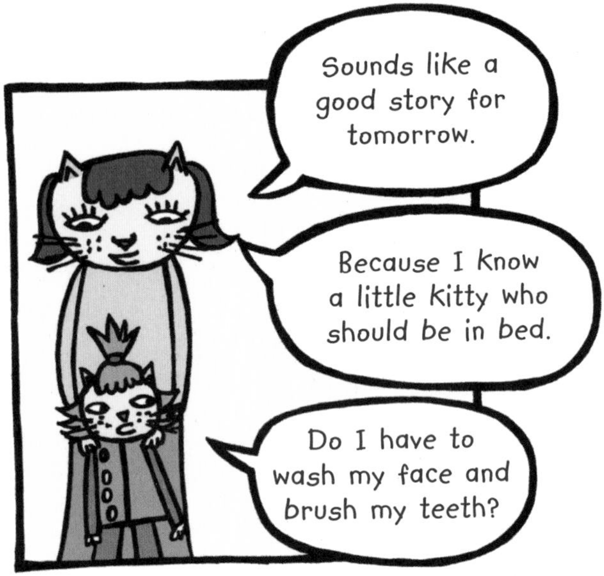
Sounds like a good story for tomorrow.
Because I know a little kitty who should be in bed.
Do I have to wash my face and brush my teeth?

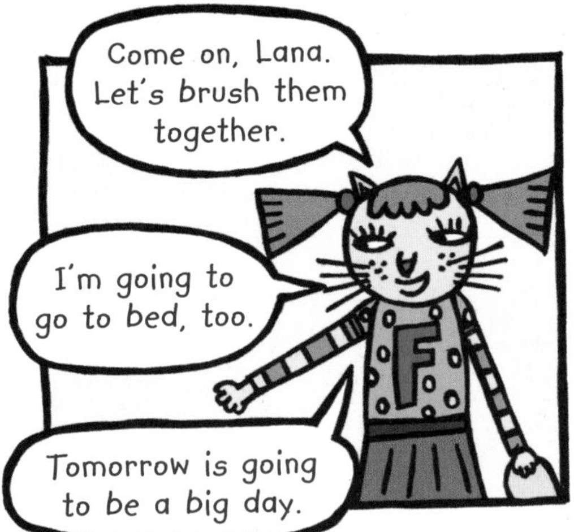
Come on, Lana. Let's brush them together.
I'm going to go to bed, too.
Tomorrow is going to be a big day.

The next day was a big day. It started off as a big black-hat day.

I have never *seen so* many *black* hats.

Cassandra was overjoyed.

So many *black* hats!

This is amazing!

It was not surprising that her hat looked very much like a crown.

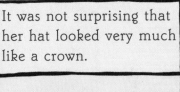

What a day!

Everyone has a *black* hat on.

And then Cassandra spotted Carol Anne.

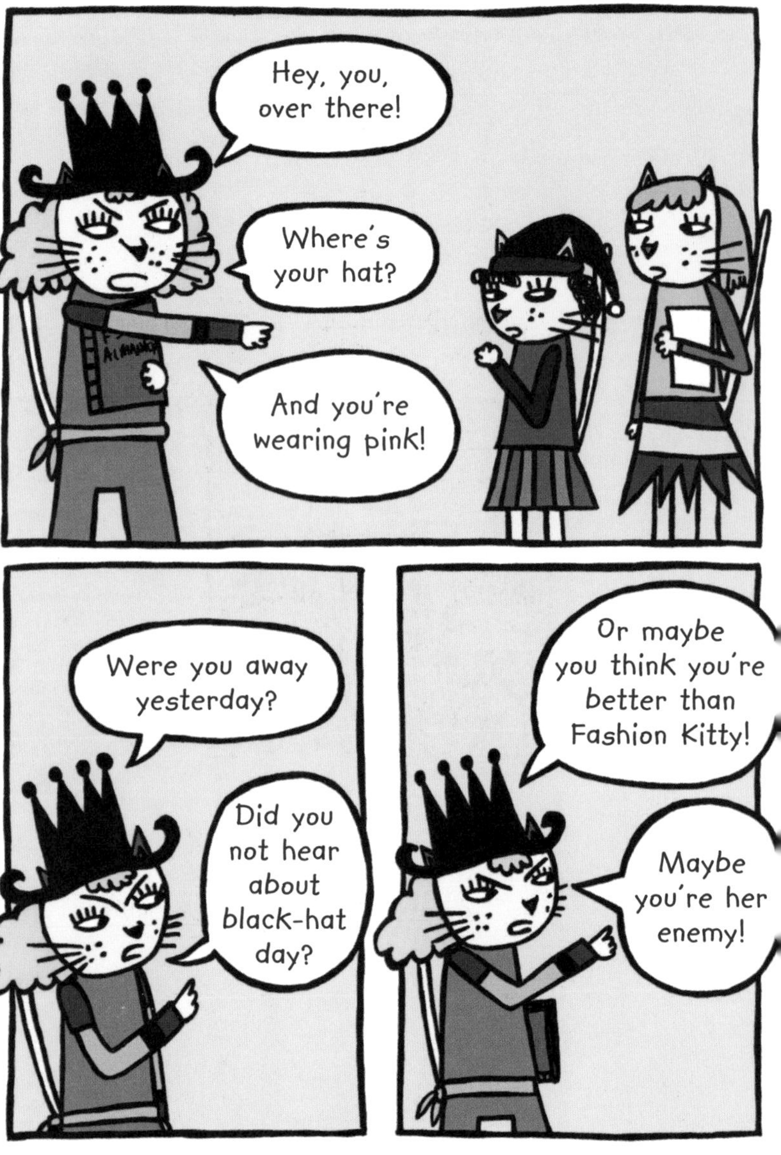
Hey, you, over there!
Where's your hat?
And you're wearing pink!
Were you away yesterday?
Did you not hear about black-hat day?
Or maybe you think you're better than Fashion Kitty!
Maybe you're her enemy!

All the kitties gasped in horror.

Cassandra was happy that everyone was watching her. She was going to make an example out of Carol Anne. She was going to teach her a lesson.

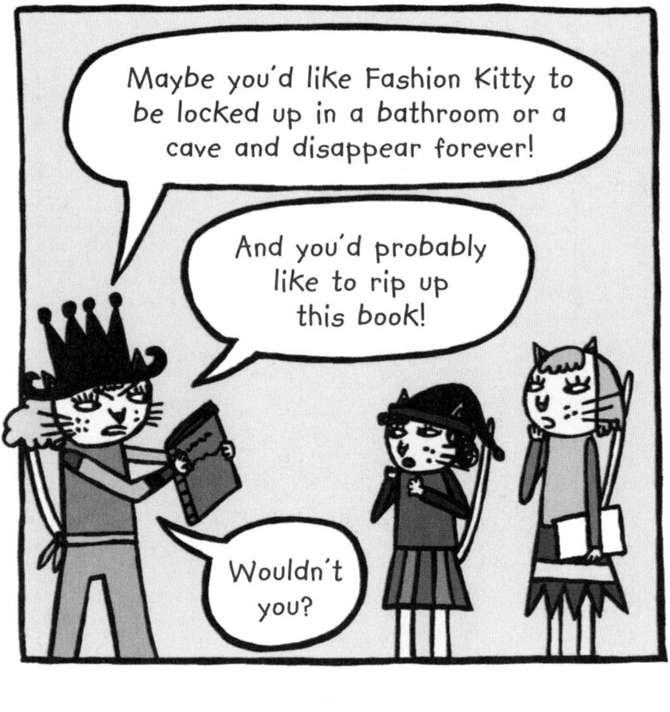
Maybe you'd like Fashion Kitty to be locked up in a bathroom or a cave and disappear forever!
And you'd probably like to rip up this *book*!
Wouldn't you?

Carol Anne looked nervous, but she took a deep breath and said:

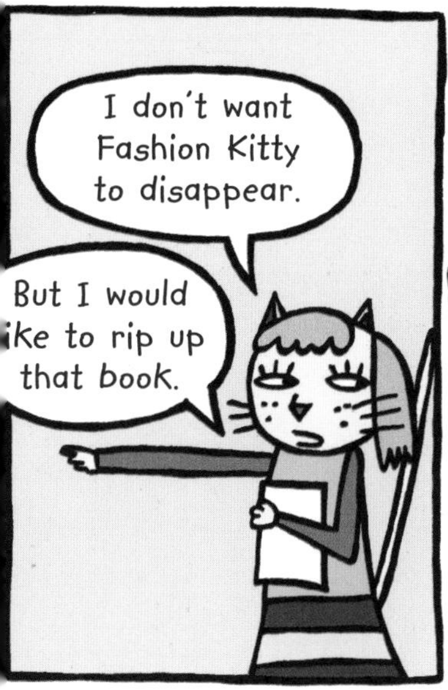
I don't want Fashion Kitty to disappear.
But I would ike to rip up that *book*.

The crowd of kitties started mumbling excitedly.

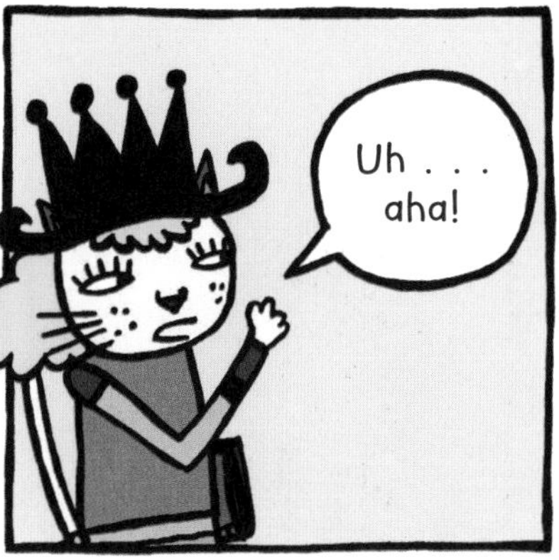
Uh . . . aha!

Cassandra was a little confused. What Carol Anne had said was not what she had expected.

If it had been the olden times she would have said:

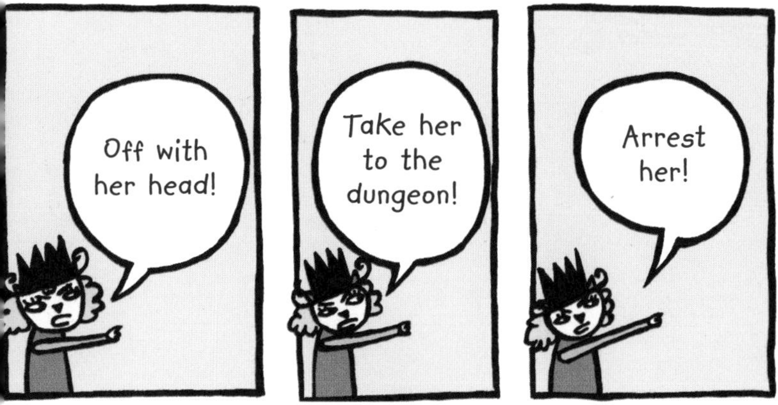
Off with her head!
Take her to the dungeon!
Arrest her!

But you couldn't really do that kind of thing today, in a modern school yard. Cassandra couldn't think of what to say, so she said:

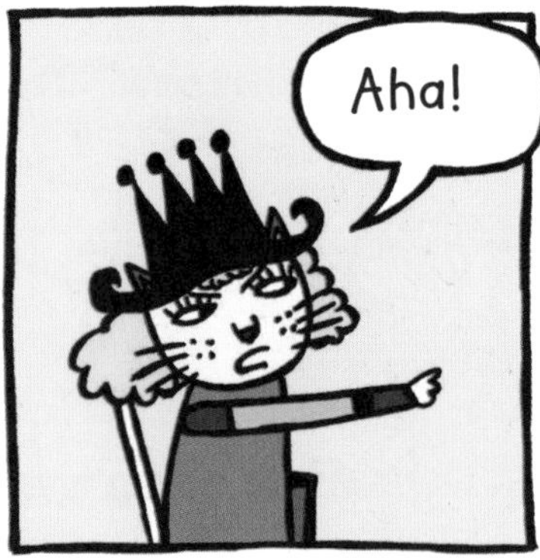
Aha!

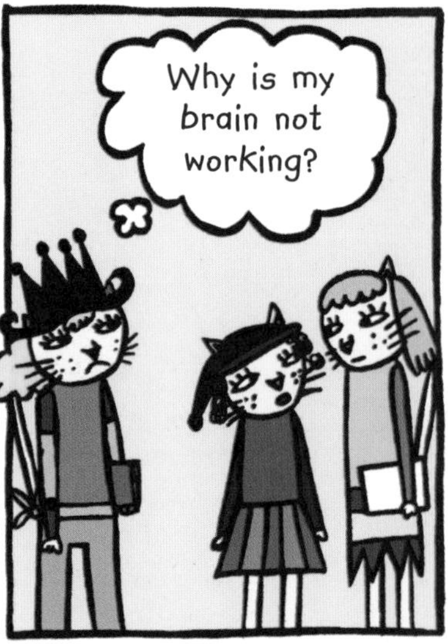
Why is my brain not working?

one more time while her kitty brain tried to think of something clever.

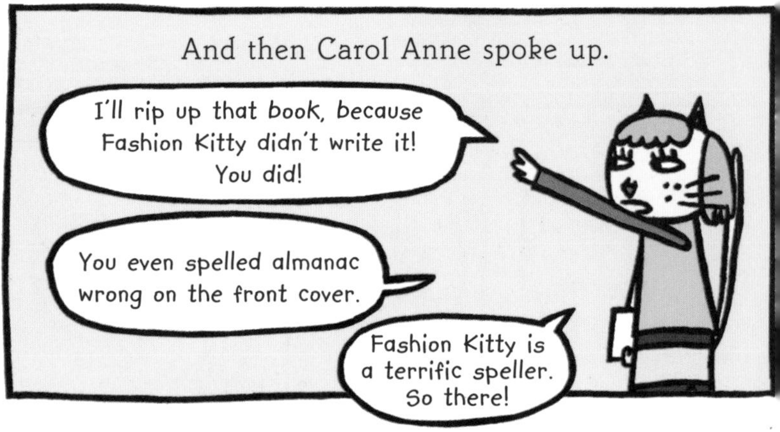
And then Carol Anne spoke up.
I'll rip up that *book*, because Fashion Kitty didn't write it! You did!
You even spelled almanac wrong on the front cover.
Fashion Kitty is a terrific speller. So there!

Everyone tried to get a peek at the cover to see if Carol Anne was right.

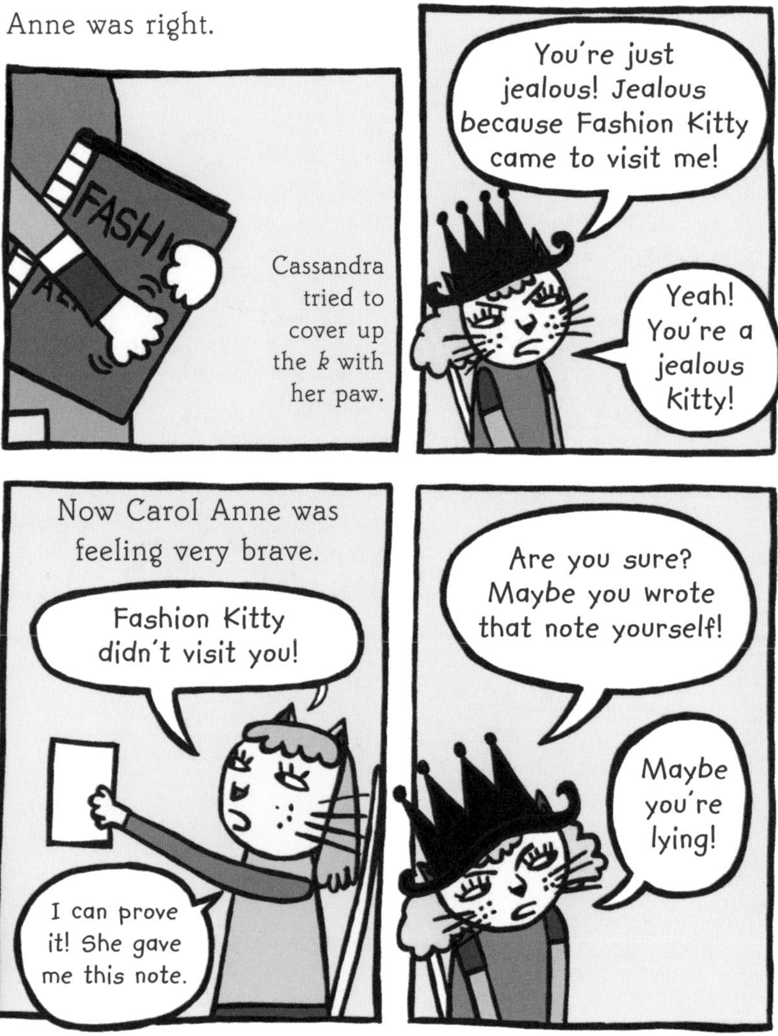
FASH
Cassandra tried to cover up the *k* with her paw.
You're just jealous! Jealous because Fashion Kitty came to visit me!
Yeah! You're a jealous kitty!
Now Carol Anne was feeling very brave.
Fashion Kitty didn't visit you!
I can prove it! She gave me this note.
Are you sure? Maybe you wrote that note yourself!
Maybe you're lying!

What Carol Anne said next shocked and excited everyone. It shocked Cassandra so much that she dropped the fashion almanac and ran all the way home.

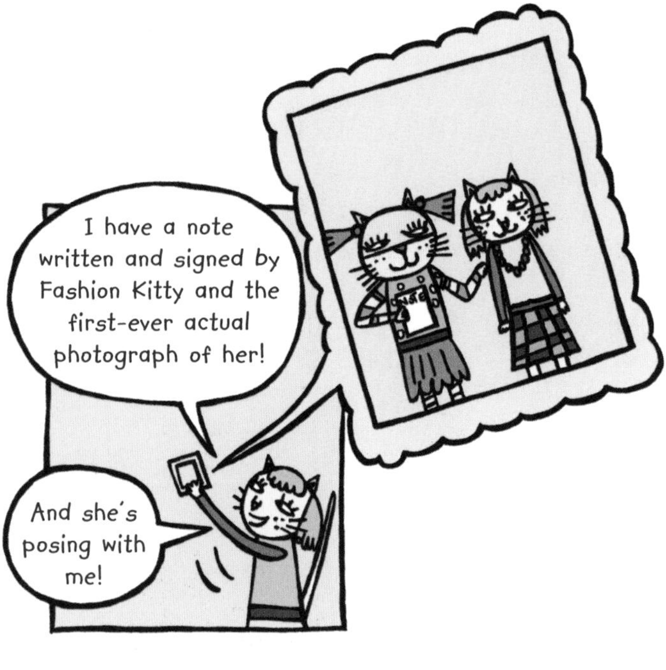
I have a note written and signed by Fashion Kitty and the first-ever actual photograph of her!
And she's posing with me!

Everyone wanted to see the photo, and everyone wanted to see the note. The principal put them both on display in the gym for the last two hours of school. They were all way too excited to work anyway.

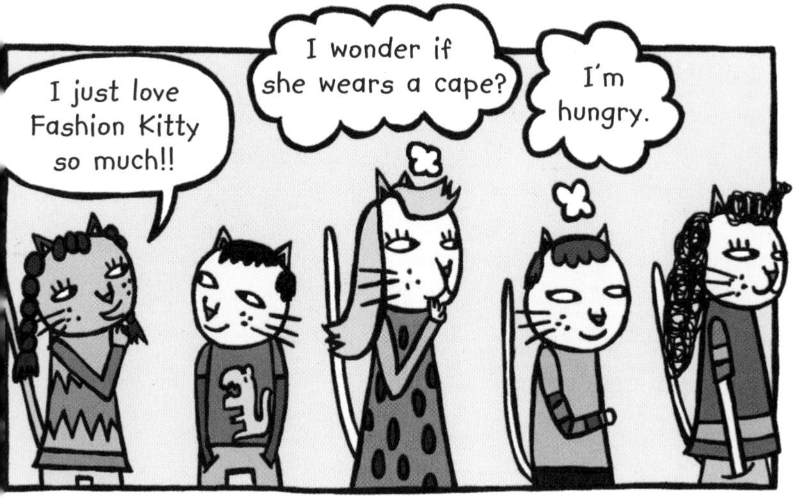
I just love Fashion Kitty so much!!
I wonder if she wears a cape?
I'm hungry.

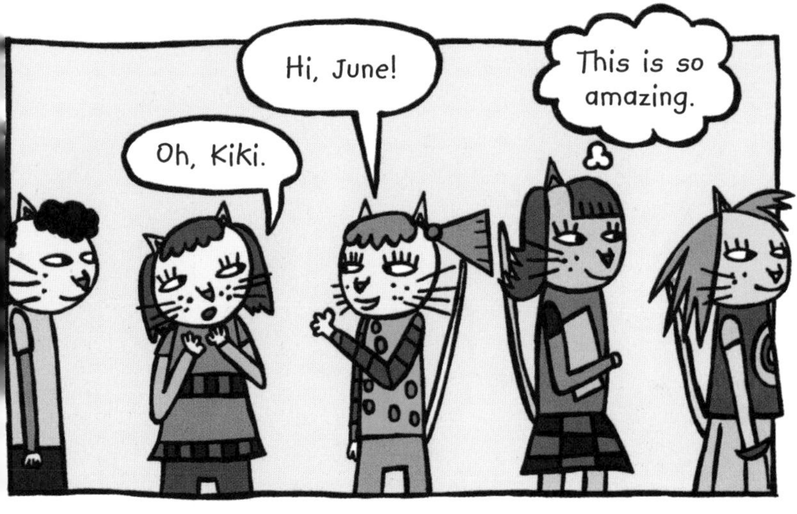
Oh, Kiki.
Hi, June!
This is so amazing.

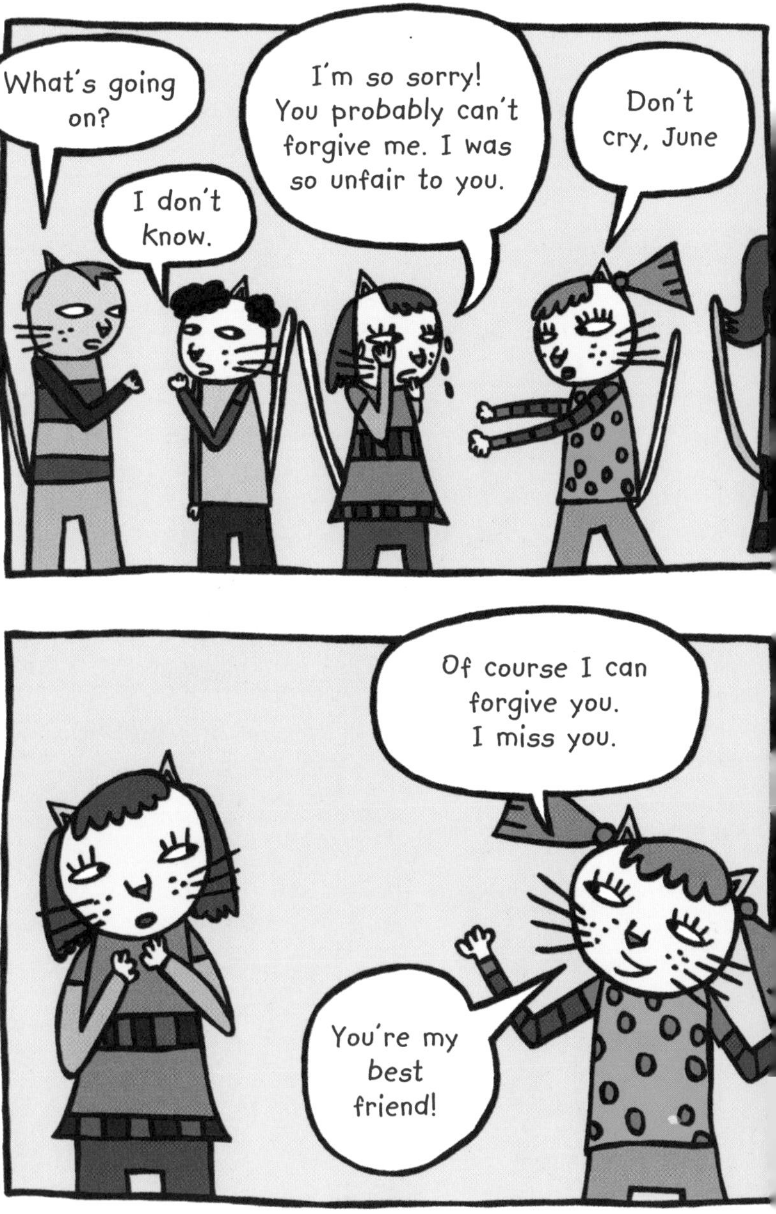
What's going on?
I don't know.
I'm so sorry! You probably can't forgive me. I was so unfair to you.
Don't cry, June
Of course I can forgive you. I miss you.
You're my *best* friend!

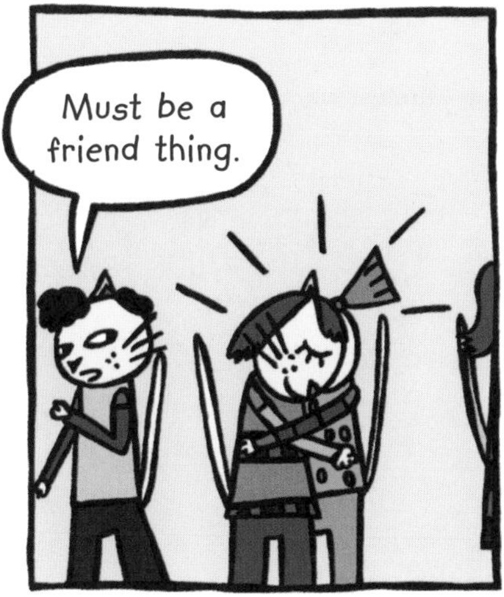
Must be a friend thing.

Epilogue

which means
this is what
happened at
the end of
this story.

To show how angry they were with Cassandra, all of the students marched to her house and threw their black hats on her front lawn. It wasn't a nice thing to do, and it wasn't a supermean thing to do, but it was something to do with all the extra black hats that made sense.

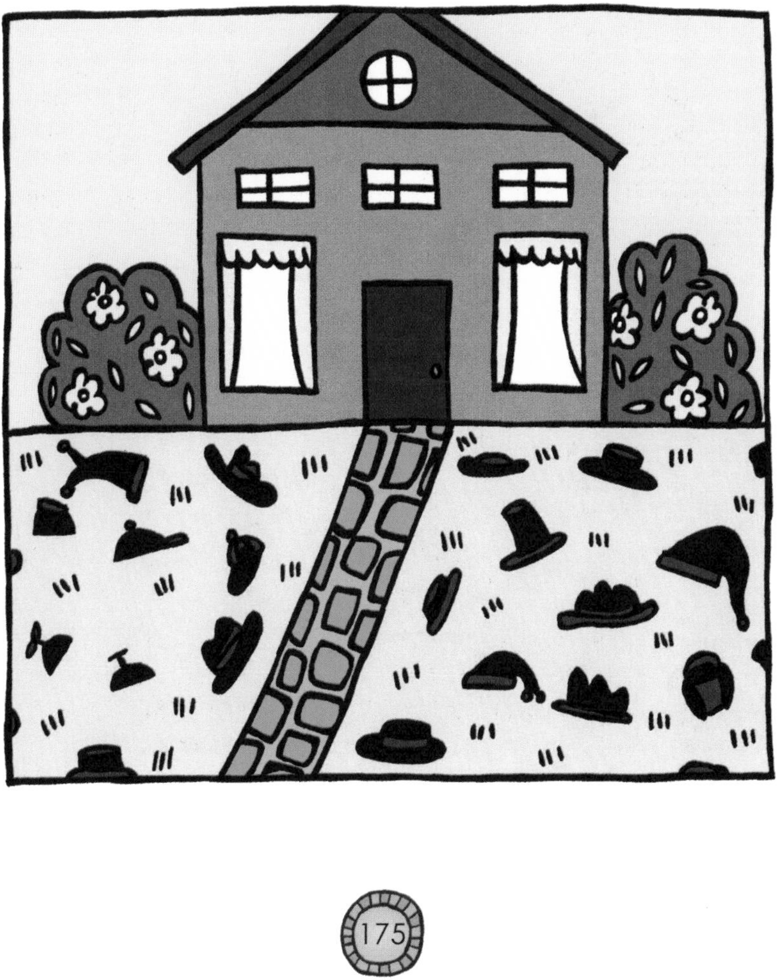

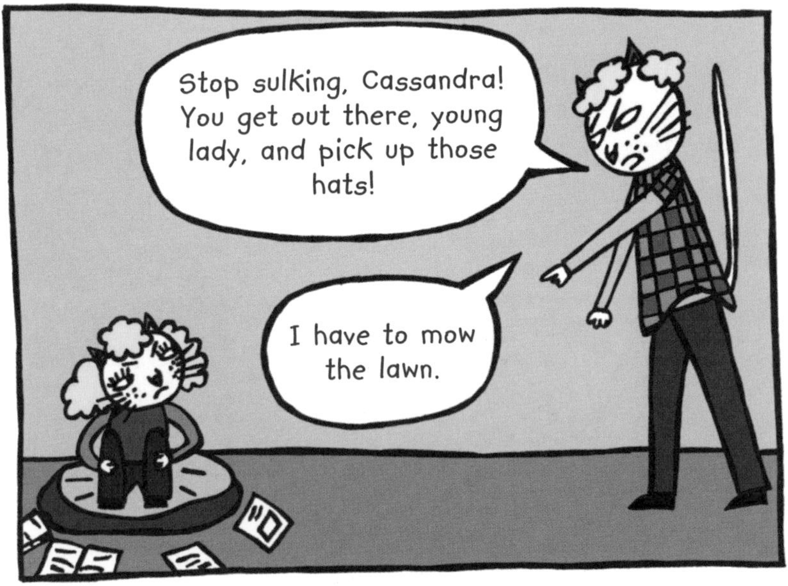
Stop sulking, Cassandra! You get out there, young lady, and pick up those hats!
I have to mow the lawn.

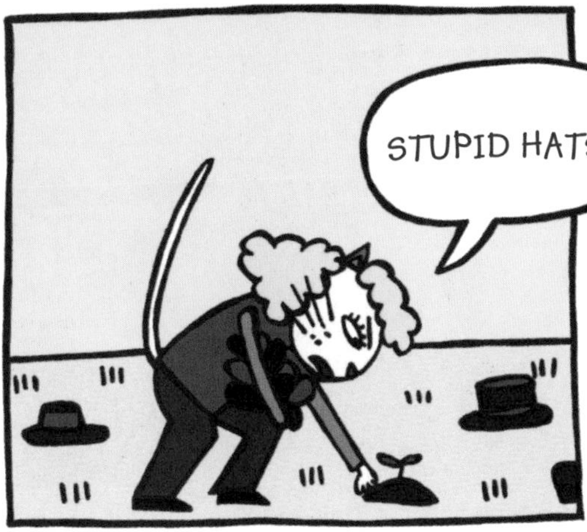
STUPID HATS!

The next day when Cassandra went back to school, she pretended like nothing had ever happened.

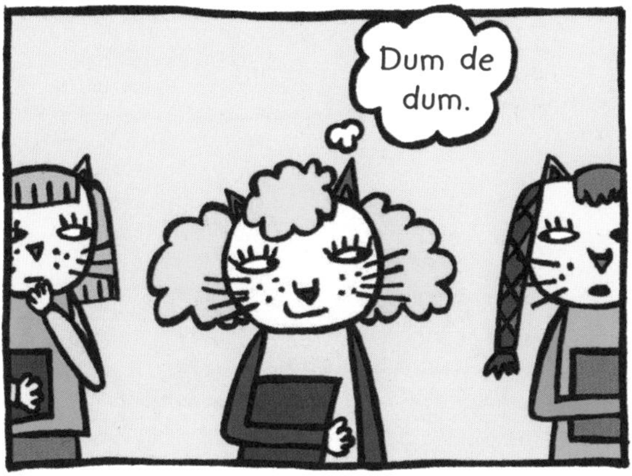
Dum de dum.

She was a fantastic actress. The drama teacher heard about her talent and soon had her busy rehearsing for the Thanksgiving play.

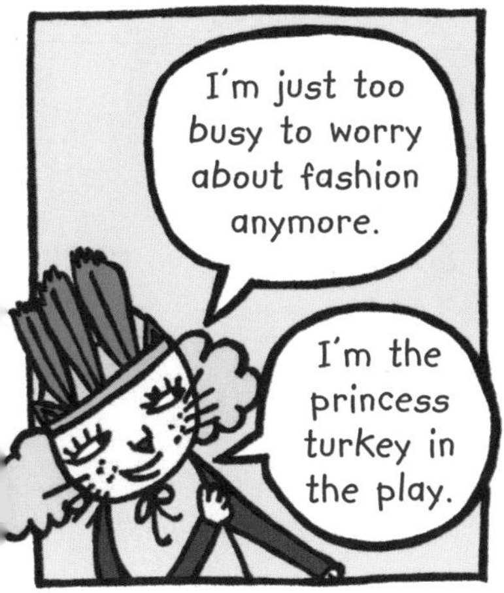
I'm just too busy to worry about fashion anymore.
I'm the princess turkey in the play.

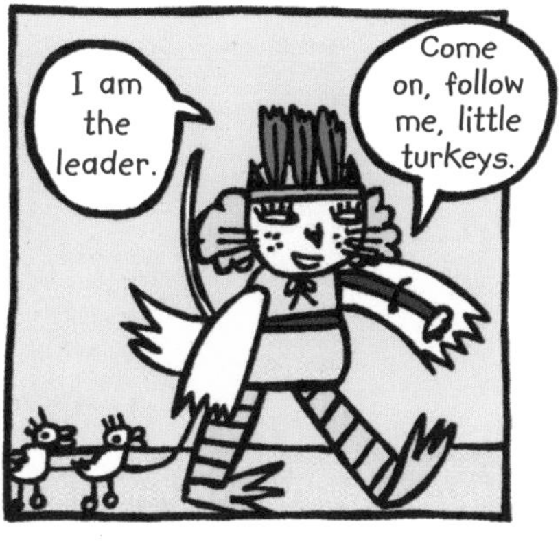
I am the leader.
Come on, follow me, little turkeys.

She was perfect for the part.

Kiki and June were best friends again, and Kiki was even making a special effort to be nice to Lana.

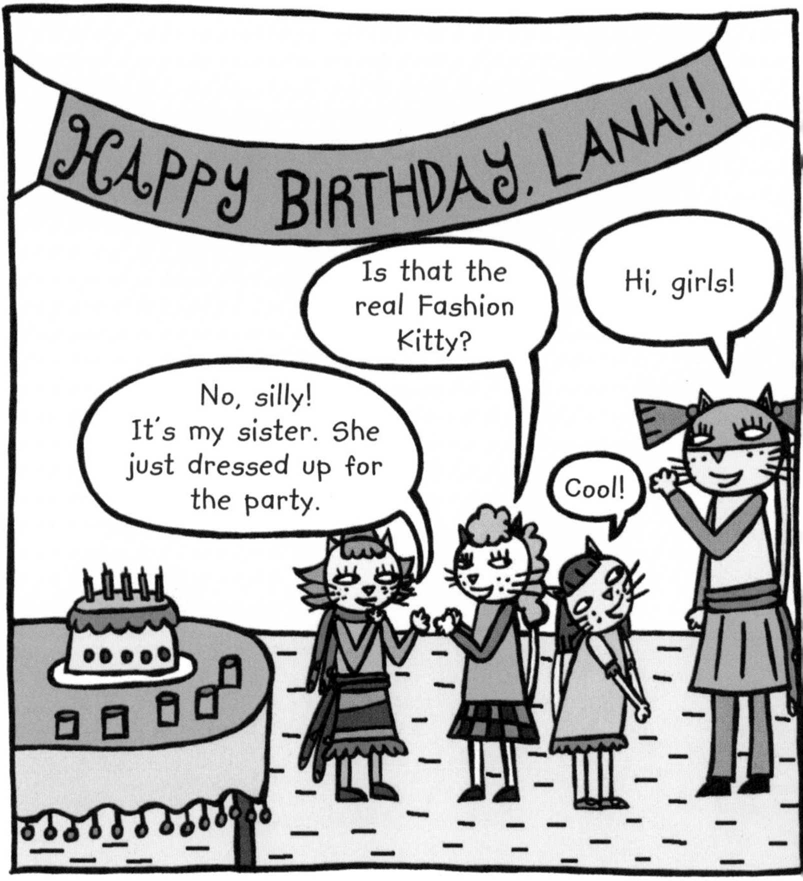
HAPPY BIRTHDAY, LANA!!
Hi, girls!
Is that the real Fashion Kitty?
No, silly! It's my sister. She just dressed up for the party.
Cool!

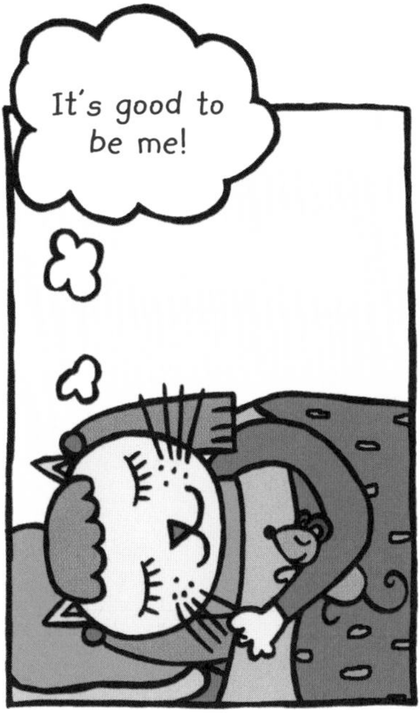
It's good to be me!

Thought Kiki Kittie, and that was a very nice thing to be thinking right before falling asleep.

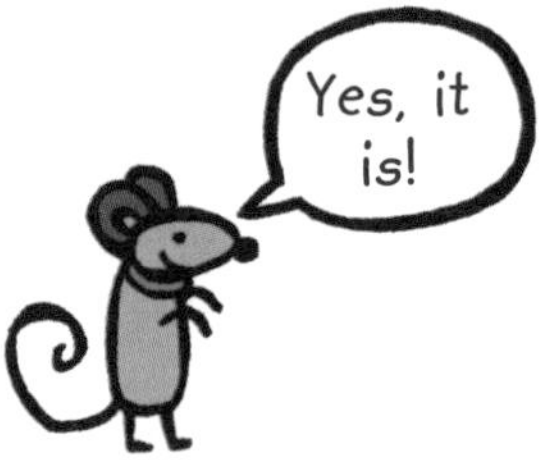
Yes, it is!

NOTE:

I, Fashion Kitty, did not write *The One and Only Fashion Almanack*. (And please remember, there is no "k" on the end of the almanac.) FIGHT FOR FREE FASHION

Fashion Kitty

The End,
or is it . . . ?